WORLDWIDE PRAISE
FOR AWAKEN THE DAWN

"Ellis K. Popa (delivers) an amazing story full of mystery, intrigue and romance."

— JOHN BENEDICT, BESTSELLING
AUTHOR OF *ADRENALINE*

"(Simply) one of the best books I've ever read."

— HEATHER BROWN, BOOK GIRL BROWN
REVIEWS (US)

"A gripping and unforgettable read that heralds Popa as a rising star in the genre."

— ELICIA MEIERS, NETGALLEY (US)

"This book is an adrenaline rush, with every twist sharper than the last."

— ALEXANDRIA W, BOOKSTAGRAM (US)

"A fast-paced mystery with a strong, likeable protagonist to root for."

— THE WISHING SHELF (UK)

"Go ahead! Go add this to your TBR!"

— BOOKS WITH CATS (CYPRUS)

"(*Awaken the Dawn*) will have you hooked from page one."

— NESSA'S BOOK REVIEWS (UK)

"This is an absolutely delicious book. I both devoured it in one day, and savoured every word!"

— BLUE FAIRY BUGS BOOKS (UK)

"Kat was amazing and a kick-ass character."

— KRITI, THIS READER GIRL (INDIA)

"(Popa) builds a world charged with grief, secrets, and the urgent need to uncover the truth."

— JOHN RANDALL, POSTMODERNISM &
BEYOND (US)

"Popa's vivid prose (invites) readers to actively participate in the unfolding story."

— ROGUE BOOK REVIEWS (US)

"(*Awaken the Dawn*) is unputdownable..."

— JAME_EREADER, GOODREADS (US)

"The book thrilled me."

— SOPHIA, GOODREADS (CROATIA)

"I loved the twists in the tale."

— HELEN FOX, LIBRARIAN (UK)

"The book was absolutely amazing and I couldn't get enough of it. I can't wait to see what happens next."

— SCARLET LE CLAIR, NETGALLEY (UK)

AWAKEN THE DAWN

THE AWAKEN SAGA
BOOK ONE

ELLIS K. POPA

COPYRIGHT

This book is a work of fiction. Names, characters, places, and incidents are the product of the author's imagination or are used fictitiously. Any resemblance to actual events, locales, or persons living or dead, is coincidental.

PUBLISHER'S NOTE

Awaken the Dawn touches on sensitive subject matter such as kidnapping, non-graphic violence, and substance abuse. Young readers or those sensitive to such material should be advised.

The story also contains the term *țigan* ("gypsy"). Derivatives of this word are found in many countries—*Zigeuner* (Germany), *tsygan* (Russia), *cigány* (Hungary) and countless others. These are commonly used terms, spoken even among those in the Roma or Sinti ("Gypsy") communities, but readers should note the etymological meaning, which is derogatory and amounts to "untouchable" (originating from the *dalits*—untouchables—of India's caste system).

As part of her research, the author consulted a Romani leader, members of the Roma community, and an advocate for the Romani people. Their feedback was instrumental in deciding how best (and most sensitively) to present certain beliefs, misconceptions, and true-to-life scenarios within the framework of the story.

HOW TO SAY THE ROMANIAN WORDS

Examples of how to pronounce the Romanian words can be found on the author's website in the **How to Say** section.

DisappearWithEllis.com/HerWriting/How-to-Say

NOTE FROM THE AUTHOR

Romania is like a beautiful woman with a difficult past that has left her with scars. Like many of us, she might be inclined to hide those scars, ensuring she's never too exposed, never too vulnerable, to those who may be looking to harm or criticize her.

But it's our vulnerability that makes us strong, and this woman's scars—though they are many—aren't a picture of her failures. They're the afterglow of all she has endured and the ways she has overcome great adversity. They're markers, showing us who she was long ago and the journey she's been on since. They speak of this woman's will to survive, to flourish, and they provide deep and meaningful insight into the hows and whys of who she is today.

When I wrote this book, I didn't do it with the intent of focusing on Romania's scars. Instead, it's been my hope that people will focus on her—on beautiful Romania—while letting the scars point them to the deeper things about her.

Because those scars tell a story, and her story is worth telling.

THE PLAYLIST

Listen to the playlist for *Awaken the Dawn* as you read. You can also listen to music from the club scene and Kat's summer mix.

www.Linktr.ee/BookishMood

It will be many years, or perhaps soon,
    Before your hands find my song.
    Where did you get it?
    Is it day or night?

I sing, and remember.
    Was it a fairytale? Was it true?
    And my songs: everyone will forget.

— BRONISŁAWA WAJS ("PAPUSZA")

PART ONE

ATLANTA

PROLOGUE

Wednesday, December 19

The wind scraped at my cheeks and whipped my ponytail around. I laced up my cleats, shivering, and zipped myself into a Lady Knights hoodie. The soccer field stretched around me. Silence rested on the empty stadium.

I turned away from the goal and jogged up the sideline. My thighs protested. Cold air hit my lungs and caught fire in my chest. I pushed harder, commanding myself into focus.

District. Regionals. State. State champs.

A blip of movement drew my attention to the bleachers. I turned, expecting to see Brandy—but why would she be in the bleachers? We were supposed to be practicing.

I paused my warm-up, scanning. The announcer's box fortified the top, and I could see straight through the large windows. There was nobody in there.

There was nobody anywhere. I was alone.

My pocket vibrated. I pulled out my phone and checked the message.

Hello dear

I blinked. The text was from Dad, but... he never called me dear. He also never wrote messages shorter than fifty words.

I swiped a reply.

> Did you see my text? Need to know when your flight gets in.

I pressed Send and dropped into a lunge.

The phone vibrated in my hand. The screen brightened.

> U can find it dear

I straightened. Dad never abbreviated anything. Ever. He also used perfect grammar and punctuation in all his text messages. These didn't have any of that.

A scuff broke the silence. My attention moved to the stands, then to the cyclone fence that wrapped around the stadium. Somebody was here. Whoever it was didn't want to be seen.

"What are you doing?" The muffled voice came from behind me.

I wheeled around.

Brandy stood there, padded goalie gloves held between her teeth while she yanked her auburn hair into a ponytail. She was layered up in bulky clothing, and the gray weather dulled her normally warm freckles.

When she finished, she spat out the gloves. They landed in a heap on the grass. "You're looking paler than usual. You're not sick, are you?"

"N-no, it's just— Never mind." I stilled my heart, which pounded at a full sprint. "Trying to figure out my dad's itinerary. Almost done." I held up my phone.

She shrugged, plunking herself on the grass.

Her neon-pink cleats were tied together and slung over one shoulder. She pulled the shoes onto her lap and picked at the knot.

I headed for my bag, swiping a reply to Dad.

Have to go. Shooting drills with Bee.

I hesitated, thumb hovering. Dad had been acting weird since Thanksgiving, and he was acting extra weird now.

Unless I was imagining things. Was I? How could I know for sure?

An idea breathed across my thoughts. It wasn't the greatest idea, or the nicest, and it might get me in trouble. But...

I gnawed my bottom lip and added to the message.

Ty's coming over to help me study. Hope that's ok.

Ty wasn't allowed over at night. Not ever, but especially not while Dad was out of town. If I didn't get a reply with all caps and threats of being grounded for life, I'd know something was up.

I held my breath and pressed Send.

"My mom needs the car tonight."

I pivoted, insides heavy. "Huh?"

"My mom's covering the overnight at the nursing home." Brandy flexed her fingers in the padded gloves. "Can you follow me home and then drop me off at Dave's?"

"I... can't. Have to study. Chemistry midterm." That part was true. I really did need to study.

My gaze landed on the phone. No reply from Dad.

"Come on, Kat. We have to study, too."

"Right. 'Study.'"

Brandy cocked her hip and used it as a handrest. "Dave and I have pre-cal."

"Then take the MARTA."

"You know that station by my house is sketch, and I'll have to connect by bus. That'll *suck* in this weather. Please, Kat?" She blinked out puppy-dog eyes. "Pretty please?"

I rubbed my forehead. Dave and his dad lived forty-five minutes away. Double that with rush hour traffic. I couldn't afford to lose that much time.

But I also couldn't let my best friend end up cold, stranded, and stuck at a sketchy train station.

"Yeah, okay. We won't have time for sprints or crunches—"

"I'll do crunches before bed and sprints up and down the staircase." Her mouth tipped up. "What's the deal with chemistry, anyway? You're not at risk of getting a B, are you? Or dare I say... a B-minus?" She waggled her eyebrows.

I rolled my eyes and started for my athletic bag.

She angled to cut me off. "Hold up. For real, what's going on?"

"I wasn't going to say anything yet, but... Coach Jules got a call." I fought a smile. "From Georgia State."

Brandy's mouth dropped open wide enough for a small plane to land. "They called about you?"

"Sort of. They're sending scouts when the season starts, and they had a lot of questions about me. They even asked about my academic performance. Coach Jules thinks they might offer me a full ride."

"A full-ride scholarship? *What?*" Brandy squealed and spun me around.

Georgia State checked off all the boxes. I could live with Dad rent-free, and I'd be close to Brandy and Dave, who were planning to stay in Atlanta for community college.

But without that scholarship, my college horizons were bleak. I hadn't wanted to jinx myself.

"Okay, okay." I anchored my feet, bringing us to a stop. "But I have to practice. Shooting drills every day, even on crap days like this one."

"Don't worry, babe. I got you." Brandy glanced around. "Where's the ball?"

I tipped my chin toward the goal. My soccer ball rested against the post. Brandy took off in that direction. I closed the distance to my bag.

I stooped and tugged on the zipper. No more distractions, not from Dad or anyone else. My phone would go in the bag. I would focus. Everything else would fall into place. It had to.

District. Regionals. State. State champs. My smile tugged harder. *Georgia State. Scholarship.*

The smile faltered. I checked the phone one more time, and my chest tightened. The message light was off. The screen was still black.

I. DELIVERY

TWO WEEKS LATER

More people die from selfie accidents than shark attacks. Vending machines kill an average of thirteen people per year.

A Brazilian man died after a cow fell through his roof, crushing him while he was asleep.

Of all the statistics I'd seen, that death-by-cow incident had to be the weirdest, but I couldn't say it was the absolute worst. That honor surely belonged to selfie accidents, especially those involving heights.

Imagine the regret someone would have as they fell, knowing what's about to happen, knowing they can't stop it. What would they be thinking about? Would they have enough time to ponder their life's decisions (or at least their last decision)?

There's a saying in Romania: *"The life of one who fears death is a kind of death."*

In other words, the person who's afraid of dying is the one who really loses his life. But how can that be true? Because if the selfie-accident people had been afraid to climb up to that height, they'd still be alive.

And if Dad had been afraid to return to his homeland, he'd still be alive, too...

I pushed a stack of dirty dishes aside and dumped an armful of mail on the counter. The words PAST DUE in blood-red ink glared up at me. I picked up the envelope, and the one beneath it had an identical, inky-red twin.

My eye twitched. I rubbed it and reached for a padded mailer. Probably something from Mom, a late Christmas gift no doubt. I was surprised she remembered at all.

I tugged on the junk drawer and reached for the scissors. My attention skimmed a postmark on the back of the mailer.

BRAŞOV – POŞTA ROMÂNĂ

My brow dipped. Braşov?

The front door to the apartment creaked, and cold air settled around me.

"Kat?" Brandy's husky voice drifted into the kitchen. A quick double knock followed. "Hello?"

"In here."

The ceiling fan blinked on, drawing my attention across the breakfast bar.

Brandy breezed into the living room, striding past the Christmas tree, then the couch, before stopping next to the one-and-only box I'd managed to pack—Dad's programming books.

She yanked off her beanie, leaving a trail of static in the wake, and surveyed the living room. Her smile crashed and burned. "What the hell? Kat, you're supposed to be packed." She marched into the kitchen. "Dave's coming with the truck. He could only get it for tonight."

"I was about to, um..."

Brandy leaned sideways, trying to see past me. I sidestepped, putting myself between her and the mound of dirty dishes.

"I'm sorry." I wrung my hands. "I-I meant to do more."

Her eyes found mine, and her expression softened. "You don't need to apologize, okay? You just lost your dad." She took my hands. "Don't worry, babe. We'll figure this out." She marched out of the kitchen.

I wiped a stray tear and followed her.

The Christmas tree sprayed the living room in blue, gold, and red. The lights splashed across the wall and spilled onto the carpet. Homemade flag ornaments dotted the branches.

My feet stalled. I hadn't thought Dad would let me do a Romania-themed tree. He never had before. Why this year? Why the change of heart?

I looked down at the padded mailer I was holding. My fingers detected something hard and clunky inside. Had the cleanup crew found something in the wreckage?

"Today's Wednesday." Brandy stood beside the couch, massaging her temples. "School starts Monday. I'm working tomorrow, Friday, and Saturday. Shoot, and I think Sunday, too. We've gotta get this done tonight."

"We could take the big stuff to your house first, couldn't we? I-I'll move the smaller stuff by myself this weekend."

Brandy slanted an eyebrow.

"What? When we moved into this place, I packed everything we owned into our car. It's a compact, but it holds a lot." The real reason was because we hadn't owned much back then. Even less than we owned now.

Correction: Than *I* owned. There was no more "we."

Brandy whipped out her phone and punched out a text. Probably to Dave. I let my stare drift over the living room... over Dad's TV... over our ratty couch.

I paused on Dad's poster of Rosie the Riveter. Her red bandanna wrapped around her head and tied at the top. She pursed her lips, expression serious and kind of intense. She was confident in her mission, in herself, with her sleeve rolled up and her biceps flexed.

WE CAN DO IT! The World War II slogan filled a dialogue bubble.

Dad had other posters, but Rosie had been his favorite. She was the screen saver for his laptop, too.

Grief dragged my heart into my rib cage.

"Hey, Bee?" I swallowed my emotions and held up the mailer. "This might be from the government liaison I've been working with. I think the cleanup crew might have—" I looked down and nearly choked.

My name and address had been scribbled in a familiar, left-handed slant. Hope sprang up. "Dad?"

"The cleanup crew, what?" Brandy peered back at me. "Babe. You've got to start finishing your sentences. I don't know what you're talking about half the time."

I bolted into the kitchen. The package had been taped solid on both sides. I grabbed the scissors and ripped through the semi-soft material. Something gold and shiny clattered to the linoleum. A folded-up sheet of paper followed, landing on my shoe.

I picked up the paper and unfolded it.

This looked like the scavenger hunts Dad used to make, and it was all in his handwriting.

I scooped up the other item that had fallen out—a gold locket with a wagon wheel stamped on the back and flowery vines engraved on the front.

I pressed a latch, and the locket opened to an inscription.

"That wasn't a bad idea." Brandy's lean frame appeared in the kitchen. "We'll take the big stuff tonight. Dave's bringing the truck for that, and then he's gonna swing by this weekend for everything else."

I stared, lips parted. My vocal cords wouldn't work.

"I'll start on your room, okay? Take your time, do what you need to do, then come help me." She stripped off her fleece jacket, tossed it on the dining room table, and hauled a stack of flattened cardboard boxes into my bedroom.

The screech of packing tape hit my ears and sank to my stomach. My room, my entire life, was being dismantled, and no amount of procrastinating had been able to stop it.

I clutched the locket. The thing was sturdy, an antique from the looks of it—but Dad hadn't been into antiques. And when could he have sent me this? He'd been dead for two weeks.

Two weeks. Was that enough time for mail to arrive from Romania? I didn't know the answer, but I thought of someone who might.

2. DJANGO

I peeked behind the potted plants stacked around the entrance. The diner's pale lights reflected off crinkly plastic.

"Sour candies!" I squealed and clapped. "Daddy, I found them, I found them."

"That's my girl. Up we go now." He scooped me up. The list of clues slipped from my hands and floated to the floor.

He spun me around. I giggled, clutching the candies.

"Has the explorer found her big prize?" Mr. Kotfas came through the kitchen doors and wandered into the dining area. He'd been in America as long as Daddy, but he still rolled his R's and sang his words together. Sometimes I couldn't understand him.

"She certainly did. Ohh, but our game required a bit more work this time." Daddy set me down. "Didn't it, my darling?"

HIGHWAY LIGHTS RUSHED past my window. I gripped the steering wheel, pressing the grooved vinyl into my palms. The sensation helped sharpen my focus.

Eighty percent of car accidents were caused by distracted

driving. Nearly three thousand of those resulted in deaths. I needed to concentrate.

Downtown Atlanta glittered against the black horizon. Skyscrapers towered over the freeways, glass giants standing guard over their neon-lit kingdom.

I veered onto Peachtree Street and skidded to a stop behind a line of traffic. "Seriously? Ughh." I hadn't told Brandy where I was going, just that I needed to step outside. She was going to be pissed if I didn't get back soon.

A parking space opened up near restaurant row. I swung into the spot and hopped out. The meter had twenty-two minutes left. Hopefully that was enough time.

The wind blasted me, whipping my hair into curly black chaos. I zipped myself into Brandy's fleece jacket, which I'd borrowed without permission, and jogged up the sidewalk. A heady mix of hot oil and fried chicken swirled.

Memories rushed back to me. Dad and I used to come down here when I was a kid. Sometimes we would race each other on this sidewalk.

I stifled my emotions and stopped at the corner. Gold letters twirled across a backlit sign. GYPSY DJANGO. It wasn't the sign I remembered, but there wasn't another Gypsy Django in Atlanta.

I tugged on the sturdy black door—also new—and then hesitated. I hadn't been here in... how long? Five years? Six? What would I say to Mr. Kotfas? *Sorry I stopped coming to your restaurant. Dad's dead, but can you help me figure out if he mailed this stuff?*

Yeah. I hadn't thought this through. Not even a little bit.

I released the door as the hostess appeared. Her jewelry glistened beneath diamond-white lights. Glossy tiles stretched around her stiletto heels, her curves wrapped in a chic dress.

The door swung shut. I yanked it open. Since when did Gypsy Django have a hostess? Mr. Kotfas had always done everything. He even helped the line cooks.

The hostess gathered a stack of leather-bound menus and led

a party of four into the dining room. Classical music drifted from that direction.

I hurried inside, grabbed a menu, and skimmed the glossy pages. A tiny black *47* marked a veal dish. Was that the price?

"May I help you, miss?" A man stationed himself behind the host stand. The lights burned above him, casting a shimmery glaze over his red silk tie.

"I'm here to speak to Mr. Kotfas." I studied the menu. "Real quick, do y'all still serve burgers? I'm trying to figure out—"

"We do not serve *burgers*." He said the word like he'd been chewing on a lemon. "And I am unsure who you wish to speak with. We have no staff by the name of Kotfas."

"He's not staff. He's the owner."

Understanding crisscrossed the man's face. "This establishment underwent a change of ownership last fall. I do not know the previous owner, but none of the present owners—there are three—are named Kotfas."

I fumbled with the menu. The man scowled.

"I-I guess I'm more interested in one of your customers. His name was Nicholas Barrett. He was a regular on Mondays. I should have a picture." I patted my pockets. Where was my phone?

"That name likewise does not sound familiar, nor are we open on Mondays."

I froze. "You're not?"

"We are open to the public Tuesday through Sunday. Mondays are reserved for staff meetings."

"Since when?"

"Our grand reopening. That was in November." He pried the menu away from me. "Is there anything else I may assist you with?"

"Um, no. I-I don't think so." My shoulders sagged as I ambled outside.

A blast of cold air tunneled through downtown. I stuffed my hands into the fuzzy pockets of Brandy's jacket. The locket and scavenger hunt took up one side. Dad's keys scraped my knuckles in the other.

Gypsy Django had been Dad's favorite restaurant. Mr. Kotfas was his friend. Why hadn't he mentioned any of this?

Then again, maybe I hadn't been paying attention. That was possible, but it didn't explain everything—like where Dad had gone the Monday before his trip.

And where he'd gone every Monday since November.

BACK AT THE APARTMENT, the ceiling fan shed light on my deconstructed living room. Dad's TV, with its dusty stand, had been staged by the door. The wall was blank, no more Rosie, and the Christmas tree was off for the first time in two weeks.

My teary gaze lingered on the bundle of plastic branches. Dad and I had this habit of leaving the Christmas lights on for whoever was coming home last. I'd left them on this entire time.

An ache penetrated my chest.

Brandy's five-ten frame filled the doorway to my room. "There you are." She crossed to the den in three strides. "Where were you? We were getting worried."

"I wasn't worried," a male voice called.

Dave traipsed out of my bedroom. A guy with dark skin a tinge lighter than ebony followed—Dave's latest recruit for his parkour and free-running team.

"Hey." I couldn't remember the guy's name. "Thanks for helping out tonight."

"Welcome. It's not a problem." He pushed up his sleeves. "We're goin' pretty fast. You don't have much stuff."

My stomach soured. He'd made the comment offhandedly, not as an insult, but it reminded me of how broke Dad and I were. How broke *I* was.

"We tried to call." Dave held up my phone and gave it a jiggle. "It was plugged in by your bed."

I took the device. "Thanks."

"Ty texted you." One of Dave's pale eyebrows slid up. "Figured you'd wanna know."

The twitch in my eye returned with a vengeance. Ty had gone skiing with his parents and their family friends, some kind of stupid tradition they had. He knew about Dad. They all did. Ty was fully aware I had a deadline to move out, but he'd gone anyway.

Jerk.

"Well?" I woke up my phone. "Has he apologized yet?"

Brandy snorted. "Doubt it."

"Listen, I wouldn't know," Dave said. "I only saw the notification."

I did a double take. My app had marked the message as read. "You didn't open this?"

"Not me." Dave sent a questioning look to Brandy. She raised her hands in a show of innocence.

This happened the other night, too. With an email. The message had been marked as read, even though I hadn't seen it.

"You never answered my question." Brandy pushed through the messy den, ponytail swinging. "Where'd you go?"

I grimaced. "Gypsy Django."

"That place your dad used to go?" Her eyes narrowed. "Isn't that downtown?"

"More like midtown, I'd say."

"You drove to—?" Brandy squeezed a fist. "How could you do that when you *knew* Dave was on his way with the truck? After I explained, in great detail, that we're out of time. If we don't get this stuff out—"

"Okay!" Dave clapped his hands and rubbed them together. "Time for us to keep packing." He nudged the new guy, and they retreated to my bedroom.

"I'm sorry," I said when they were out of earshot. "I know I shouldn't have left, but I had to do something. It was important."

"I get it. I do, but—" She gathered a breath, like whatever she was about to say required new strength.

"What?"

"Something's going on with my folks. Really with my mom. She doesn't think we're equipped to handle this situation."

"What situation? Me moving in with y'all?" My guts twisted. "Did you tell them I'm willing to pay rent? The movie theater by your house is hiring. I'll apply this week. Whatever I need to do."

"My dad's fine with that, but my mom... I haven't known how to talk to you about this."

"About what? Bee, tell me."

"After I left for work the other day, my mom heard you talking to someone." Brandy averted her gaze. "She thought you were on the phone, but then she found you digging through my closet. You were looking for something, and you were frantic over it. Then she realized—" Her eyes met mine. "You weren't on the phone."

My jaw slid out of place.

"You were saying stuff about your dad, about how he couldn't be dead. She said it sounded like crazy talk, like you weren't mentally there or..." She punctuated her explanation with a sharp sigh.

"I-I don't remember doing that."

"It's gotta be trauma. You've always had hang-ups because of your mom's— You know. Stuff. My parents think your dad's death sent you over some proverbial cliff." She gripped my shoulders. "Do you get what I'm saying?"

"No. I don't. Does your mom think I'm crazy? Do you?"

"What was in the package?" The edges of her mouth turned down. "It wasn't from the liaison, was it?"

I shook my head.

"Kat, what's going on? And don't say it's nothing. I know you."

I pulled out the list of clues and handed it over. "It's one of my dad's scavenger hunts. It was in the package, and this was with it." I set the gold locket in her other hand. "I went to Gypsy Django to talk to my dad's friend about this stuff."

"You think your dad sent you a scavenger hunt?" She held up the paper. "In the mail?"

"It's all in his handwriting."

She didn't say anything for a long moment, but she didn't need to. The lines sinking into her tan face—across her forehead, around her pear-green eyes—spoke louder than words ever could have.

Everyone thought I was crazy. Maybe I was.

The ceiling fan added a *swish swish swish* to the tense silence. Dave's voice floated out of my room, followed by the rustling of clothes and the scraping of metal against metal. Sounded like the guys were in my closet.

"I'm not saying my dad mailed this stuff from the grave." My voice turned raspy, threatening to crack. "He must have sent the package before his flight."

"I want you to see something." Brandy scooted past me and retrieved the mailer. "This is a customs form. See?" She placed her finger on a thin square piece of paper. "Look at the sender's name."

I examined the gray letters scrawled into the carbon-copy paper. The return address was illegible, but the sender's name was crystal clear.

Levi Pavel.

My pulse quickened. Impossible.

"I know how badly you must miss your dad." Brandy wrapped an arm around me. "But babe? There's been no mistake. He didn't survive that plane crash—"

"Bee."

"—and he didn't send you this package."

"Bee, listen to me. Dad lived in Brașov. He told me a bunch of stories right before his trip." I flipped the mailer and showed her the postmark. "That's where this package was sent from."

"That doesn't mean he sent it."

"I know, but there has to be a connection. Somehow." I shook my head, trying to organize my thoughts. "Levi Pavel was a friend of my dad's, but this package can't be from him."

"Of course it can. It is. He heard about the plane crash, saw it on the news or whatever, and sent you this stuff. The locket is a condolence gift."

"I went to Gypsy Django tonight to see Dad's Romanian friend. His *only* Romanian friend. Everyone else he knew, all his other friends and family, are dead."

"All?" Her brow pinched. "What do you mean by that? How's that even possible?"

"Because they died in the revolution that happened over there. That's what I'm trying to tell you. Levi Pavel couldn't have sent me anything. He died in 1989."

BUCHAREST

HUNGARY
UKRAINE
MOLDOVA
ROMÂNIA
Brasov
București
SERBIA
BULGARIA

3. VOYAGE

"Ladies and gentlemen, it's my pleasure to welcome you to Henri Coandă International Airport." The flight attendant's delicate voice peeled through the PA system.

The plane rocked, touching down. I death-gripped the armrests.

"Do exercise caution whilst opening the overhead lockers," the flight attendant purred. "We ask that you wait until the captain has turned off the Fasten Seat Belt sign before moving 'round the cabin. Thank you for flying with us."

I released the armrests and watched the color return to my knuckles. Turbulence. All the way from London. The chances of an accident were low, statistically speaking, but turbulence was the reason Dad's flight had crashed.

Well, one of the reasons.

The plane ground to a halt, and the seat belt light dimmed. *Ding!* An orchestra of snaps filled the cabin. Two blondes in my row moved to the aisle. The younger one made eye contact with me and pointed at the overhead bin.

I thumbed behind me. "My stuff's back there."

The girl nodded and helped her mom with their carry-ons. I powered up my phone.

A tiny blue envelope appeared on my screen. I figured it was a message from Brandy and opened it.

> You make it to Romania? Miss you. Thinking of you. Xx

Bitter, inky blackness filtered into my stomach. My phone indicated the sender was a former classmate of mine, but the "Xx" was Ty's trademark. Shorthand for *kiss kiss*.

A second message chimed.

> Had a chance to hit the bike track. Couldn't stand the thought of going without you… Can't we talk?

Yep. Definitely Ty.

I stared at the empty seats. Passengers had smashed into the aisle and were pressing forward little by little.

"Do not text him back," I warned myself, tears rising. "Don't do it."

My thoughts shifted from Ty to the girl he'd slept with. Someone had sent me a pic of them together, and I had decided to keep it—an ever-present reminder that my ex, with his pathetic excuses, could not be trusted.

I navigated to the folder and tapped the icon, launching the god-awful pic onto my screen. My eyes heated, but I refused to look away.

The girl sat on Ty's lap, head tipped back while he kissed her slender neck. Honey-brown hair, streaked in lowlights and high-lights, cascaded down her back. Her lips were over-Botoxed. Her sweater looked like it had been painted on, the neckline scooping low and showing off her cleavage.

I firmed up my chin. Tried to. Why couldn't European snow bunnies be gross and ugly or—at the very least—repulsed by my cheating boyfriend?

Ex-boyfriend, I reminded myself. For nearly five months now.

Warm streams spilled. I navigated to my contacts. That former classmate was likely an innocent bystander, but I deleted his number anyway. It was either that or manually block him. Either way, Ty wouldn't be able to reach me from that number again.

Somebody cleared his throat. Might have been the second time he'd done it, actually. I wiped my face and twisted around.

A guy who looked about my age stood in the aisle, adjusting his huge, thick-rimmed glasses—what Brandy called "grandpa glasses," even though people our age wore them. He gestured for me to go ahead.

"Uh, *vorbiți engleză?*" I was trying to ask if he spoke English.

The guy fought a smile, and I knew I'd butchered the pronunciation. Dad had never taught me Romanian, and I couldn't afford language programs. Had to settle for YouTube videos in the months leading up to this trip.

The guy erased his amusement and nodded. *"Da."* Yes.

I pointed at an overhead bin at the back of the plane. It was the only bin still closed. "My backpack's in there."

He glanced at the bin.

"I was going to let everyone else go first..." My explanation trailed off as the guy pushed through the line of passengers and angled for the bin.

A woman huffed, squeezing past him. I had one foot in the aisle when she brushed past me, her frumpy heels *thump-thump-thump*ing. Other passengers followed her lead.

Lava rose in my cheeks.

Grandpa Glasses retrieved my backpack and returned it to me. I mumbled thanks, did a one-eighty, and fast-walked off the plane with my head down and my face hot.

Thankfully, nobody seemed annoyed by the time I processed through Customs. The terminal funneled into a baggage claim filled with duty-free shops, souvenir kiosks, and luggage carousels.

The passengers from my flight gathered around a carousel labeled with a yellow number four. Not a digital four. An actual printed sign. The conveyor belt cranked to life, and a horrible noise, like metal being forced into a meat grinder, dampened all other sounds.

Five minutes ticked by, then ten, and not a single bag had appeared. Was this normal? No one else seemed alarmed.

I took a calming breath and decided to work on the scavenger hunt. The paper had thinned along the creases from where I'd folded it so many times. I unfolded it yet again and reviewed the clues.

→OTP

The first one showed an arrow pointing to the letters OTP— the code for Bucharest's main airport. The arrow was Dad's shorthand for "go to." **Go to Bucharest.** That was what he'd been saying.

The next clue:

„AM FOST PROFESOR LA UNIVERSITATEA POLITEHNICA DIN BUCUREȘTI"

„Am fost profesor la Universitatea Politehnica din București." Translation: **"I was a professor at the Polytechnic University of Bucharest."** Dad had worked at that school before moving to America. He was talking about himself.

The next part was harder and had taken an entire weekend to solve. I had been reading **DRS SADE** as *Doctors Sade*. Were these professors at the university? A husband and wife, maybe? Siblings? Those had been my initial thoughts, but when I'd researched the faculty, I didn't find any professors with the name "Sade."

The next part of the clue was **DREADS FINDS**. That was even more confusing. So, basically, none of this made sense... until I realized these were anagrams. After shuffling the words around, it became clear that **DRS SADE** was *address* and **DREADS FINDS** was *find address*.

But what address had Dad been referring to? That answer had taken me a whole month to figure out.

The first bag tumbled onto the conveyor belt, yanking me out of my thoughts. Other bags followed and filled up the metal carousel.

I folded the paper and stuffed it into my jean pocket. As I withdrew my hand, my attention shifted to a familiar rugged face.

Grandpa Glasses stood on the other side of the carousel. Belted khakis rested low on his waist. A powder-blue shirt, sleeves rolled at his elbows, hugged his lean frame. He might have been older than me, actually—twentyish maybe?—and he was a head taller than the other passengers.

He folded his arms and sighed, gaze drifting. He busted me staring at him.

I slid a hand under the strap of my backpack and pretended to stretch my neck. His eyes glimmered with amusement.

Yeah. He wasn't buying it. My stare locked with his, and he winked.

My cheeks caught fire a second time. I burrowed into the crowd, letting other passengers slide into my spot.

Bags trickled in from whatever luggage purgatory they'd been trapped in. Twenty minutes later, I had my suitcase and rolled it to a set of glass doors. Yellow cabs lined up outside. Most people bypassed the taxis and continued to a parking lot.

I paused at the doors, cross-bodying my travel purse and cinching the straps of my backpack. I was about to continue outside when a tall frame veered my way.

Grandpa Glasses.

He shouldered a leather duffel, his stride long and relaxed, his smile easy. Was he flirting? He had to be.

Then something utterly terrifying rattled its way into my thoughts. What if he was up to no good? He could be trying to gain my trust when in reality he was planning to rob me. Or worse. I'd seen *Taken* and had always wondered if that kind of thing really happened in Europe.

"I hoped I could ask you—"

"I have a boyfriend," I blurted.

He pulled up short.

"He's... going to be here any minute. I'm meeting him. He's Romanian." I tried to sound sure of myself—*not* like a solo female traveler—but everything came out rushed and with a slight quaver.

I gripped the handle of my suitcase for resolve. "Also, I... didn't need help with my backpack. You should have asked before you, um, did that."

The guy stayed quiet, and guilt pricked me. Was this whole thing really necessary?

Maybe. But maybe not.

He offered up a weak smile and filed outside with another wave of passengers. I took a step in that direction, about to call out to him, about to apologize. Fear rooted me in place.

The homicide rate in Romania was 1.25 per every one hundred thousand. That was low compared to the US, but I couldn't afford to let my guard down.

I also couldn't afford any distractions. I had a meeting at the university this afternoon, and it was going to take all my energy to shake off this jet lag and solve the next clue.

3½. PORTENT

I stood on a ridge and looked out over rolling mountains. The landscape dropped down into a long, deep valley. The sun hovered at midmorning.

I closed my eyes, tipped my face up, and let the golden warmth soak into my cheeks.

"Isn't it wonderful?"

I opened my eyes. Dad stood beside me, his skin bronzy in the sunlight. A breeze rustled his short black curls, shaking them in a happy greeting.

He held his attention on something in the valley. I traced his line of sight. Whatever he was staring at crawled along at a snail's pace.

"Ox-drawn carriage." His mouth hitched up. "A common means of transportation here in Transylvania, and so much more stylish than horses, don't you think?"

I grinned. "Sure. If you say so." When I was a kid, I used to beg Dad to tell me about his homeland, about what it was like growing up in a communist country. He never shared much. Sometimes he became angry.

Not anymore, apparently.

The wind changed direction, blowing in sharp gusts. Dark

clouds rolled in, and the emerald landscape morphed into rocky, barren terrain. Lightning popped. Thunder clapped.

A funnel cloud slipped out of the storm, a black ribbon let down from heaven. The strand glided toward the earth, moving, dancing, twisting this way and that.

Finally, it touched down, spraying up dirt and mowing down everything in its path. Three more funnels descended.

"How many are there?" Dad slanted a look at me. "Total."

"Four." I knew the answer was important. I didn't know why.

A gust swept over the ridge, swirling, carrying bits of earth. Dirt peppered my face.

I rubbed my eyes. "We need to take cov—" My eyes cleared before I could finish. Dad was gone.

Of course he was gone. He was dead. He'd been dead for more than five months.

Pain bloomed between my ribs. Tears, the kind that are big and fat and full of regret, flowed down my cheeks. *I'm sorry. Dad, I'm so sorry.* The words bubbled up, aching to be said, to be heard, but I couldn't speak past the tightness in my throat.

The ache swelled, tumbling down into the depths of me. My legs gave out, and my knees slammed against rocky ground. Dirt and pebbles dug into my skin. Dust swirled around me.

As I shielded my face, I caught a glimpse of something shiny and silver in the distance. A jumbo jet had entered the valley.

Dad's plane.

A chill settled. Puffy clouds rolled across the valley, dumping a flurry of white over the landscape. Snowflakes accumulated in my hair. My damp cheeks turned frosty.

The tornadoes twisted around the plane. The aircraft rattled from head to tail, and a metal sheet peeled away from the frame.

"No," I whimpered. "Please, please no."

One of the wings caught an updraft. The plane tipped forward and entered a nosedive. "Daaad!" I watched, horrified, as the aircraft collided with the mountain.

Metal crunched. Flames burst into a pillar of smoke.

I screamed and bolted upright. Hair matted my neck and face, sweat soaking my shirt. The fabric clung to me.

Warm air smothered my lungs as I took in my surroundings—suitcase, dresser, backpack, travel purse.

I was at the hostel.

Sunlight poured in through the window. This room was supposed to be warm, being on the third floor, but I hadn't realized it would be this hot. Not this early in the day.

It was still early, wasn't it?

I found my phone and checked the time. It was two thirty in the afternoon. I'd been sleeping for more than *three hours*.

"Crap. My meeting."

4. DETOUR

"Can't believe this is happening." I pressed the cordless phone to my ear and used my other hand to fan myself. The hostel didn't have AC, and the building had become a brick oven as the afternoon had progressed.

A monotone ring pealed through the receiver. I held my breath and willed the professor to answer this time. His name peered up at me from a notepad lying face up on the reception desk.

IONESCU MARIUS—GONE TO FRANKFURT, EMER-
GENCY (COLLEAGUE ILL)

The ringing stopped. I snapped to attention. "Professor Ionescu, it's Kat Barrett—"

The professor's voicemail cut me off. I slouched and set the phone on its charging cradle.

"Were you able to reach your friend?"

I pivoted toward the voice, which sounded like a female Dracula. The hostel worker who'd talked to Professor Ionescu entered the reception area.

"He's more of an acquaintance. And no, he's not answering."

"Perhaps he has not yet reached his destination." She stationed herself behind the reception desk. "I hope he will return your calls. I think he will. He sounded very sorry for missing you."

"Great." I tried to sound optimistic, but a headache had been slinking through my skull all afternoon, ever since I'd woken up. The throbbing settled behind my eyes. "What did he say the emergency was again?"

"He is conducting quality management training on behalf of his sick colleague."

That was the part I didn't understand. Marius Ionescu was a computer science professor. What did quality management have to do with that?

"He didn't say when he'd be back?" I asked, massaging my temples.

"He said only that you may be returning to the United States before he could meet with you."

That didn't make sense, either, since I'd never given him my full itinerary. Just the date and time I'd be arriving in Bucharest.

"Do not worry, dear. There is much to see in my city." The girl lifted a shoulder, blasé. "You will have no shortage of activities."

"But I was supposed to leave for Braşov tomorrow, and I can't go unless I find what I'm looking for. The professor was supposed to help me."

"The university has other employees. Perhaps if you visit them you will find better luck."

I resisted the urge to argue. I'd talked to plenty of those employees these past five months, and none of them had been very helpful. None except Professor Ionescu.

A crowd of people herded into the reception area. One girl—an Aussie, based on her accent—wore cutoff khaki shorts and brown hiking boots that accentuated her tan legs.

My thighs sweated jealously in my jeans.

Crocodile Huntress pushed open the back door and held it

for the others. Amber sunlight spilled inside the reception area, hitting me square in the eyes while the group poured outside.

I winced. "Do y'all keep any headache medicine?"

"I would suggest for you to buy this at a *farmacie*. Here, I will show you." The hostel worker pulled out a tourism pamphlet and opened it to the map.

My stomach rumbled.

"Are there any fast-food restaurants near that pharmacy?" I pressed on the bulge in my pocket—leftover lei from the over-priced taxi I'd taken from the airport. "Something cheap."

"I know the perfect shawarma restaurant. It is inexpensive, and the food is good." She circled a street called Strada Olimpului. "This is where we are. You will follow this path"—she drew squiggly lines and arrows—"until you see Piața Unirii. Union Square. It is a busy area with a mall and a park. Impossible to miss."

I traced the squiggles. "That seems… far."

"You can order a taxi, of course. But with traffic, at this hour, walking is faster."

I dug out my phone—Brandy's phone, technically, an old one she'd let me borrow for the trip—and checked the time. It was six p.m. Paying to sit in rush hour traffic was a hard no on my budget.

"Walking it is."

———

MY HOSTEL RESTED in a pocket of peace and quiet deep in the city center. Parked cars stacked both sides of the narrow street. A long row of metal gates cordoned off old stucco homes.

Tower-block-style buildings rose up on the next street over, hiding the sinking sun and casting long shadows over the pave-ment. Black wires crisscrossed the space overhead.

The lines gathered in tangled wads attached to telephone poles and buildings. I marveled at the organized chaos until the street dead-ended in front of me. There weren't as many parked cars in this section, and rubble lay piled up where homes—maybe apartments?—must've once been.

A communist-era tower block, dull gray and made of cement, loomed over the cul-de-sac. Rebar jutted through the crumbling walls. Graffiti wallpapered the exterior, and most of the balconies were gone or in need of repair. A stepping balcony hung lopsided, dangling by a single screw.

Heaviness settled in the pit of my stomach. Had the hostel worker given me bad directions?

I studied the map. The squiggles pointed left, but there wasn't a street on my left. Just a cement staircase in an alley.

Glass clattered, and the clink of a bottle rolling across pavement echoed. I wheeled around. "Is someone there? I-I think I'm lost."

My voice dispelled, leaving behind eerie silence. A shiver dragged up my spine.

I swore under my breath, sprinted for the alley, and climbed the steps two at a time. The staircase dumped me onto a sidewalk that led downhill. Honks and the rumble of motors grew louder.

I reached the bottom and discovered rush hour traffic pushing through an intersection. The stench of hot pavement burned my nose.

Pedestrians gathered at a crosswalk. I burrowed into the crowd and slid a glance over my shoulder. The top of the stairs came into view, and I half expected someone to be there.

There wasn't.

I smoothed the tourism pamphlet and used it to fan myself. Of course there wasn't. Why would someone be there? "Chill," I told myself. "Everything's fine. You're perfectly safe."

An elderly woman waited in the crowd. She was short and pudgy, and coarse hair poked out from beneath her headscarf.

I mustered up a smile. *"Bună ziua."* Good day. "Do you know where I can find Union Square?"

She cut a sideways look.

"Union Square," I repeated, louder.

She gripped her cane the way I had gripped my suitcase when that guy at the airport had been bugging me. The other pedestrians were busy with kids or phones. I was on my own.

Traffic skidded to a stop, and everyone filtered into the crosswalk. I moved with the crowd, studying the stone buildings and watching for landmarks. Water arced through a line of fountains in front of us.

A swath of green appeared amid the concrete, and happy voices drifted from that direction. The hostel worker had mentioned something about a park. This had to be it.

I turned in.

The grit of the city disappeared as natural green enveloped me. Well, it was more of a dusty green-brown. Hedges lined the exterior, but they were sparse, their leaves crispy and sprinkled over the crunchy grass.

After everything the liaison had told me, I hadn't been expecting dry weather. Not that I was complaining. I'd forgotten to bring an umbrella so... better if I didn't need one.

Walking paths weaved through the park. I picked one, squeezing past people in line for ice cream, when a blur of movement drew my attention to the right. Several guys darted back and forth, chasing after a soccer ball.

I slouched and continued on my way. I didn't want to think about soccer. Not right now.

One of the guys shouted.

I turned in time to see the ball sail into the corner. The players quickened their movements, and someone's foot connected. The keeper dove, blocking the shot.

My pulse ratcheted. Okay, maybe I could use a break. Just for a minute.

I found a bench and let the rhythm of the game sweep me up. One minute turned into ten, turned into twenty or thirty.

The sun slipped away, coating the sky in deep gold with splashes of scarlet. I hadn't meant to stay out this late, but I could feel the stress leaving my body. The pounding in my head abated.

"Where is it? Come on, come on. You gotta find it."

My ears tuned into a voice—male, no accent. Was he American?

I scanned the park and noticed a young guy calling people over to him. He was wearing a polo shirt with slacks, his sooty-blond hair wavy and swept to the side.

My focus returned to the soccer players. They wiped their faces and fist-bumped each other. The game was over.

I pushed up from the bench and made my way into the growing crowd.

"Keep your eyes on the ball." The young guy shuffled three matchboxes on a table. "You gotta find the ball to win. Where is it?"

A stocky guy stepped forward and handed over a neatly folded stack of bills. His knit shirt strained against bulky arms and a broad chest.

The young guy lined up the matchboxes. Beefcake pointed at the middle one.

"Our player has made his selection." The young guy lifted the box, and a ball the size of a marble appeared. "We have a winner!"

Whispers circled through the crowd as Beefcake made his money back, plus some. Huh. Must've been a game.

The crowd held a collective breath each time Beefcake placed a bet. I had to stop myself from calling out one time. The ball was on the right, but Beefcake had selected the matchbox on the left. He was about to lose his—

"Winner!"

Cheers went up.

I blinked. The ball should have been on the right. I'd been sure of it. So sure, I would have bet money.

My brow dipped.

The young guy did a dramatic slow clap. "*Merci beaucoup,* Émilien."

Beefcake—or Émilien?—responded with a glare. Did these guys know each other?

Onlookers stepped forward to play, but only one of them managed to win. The man was lanky, with dark hair that fell at his shoulders and a perfectly coiffed five-o'clock shadow on his chiseled cheeks. His clothes—slacks, dress shirt, dress shoes—were better suited for a nightclub than a park.

The young guy was dressed similarly, come to think of it. So was Beefcake.

"Hang on," I said as the puzzle pieces snapped into place. These guys *did* know each other. Because this wasn't a game. It was a scam.

Parkgoers strolled past, and I considered asking someone to call the cops. But not all Romanians spoke English, and I wasn't sure how to overcome this type of language barrier. I mean, what if I said "police" and they freaked out?

I couldn't ask them to call 911, either, because Europe was on a different emergency system. Finding an English-speaker would be better.

My attention landed on a guy standing beneath a tree. He leaned back, bracing a chunky black boot against the trunk, and I noticed he was wearing a Post Malone shirt. Maybe I'd found my English-speaker.

I edged through the crowd.

The guy pocketed his phone. As he folded his arms, the sharp lines of a tribal band peeked out from beneath his shirtsleeve.

The tattoo flexed with the cut of his biceps. My heart pitter-pattered.

I made myself pause. Okay, if I was going to approach this guy, I needed to have my wits about me.

But as I stood there, trying to convince myself he wasn't all that hot—even though he totally was—I realized there was something kinda familiar about him.

My stare traveled to the top of his head, and my guts twisted. He'd styled his chestnut-brown hair into a thick, short faux hawk —exactly the way Ty had worn his hair last summer. It'd been his "thing" on days we'd gone to the motorcycle track.

That was what seemed familiar. Not the guy. His faux hawk.

He scanned the crowd, his stare drifting over each person. His eyes held a glazed look as they passed over me, but then he did a double take.

I wrinkled my nose, thinking of Ty.

Amusement lit the guy's face. He gestured at himself as if to say, *It's me.* So I did know him. But from where? The hostel?

I shrugged and shook my head.

He rubbed his chin, expression thoughtful. Then a knowing grin played across his lips.

He dipped into his breast pocket and pulled out a pair of huge, thick-rimmed—

Oh. They were thick-rimmed glasses. He slid them on and winked.

It was Grandpa Glasses. From my flight.

5. INVITATION

The crowd booed, severing my connection to Grandpa Glasses. A middle-aged man was shouting about something, and everyone was glaring.

The young guy chuckled, smiling through clenched teeth, and took a measured step backward. They were on to him.

The young guy turned to run. His shoe caught, and he belly flopped onto the ground. The crowd rushed him. He had something in his hand and tossed it.

Correction: two things. The objects bounced across a scrubby patch of grass and settled by my feet. Were those... balls?

They were. Extra balls.

So that was how Émilien and the bearded man had been winning. Whenever they played, the young guy must have used all three balls. For everyone else, he probably used one. Or none, ensuring a loss every time.

I pointed at the balls, about to scream, about to bring their scam to an end.

The young guy cried out. His voice bordered the upper end of puberty—not quite deep, not quite squeaky. He couldn't have been older than fifteen.

My thoughts carried me back to three years ago, when I was

that age, and heaviness crept into my being. Life had a way of thrusting people onto dark paths. I knew that firsthand. Plus, I was willing to bet Émilien and the bearded man were the real masterminds. They were likely taking advantage of this poor kid.

But I might be able to help him.

Without thinking, without even considering the consequences, I walked forward and stepped on the balls. They pressed against the soles of my shoes and sank into the dry earth.

There. Nobody even noticed.

Except someone did notice. Three people, actually—the bearded man, Émilien, and Grandpa Glasses. The trio shared a questioning look.

Émilien said something in French. Grandpa Glasses replied with a warning shake of his head.

Fear choked me. Grandpa Glasses was with the scammers.

"I said I don't have anything!" The kid was on his feet, hands raised while everyone frisked him. He scanned the ground, probably wondering where the balls had gone.

His stare reached my feet and climbed. He met my gaze, and his forehead creased.

I squatted, pretending to search like everyone else. Four sets of eyes burned a hole in my head.

The mob found one ball and three matchboxes, nothing else. Everyone dispersed, muttering to each other. Émilien watched them go, his mouth drilled down in a scowl.

The kid peeked over at him. "What?"

The Frenchman gave a slow, disgusted shake of his head. He swatted the bearded man, and they slinked off. The kid sighed and started toward me.

I plucked the balls from their hiding place and lobbed them. The kid caught one and fumbled the other. "Those guys are taking advantage of you," I said. "You should find better friends."

He blinked, mouth hanging open. Grandpa Glasses had about the same expression, although slightly more amused than perplexed.

I did an about-face and headed for the park's main entrance. My heart shook. Couldn't believe I had nearly asked Grandpa Glasses to call the cops. On his *friends*.

Footsteps pounded behind me. Someone gripped my elbow and pulled me around. It was the kid. "You hid those balls."

"Yeah? So?"

"That was awesome. I thought I was busted for sure." His mouth twisted up in a smile. "Thanks."

I wasn't sure what to say. *You're welcome. No prob. I love helping scammers get away with their scams.*

"I'm Andrei, by the way."

"I'm... Kat." I knew better than to give my real name, but I couldn't think of a fake name fast enough. *Do not tell him your last name.*

"Nice to meet you, Kat. That's Maksim." He jerked a thumb toward Grandpa Glasses.

"We've been over this." Grandpa Glasses stopped in front of us. "It's Răzvan."

Andrei waved him off. "Don't listen to him. They go by family names here, but his first name is Maksim."

"I suppose she can call me that. If she wants to." His Post Malone shirt strained as he reached up and removed his glasses. "So. We meet again."

His voice tolled like a bell, reverberating in my chest, and my cheeks warmed without permission. I looked down, hiding the blush.

"Again?" Andrei asked. "You two know each other?"

I mumbled no as Maksim said yes.

"We saw each other on a flight." I brought my gaze up. "Briefly."

"It was you and someone else, wasn't it? A boyfriend, I believe?" Maksim's lips quirked. "I hope you'll convey my apologies to him. For the miscommunication."

The heat in my face cranked. I'd said something about having a boyfriend. He was calling my bluff.

"Hey, Kat? Is that your name?" Andrei motioned at his friend. "Maks doesn't run these hustles anymore, just so you know."

"Why do I care? I mean, I *don't* care." I fidgeted, crossing and uncrossing my arms. "I'm—not sure why you're telling me any of this."

"Because you said these guys were taking advantage of me. But Maks was trying to make sure I didn't get in trouble." Andrei shrugged. "He was watching out for me."

Maksim gave a bounce of his eyebrows—which, by the way, framed his eyes pretty stinkin' perfectly. My stomach flipped.

I turned and beelined for the exit. "Gotta go," I called over my shoulder. Then I mumbled, "Please don't follow me."

Sunlight faded, dusting the city in hazy purple twilight. Streetlamps lit up the sidewalk like giant fireflies. Digital billboards glittered atop the massive stone buildings.

Cars jammed the one-way street, filling the air with exhaust fumes, the whirr of idling motors, and a mix of music and Romanian talk radio.

My stomach rumbled as I trekked alongside the traffic jam. I swore and reached into my pocket, yanking out the tourism pamphlet. It was official. I had lost a day, my entire first day in Romania, and I hadn't even eaten yet.

Also, the headache was back. With a vengeance.

I pressed on my temple and continued up the sidewalk. A sweet fragrance followed two ladies out of a candle shop. If I didn't find that shawarma place soon, I might settle for a vanilla-scented candle.

Someone slid into step beside me. I looked over and found happy, denim-blue eyes and a sunshiny grin. "Where ya goin'?" Andrei asked.

"Dinner. Did you follow me from the—?"

"Hey, why don't we grab dinner together? My treat." He glanced at Maksim, who trailed us by two steps. "You, too, pal. I owe you for last week."

"You're offering to pay for my meal?" My feet dragged to a stop. "Why?"

"Eh, seemed like a good idea." Andrei pulled me to the side, allowing other pedestrians to pass. "I'm hungry, too. Haven't eaten all day."

My eyes went squinty. "Is this another scam?"

He dropped the smile. "No."

"It is. You two are going to trick me into paying for your meals."

"We wouldn't do that!" Andrei turned to Maksim. "Tell her we wouldn't do that."

"*I* wouldn't do that." Maksim stuffed his hands into his jean pockets, shoulders rising. "You trick me into paying for you all the time."

Andrei huffed and squared up to me. "I owe you for what you did back there. Let me pay for your dinner, and we'll call it even."

His offer was tempting, but I was battling some serious doubts.

Then again, free was free. I could order a big meal and save half for tomorrow. Two meals for the price of none.

"Let's go." Maksim nudged Andrei. "She's not interested."

"Sure she is." Andrei looked at me. "Aren't you?"

"I—"

"She doesn't know us," Maksim said, cutting me off. "She's afraid."

I straightened. "I am not."

"Oh, come on," Andrei said. "We'll be in a public place, plenty of people around." His eyes brightened. "It'll be fun. You'll see."

I FOLLOWED Andrei and Maksim into a neighborhood paved in cobblestones. We skirted a bunch of tourists snapping selfies in front of a white-stone building. The sign read Librărie, but it looked more like a bookstore than a library.

The upper floors looked like apartments, with flower boxes dotting the windows and wrought-iron railings curling across each balcony. The building, the whole neighborhood, had a neoclassical vibe. Like photos I'd seen of Paris. The touristy section of Bucharest was supposed to look similar.

"Is this Old Town?"

"Sure is." Andrei steered us into a wide cobblestone alley. We merged with the foot traffic flowing through the corridor. "Thought you said you hadn't been here before."

Had I said that? I didn't recall saying that.

"I've read about it online."

He replied with a *hmph*.

We continued past a row of eateries with outdoor patios full of sweaty, talkative patrons. A melody of accents echoed through the corridor. String lights burned into the thickening darkness.

We turned a corner and passed beneath a sign that left a red imprint on the night. Long cracks and peeling paint marked the building. The windows were shuttered.

A sign out front flickered. Massage Parlor. Guess that explained the windows.

A burly guy stood at the entrance, sizing people up as they approached. Maksim made eye contact and offered a subtle nod.

The bouncer, or whoever he was, nodded back.

I focused forward. Did Maksim go there? Was he one of their *customers*?

I couldn't say for sure, but there was an unmistakable familiarity between them. One more reason I shouldn't let my guard down.

We pushed through dense crowds until a green bubble of light appeared. Some kind of restaurant. Patrons filled every table on the patio, and a long line spilled outside and snaked around the building.

Andrei and Maksim stationed themselves at the end of the

line. The name Kebap plastered the windows and doors while a neon Shaorma sign glowed at the entrance.

Shaorma? As in shawarma?

I checked my tourism pamphlet. Sure enough, the hostel worker had jotted Kebap above the map. She had even circled two pharmacies, both of which sat kitty-corner from the restaurant, matching her notations.

I pointed a look at Andrei. "Did I tell you I was coming here?"

"You were coming here?" Maksim and Andrei said in unison.

"Great choice." Andrei pulled me into the line. "Food's decent, and Maksy Boy here knows the owners. That should get us a discount. Been a slow week for me." He said it like he waited tables for a living.

Maksim seemed distracted, his gaze drifting over our surroundings. Then, for a reason I couldn't understand, he looked at his arm.

Not the arm with the tattoo. The other arm.

He rotated it one way and then the other. His sleeve hitched, and puckered skin appeared. A scar?

His eyes met mine. He tugged on the sleeve and focused on Andrei. "I have somewhere to be."

Andrei sent up a disbelieving eyebrow. "Where?"

"A prior engagement. Forgive me, I... forgot." He did a one-eighty and shouldered through the crowd.

"Maks. Maks!" Andrei cupped his mouth. "What about the discount?"

Maksim cast a backward glance. His gaze came to a rest on me, and my center pinched.

I wheeled around and bumped straight into Andrei, who blinked out a confused look. "That was weird," he said.

"Yeah. Totally." I traced the path Maksim had taken. He would have disappeared by now if he hadn't been a head taller than everyone else. "Does he always act like that?"

"He was spooked. But Maks never gets spooked by anything."

Andrei tilted his head. "How'd you say you met him again? On a flight?"

"I had a flight from Atlanta to London, then another from London to Bucharest. I met him on the second leg coming from London."

"That's a funny coincidence, don't you think? That you two were on the same plane and then you saw him at the park? Bucharest is huge. What are the odds?"

What *were* the odds? Slim to none if I had to guess. But it wasn't like Maksim had known I would be at the park. I hadn't even known that. That meant it had to be a coincidence.

Right?

"So what are you doing in Romania?" Andrei inched forward as the line moved. He gestured for me to do the same. "I'm guessing you're American."

"My dad was born here, but he moved to America during the revolution. My mom's American." I wasn't up for talking about Dad's death or the scavenger hunt. Hopefully, he didn't catch on that I was sidestepping. "You're American, too, I guess?"

"Me?" Andrei pointed at himself. "I'm not American."

"Are you Canadian or...?"

"I'm Bulgarian. Taught myself English by watching American TV shows and movies. The accent's easy now, and the ladies seem to like it." He perked up. "You really think I sound American?"

"Uh, yeah. Fooled me."

Pride shone through in his smile. "Listen, I'd be happy to help you out while you're in town. I know the best places to eat, and I can take you around to the most famous sites. You'd have to pay for both of us, of course, and I do charge a small fee—"

"I'll keep that in mind." Solving the scavenger hunt in a week —less than a week now—was going to be difficult. I didn't have time for sightseeing, and I didn't have the budget for my own personal scammer-tour-guide.

Andrei prattled on while we waited. He was older than I'd

thought—sixteen rather than fifteen—and his parents weren't "around" anymore. Whatever that meant.

He wouldn't elaborate, but he did say he'd traveled a lot for his age. "I lived on the Ivory Coast. Do you know where that is?"

"Africa?"

"West Africa, the French-speaking part. That's where I met Maks. He was in charge of my training. But like I said, he doesn't do that stuff anymore."

"The scams? Or the training?"

"Either. He thinks it's bad karma or something. Anyway, one of the other guys is helping me now. We're foreigners, and we don't know much Romanian. That's why we were sent to the park today. Bigger crowds mean better chances at finding English speakers."

We reached the entrance, and Andrei held the door for me. I stepped inside. Bodies filled every table and booth. Cooks busied themselves behind the counter, spinning and shaving chunks of meat on vertical skewers.

A savory aroma tickled my senses. My salivary glands melted.

"West Africa," I blurted, trying to distract myself. We still had four people ahead of us, and they were taking their sweet time. "Is that where you met the French guy, Émilien?"

Andrei studied a backlit menu mounted above the cashier. "Yep. That's— Wait, how do you know his name is Émilien?" He focused on me. "And how do you know he's French?"

"You called him Émilien at the park. You said *merci beaucoup,* and I know that's French for—"

"*You heard that?*" Andrei face-palmed himself. He seemed to realize something else, and his eyes bulged. "Do you know if Drago heard? That was the tall dude with the—" He pulled a hand down his face, indicating a beard.

"Probably. Why?"

"He hates me. He *looks* for reasons to report me, and I just gave him one."

"Report you to who? The police?"

"To the underboss of our operation, Ştefan." Andrei pronounced the name with a *sh* and added emphasis to the second syllable: *shteh-FAHN*. "Maks and Émilien won't rat me out, but Drago will. Ohh man, oh man." Andrei fidgeted, then braced his head. He looked at me and sighed. "Sorry, Kat. I gotta go." He shouldered through the line.

"What about dinner?" I chased after him. "You said you wanted to pay me back. You said— Andrei, wait!"

He was already outside, sprinting up the corridor. The glass door shut in my face, and I watched until his five-six frame dissolved into the crowd.

6. WALLS

The cab accelerated, drawing me back into my seat. My driver cut into the next lane, carving a path through midmorning traffic. Honks went up around us.

I jerked the seat belt across me, about to buckle myself in, until I noticed... There was no buckle. Anywhere. Not even on the other side of the backseat. There wasn't a handlebar above the window, either, so I had nothing to hang on to.

I looped the seat belt around me and hoped for the best. Should have taken a bus. It was cheaper—and safer, apparently— but I hadn't been able to decipher the bus routes.

"How long do you visit my country?" The cabbie peered at me through the rearview mirror. "You are a student?"

"Tourist. I'm here for a week."

"Will you visit our Palace of Parliament?" He motioned at a rectangular building that filled the horizon. The shape imitated building blocks, extended out to the sides and stacked higher in the middle.

Kinda like the White House except bigger. And boxier.

"Fifth largest building in the world, but *first* in ugliness." The man held up a finger, making his point. "Built by the blood of

Romanians like my father and grandfather, slave labor at the hands of Ceauşescu. Do you know this name?"

I settled back. "He was the dictator."

"Communist 'president' of Romania until our revolution. *If we are permitted to call it a revolution.*" He said the last part with a guffaw.

I stiffened. "My dad's family died in the revolution."

"I am sorry to hear this." The man slouched. "Please understand. I express only my frustration over the findings of a new report, which is concluding that our revolution was a coup d'état orchestrated by members of the Nomenklatura."

"Whoever that is, I'm glad they did it. Any dictator who kills hundreds of thousands of people deserves to be overthrown. I don't have any family because of that tyrant."

Silence filled the cab.

My gaze lingered on the so-called palace. Stone columns framed the first floor while hundreds of windows reflected the midmorning sun—but even the scorching daylight did little to offset the dull-gray dreariness. Truthfully, the building looked like it needed a dose of antidepressants.

"Pardon me, *domnişoară*." The driver's cautious tone reeled me inside the vehicle. "When you are saying 'hundreds of thousands,' what is it you are speaking of?"

"What we've been talking about. The revolution."

"But this information you have is incorrect. There was a report used to gain support for the swift trial and execution of Ceauşescu. However, the death toll was inflated, and this report was later found to be... How do you call it in America? Fake news?"

"My dad was here. He witnessed all those people being killed."

"Perhaps it appeared to be hundreds of thousands to those who were being fired upon. But truth is important, and I must emphasize to you... This information you have is incorrect." He followed a line of traffic into a left turn. "Can we not agree that one thousand deaths were too many? Why must this number be inflated? We know of the many other crimes—"

"S-sorry, can you repeat that?" I unhooked myself from the seat belt and leaned forward. "How many deaths did you say? One thousand?"

"During the ten days of fighting, the death toll reached 1,104."

"Ten days?" Dad had always acted like the revolution dragged on for months. I'd never checked into it. Never had a reason to. He'd been a history buff with a knack for memorizing names, dates, locations. How could he have gotten such basic information wrong?

He couldn't have. This man was mistaken.

"Politehnica is there." The cabbie pointed ahead and to the right. A set of buildings peeked out from behind a tree line. "To which part of campus should I take you?"

"The rectorate." I grabbed my backpack.

"Administration building. I know where this is." He smiled into the rearview mirror. "Do not worry, *domnişoară*. Sometimes the truth is hidden, but we are learning more about it all of the time."

A ROUND CLOCK sat on the desk in front of me. The second hand *tick tick tick*ed, measuring the distance between my sanity and when the student assistant had gone to look for Dad's file.

That was twenty-six minutes ago.

Sweat leaked from my hairline and slid down my neck. I wiped the stream and reached for my backpack. Brandy had texted early in the morning—late last night for her—and I decided to text her back.

> Send good vibes and positive thoughts. At the university. They're trying to find Dad's file.

I pressed Send.

A red exclamation mark blinked onto my screen. Unable to send message. Tap to resend. No signal. I'd have to use a messaging app.

"Ma'am? Do y'all have Wi-Fi?"

The head secretary sat across from me, drilling her stare into a computer screen. She halted her rapid-fire typing. "I cannot give you the password unless you are a student or employee." She situated her spectacles and went back to typing.

I'd dealt with this woman before, by phone and email, and she'd always been unhelpful. Half the time she hadn't bothered to get back to me.

A girl with deep bronze skin and black hair—as thick and black as mine, but straight—rushed into the office. A mishap with bleach had stripped the brown from her frumpy shirt, leaving behind splotches of pinkish-orange.

My attention moved to her name tag, which hung lopsided over one of the splotches. Her name was an alternate spelling of Patty with one *t*.

Paty.

The girl passed a manila file to her boss. My pulse thrummed. Dad's old address was in that file. As soon as I had it, I could solve the current clue and head to Braşov. Trains ran all day. I could be there by this evening.

The secretary barked in Romanian and snatched the file from her assistant. Paty flinched.

"Now." The woman flipped open the file. "I must see the certificate of your father's death. I will need your passport *and* his for confirming identity."

I reached into my backpack and retrieved the folder with all my paperwork. Dad's death certificate was inside. I pulled out the paper and passed it to the secretary.

"What is this?" She squinted at the certificate. "This is not an official copy."

"It is. From the Ministry of the Interior." My fingers

connected with Dad's frayed passport. Mine was beside it. I pulled them out and pushed them across the woman's desk.

"I assure you this document is not official." She passed it back to me, refusing to even look at the passports. She closed Dad's file, and my throat clenched. "An official copy of the death certificate is required. I cannot release the records without it."

"What makes you think it's not official?"

She leaned across the desk and pointed at the word TEMPORAR, which was printed below the phrase CERTIFICAT DE DECES. "This means temporary. It is a temporary death certificate! Who has ever heard of such a thing?"

"My dad died in a plane crash." I wrenched a handful of papers out of the folder. "The investigation is complete, the investigators know what caused the crash, but they haven't recovered all the, um— The—" I bit back the urge to cry.

"The remains," I finished with a loud swallow. "The recovery efforts are ongoing. It's all in this report." I handed her the papers.

She read through the first page, and her head tilted. "This appears to be the aviation accident our media have been reporting."

"Probably. I don't speak Romanian, so I haven't been able to follow any news reports."

"I believe it is. The delay must be because of the controversy."

"The controversy with the cleanup and recovery efforts?"

"I am referring to the aircraft." She skimmed the first page of the report. "Everyone says something different—the pilots were not trained well or the aircraft experienced a malfunction." She flipped to the next page. "We have many problems with our government. No one wishes to accept the responsibility."

She must have been talking about the captain. Plane crashes from turbulence were rare, but pilot error was involved in this one. Then the plane started having problems...

The papers rustled, drawing me out of my head.

"As I understand this report," the secretary said, "it seems the death of your father has been declared—officially—but the circumstances of this documentation are extenuating."

"I know it sounds strange. Believe me. I haven't even been able to plan the funeral, but the liaison says his department needs more time. The problem is, I need my dad's records now."

"For what purpose? Why do you desire such outdated records?"

"Professor Ionescu said my dad's old address should be in the file. That's all I need. The address."

The woman sighed and set the papers on her desk. A hint of sympathy, the first I'd seen, softened the lines of her face. "This is a minor request. I feel confident to speak with our vice-chancellor. He has the authority to make a special exception for you."

"That would be amazing. Thank you."

"Allow me one moment please." The woman reached for her phone.

I directed a smile to Paty. She stood to the side, fingering a wooden crucifix fastened around her neck. It looked like one Dad used to have. We'd never been religious, but he'd kept the necklace hanging on his mirror. "A gift from a friend," he used to say. And that was all he would ever say.

Paty responded with a quiet smile. She seemed to understand the importance of the records.

The secretary noticed our silent exchange and divided a questioning look between us. Her scowl returned as she lowered the phone into its cradle.

Paty dropped the crucifix. The necklace fell taut around her neck.

"Excuse me, ma'am? There's one more thing." I was attempting to distract the woman.

It worked. The secretary focused on me.

"Professor Ionescu promised to help with something else." I fished the gold locket out of my backpack. The chain slipped between my fingers. "There's an inscription inside," I explained, handing her the necklace.

She pressed the latch, and the locket opened to the gold inner plate. "What language is this?" she asked, studying the inscription.

"I'm not sure. Professor Ionescu said he had colleagues who were multilingual. He thought they might be able to help, but he didn't tell me their names."

"Many Romanians are speaking four and five languages. I have fluency in French, German, Russian—" She flipped the locket over and examined the circular design. Her back stiffened.

She returned to the inscription, and her entire body went rigid. "How did you come into possession of this jewelry?" Her voice cooled and hardened at once, a steel blade forged in fire and then doused in water.

"M-my dad sent it to me. Before he, um... Before—" My attention shifted.

Paty was craning her neck, trying to get a look at the locket. Her stare widened. She gasped.

The secretary popped up in her seat and spun around. She stabbed a finger at her assistant and breathed fire. Paty's wide-eyed stare didn't budge from the locket.

The secretary aimed her tirade at me. I caught one thing she said—*zigany? sigany?*—and then she slammed the locket on her desk.

I jumped. "Hey! That's an antique."

"Why are you here? Are you spying on us?" A glimmer dawned in her eyes. She scooped up Dad's passport, and her jaw tightened. "How foolish of me. I should have inspected these documents more closely."

"I don't know what you're talking about."

"These names do not match. You are attempting to obtain records illegally." She tossed the passports at me and shoved everything else across her desk.

My papers scattered. I lunged for them.

"Liars and criminals, all of you." She grabbed the file and stuffed it in a drawer.

My heart skidded to a stop. "What are you doing?"

"Since you cannot prove a familial relationship, you will not be permitted to view this file." She tipped her chin toward the locket. "Now take with you that *thing* and leave. Do not return."

She swiveled toward her assistant and uttered something low and menacing. Tears slipped down Paty's face. The assistant raced out of the office.

I jumped up and followed her to the doorway. "Paty!"

She turned a corner. Her footsteps disappeared down the staircase.

I wheeled around. "Why would you—?" My question evaporated as I came face-to-face with a smartphone.

The camera light flashed.

7. LOST

"Sir?" The bus lurched. I gripped a metal pole, swaying. "Can you let me off?"

The driver met my gaze through his rearview mirror. "You don't want Piața Unirii?"

"I have to get off. Now." My lips stuck together, peeling apart on each word. I'd been riding un-air-conditioned buses for two solid hours, trying, with mixed success, to reach Union Square. If I didn't get something to drink soon, I was going to become a death statistic.

The driver tugged on the steering wheel. The bus eased over, hydraulics hissing.

I squeezed between sweaty bodies and stepped off. The bus chugged away, leaving behind a trail of smoke.

A canal ran up the middle of the street, dividing traffic in each direction. I pushed out a breath, donned my backpack, and started up the sidewalk, keeping alongside the canal. Sweat glazed my body. My mouth felt like I'd swallowed a cupful of sand.

I peered over the railing. A water demarcation line was visible, but most of the water was gone. That had to mean the flash-flooding had stopped. So then why hadn't the liaison said anything?

His email came back to me.

```
The storm system continues to delay our
recovery efforts. Romania is experi-
encing many unusual events due to
climate change. This phenomenon is
predicted for the foreseeable future.
```

The man had provided a link to a video, which showed flood-water sweeping through a village. That was in March. Now we were in May—granted, the end of May—and the weather had become arid enough to dry up a canal?

Extreme thirst elbowed its way into my thoughts. I scanned the stone buildings on my right, searching for a convenience store, a corner grocer, any place that might have something to drink.

My attention wandered to the other side of the canal. Modern glass buildings towered over the area, and several shops occupied the first floors. Most of the shops were boutiques. One showcased food in a display case.

Was that... bread?

It was. Different kinds of bread. The place was a bakery.

Bakeries sold drinks, right? If nothing else, I could ask for water from the tap.

I moved at a fast clip, feet smoldering in my running shoes. A group of tourists in matching shirts and khaki shorts loitered on the sidewalk, fanning themselves, their faces red and glossy. Several of them gathered around a map.

"Excuse me, please." I maneuvered through the crowd. "'Scuse me. Coming thr— *Oof.*" Someone rammed into me from behind. I stumbled forward and collided with a woman who was taking a selfie. She glowered.

I lifted an apologetic hand before turning toward the perpetrator—a Romanian man going the same way I'd been going before he plowed into me.

"Don't worry. We're fine," I called. A hum of chatter drowned out my voice.

The man found a break in the crowd, slipped through, and jogged up the sidewalk. His black curls waved goodbye as he picked up speed.

My heart wrenched. Dad used to have a shirt like that. He'd always joked about looking like a Georgia peach whenever he wore it. The man who'd bumped into me had the same bulgy waistline. He was Dad's height, too.

The man continued up the sidewalk, putting more distance between us. His hair was a little longer than Dad's had been the last time I'd seen him. Apart from that he could have passed for Dad's twin. Unless...

No. It couldn't be.

"Dad?" The word lodged itself in my throat. I swallowed and tried again, louder. "Dad? Dad!"

His head turned like he might've heard me. Hope sparked in my chest. I shouldered through the tourists, pushing my way to the edge of the crowd.

My feet stalled. What was I thinking? Dad was dead. Everyone had said so—the liaison, the airline, the investigators.

But what if they were wrong? What if he had survived the plane crash and found a way down the mountain? What if that was why they'd only found his passport?

But that didn't make sense. Because if Dad had survived, he would have texted or called—unless he'd been too disoriented.

An explanation bubbled up. It was a subtle thought, a glimmer, like the possibility had been there all along but hadn't occurred to me. Amnesia. What if Dad had amnesia and that was why he'd never contacted me? He hadn't known to.

My feet exploded in a run. "Dad!" My backpack flopped around. I cinched the straps and pumped my arms. My thighs burned, legs carrying me up the sidewalk.

Dad was a speck in the distance. I pushed myself harder,

tracing the peach color to a cross street. He was crossing over the canal.

The sights and sounds of the city grew louder. Traffic scooted through an intersection.

I turned left and barreled through pedestrians milling around on the sidewalk. The people glared at me. One of them shouted, but I barely heard him over construction in the area. Workers drilled into a slab of cement, their equipment banging and rattling and sending up plumes of dust.

Stone apartments towered over the neighborhood. Was that where Dad had gone? Maybe he lived around here.

Business suits streamed through a crosswalk. The people were headed for a restaurant. I trailed behind them, intending to check out the first apartment building.

Peach tugged at my vision.

I peered inside a window overlooking the restaurant's main dining room. My next breath caught. Dad was in there. He was *right there,* sitting at a table. Two men sat across from him. A blonde cozied up at his side.

Dad rested a hand on the woman's thigh, and I felt the blood drain from my face. Had he gotten married? He must have started a whole new life here.

That didn't matter. He was still my dad, and even if he'd forgotten about his life in America, seeing me again would jar his memory. It had to.

I shouldered through the suits and entered the restaurant. The maître d' stepped in front of me. I brushed past him.

He raced ahead of me and blocked my path. A woman in a delicate blouse and long pencil skirt joined him.

"I need to speak to one of your customers. He's in the dining room." I pointed in case they didn't speak English.

A hand came down on my shoulder. Another hooked my arm.

I looked up to find a man in a chef's hat standing on one side of me; a businessman stood on the other. They turned me around and escorted me to the door.

I tried to turn back, but the other suits joined in. I was surrounded, being pulled from the front and pushed from behind. "What are you doing? Let me go!"

I was outside, in this cluster of chaos, when broad shoulders appeared. The guy's eyes were hidden by a pair of sunglasses, but his other features—square jawline, strong nose, supple curve of his mouth—rang a distant bell.

He wedged himself between the suits and me.

"I don't understand." A tear slipped out. "I need to talk to someone in the restaurant, and they won't let me."

His mouth slipped open. I could almost see his eyes go wide behind the dark sunglasses. He faced the men and ushered them away.

Peach flashed in my peripheral. Dad was on his feet, chair pushed back. I raced to the window and rapped on the glass. Everyone in the dining room jumped.

The man in the peach shirt wheeled around, eyes wide—but they weren't Dad's droopy hazel eyes. My heart flipped and shattered.

Tremors moved up my legs and deposited into the rest of me. I braced a hand against the window as the mystery guy removed his sunglasses.

Maksim.

"Kat? Are you all right?"

I inhaled a shaky breath and burst into tears. Didn't matter who saw me, him or anyone else. I wanted Dad to be alive more than anything, more than absolutely anything.

A minute ago, I had him.

Snot and tears drained down my face, the full weight of disappointment crushing me. Tightness squeezed my chest and lungs.

I tried to inhale a breath. The air stopped at my throat. I tried again. Again.

Darkness edged into my vision. Fear hissed in the background, taunting me. I clutched my chest. I was having a panic attack, my first in months.

Maksim touched my shoulder. "Kat?"

"C-can't... b-b-breathe."

He worked the backpack off my arms and helped me sit down. Warm air kissed my face. He was fanning me, whispering. I leaned forward and held my head, trying to think, trying to focus on my breathing.

In through my nose. Out through my mouth.

Maksim's voice walked the line between bass and baritone, his words ebbing and flowing—like a song, except he wasn't singing. It was more like a poem. A secret poem only he knew the words to.

The heaviness lifted. I drew in a breath, and fresh air washed through my lungs. Another breath, deeper. I pushed the air out in a slow, steady stream.

Maksim pressed pause on the poem. "How do you feel?"

I lifted my head. He sat beside me, worry penetrating his otherwise smooth features. Something about him was different today. He wasn't wearing the grandpa glasses, but also something else.

His hair, I realized. He'd styled it into a soft, brushed-back look that highlighted his strong features. Was that how he'd worn it that day at the airport? I couldn't remember.

An angry voice intruded. I risked a glance and saw the maître d' marching toward us.

"He wants us to leave." Maksim stood and helped me up. He reached for my backpack, then hesitated. I stared at him for three beats before understanding why.

"I'll—get it." I scooped up the bag and followed him up the sidewalk. "I, um, can't decide if I owe you an apology or a thank-you. I guess it's both."

His attention returned.

"Sorry I got pissy about my backpack. Yesterday, I mean. It's my first time out of the country and— Anyway, thanks for helping me. Twice now."

A phantom smile touched his lips. "I have somewhere to be, but I can spare a moment if you're willing to talk." He sent a glance over his shoulder. "Preferably somewhere private."

I traced his gaze to the maître d'. The man stood with his arms crossed and his expression cinched into a glower.

Shops lined the next street over. Maksim entered a cobblestone alley that ran behind them. "They have a dress code."

I stopped at the mouth of the alley. "Who?"

"The restaurant." He faced me and propped one shoulder against the building, arms folded in front of him. "They're expecting an important visitor. I didn't gather who, but they didn't want him to arrive and see— Well." His attention fell to my clothes.

Wet splotches soaked my tank top. My khaki shorts, freshly unpacked that morning, held fast to wrinkles. No wonder those people hadn't wanted me in there.

"Kat, what happened? Who was that man you were trying to speak with?" Maksim's eyes shifted toward the restaurant. "Did he do something to you?"

"N-no. I've never met him before."

"Then why were you trying to speak with him?"

Should I tell him about Dad? The scavenger hunt? Maybe I should start with what happened at the university today. Not only had the secretary kicked me out, *with* a security escort, she'd sealed our nightmarish meeting with that photo she'd taken of me.

"Never return to my university. Our staff can identify you, and they will call the police."

That was why she'd taken the photo. She was going to share it with her colleagues to make sure I never got Dad's file.

The thought of coming all this way only to be thwarted by the Wicked Witch of Bucharest had wrecked me. Then seeing Dad— thinking I'd seen him—must have sent me over the edge. Any normal person would understand.

But I didn't know Maksim. I had no idea if I could trust him with such deeply personal information. Plus, rehashing the incident wouldn't fix my problem. Dad's file wouldn't magically appear because I detailed the whole humiliating experience.

That last thought boomeranged back to me. Dad's file. I needed it for the scavenger hunt, but I had no way to get it now. No *legal* way.

An idea burned through my brain, a lit fuse on a stick of dynamite. It blazed past every bar and barrier, and I knew, with everything in my being, it could work.

All I needed was a little help. From the right person.

"You're not required to provide an explanation, of course." Concern rested in Maksim's features. "I suppose I'm wondering if you may need—"

"Andrei," I blurted. "I need Andrei. I need his... help."

"Why?" Maksim straightened, hands falling at his sides. "When was the last time you spoke with him?"

"When we were at Kebap last night. He left suddenly without sharing his contact info, and I-I need to talk to him."

"About what?"

"It's... personal. And complicated. I'd rather discuss it with him."

"I'm hopeful you can *un*complicate it. Otherwise I won't be able to assist." The corners of his mouth turned down as a dark cloud cast a shadow over his mood.

His phone chimed from his pocket. He retrieved the device and checked the message. "I'm late for something." He focused on me. "Why do you need to speak with Andrei?"

Uncertainty held my tongue. I'd been expecting Maksim to respond with something like "sure, no problem" and "here's how to reach him." What I had *not* expected was the Spanish Inquisition.

He waited. When I didn't answer, he gave a slight guffaw and brushed past me.

"Wait, where are you going?" I shouldered my backpack and

hurried after him. "Okay, clearly there's been a miscommunication here. I need Andrei's contact info so I can talk to *him* about something *private.*"

Maksim rolled his eyes. "I understood you the first time. But unless you're willing to disclose this private matter, you will not be speaking with him."

"Why not?"

Maksim stopped midstride and wheeled around to face me. "Because Andrei is *my* responsibility. I answer for everything he does—his recklessness, his mistakes—and he has me in a precarious position if you must know."

I bit my lip. My idea for getting Dad's file involved devising a scam. I didn't know how to do something like that, but Andrei did, and he still owed me a favor.

But what would Maksim think of that? I wasn't sure, and I wasn't going to risk finding out, especially after what Andrei had said last night. *"Maksim is kind of opposed to certain things, like it's bad karma or something."* Those had been Andrei's exact words.

Construction equipment rattled and clanged from across the street. Maksim glanced that way, then at his phone. "As much as I would like to continue—"

"Did you know your chances of dying can increase by ten percent around the holidays?" The question tumbled out so fast I wondered if he'd caught it.

But he had. And he sighed. "Should I know that?"

"Not specifically. But that man in the restaurant looked like my dad, and I freaked out when I saw him because—" My heart crashed. "Because my dad died. Right before Christmas."

Surprise rolled across Maksim's features.

"He was from Romania," I continued, "and I came here to— You might say I'm dealing with family business. That's why I need Andrei's help. He offered to help, actually."

Andrei had offered to help with tourism stuff, not family business. Maksim didn't need to know that.

I waited for him to pepper me with more questions. To my

surprise, he navigated to his keypad and dialed a number. "Andrei's mobile has been off today." He placed the phone to his ear.

A moment later, he shook his head. "Still off."

"Is that normal? You think he's okay?"

"I'm certain he's fine. But I may not be." He muttered the second part and accessed a menu on his phone. "Give me your telephone number. I'll have him call you."

I unzipped my backpack and dug out my phone. "You'll have to give me your number first. I have an app that blocks unknown numbers."

Maksim flagged me with both eyebrows.

"Long story." I navigated to my contacts and handed him the phone.

He entered his number, and his phone vibrated. "I've SMSed myself so I have your number, as well." He returned my phone. "I'll call you as soon as I've located him... if that's all right?"

The way he said it created a flush of heat under my sternum. My neck and face warmed. "Calls are... expensive."

"Should I SMS you, then?" His expression remained stoic, but his eyes glimmered. This guy had been flirting with me at the airport, and now I'd given him my number.

"Texts are twenty-five cents per message." The explanation escaped as a whisper.

"Uh-huh." His mouth slipped into a smile. "We're running out of options, *dragă*."

I was about to offer my email when he said, "Would you like to speak with Andrei in person? Perhaps we could meet you somewhere."

"That's... perfect." And it really was. Because even if Maksim passed along my message, that didn't guarantee Andrei would email me. Meeting in person was better.

My excitement sank as I processed the rest of his offer. "You said *we*. Does that mean you're coming, too? You don't have to."

"I don't mind." He held onto the smile.

"It's a Thursday, practically the weekend. You probably have plans. A date, maybe? Guys night?"

"My evening is wide open as it so happens." His eyebrows gave a bounce, and my smile crumbled.

His phone vibrated two times in succession. As he checked the messages, I peeked at the one he'd sent to me. His number appeared with a +40 country code. He'd listed his name as Răzvan (Maksim), and his message made my blush burn a shade hotter. He'd sent the winking emoji.

"Do you remember how to get to Kebap?"

My eyes flashed to his. His gaze held steady, his smile once again hidden.

"It's on Strada Franceză," he continued, "in case you need to look it up. Be there by twenty." He turned to go.

Twenty? What was he talking about?

Oh yeah. Europeans told time in twenty-four-hour format. I counted to twenty on my fingers, and my eyes widened.

I lunged and caught his sleeve. "Twenty is eight o'clock. *At night.*"

"I'm aware." He let a questioning look fall to my hand.

I let him go. "Sorry."

"I'm not free until the evening." He smoothed his sleeve—a long sleeve, I realized. But why? Who would wear long sleeves on a day like this? The temperature had to be pushing one hundred. "I have a meeting now and errands this afternoon. They're important."

"So is this."

"I understand, and I'll search for Andrei when I'm finished." Maksim's phone vibrated again. He muttered and started across the street.

Halfway there, he called over his shoulder. "See you tonight."

8. SEARCH

I cradled my chin and zoned out on RomaNIA's GoT TALENT. The volume was low—lower than the noisy restaurant—and captions scrolled across the screen.

Steak-cut fries and bits of shredded cabbage poked out from my half-eaten lamb kebab. A guy in a lime-green shirt walked over and pointed at my plate. I nodded that he could take it.

The front pocket of my shorts vibrated. That had to be Maksim. I'd texted him four times in the past hour. What was taking so long?

> Make any headway?

Not Maksim.

I set my phone on the table and stared at Brandy's message. I'd meant to text her earlier, but I'd spent the afternoon researching scams. Everything I'd found required at least two people, oftentimes three or four. I needed Andrei's help. There was no way around it.

My phone vibrated again. An old picture filled my screen, and surprise pricked me. It was a pic of Brandy and me from my twelfth birthday. I was midlaugh, one arm wrapped around her neck. Her eyes were closed, lips stretched in a smile that showed off her rainbow braces.

Tightness wound its way through my abdomen. This wasn't a digital copy of the photo. Brandy had taken a pic of the printed copy. But how? I didn't have that copy anymore. Hadn't in years.

Also—and this was the really strange part—why would she send it? She knew what happened that night. She knew I hated thinking about it.

"Good. You're here."

My ears perked up at the timbre of baritone. Maksim emerged from the bodies crammed around the entrance.

"What happened? I've been texting you."

"Forgive me. I've been making calls and searching for Andrei." Maksim pulled out a chair, spun it around, and straddled it. "As you can see, I haven't found him."

I slouched. Could anything else go wrong?

"I did happen upon an acquaintance of his." Maksim rested his arms on the back of the chair. "It seems Andrei is hiding out."

"From who?"

"Our boss."

Hadn't Andrei said something about their boss? That wasn't the term he'd used, though. It was something else, something similar.

"Do you mean underboss?"

Maksim was scanning the restaurant, his expression soft but alert. He snapped to attention when I said that.

"Andrei mentioned a name," I said. "Ștefan. But he called him y'all's underboss."

Maksim forced a smile that never reached his eyes. "Ștefan *was* our underboss. He has taken over the operation since the death of his father last summer."

"His father? So this is a family-run scamming operation?"

"Something like that." Maksim stood. "I know of some places Andrei may be tonight. If you're set on finding him, we'll have to go in person. His mobile is still off." Maksim crossed the restaurant.

I stood. "How are we getting there?"

"Taxi." He paused at the crowded entrance. "Metrou, our subway system, doesn't reach the places I have in mind."

I was nudging my chair under the table and froze. Public transit would have been fine, but riding around in a car could be dangerous.

Couldn't it? Was I overreacting?

One of the cooks called out from the prep area.

Maksim called back, his accent thickening under the influence of his native language. He spoke rapid-fire, his words popping across each syllable. Almost like Italian with a Slavic accent.

He made his way to the cashier. Same woman from last night.

She greeted him with a mom-kiss, leaving a splotch of raspberry on his cheek, and nodded in my direction. I heard her say something about the *americanca*. Female American. Maksim replied, and the woman brightened.

She leaned across the counter, ushering customers aside. "He is a good boy. He visits my mother." She patted Maksim's arm. "He is good to our family."

Maksim said something else, mouth bent in a playful smirk. The woman laughed and gave him a push toward the door.

He paused and looked over at me. "Are we going?"

OUR CAB SCOOTED through evening traffic. Maksim kept to his side of the back seat. His cologne, however, did not. I caught a whiff of musk and wood with hints of citrus and sage.

It was probably designer. Like his outfit. Tonight he was winning best-all-around in a white dress shirt, slim navy chinos, and lace-up leather chukka boots. Oh, and a Louis Vuitton belt.

I wasn't familiar with designer stuff, but I recognized the LV buckle from a reality TV show. That thing cost more than my entire wardrobe—the stuff I'd brought on this trip plus everything at home.

"I apologize for all this trouble." Maksim unbunched his chinos, which fit him like a glove. "Andrei isn't permitted to turn off his mobile. He knows that."

"Then why do it?" I held a steady gaze on Maksim's face, away from his perfectly snug pants.

"His mistakes have consequences he'd likely rather avoid. Unfortunately, turning off his mobile doesn't provide the kind of privacy he thinks."

"Why not?"

Maksim didn't offer an immediate answer. Our taxi maneuvered through traffic, and a band of light fell across him. He maintained a stoic expression, his attention straight ahead.

"My dad was a computer programmer. He told me about malware that can monitor people's activities. Is that what this is about?"

"I'm sure you can understand"—Maksim slanted a look—"this isn't a conversation I can have with a sweet, innocent tourist."

"I'm not sweet." I folded my arms. The movement jostled my shirt, and the oversized neckline slipped off my shoulder.

"Yes, well, I can't discuss it with cynical tourists, either, even cute ones." His gaze brushed my bare shoulder.

He checked himself and focused forward. My body twinkled.

I dragged my neckline into place and turned my attention to the city rushing past my window. Cement tower blocks gave way to stone buildings highlighted by sharp lines and soft round curves. Two of the buildings, set on two different streets, came together at the corner. Their curved balconies connected, creating a cylindrical end-cap.

Our cab accelerated, moving with the flow of traffic. I cranked the lever beside me and lowered my window in jerky movements. Warm air swept through the car. I folded my hair back, and the wind on my face carried me into memories of last summer.

I closed my eyes and let myself drift into a time when I was riding motorcycles with Ty and playing soccer with Brandy, when Dave was teaching me parkour... things that had made me feel alive. These days I felt dead, numb. But as the hot night blew over me, I could taste the way my life had been before. Everything had been sweeter back then, sprinkled with happiness and accomplishment instead of cold, empty sadness.

Maksim's voice interrupted my daydream.

I swiped at the dampness under my lashes and opened my eyes. "Are you talking to me?"

"To myself more or less." Streetlights splashed across him in a steady rhythm. He rolled his sleeves higher, and the tribal band peeked out. "This heat is intolerable. Rarely do we ever experience this kind of weather." He unfastened his top buttons, revealing a sculpted chest.

"Oh?" I made myself look the other way. "What's it normally like?"

"Springtime has plenty of rain so that even on hot days the showers cool off the city. But we haven't had much rain this year, so the weather has been sweltering day and night."

My brain buzzed with everything he was saying—and everything I was trying *not* to look at—but something rattled my thoughts into place. "Not much rain this year? What do you mean?"

"Romania is experiencing a drought and heat wave."

I straightened. "Since when?"

"It began last year and has been growing more critical in certain parts of the country."

"What about the western part?"

"There, as well. The drought has affected Timișoara, Arad, Oradea—"

"*Timișoara?*" I practically shouted the name. That government liaison had said the entire country was flooding. He'd said it was bad around Timișoara, where Dad's plane had crashed.

Maksim held me with a curious gaze. I looked away. I'd have

to email the liaison next time I had Wi-Fi. There had to be a logical explanation.

The cabbie said something from the front. Maksim leaned forward, listening. "We're nearly there," he said, translating for me.

"Where?"

"A pub. In case we don't find Andrei, the driver has offered to take us to a few more places."

"How many more?" I pressed on the lei stuffed in the pocket of my shorts. I'd left my purse behind because, well, scammers.

Maksim caught a glimpse of my hand. "We won't be paying the fare if that's your concern."

"We won't?" My attention flicked to the cabbie. "Do you know him?"

"He knows my cousin."

Our driver pulled into a parallel space outside a row of eateries. The front facade was made of glass, revealing dark-wood tables, a bar, and an upright piano inside. Patrons packed the dining room.

Maksim reached for his door handle. "You're welcome to wait here."

"Actually, I need to email someone." I held up my phone. "Think they'll have Wi-Fi?"

"They should."

Headlights flowed past us. The stream broke, and Maksim pushed open his door. I climbed out on my side. We met on the sidewalk, and I followed him into the pub.

9. Harbinger

We searched the city for Andrei—his favorite restaurants, bars, pubs. Hours later, we entered a residential neighborhood full of narrow streets, broken-down cars, and...

The cab bottomed out. My head smacked the window and bounced off. "Ouch!"

...potholes. Big ones.

I rubbed the side of my head as our cab eased to a stop. Maksim climbed out and left the back door open for me.

"You go ahead." I peered up at him. "I'll wait here."

"Not this time." He beckoned me out.

I sighed, scooting across the seat, and stepped out. My shoe crunched something.

A rickety streetlamp blinked out enough light to reveal garbage strewn everywhere, all over the street and sidewalk. Gangster rap blasted from an apartment building so decrepit I wondered if it had running water.

A pack of dogs trotted through the cabbie's headlights. One of the dogs growled.

"Okay, getting back in the car now." I edged behind Maksim.

He held me in place while he shouted at the dogs, something

along the lines of *"Hei! Mursh!"* He stomped twice, and the dogs scattered.

The cabbie had his window down, arm resting on the door. He nodded at us, shoved his transmission into gear, and pulled away.

"Is he going to park?" I asked.

"He's going home."

"What?" I stared after the cab.

The taillights shrank to glowing cherries. He reached the end of the street, turned, and disappeared.

"It's the end of his shift," Maksim said. "I'll order another when we're done."

I pinched my lips together, thinking. Worrying.

"Unless you prefer to leave now." He glanced in the direction the cab had gone. "I thought you wanted to find Andrei."

I did. But I didn't like the idea of being alone with a guy, someone I barely knew, in a sketchy neighborhood like this.

On the other hand, Maksim hadn't crossed any boundaries. He'd been the perfect gentleman, waiting for me, holding doors, giving me plenty of physical space. I couldn't say I trusted the guy, but he didn't strike me as the murderous type.

"I understand this neighborhood is a bit... unconventional." He offered up a sympathetic smile. "However, this is our last stop. If we don't find Andrei here, I have nowhere else to look."

"Where's 'here'?"

"Sector Five, a neighborhood called Ferentari. There's a club nearby. I don't go there anymore, but Andrei does. Sometimes."

My insides squeezed until I thought an organ or two might burst. We were going to a club, in the middle of the night, in a sketchy neighborhood, and Andrei only went there *sometimes*?

The records, I reminded myself. I needed Dad's records to solve the current clue. After that, I could go to Braşov and finish the scavenger hunt. Andrei was the first step to accomplishing all that.

"Okay, fine." I pushed out a breath. "Let's get this over with."

We worked our way into the neighborhood, passing cement tower blocks and abandoned, stripped-down cars. Shouts and the occasional sound of glass breaking echoed in the night.

The shadows thickened on the next street. I grabbed Maksim's arm and brought us to a stop. "Sorry, I-I need a second." I blinked, coaxing my vision to adjust. "Why is this street so dark?"

"Nobody lives in this section. Not officially." Maksim pointed ahead of us. "Are you able to see that building?"

Light pollution created a dim backdrop around a tower block. "I see it."

"The government condemned the building last year. That one, too." He pointed at another. "The residents were evicted, but I assure you, people are making use of the space."

A golden glow flickered in a window several stories up. He was right. Someone was in there.

We reached a street untouched by even a shred of light. My ears strained to hear something, anything, while the stench of rotten food and dirty diapers invaded my nostrils.

My stomach folded in on itself. I yanked my shirt up and over my nose. "Gross."

White light streaked the blackness.

Maksim had activated the flashlight app on his phone. The LED light revealed a mound of garbage in front of us. Trash carpeted the pavement.

"We can't go this way," he said.

"Are you sure? I know it stinks, but—"

"It's not the smell I'm concerned about." He aimed the phone, and my gray canvas flats appeared under the light. "Heroin is rampant in this sector. Those shoes won't do much if you step on a needle."

My toes curled up. "Th-there are needles on this street?"

"And on the sidewalk. They're everywhere in this trash."

Fear drained the strength from my knees.

His light traveled up my body and settled below my face, like he was trying to see my expression without blinding me. "We can turn back if you'd like." He glanced around. "Perhaps we should."

"N-no. I'm fine." I forced a smile. "All we have to do is find a way around the garbage, right? We came all this way. It'd be a waste to give up now."

He didn't seem convinced. But he didn't argue.

We doubled back to the last set of apartments. An alleyway divided the buildings, and Maksim said it would lead us past that one part of the street.

"I'll go first," he said.

Glass crunched beneath his boots. He swept the shards aside, making a path, and then waved me through. The alley funneled into a courtyard.

Maksim stopped short.

I bumped into him from behind. "Why'd you—?" My question snapped off.

Four men gathered around a metal trash barrel, fire blazing. Smoke rose and carried a strong odor of burnt wood and melted plastic. The tang of hot metal reached me from across the courtyard.

The men glared, and a twist of fear wound through my abdomen.

Darkness cloaked the apartment buildings around us. I held my breath, listening. The amber flames crackled and licked at the still night. I heard nothing else. No voices or music. No TVs.

Maksim pointed ahead of us. The firelight cast an orange glow over a walkway that looked like it led out of the courtyard. "That's where we're going. Stay close to me."

"Okay."

Our shoes scuffed dirt and crispy grass. Weeds skimmed my ankles.

The men angled to cut us off.

"Maksim." I tugged on his shirt.

He stopped again and addressed the men in a calm, serious tone. Whatever he said brought them to a standstill beside a cracked, dried-up fountain. That fountain was the only thing standing between them and us.

We continued toward the walkway. Maksim kept our pace slow, his steps measured. His navy pants blended with the shifting shadows. I focused on his crisp white shirt, which was the brightest thing in the courtyard.

We cleared the fountain, and my attention drifted. One of the men was sucking on a plastic bag filled with something gooey.

He lowered the bag, eyes glassy, and a metallic substance coated his mouth and chin.

My legs went numb.

I wasn't sure how long I'd been standing there—frozen, unmoving—before panic jolted me.

I looked around. Maksim had reached the walkway and was continuing out of the courtyard. I tried to call out. My throat closed over his name.

One of the men walked forward. His leather vest revealed bulky arms and a bare chest. He wore matching leather pants and a vintage military officer's hat. A five-point star—the communist red star—left a blood-red imprint on the service cap.

The man locked onto me, his eyes black, void of emotion—a great white shark circling its prey. I'd seen eyes like that before. When I was a kid.

One of those memories spun across my thoughts. Same memory I'd recalled earlier when Brandy sent me that pic.

Every muscle in my body locked up.

A LADY in scrubs sat perched behind a computer. She held a phone to her ear, fingers striking a keyboard. Dad tried to get her attention.

I surveyed the waiting room. Sick people sneezed and rattled out coughs. One guy held a blood-soaked towel to his head.

My stomach flipped. I hated hospitals. I hated how depressed everyone looked and the sharp, sterile smell that failed to cover up whatever diseases lurked here.

Why did she have to do this again? Why tonight?

My thoughts rewound to my birthday party, to Mom's erratic behavior and how everyone's mood had shifted.

We'd been watching a movie when Brandy scooted closer. "I saw her go into the bathroom," she whispered. "She's been in there awhile."

The memory of what happened next flashed, mental images I wanted to shred and burn but couldn't—Dad busting through the door, Mom lying there, the orange syringe hanging from her arm.

Pressure coiled in my chest. I hugged myself, tears pouring while Dad ushered me into the waiting room. I felt sure he chose the same two chairs he'd chosen last time. These trips to the ER were becoming routine.

Three men entered the waiting room. Scabs marked their hands and faces, their hair matted and greasy. One of them spotted us and swatted the others.

I slumped in my seat. No. Please don't be here for us. Please.

The stench of their body odor reached us before they did. My insides hardened like fast-drying cement.

"You Evelyn's husband?"

Dad dragged his attention from the TV. His olive complexion paled.

The man hauled him out of the chair. Another man grabbed me. Shouts went up, and the people in the waiting room scattered. I screamed.

The man placed a hand behind my head and shoved me to the floor. Pain exploded in my nose and gums. Blood poured into my mouth.

THE MEMORY PLAYED LIKE A MOVIE, tangling with the scene in front of me. The taste of blood filled my mouth, and for a nauseating moment, I thought I was back in that emergency room six years ago.

The man in the officer's hat approached. I managed a step backward. Then another.

He lunged, snatching my arm. I opened my mouth to scream. My vocal cords constricted.

Broad shoulders cloaked in fiery white appeared. A sturdy arm crashed down on my attacker's wrist. The man grunted and let me go.

Maksim stepped between us. He swatted the officer's hat, knocking it to the ground, and shoved the man. Then he rumbled what sounded like a warning.

The men lifted their hands in surrender. The druggie sucked on his bag, smearing the metallic substance.

My insides twisted into a suffocating knot.

Maksim hooked my arm and dragged me toward the walkway. "Why didn't you say something?" He held his attention on the men. "You should have screamed."

I wanted to say I'd tried. I couldn't.

He caught a glimpse of my face, and his expression softened.

He slowed our pace and wrapped an arm around me, holding me up. I staggered along until the knot in my stomach ruptured. Nausea crashed into me.

I broke away. Yellow light bloomed in the darkness up ahead, and desperation swelled within me. I had to get there. I had to get to the light.

The walkway connected to a sidewalk in front of the apartments. The light turned out to be a streetlamp. I reached the pole, snapped forward, and retched lamb kebab all over the pavement.

Bile seared my throat. My stomach convulsed.

I closed my eyes and clenched my muscles, fighting the urge to dry heave. Three beats passed. Four. Five.

I opened my eyes. I was on my hands and knees, hunched over, while a gentle hand gathered my hair. I wiped my mouth and looked over.

Maksim knelt beside me. "Can you stand?"

I answered with a weak nod.

He helped me up and guided me away from the vomit. I used the back of my hand to dab my eyes and the inside of my shirt to wipe my mouth.

Standing there, on the other side of these buildings, I detected the thump of bass in my body. We were getting close to the club.

Maksim pulled out his phone.

"Who are you calling?" My voice rasped. "I-I don't need an ambulance."

"I'm calling for a taxi. We're going back to the drop-off spot."

"What? No." I swiped at his phone, but he pulled it out of reach. "What about Andrei?"

"I will look for him tomorrow. Alone. If I find him, we'll try again for Kebap."

Our original plan? Would that work?

Not likely. If Maksim didn't find Andrei by the end of the day, the university would be closed for the weekend.

Then I'd have to wait until Monday. That would be too late.

"Maksim, I'm going home next week. If tomorrow doesn't work out... Please. Can't we talk about this?"

"You want to talk? All right. You first." He folded his arms. "What is this family business of yours, and why is it so critical? What is it you're not telling me?" He held up a stern finger. "Do *not* lie to me."

His warning collided with my guilt. I hadn't intended to share my plan with him. I was afraid he would hate the idea and forbid Andrei from helping me. What would I do then?

The streetlamp cast hazy light across his tense features. I couldn't keep sidestepping his questions. But I might be able to buy myself a little more time.

"You're right. There's more to the story. I think that's what you're sensing."

His brow dipped.

"I don't like to talk about certain things, for a lot of reasons, but I'm willing to tell you everything. *If* you'll take me to the club."

"You'll answer my questions?" Maksim pocketed his phone. "All of them?"

"All of them, whether we find Andrei or not."

"We might not." Maksim glanced in the direction of the distant bass. "I wouldn't think Andrei is stupid enough to go to this particular club. But his stupidity has never ceased to amaze me, either, which is why I thought we should try."

"Then let's try. Maksim, whatever happens, I have to know we did everything possible to find him. It's that important."

10. ENVY

Bright lights pierced the darkness. People flocked in the direction of a warehouse, and they were all on foot. I didn't see any cars, not even the yellow taxis.

"This way." Maksim led me around a sinkhole and up onto a janky sidewalk. No wonder people were walking. There was nowhere to drive.

Decrepit shops ran alongside us until we passed BETMAX PLUS. The building was small, but the marquee sign created a halo of light over the street corner.

A man ducked out of the building, his clothes disheveled, his eyes bloodshot. An array of *ding*s and *beep*s followed him out, and one of the clues blinked into my thoughts.

A number three scrawled into a black suit of clubs. The same suit of clubs used in playing cards. This particular clue was farther down the list—in the Brașov section—but it might be helpful to know if this was a track to follow.

I turned to Maksim. "Hey, so... gambling is legal in Romania?"

He'd been eyeing the guy who exited the casino. When I said that, he shot an annoyed look at me. "I am *not* taking you to BetMax."

I drew back. "I wasn't—"

"No." A muscle jumped in his jaw. "I agreed to take you to the club, and I'm happy to accompany you to Kebap. You'll have to visit a gambling den on your own time."

"Gambling den? I don't—" I nixed the explanation and sealed my lips. I was beginning to see what Andrei had meant last night. Did Maksim think casinos were "bad karma"? He must have. So much for a casual-sounding inquiry.

Pink lights glistened on the warehouse. Frosty-white letters spelled out CLUB ENVY. The bass I'd felt earlier intensified, thumping against my midsection.

Maksim bypassed the line and went straight to the entrance. A bouncer unlatched the velvet rope.

"I don't have my ID," I said.

"You don't need it." Maksim led the way into a sleek foyer. The music grew louder the closer we drew to a set of doors.

A redhead sat at the reception desk, holding a smartphone in one hand and a portable fan in the other. Wisps of air ruffled her bangs.

She looked up, expression lifeless.

Maksim's mouth rested in that easy smile of his. *"Bună seară."* Good evening.

The girl dropped everything, scrambled around the desk, and forced one of the doors open. Techno crashed into us. Lights swirled, breaking through a haze of smoke.

Maksim asked her something.

She smoothed her pencil skirt, keeping her eyes downturned. *"Da, Domnule* Răzvan."

My jaw collapsed. "Did she call you *Mister* Răzvan?"

He hesitated. "Yes."

"How old are you?"

"Younger than she is, but this is my cousin's club. I've asked her about Andrei. She said he's here."

My pulse trilled. We'd found Andrei.

Maksim and the girl had a back-and-forth. Sounded like he was asking questions. She answered respectfully each time.

Finally, Maksim returned his attention to me. "Come on."

We crossed the threshold and entered the haze. Shouts went up from a dance floor on our right. Lasers pierced the darkness overhead. We passed beside a railing, and I peeked over.

A massive stage, complete with red velvet curtains, ran the length of the lower level. Dancers strutted around in eccentric costumes, performing a weird, theatrical burlesque. Tonight's production? A seedy version of *Cats*. The women had poured themselves into leather catsuits so tight they defied science.

Maksim led me through a section of tables. People toasted and took shots. Smokers ashed in shimmery ashtrays.

I fanned my face. "We're not staying long, are we?"

"Hopefully not." Maksim tapped an empty table. "Have a seat. I'll be a moment."

"Are you going to find Andrei?" The music drowned out my question.

Maksim maneuvered between tables, slipping between light and shadow, until he reached... the bar? He was getting a *drink?*

I flopped in a chair. All we had to do was find Andrei. Was that so hard? Maybe I didn't need Maksim for that.

My attention moved from table to table. Andrei wasn't at any of them, and he didn't appear to be on the dance floor.

Track lighting fashioned a walkway, which led to a staircase that went one way. Down. A waitress crested the top stair, tray in hand, and made her way toward the bar.

I stood, trying to glean where she'd come from.

The stairs accessed the lower level. I could see couches down there, a second dance floor, and tons of people.

My attention returned to Maksim. He was leaning against the bar, talking to the bartender.

The waitress sashayed over to them. I thought she was going to scoot past Maksim, but she actually hip-checked him.

They had a back-and-forth, and something Maksim said made her laugh. She plunked her tray on the bar, gripped his sleeve, and gave a playful tug. The black lines of his tattoo appeared.

He caught her hand, and a stab of jealousy wedged itself between my ribs. Why? Maksim and I weren't anything. We weren't even friends. So then why did I care who he flirted with?

I didn't. I was annoyed.

Maksim left her with a killer smile, grabbed his drink, and made his way over to me.

I sat straight, buckling down on a glare. "You couldn't have waited until later to get a—?"

He set a bottle of water on the table.

My accusation crumbled. "What's that?"

"It's been a long night. I thought you may be thirsty." He tossed a cellophane-wrapped candy next to the water and gestured for me to have a seat.

I lowered myself into the chair.

He took my wrist and drew my arm into a spray of lights. Black marks smeared my forearm. There was also a cut I hadn't noticed before.

From that man's fingernails. Gross. His hands must've been filthy.

Maksim released me and tore into a flat white packet. Pre-cut gauze? He took the gauze and wiped around the cut. The black marks vanished, and cool moisture seeped into the wound.

Fire ignited.

"Ouch!" I yanked my arm away.

He offered an apologetic look.

"Alcohol pad." I fanned the cut. "A warning would have been nice."

Maksim reclaimed my arm. "He who knows does not speak."

"Mm, so deep. Thanks, Lao Tzu."

He chuckled.

The DJ mixed to a new track, and female vocals purred across a muted bass line. Bright lights and lasers vanished, replaced by soft purple that bathed everything in an amethyst glow.

UV light. Maksim's eyes looked like a nuclear fallout zone.

"You like this music?" He bent his eyebrow.

"Hm? Oh." I'd been nodding along to the beat. "Uh, yeah. It's called Deep House. I love it."

His attention shifted to my hair. He reached out and swiped the alcohol pad over a tendril.

I drew back. "What are you doing?"

"Cleaning a bit of residue."

"Residue? You mean... vomit? I've been walking around with *vomit* in my hair?"

"You have a bit here, too." He licked his thumb and brushed it across my neck. Electricity sparked at his touch. Warmth filled my body.

I pulled a soft breath. Maksim went still.

We held each other with a stare so soft yet so steady I felt like a balloon tethered to the chair. He withdrew his hand—but then, as if second-guessing, he reached out again and let the tips of his fingers come to a rest on my cheek.

My heart broke into a gallop.

I pulled myself away and snatched the candy. "I'm sure you got it all." I fumbled with the wrapper. "Thanks."

He tossed the spent alcohol pad on the table. "Forgive me. I didn't meant to—" His Adam's apple dipped. "I had a strange dream recently. It came to my remembrance just now."

"Uh-oh. You're not having déjà vu, are you? Have we been here before?"

That was supposed to be a joke. He didn't laugh.

"Never mind," I mumbled, popping the candy in my mouth. It crumbled like chalk, and a burst of menthol cooled my tongue.

Breath mint. He'd given me a breath mint, probably because I had vomit breath in addition to vomit hair. The epiphany made me want to crawl in a hole and never come out.

Before I could decide how best to un-embarrass myself, a blur of red rushed past us. The blur stopped. And swore.

"Maks. Pal." Andrei stood in the walkway, gaping. "What are you doing here?"

Maksim went rigid. He rose from kneeling, his gentleness folding into a glare.

Andrei backed up, hands raised.

He wheeled around and stumbled between tables. Maksim chased him down and hauled him to the walkway. Onlookers swatted each other and pointed.

"Okay, okay, okay. Maks, I'm not gonna run!"

Maksim stopped short of the staircase. I met them there.

"I panicked, man. I'm sorry." Andrei spun around. For the first time, I detected an east-European accent. "I'm on a date with Anca."

"I heard." Maksim nodded toward the staircase. "Go."

"I-I was on my way to the toilet." Andrei swayed, cheeks puffing under a belch. "Don't wanna get sick in front of her."

"You're drunk? You've been here two hours!"

"I got carried away."

Maksim gripped Andrei by the shoulders and stooped, bringing them nose to nose. "I have been trying to reach you all day and searching for you all night. If you dare to leave this club without my express consent, you *will* regret it."

Andrei went to answer.

Maksim silenced him with a stern finger. "Ştefan has been

inquiring about the park, among other things. I have been covering for you. Cross me, and I will feed you to the wolves."

"Okay, I get it." Andrei held his stomach. The UV light illuminated a sprinkling of freckles on his nose and a dusting of lint on his black pants. "Can I go to the toilet now?"

"Make it fast." Maksim released him. "Kat needs to speak with you."

Andrei pointed a look at me. His expression ballooned, as if he hadn't noticed me until then. "Uhh, hey. I—" His face blanched.

He turned and stumbled up the walkway.

"I know Andrei's date. She works here." Maksim peered down at the lower level. "A friend told me where they're sitting."

"Your 'friend' the waitress?" I didn't make air quotes, and I hadn't meant to imply air quotes in my tone. But that was how it came out.

Maksim brought his stare around, head tilting.

"Think I might've forgotten my water. Be right back." I doubled back to the table. Ugh, why would I assume he was referring to the waitress? He could have been talking about the bartender, the door girl, literally anyone.

I wasn't surprised to find him gone by the time I returned. I leaned over the railing and spotted him on the lower level. At least he hadn't left.

I clambered down the stairs and sprinted after him. He didn't even look at me when I caught up. Great.

The DJ switched tracks to something fast. The purple vanished, and bright beams of orange and yellow splashed across the club. Waitresses hustled past us. Dancers strutted on the stage.

Maksim stopped beside a curved couch. A blonde sat perched on one side. A beefy guy with dark hair and a sharp nose guarded the middle. Spent shot glasses and champagne flutes scattered a coffee table.

The blonde stood, and the sequins of her minidress winked

fire under the lights. She must have been Anca. She greeted Maksim with a peck on the cheek, reserving a cutesy wave for me.

The beefy man scowled. I recognized him—the Frenchman from the park. What was his name again? Émilien?

A waitress swung in and cleared the coffee table. Maksim gestured for me to have a seat.

"I'd rather not get too comfortable," I said, "if you catch my drift."

"Sorry, can you repeat that?" Maksim tilted his ear toward me. "It sounded remarkably like, 'Thank you for bringing me here, Maksim. I would be happy to wait a little longer.'"

I frowned and flopped onto the cushions, scooting over to make room. Maksim parked himself on my left and relaxed against the couch arm.

Émilien held a glass filled with ice and some kind of clear drink. Not water based on his glazed expression. His top four buttons were undone, revealing a smooth, tanned chest, and his gray pants—the same shade as his eyes—outlined thick, muscular legs.

"What is she doing here?" The Frenchman tipped his head toward me. I wouldn't have thought the question was an accusation, but his tone said otherwise.

"We're here to see Andrei." Maksim remained cool and composed. I almost couldn't hear him over the music.

"Andrei." Émilien guffawed. "Ştefan knows of this?"

Maksim didn't answer.

Émilien straightened. "She has seen our faces, Răzvan. She knows our names. Now you bring her here?"

Maksim switched to French. Their exchange escalated.

"You can trust me."

I wasn't sure the guys had heard me—I could barely hear myself—but I knew they had when Émilien stopped midsentence.

"What did you say?" His eyes narrowed to silvery slits. "You dare to speak to me?"

"I-I was saying you can trust me. That's all."

The Frenchman plunked his drink on the table.

Anca's eyes widened from behind her champagne flute. She hopped up and circled around the couch. The shimmer of her dress vanished between the mass of bodies on the dance floor.

I gripped my water, fingers denting the thin plastic.

The Frenchman slid closer. His eyes pierced mine, a knife sliding into my being and twisting until every ounce of resolve bled out of me.

This was a mistake. I shouldn't have come here.

II. SNAKE

"You say we can trust you, mm? How can we be... assured?" Émilien plucked at the neckline of my shirt. The fabric slipped off my shoulder.

I gasped and jerked away.

The cushions on my left jostled. Maksim's hand shot across me. He held Frenchie by the forearm. "That's enough."

Émilien slurred a response in French.

"I said"—Maksim redoubled his grip, veins bulging in his neck—"that's enough." He shoved Émilien. Hard.

The Frenchman jolted backward and nearly toppled off the couch. He jumped up. Whatever he said next brought Maksim to his feet.

The guys stood toe to toe. Maksim was a head taller, lean and cut, but Émilien was pure bulk and muscle.

They had an exchange.

Émilien leered in my direction—but then his foulness melted away. He backed up, hands raised. This was a trick. It had to be.

But it wasn't. Swaying, he started up the walkway and made his way to the metal staircase. He hadn't bothered to take his drink, which sat in a puddle of condensation.

"He's leaving." Maksim lowered himself to the couch.

We watched Émilien stagger up the staircase. He reached the top, and we both exhaled. Maksim's posture relaxed—but then his attention wandered to the stage.

One of the dancers had painted herself into a strawberry-red catsuit. She held him with a sultry stare, swinging around and rolling her hips.

Their gazes rendezvoused with unspoken familiarity, and her lips lifted in a seductive smile. She reminded me of Ty's snow bunny. Every blood vessel in my body constricted.

Maksim pulled—i.e., *dragged*—his stare away from her. "This wasn't wise." He looked down at his hands. "I shouldn't have brought you here."

"That's the understatement of the year." A tremor moved through my legs and arms and spread to the rest of me. My voice quavered. "Why didn't you do something?"

He cast a surprised glance, forehead creasing. "I did."

"Not really. Not like you did with that guy in the courtyard. I get that Frenchie's your friend, but what he did just now—"

"Émilien is *not* my friend." Maksim spat the response, jaw tight. "But he is my colleague, and I'm required to abide by a certain decorum."

My jaw slacked. "You can't be serious."

"He has rank. And if you believe I could handle him as easily as the other man, you're mistaken. Émilien is short, but he's an ox." Maksim shoved a hand through his hair. "Do not forget I brought you here tonight at *your* insistence."

"Then please, don't let me keep you from whatever you'd rather be doing." I sent a fleeting look to the stage. "Or whoever," I mumbled.

He held me with a burning stare. Burning and deeply perplexed.

I clutched my neckline. Some part of me expected him to apologize, to say Frenchie was a drunk, an idiot, and that my anger was justified. In my wildest dreams, he might have even apologized for ogling the dancer.

Instead, he pushed up from the couch. He didn't hesitate, and he didn't look back.

My anger wilted.

I watched him follow the same path Émilien had taken—past the stage, past the couches—until he reached the metal staircase. He ascended, then his white shirt and navy pants disappeared on the top level.

"It's fine. Everything's... fine." I unscrewed the lid to my water. There was no need to panic. I needed to talk to Andrei alone, and now I could. I just needed a second to compose myself.

I lifted the bottle, hands trembling, and took a drink. Lukewarm water filled my mouth. I swallowed, attention drifting.

The red catsuit crossed my line of sight. Pain dug a grave between my ribs and buried itself there. I couldn't believe how much that dancer looked like Ty's snow bunny.

I held back tears and forced myself to take another drink. Why was I thinking about Ty and his stupid—?

Bright lights washed over the dancer, revealing a cascade of honey-brown hair streaked with highlights and lowlights.

I coughed, spewing water. Was that *actually* Ty's fling?

No. It was a coincidence. A similar hairstyle.

She pranced in the other direction, revealing her profile—over-Botoxed lips, slender neck, delicate nose and jawline. The only difference was a tattoo.

Black and white ink trailed up the dancer's neckline and stopped short of her throat. It was a white tiger, claws extended.

The snow bunny had been wearing a low-cut sweater in the selfie she'd taken with Ty. Wouldn't I have noticed such a gaudy tattoo?

I leaned back and dug into my pocket, fumbling for my phone. I'd seen the pic of Ty and that girl a thousand times. A million. I had to see it again. I had to know for sure.

Someone flopped onto the couch. I glanced over, expecting to see Maksim. "Do you know that danc—?" I froze with the phone halfway out.

Silver eyes glared at me. My blood froze.

"Where is your boyfriend? Mm?" Émilien's meaty fingers hooked my arm. He squeezed, and I whimpered. "Răzvan did not like my idea to share you tonight. But this is not a problem now, you see, because Răzvan... is gone."

"M-Maksim went to get Andrei. He'll be back any second." I had no idea where Maksim had gone, and I certainly didn't think he was coming back. But it was the first thing that popped into my mind.

"Ohh, but he won't, *ma petite belle.*" Émilien clucked his tongue. "Your 'Maksim' has—how do you say?—left zee building." The Frenchman raked his gaze over me. Then he leaned in and placed his mouth by my ear. "So much the better, mm? Now I have you all to myself." His hot breath, sharp with alcohol, fogged my senses.

I shoved him and jumped up.

He caught my waist, threw me onto the couch, and climbed on top. I sank into the cushions, fully pinned beneath him.

I yanked an arm free and brought my fist down on his head and back, his shoulder. It was like hitting a block of cement.

A waitress angled in our direction. I waved frantically.

The woman stopped.

Other waitresses started toward me. The first one ushered them away.

Tears plucked at my eyes. "Wait!"

Émilien moved to my shorts, and my adrenaline spiked. I needed a gun or a knife, something hard like a baseball bat or—

A glass.

My attention swung to the coffee table. Émilien's drink was still sitting there.

I reached over. My fingers grazed the glass, and hope sparked within me.

I grunted, lunging. My fingertips bumped the glass and rocked it back. Dread sank to the core of my being. It was even farther away now. By an inch.

I tried again. Again.

Émilien had my shorts unbuttoned. The panic I'd been fighting leveled up. I pictured Brandy getting a phone call from Romanian police and finding out I'd been assaulted in a nightclub —and what if Émilien didn't stop at assault? What if he killed me and dumped my body somewhere?

Fear and desperation collided within me. Sorrow flowed down my face.

White strobes flashed, pulsing in time with the music. I squeezed my eyes shut, mustered my last bit of strength, and lunged for the coffee table.

My shoulder strained.

My elbow popped.

My palm struck the glass... and knocked it back several inches. *No!*

Frenchie caught my arm and pinned it at my side. He reared back.

The strobes turned everything into an optical illusion, and I watched his fist bear down on me in sharp, jerky motions.

Knuckle connected with cheekbone, and fire exploded in my cheek. Pinpricks ruptured in front of my eyes.

A shout rang out... then Émilien was gone, as if he'd dissolved into the strobes. My left cheek burned. Red dots clouded my vision.

Glass shattered. People screamed, and the smack of skin on skin, of knuckle against bone, roused me.

I rolled off the couch and hit the floor. *Oof.* I strained against the strobe lights, willing my vision into focus.

Broken glass and splintered wood lay strewn across the floor. Maksim stood at the epicenter, unleashing blow after blow on Émilien.

"Cool it, Maks!" Andrei raced in and jumped between them.

Maksim backed up, wincing and grabbing his shoulder. Guess he'd been hit there.

A swirl of color replaced the strobes. Everything was suddenly covered in rainbows, and I couldn't tell if it was my hazy vision or the lights in the club.

Émilien pushed himself up. Dark liquid dripped down his chin. He wiped his face, and the liquid smeared.

Blood.

The Frenchman let out a low, menacing growl and staggered to his feet. Maksim released his shoulder and widened his stance, fists ready.

Before round two could commence, Andrei whipped something out of his back pocket. Light glinted off burnished metal. He tightened his grip, came alongside Émilien, and threw a punch.

Thwack! Fist connected with face, and the Frenchman collapsed.

"Sorry, pal." Andrei tucked away the mystery object while spectators encircled them.

Maksim pushed through the crowd, searching for someone. Me, apparently. "Are you hurt?"

"I thought you left." My voice cracked. "He said you left."

"I was outside taking a call. Kat, I wouldn't leave you in a place like this." His answer broke across me, a whisper somehow rising above the music. Relief swelled in my chest.

He gathered me up and helped me onto the couch. I held my cheek.

"Let me see." He tugged at my hand.

"Don't."

He removed my hand and pressed on my cheek. Heat ignited deep in the bone.

I shrieked, knocking his hands away. His expression hardened.

He stood, shoulders rigid, hands fisted, and returned to Émilien. The Frenchman pushed himself onto all fours.

"What were you thinking?" Maksim grabbed Émilien by the collar and yanked him around, screaming in his face. *"Have you lost your mind?"*

Andrei rushed to separate them.

The crowd thickened. Someone held up a phone, taking video from the looks of it. A waitress swooped in and snatched the device. The guy shouted but otherwise didn't put up a fight.

These people wanted to hide what was happening. They didn't want this getting out.

Émilien climbed to his feet. I scrambled behind the couch.

A slender figure squatted beside me and touched my arm—the waitress Maksim had been talking to. "My coworker is distracting the security team. We must go."

I clutched her arm. "Don't we want the security team to help us?"

"They are not here to help. They are here to deal with people who cause big problems for loyal customers. Do you understand?"

My eyes widened. I nodded.

She led me across the club, pulling me through the shadows until we reached a door in the far corner.

Shouts rang out. *Thud-thud. Thump.* The crowd stirred. I gasped and looked back.

The waitress tugged on me. "You must not wait for Răzvan. It is too dangerous."

"Will he—?"

"Look." She pointed at my shorts, which were hanging open.

I rushed to button them.

"Your life is in danger by the man who did this to you. He is evil, the son of the devil." She entered a numeric sequence on a keypad, and the door opened to a stairwell. "This will lead you to the street level." She pushed me into the stairwell.

Warped, rickety stairs disappeared into the darkness above my head. The trembling in my legs magnified.

"The code to open the door is eight, one, zero, nine," she said. "Do not forget it."

"You're not coming?"

"I cannot." She caught a glimpse of my expression and

gripped my shoulders. "You must stay calm and think clearly. Repeat the code to me."

"Eight. One..." Dammit.

"Zero. Nine," she finished.

I repeated the code three more times. My memory used to be great. Better than great. Coach Jules had thought I might have a photographic memory. But ever since Dad died, I couldn't seem to retain anything for longer than a millisecond.

"The door will open to an alley," the waitress said. "Go to the street and turn left. The road will lead you out of Ferentari." She went to shut the door but paused. "Run. Quickly. For your life."

12. RESERVATIONS

Steam followed me out of the tiny bathroom. Water dripped down my back, my curls stacked high in a wet bun. My skin radiated soft pink.

I'd scrubbed myself raw in the shower, water cranked to boiling, but still hadn't managed to wash off the night.

Everything the waitress had said was true. There'd been a door at the top of the stairwell, and that door had opened to an alley. The only problem had been my escape route.

That street she'd mentioned, the one leading out of the neighborhood, had more potholes than any of the others. The sidewalk was even worse, and the area had grown pitch dark the farther I'd gone.

I had limped along, zigzagging up the block, passing shadowy buildings and broken-down cars while trying not to break an ankle. And all the while, my cheek felt like the launchpad for the space shuttle.

It wasn't until I reached a crossroad that I'd found my first ray of hope.

A sedan lit up the night like an angel, headlights swinging toward me. A ride-sharing sign glowed in the window. The guy was picking up someone from the club.

I had never bribed anyone before. Guess there was a first time for everything.

I plunked myself on the bed, powered up my laptop, and selected an app for video calls. My image appeared in a microsized window.

I leaned in, examining the cream on my face—men's shaving foam from a convenience store.

Brandy would freak out if she knew what happened tonight. I could not, under any circumstance, let her see my cheek.

Auburn hair flashed onto my screen. Blue mats and a balance beam filled the background.

"Kat?" Brandy panted. "That you?"

"Hey! What are you—?" Pain ground through my cheekbone. I sucked air between my teeth and tried not to moan.

Brandy dabbed a towel to her face. "You there? Hello?"

"Mm-hm. Yep." I clenched a pillow out of view. "Are you at the gymnastics center?"

"Am. Dave's team has a competition coming up, and the guys wanted to practice on the obstacle course. I decided to join."

"I didn't know they were competing this summer. Did they find a new league?"

"Babe. They've been talking about this for months. You don't rem—" Understanding flickered in her eyes. Her mouth softened. "They did find a new league, yeah."

She'd explained all this before. I must have forgotten. "I'm sorry."

"It's okay, babe. You've had a lot going on." Brandy pushed up a smile. "How's Transylvania?"

"I wouldn't know. I'm still in Bucharest."

Dave said something off-screen.

Brandy pointed the camera at him. I summoned a fresh smile —a small one that wouldn't send me to the emergency room. "Hi, Dave."

"Kat. Good to see ya." Sweat slicked his face, his sandy-blond hair pushed back by a folded-up bandanna. "How's the trip goin'?"

"Everything's... great. Never better."

"That's good. 'Cause Brandy's been worried sick."

"I haven't been." Brandy centered the camera on herself. "Okay, I have a little. I couldn't tell if you were getting my texts." The side of her mouth tipped up. "My dad was joking that you must be distracted by all those cute European guys."

Thoughts of Maksim crash-landed. He'd rescued me, and I hadn't been able to thank him or say goodbye. I'd also lost my phone—Brandy's phone—so I couldn't check on him, either. What if he'd been injured or... worse?

A tear slipped out.

Brandy grinned, waiting for me to laugh or crack a joke—whatever she expected me to do. Her gaze traveled to the tear, and her smile did a sudden U-turn.

I swiped at the moisture.

Dave pulled his head into view. One of his dense blond eyebrows flew high, creasing that side of his forehead. "Uhh..."

"Bro." One of Dave's teammates trotted over. "Gonna try out a new flip. Can you film?"

Dave nodded, and they disappeared from view.

Brandy's attention stayed on me. She looked like she had a dozen question marks flying above her head. "Is there something you'd like to—?"

"Hello? You there?" I leaned in, ear angled toward the camera. "We must have a bad connection. I-I can barely hear you."

Her mouth twisted. She glanced around and then crossed the gymnastics center.

The obstacle course came into view. Another of Dave's teammates launched himself over a railing and down a long staircase—special obstacles for parkour and free-running.

The guy landed, ran at a twelve-foot wall, and scaled it with a parkour wall climb.

Brandy stepped outside. Daylight waned, casting ribbons of golden light over her.

"What time is it there?" I asked.

"Eightish. You?"

I counted on my fingers. "Three, I think."

"In the morning? What are you doing up so late?" She stationed herself against the building. "Something involving *cute European guys,* by chance?"

I thought she'd missed that. Apparently not.

"No European guys," I lied. "Just a lot going on."

"Like what? And what's that gunk on your face?" She squinted. "Is that shaving cream?"

"Face mask. My skin is superdry." *Please don't make me lie about anything else.* "I've been meaning to text you. My meeting at the university was a bust."

She popped up straight. "Why?"

"Some kind of miscommunication. The head secretary was pissed, and she wouldn't let me have Dad's file."

"What are you going to do?"

"That's why I'm calling. I thought we could brainstorm. There's got to be a way of sneaking past the admin staff with a disguise or—"

"Sneak? Disguise? What?" Her mouth flopped open. "Kat, what did you do?"

"Me? Why would you think I did anything? It was the secretary. She made her own assistant cry."

"Then why haven't you texted me back?" She cocked her head, lips pursed.

"I... lost your phone, the one you loaned me for the trip." That was technically true. She didn't need to know all the gritty details of *how* I'd lost it. "I'm really sorry. I'll replace it when I get home."

Brandy's expression fell somewhere between OMG and WTH.

Tension stretched between Atlanta and Bucharest, between

my best friend and me. Finally, she said the ugly part out loud. "This trip was never meant to be."

"What? No." Maybe.

"Kat, you barely graduated high school. You threw away soccer. You don't have any money. Now you're trying to solve a supposed scavenger hunt, and you don't even know who it's from."

I switched off the argument flowing to my tongue. Brandy had never believed Dad sent the package. For one, she thought he would have included a note. She also didn't think he would have written a dead guy's name on the customs form.

But it wasn't just any dead guy. It was his old friend. And that business trip had been his first trip home in twenty-nine years. Dad might have been overwhelmed with nostalgia. He might have zoned out and listed Levi's name by accident. Wasn't that possible?

"You bought insurance, didn't you?" Brandy's question interrupted my thoughts.

"For the phone?"

"For the flight. The insurance that covers trip interruptions. I was thinking you might want to come home early."

I snorted. "Yeah right."

"I'm serious. Say someone in your family died. You can use my grandma's obituary."

"Your grandma died two years ago, Bee."

"I'll photoshop the date. No one'll ever know."

My flight home was next week. Leaving before then had never occurred to me. But... without the records, and no way to solve the other clues, I had no reason to stay.

"In case you might not've realized," Brandy said, "you do know what Sunday is, right?"

I rolled my eyes. "Cut it out."

"Why? It's your birthday, and I'm your best friend."

"As my best friend, you should know better than to bring it

up." I huffed and folded my arms. "You definitely should have known better than to send that pic."

Brandy's expression blanked. "What pic?"

"You and me? My twelfth birthday?" It was the only pic she'd sent since I'd been here. How was she not remembering? "Forget it, look, I don't want anything to do with my birthday. Can we drop it?"

"What if we keep it simple? You and me, movie marathon and my dad's homemade pizza. Not birthdayish. Just chill."

My mind did a rewind across the night, pausing on the horrible things that had happened. And the things that *could have* happened. Going home would be a way to take control of an out-of-control situation.

"Promise me you'll contact the airlines," Brandy said, "even if there's a fee to use the insurance."

"Fees. For two different airlines."

"Doesn't matter. I'll scrape the money together, whatever it takes to have you home this weekend." Her mouth settled into a gentle smile. "This isn't failure, babe. You tried. I know you did."

Yeah. I really had.

"Better go. Dave'll wonder where I went." She moved to the door. "Keep me posted?"

I nodded.

"And hey. Stop looking up those death statistics. I know you're still doing that, but it's not good for your mental health."

"I haven't been. Not lately." Yet another lie. "Love you."

"Love you, too. Send a message after you talk to the airlines." She ended the video call.

13. REROUTE

I knotted my hair in a bun and zipped my suitcase. A clean floor stretched around me. Now I needed to find a hostel worker.

I shuffled down the stairwell and entered the hallway on the first floor. I was mentally rehearsing what I planned to say—asking for a partial refund, only for the unused days—when my ears tuned in to a conversation.

"...about my height, blue eyes, black hair. Big hair, wild."

Huh. Sounded like me.

I entered the reception area, and my stomach bottomed out. Andrei stood in the foyer, talking to a hostel worker. A dark bruise, like football eye-black, colored the underside of Andrei's eye. A laceration marked his cheek.

He pivoted toward me. "There you are. I was asking about you."

"How did you—?" Nothing else came out.

"How did I know where to find you?"

I nodded stupidly.

"The cabbie who picked you up last night. He told Ştefan he dropped you off at this hostel."

"He told Ştefan— *Huh?*"

"Guess you'll be wanting this back." Andrei crossed the room and handed me something.

My phone.

I ran my thumb over a crack splayed across the top. A deep scratch scored the center. I pressed the Power button, and the phone started up. "It's charged."

Andrei shrugged.

"Where—? How—?" I shook my head. "Andrei, I didn't take a cab last night."

His grin lost steam. "You didn't?"

"I came across a guy who did ride-sharing, and he didn't even drop me off here. I needed shaving cream, so he took me to a convenience store. I walked the rest of the way."

"Weird. I thought Ştefan only had cabbies working for him. He was upset when ride-sharing came to Romania."

"Why would cabbies be working for your boss? I thought y'all have a scamming operation."

"We shouldn't be talking about this." Andrei pinched at his throat. "Don't tell anyone I said that, okay? I'm in enough trouble—" He leaned in, brow pinched. "Are you wearing makeup?"

"I didn't bring any makeup on this trip. Why?"

He swiped a finger across my jaw.

I knocked his hand away. "What are you doing?"

"Double-checking." He rubbed his thumb and index finger together. "No makeup."

"I already said that."

"Yeah, but I saw how hard Émilien hit you. You should have one hell of a shiner—that's what it's called in America, right? A shiner? I heard it in a movie once. Anyway, I thought you must be wearing that liquid covering stuff."

"Foundation," I said absently, reaching for my cheek. In my rush to get ready, I hadn't bothered to look in the mirror. Hadn't even thought about the injury.

I fingered my cheekbone. No pain. No swelling.

My gaze drifted to my forearm, and I gasped. The cut was gone.

"Impossible," I whispered, and I might've thought I was crazy—at the very least, I would have assumed I was imagining things—but that sting from the alcohol pad had seared itself into my memory.

"Hmm, interesting." Andrei gripped my chin, checking the other side of my face. "Maks'll be happy to hear about this. He was pretty upset."

I pulled away. "He was?"

"Oh, man. Didn't you see him? He would've beat the French out of Émilien if I hadn't stopped him. I haven't seen Maks go off like that since—" Andrei tapped his chin. "It's been a while."

What else had Maksim said? More importantly, was he okay? I wanted to know, but Andrei cut me off.

"So why were you looking for me yesterday? Maksim acted like I should've known. Did we have a conversation I'm not remembering?"

Laughter echoed from down the hall. The voices tapered off, but then someone entered the hostel and ambled into the reception area.

"Mind if we go someplace quiet?" I gestured at the back door.

Andrei shrugged and followed me out. A tidal wave of heat tumbled down on us. Sweat broke out across my body. Andrei fanned himself.

Cement steps dropped down to the backyard. I parked myself on the top stair. "I was looking for you yesterday because I needed help with something."

"Oh, yeah?" Andrei joined me. "With what?"

I grimaced. "A scam."

His head jerked in surprise. "Whoa, what? Is that a joke?"

"Not a joke. My dad was a professor at the polytechnic university, and there's something in his employment records I need. The school won't give me his file, so I thought we could scam our way into the admin office and sneak a peek."

"Why won't they give you the file?"

"The head secretary got into a conflict with her assistant. She called the girl a name—zigany or something like that—then she had security escort me out."

"Zigany? Do you mean *Țiganii?*" He pronounced the word differently than I had: *tsee-GAH-nee.*

"I guess so. Sounds right."

Andrei's mouth flatlined. "That's not good, Kat."

"Why? What does it mean?"

"Gypsies."

His answer steamrolled me, and I caught myself saying the same thing Dad had always said. "Gypsies aren't real."

Andrei guffawed. "Sure they are."

"No. They're not. They're carnival characters, Halloween costumes, folklore."

"Are you kidding me? Gypsies are everywhere in Europe, especially here in southeastern Europe." Andrei leaned in and lowered his voice. "Who else was in your meeting? *Țiganii* is plural, so that lady had to be talking about other people."

"Just me and her assistant."

"So she was referring to you, too?" His expression fell a shade grimmer. "Why would she call you Gypsy?"

"I didn't realize that's what she was doing."

"You must've misheard her. I get Romanian words mixed up all the time, but I still wouldn't go around telling people that story. Gypsies aren't the most popular bunch. Even some European governments don't like them."

My eyebrows converged. "Are you making this up to scare me?"

"No way. The French government was mass-deporting Gypsies when I was a kid, and there are other countries trying to do the same thing."

Dad had never mentioned anything like this, and he used to follow European news. "Were these well-known events? Did they make headlines?"

"Yep. Trust me, if that lady was calling you Gypsy, it wasn't a compliment."

The things Andrei was saying stirred up memories from my childhood. *Mr. Kotfas. Gypsy Django.* Before I could piece everything together, a different part of the puzzle slid into place.

The secretary had come unglued while examining the locket.

No. Not the locket. The inscription.

"Do they have their own language?" I asked. "These... Gypsies?"

"I've heard they do, but they don't have their own country, so they speak the language of whatever country they're in."

"But there *is* a Gypsy language? It exists?"

He lifted a shoulder. "Supposedly."

Andrei's answer left me breathless. What if the inscription was written in the language of the Gypsies? What if that was why I hadn't found a translation?

"You never got your dad's records?" Andrei asked.

"No. But I came downstairs this morning because... See, the thing is..." I stared at the fresh cracks in my phone. I'd been so close to solving the current clue.

"Everything's my fault."

I peered over at him. "Huh?"

"Everything that happened at the club—it's my fault. I drank too much, trying to impress Anca, and that's why you ended up alone with Émilien." Andrei stared at his hands. "He's in so much trouble, Kat. Even more than me."

I recalled the way Émilien had grabbed my arm, how he'd leaned in until his hot, acrid breath filled my nostrils.

I shivered. "Your boss knows what happened?"

"Ştefan knows everything about everything, always, and he's not happy."

Scammers or not, at least these guys were taking this seriously. That was more than I could say for the people at the club. Would Maksim report what happened to his cousin? Would any of their staff get in trouble?

"I still owe you," Andrei said, "and not just for last night. I never did repay you for what you did at the park, so"—he slapped his knees and stood—"I'm going to help you get those records."

I blinked up at him. "You are?"

"Yep." He shuffled down the steps and jogged to the back gate.

"Wait a second, Andrei." I chased him down and pulled him to a stop. "I'm not— I can't—" *The plan. Stick to the plan.* "I'm... not sure where to buy a wig."

Crap.

He did the head-jerk thing again. "Why would you need a wig?"

"The secretary took a picture of me. She said if I went to the school, everyone would know to call the cops. I need a disguise to make a scam work."

"You won't need a disguise." He pushed open the gate and headed for a yellow taxi. "Nobody can know about this." He opened the door and dropped into the front-passenger seat. "You can't tell Maks, even if he messages you."

My pulse skipped. "Maksim is going to message me?"

"He knew I was bringing you the phone and, like I said, he was pretty upset. Don't let anything slip, and *don't* tell him about the Gypsy thing. Don't tell anyone, but especially not him."

"Why?"

"His parents were killed by Gypsies."

My mouth dried. His parents had been killed? *Both of them?*

Andrei pulled his door shut and rolled down his window. "I'll be back at twenty-two. That's ten p.m. in American-speak."

"The rectorate closes at five."

"I know." His mouth angled into a grin. "Wear dark clothes."

14. RISK

"Help me try these windows," Andrei whispered.

I squeezed past him, and the bush behind me rustled.

He swatted my arm. "Quietly."

I swatted him back. "I'm trying."

We'd been creeping around campus for about thirty minutes. Andrei's big plan for getting Dad's file? Breaking and entering. And larceny.

I'd been telling myself he was a pro and that I didn't have to worry about things like being arrested or having my passport revoked. He knew what he was doing. I was in good hands.

Hopefully.

"Why are we doing this?" I tested the next window. It didn't budge. "Wishfully thinking one might be open?"

"Anca stopped by the school this afternoon, pretending to be a student, and unlocked a bunch of windows. She even relatched them a certain way so they'd look like they were locked." He slid his fingers along the glass pane and gave it a joggle and tug. The window popped open. "Here we go."

"What about an alarm?" I peered inside the dark room. "You don't think they could have the silent kind, do you?"

"Anca checked for that. She said this building should be fine."

"*Should* be?"

"Shhh. Come on." Andrei was up and in before I could argue. He motioned for me to follow him.

I hoisted myself up. My room key dug into my hip. I ignored the pain, pulled my legs around, and dropped inside the room. A long table surrounded by chairs took shape in the shadows. We were in a conference room.

Andrei inched closer. "No talking outside this room. Whispering is okay. Hand gestures are better. Got it?"

How would we see hand gestures in the dark? I had no idea, but I nodded.

We slipped out of the room and tiptoed down a hallway. Andrei paused every five or six paces and listened into the darkness. I held my breath each time. The thumping of my pulse filled my ears.

We reached an open foyer.

A hazy brew of moonlight and light pollution spilled inside the building through gigantic windows. Andrei kept to the shadows as much as possible, pulling me along until we reached a staircase.

We ascended to the next floor, and the darkness thickened. I clutched Andrei's shirt while groping the wall. My fingers slid along a smooth, painted surface and then bumped against what felt like a doorframe.

Sleek wood glided beneath my fingers. This was the door to the first office.

We kept going. My fingers slid along the wall. *Bump.* Another doorframe. We were at the second door. I tapped Andrei's shoulder. "Here," I whispered.

The twist of a door handle broke the stillness. Hinges creaked.

Andrei pulled me inside the office. Dim light filtered in through the lone window. The secretary's analog clock ticked.

Andrei eased the door shut. "You're sure this is it?"

"One hundred percent." I rounded the desk.

White light streaked the darkness. Andrei had activated his flashlight app the same way Maksim had last night.

The reminder of Maksim socked me in the gut. I had busied myself with internet research all day, pretending not to care if he messaged or not. I'd proven myself wrong by checking my phone every five seconds and hearing imaginary notifications.

I crumpled the thought and tugged on the top drawer of the desk. It didn't budge. "Secretary must have locked it."

Andrei passed me his phone and fished something out of his pocket. I held the light while he jimmied a thin, flat pin and a bent bobby pin into the lock.

Click.

He opened the drawer, and a familiar beige color appeared under the light. I snatched the file and flipped it open.

"We don't want to take it and go?" Andrei asked.

"The woman knows who I am. She could give my information to the cops." I aimed the light. "I'll find what I need, and we'll put the file back. Do you read Romanian?"

"A little."

"Can you—?" My attention moved to a yellowed piece of paper with a name typed across the top. I groaned.

"What?" Andrei peeked over my shoulder. "Something bad?"

"The secretary said my last name didn't match the name in the file. I wasn't sure what she meant until now." I pointed at the discrepancy. "This name is Bariţiu Nicolae. My dad's name was Nicholas Barrett."

"That doesn't sound very Romanian. Could he have changed his name after immigrating?"

"It's the wrong year, too." I pointed at the date.

11-01-2002

"My dad left Romania in the eighties. There's no way these records are his." I dropped the file on the desk. "We'll have to check the archives."

"I'm game. Where are they?"

"I—"

Footsteps silenced me. Light seeped beneath the door, and my next heartbeat punched into my throat.

Andrei killed his flashlight app and yanked me down behind the desk. He swore under his breath and then reached up.

The file. It was still open on the desk.

Twist. Swoosh.

Andrei withdrew his arm as a draft moved through the room. Light swung above our heads while Andrei clutched the file to his chest. Papers hung lopsided, halfway falling out. I clamped both hands over my mouth.

The light swung the other way. Footsteps drew closer.

A pause.

Tick tick tick tick. I pinched my eyes shut and hoped the clock would cover the thud of my pulse.

The light made a third pass.

The footsteps retreated. *Click.*

Andrei peeked over the desk. He waited, listening as the footsteps faded down the hall. "Damn." He stood and tossed the file on the desk. "This is getting dicey. We've got to find your dad's file and get out of here."

"I don't know where the archives are. I waited in here while the assistant was looking."

He rubbed a hand through his hair and woke up his phone. "I'll SMS Anca, see if she can find anything online." He looked over at me. "Time to pray or cross yourself or whatever rituals you might have. 'Cause this is gonna be a long shot."

ANCA FOUND a social media account for Politehnica students. She posted our question, sans the incriminating details, and then DMed a bunch of people.

A handful of students replied, saying they thought the archives were on the first floor. Nobody knew exactly where.

Andrei and I slinked through the shadows, trying every door we found. Currently, we were trying one adjacent to the main foyer.

"Kill the light," he whispered.

I turned off the flashlight app, and darkness closed over us. Narrow staircases twisted through the shadows, connecting this level to the next. The security guard could have been patrolling up there, and we wouldn't have seen him.

Metal clinked, and Andrei muttered to himself.

My muscles clenched. "What are you doing?"

"Trying to pick this lock."

My lungs tightened. I sent a silent *help* into the universe.

Click.

"Got it." Andrei pushed open the door.

We shut ourselves inside the room, and a new level of darkness covered us.

I activated Andrei's flashlight app. Office desks emerged from the shadows. Bookshelves lined the wall on our right.

"Over there." Andrei nudged me and pointed.

I redirected the light to a row of doors.

The first three led to small offices. The fourth opened to a janitor's closet. The fifth—last door in the corner—opened to a large room full of rusty old file cabinets.

"I'd say this is it." Andrei ran a hand over the nearest cabinet. The LED light illuminated dust particles floating in the air.

"Are you sure?" I focused on a label fixed to one of the cabinets. STUDENȚI. "I think these are student files."

He opened the drawer, grabbed a file, and scanned the contents. "Check this out." He placed his finger next to the date.

02-07-1996

"February seventh, 1996," I said, more to myself.

"You're reading it wrong."

I did a double take. "I am?"

"The day comes first in Europe, then the month. So you'd say the second of July, not February the seventh." He closed the file. "Point is, these are past students, so we've gotta be in the right place. Look for files labeled *facultatea* or *profesori*."

We checked the file cabinets one by one. Well, Andrei did most of the checking. I held his phone. "Knew I should've brought mine," I said, adjusting the light. "I could be searching, too."

"Maybe you should write a strongly worded letter to the fashion industry. Tell them to start making women's clothing with pockets."

"Sure." My mouth twisted. "You can help me do that right after we find these records."

Andrei snorted a laugh.

He continued to the next row of file cabinets. As he turned, the LED light reflected off something clipped onto his back pocket. It looked like—

"Is that a knife?" I aimed the light.

Andrei peeked over his shoulder. "Ah, that's my switchblade. Wanna see it?" He wrenched it out before I could answer. Something about the way he did it seemed familiar, like I'd seen him do it before.

He pressed something on the handle. *Snap!* A blade swung out.

I flinched. "Did you, by chance, use that thing to punch Émilien?"

"You saw that, huh?" Andrei chuckled. "Great way to handle someone bigger or stronger than you. Just grip something before you swing." He folded the knife, gripped the handle, and threw a right hook into his palm. *Smack!* "Adds weight to your hand and reinforces your knuckles. Maksim taught me that trick before he... You know."

"No. I don't know. You never explained."

"Wow." Andrei gave a low whistle and stationed himself at the next file cabinet. "You sure are curious about him."

My jaw slipped. "I am not."

"You were asking about him earlier, too. You said you wanted him to message you."

"I did not!"

Andrei cast a sly grin. "Suuure you didn't."

"You're the one who's been talking about him. I've just been listening." Couldn't I go one stinkin' day without being falsely accused of something?

Andrei tugged on a drawer and peered inside. "Ooh, what do we have here?" He was pulling out a file when a creak reached my ears.

I wheeled around. "Did you hear that?"

Andrei froze. "Hear what?"

I tiptoed to the door, eased it open, and peered out.

"What is it?" Panic rose in Andrei's voice.

I shushed him and pointed his phone into the office. White light washed over desks, chairs, bookshelves, a coatrack. Apart from that, the space was empty.

"Kat?"

"It's nothing." I faced him. "I must have heard the building creak."

He stepped into the aisle, using the file to fan himself. "I'm nervous as hell. Can't remember if I locked the door."

"Which door? This door?" I thumbed at the door behind me. "Or the door between the office and the foyer?"

"Office and foyer."

My eyes bulged. "Andrei, how could you not lock it?"

"Maybe I did. Can you check?" He held up the file. "You'll wanna hurry. I think we've hit the jackpot."

I perked up. "Is that—?"

"Yep. I found the faculty files." Excitement twinkled in his voice. "This one's dated from the eighties."

I couldn't believe it. Finally, some luck.

I left the phone with him so he could keep searching, and then I entered the office. Furniture carved shapes into the darkness. I stalked forward, giving myself a wide berth around each desk. Turning on the overhead lights would have been easier, but Andrei had insisted we keep all the lights off.

I was fine with that if it meant we were safer. Just needed to be careful.

Halfway across the room, the floor beneath me creaked. I cringed. The noise was loud, but... loud enough to be heard outside this office?

I continued forward. The chances of a security guard passing by at that exact moment was one in a hundred. No, a thousand. Ten thousand. It was actually—

An epiphany brought my logic to a screeching halt. The creak from earlier had sounded strikingly similar to what I'd heard just now. Did that mean someone had been in here a minute ago?

Did it mean someone was in here... now?

Creeeak. The noise came from behind me, and my insides shriveled.

I spun around and slammed into a sturdy body. "Andrei, hel—!"

A large hand covered my mouth. The person grabbed hold of me and reeled me in. Whoever it was, he was surprisingly gentle, almost playful.

"I hope I'm not intruding." His deep voice cut the darkness the way a hot knife cuts butter. LED light disintegrated the shadows in my midst.

The guy released me and aimed the light at himself. His mouth lay flat, his features hard and pronounced.

I gawked at Maksim. "What are you doing here?"

"Ironically, I was about to ask you the same thing."

"We're trying to—" My explanation broke off as something slightly more horrifying occurred to me. "How long have you been in here?"

He lowered the light, letting two beats pass before he said,

"Long enough." A smile shone through in his voice, and molten lava rose in my cheeks. He'd heard us talking about him.

"I haven't been asking Andrei about you." The heat spread to my ears. "And I did *not* say I wanted you to message me."

"Uh-huh." His voice glimmered with amusement, but then a hint of soberness clouded his mood. "Are you all right? How are you feeling?"

"Peachy," I said with a sprinkle of sarcasm. "Thanks for checking on me today."

"Andrei was sent to check on you."

"Good thing you guys have Andrei to do your bidding." Rejection lodged itself in my throat, making it hard to speak.

The sole of Maksim's boot scraped the floor. The smell of musk and sweat filtered into my head, and I detected the last, lingering vapors of his cologne. It took every bit of willpower I had not to swoon.

"Would it be better or worse," he began slowly, "if I told you I've wanted to speak to you all day?"

Heat rimmed my eyes. "You shouldn't say things like that. It's... confusing."

He didn't have an immediate response, and I couldn't decide which was heavier—my heart or his silence. I bit my lip, clenched my jaw, and did mental gymnastics to ward off the waterworks.

His boot scraped again. He found my elbow, and his touch was a whisper in the darkness, his thumb grazing the fleshy part of my arm.

I pulled a soft breath.

He cupped my cheek, caressing the cheekbone. My body hummed as he tipped my head back. My heartbeat stuttered.

I closed my eyes, lips parting.

A sudden blast of white blinded me. I jerked away.

Maksim reeled me back. "Where did Émilien hit you?"

Took me a second to realize why he was asking.

I rubbed my eyes, trying to rub out the spots in my vision. "I-I thought Andrei told you— He was supposed to let you know I was okay."

"Andrei hasn't checked in today." Maksim took aim with the flashlight, and I winced. "Where were you hit? Which side of your face?"

"Left."

"Your left or mine?"

"Mine, but you won't find anything there." I pushed the flashlight away. Shadows fell across me. "It's gone."

"*What* is gone?"

"The injury. My cheek was bruised and swollen, and— It was awful. Then this morning— I don't know. It's just gone."

He checked one side of my face, then the other. The other again.

"I took ibuprofen before bed. That might explain things."

"And the cut?" He brought my forearm into the light. "Did ibuprofen cure that also?"

He was right. Nothing explained this.

I braced myself, letting him examine my cheek more thoroughly. He pressed on the bone like he'd done last night. Unlike last night, there was no pain.

"This whole thing is surreal," I said. "I keep thinking last night must have been a dream or—"

"Dream." Maksim's hand fell away. "I had a dream. About this."

I stared up at him. "About my cheek?"

"About the injury. It disappeared in the same—rather, in a similar—manner." His expression fell grim. He looked away.

"What?"

"I had the dream three nights ago."

"Maksim, we didn't know each other three nights ago. The flight from London was on Wednesday, wasn't it? And today's Friday?"

He didn't say anything.

"Hey Kat?" Andrei's voice jarred me.

I pulled myself out of Maksim's grasp as the door to the archives room opened. Light drifted toward us.

"You better get in here. You're not gonna—" Andrei froze in the doorway.

"Everything's okay," I said. "It's Maksim."

Maksim aimed the flashlight at himself, confirming.

"Whoa. Maks. I thought you were security." Andrei rubbed his forehead, which I imagined was damp. "How'd you know we were here?"

"How do you think I knew?" Sarcasm burned through Maksim's tone. "Think hard. We've been over this."

Andrei looked down at his phone. His shoulders wilted. So he *was* being monitored. But who would keep using a phone with spyware?

Unless he was required to use that phone.

"It's my fault," I blurted. "I-I needed my dad's employment records, and I didn't know how else to get them."

"I suppose this is why you've been searching for Andrei." Maksim's jaw tightened. "To solicit his help for this break-in."

"That part wasn't my idea. I thought we were going to come in during office hours. I was going to buy a wig."

"Um, Kat?" Andrei peeped.

"You involved one of our people," Maksim said. "That's bad enough."

"But why? Why would your boss care about something like this when—?"

"Kat," Andrei repeated.

I swore and wheeled around. "What?"

"I'm not sure how to tell you this. I can't find your dad's file."

"What are you talking about? I've been out here for ten minutes." I crossed the room. "There's no way you checked all those files."

"I did. A bunch of the cabinets are empty. The files I did find —I checked those twice." He sighed. "I'm sorry. Your dad's records aren't here."

15. ASTIGMATIC

I followed Maksim and Andrei across a parking lot. Nineties pop music pulsed from inside a pub. Smoke flowed from the roof vent, and a garlicky aroma saturated the air. The smell might have been appetizing if I hadn't felt like puking.

All three of us had combed through the archives—the labeled drawers, the unlabeled drawers, the empty drawers—but Andrei was right. Dad's records weren't there.

My throat tightened. I couldn't go to Braşov without Dad's old address, and *that* was in the file. There was no other way to solve the current clue. None that I'd been able to think of, anyway.

Maksim veered right, heading for a row of parked cars. He tucked the flashlight inside his leather jacket. "Do you need a ride?" He was looking at me.

"I'm okay. Thanks." The answer tasted bland. A ride would have saved me the cost of a cab, but I couldn't handle being around Maksim. My emotions couldn't handle it.

"Where do you think you're going?" He directed the question to Andrei, who had ducked through the parking lot and was striding toward the pub.

Andrei did a slow pivot on his heel. "Grabbing a bite to eat. I'll catch up with you."

"Are you insane? We have to report to Ştefan."

"Come on, Maks. I wasn't feeling good this morning. Haven't eaten all day."

Maksim's attitude softened. He slid a curious look to me. "Are you hungry?"

I wasn't. But even if I were, Andrei clearly didn't want company. He rolled his eyes, sighing so deeply I could feel the breeze change direction.

"I'm in a hurry. Have to get back to my hostel." I had postponed talking to the hostel manager about a refund for the unused days. That'd been a mistake. I should have set things in motion this morning, but I'd been hopeful about tonight.

Too hopeful.

Maksim focused on Andrei. "SMS me when you're done, and I'll meet you at the villa. If I have to search for you again—"

"You won't. Promise." Andrei gave a thumbs-up and disappeared inside the pub.

Maksim continued through the parking lot. He paused beside a van with blacked-out windows. Was *that* his vehicle? Hell no, I was not catching a ride with anyone in that.

"Before you go," he said, "do you mind if I ask you something?"

"No. I mean, you can ask, but I can't promise I'll answer."

"You can't? Even though you promised to answer all my questions if I took you to the club?"

I stopped beside him. His stoic expression had returned, along with a firm silence. My guilt festered. "One question, then I have to go."

"Why is it that you need your father's employment records so badly?"

"I don't need them badly, per se." My gaze fell. "I don't need them at all, actually. I'm going home."

"I find that hard to believe."

"What? That I'm going home?" I looked up in time to see him smirk. "Because I am. I'm using trip insurance."

"I find it hard to believe the records aren't important, especially after you broke into the university to get them." He rounded the van.

I followed him.

"That wasn't the original plan. A professor was supposed to help me, but I never could—" I cleared the van and found Maksim standing beside the sleekest, dreamiest sport bike I'd ever seen.

Smooth tires, as thick as my thighs, rested on the pavement. Sharp cuts and chrome edges gave the motorcycle a knifelike finish.

Maksim stood in the shadows, putting on fingerless riding gloves. In his all-black attire—boots, jacket, jeans—he blended into the night.

Then I realized he wasn't wearing normal clothes. That was a leather riding jacket. And those were riding jeans, which were thicker and specially lined to protect from road rash.

"Is this *your* bike?" I pointed. "Is this what you offered to— What you, um—?"

"Offered to give you a ride on?" A grin played across his lips. "Yes, it is."

"Oh." I cleared my throat. "Is it... fast?"

"It is. Very fast." His grin sharpened, and my pulse trilled. "Although, if I may be honest, I don't tend to drive very fast anymore." He gripped the bottom of his jacket and zipped himself in. "Nevertheless, the offer stands if you'd like a ride." He picked up his helmet and held it out to me.

I pictured myself climbing onto that bike—with him—and my next heartbeat skipped.

"Perhaps it would behoove me to explain something first." Gravity edged into his voice. He lowered the helmet. "That wasn't my ex at the club."

"Who? The dancer?"

His face widened, and for a sliver of a second, I could have sworn understanding dawned behind his eyes. He blinked, and the look vanished. "What are you talking about?"

"What are *you* talking about?"

"I was referring to the waitress," he said. "There was a time when she worked in a massage parlor—"

"Ew." I held up a hand. "I don't want to know anything else."

"I helped her leave that profession. Waitressing isn't the most distinguished line of work, but it's more dignified than what she did before, and she makes enough to support herself and her daughter. She considers me a benefactor, a friend. Nothing more."

"Why are you telling me this?"

He met my stare dead-on. "You know why."

Heat flooded my entire being.

Yellow blurred in my peripheral. A taxi was pulling into the parking lot, and I beelined for it.

"Kat, wait." Maksim darted in front of me. "Where are you going?"

"Home." My eyes heated, moisture forming at the corners. "I need to book my flights. I'm already packed."

He glanced around, as if needing something to say and expecting to pull it out of the air.

A blur of red emerged from the pub and hurried to the cab. *My* cab, the one I'd been planning to catch.

Maksim traced my line of sight to the person. "Hey!" He let out a sharp whistle.

The guy in the red shirt answered with a friendly wave. It was Andrei. "Anca's hungry, too. I'm gonna meet up with her."

Maksim started for the cab, helmet bouncing against his thigh.

"Whoa, whoa, whoa." Andrei made a calming gesture. "Maks, don't worry. Ştefan said I should go over there tomorrow. Just me."

Maksim froze.

Andrei gave another wave and dropped into the front-passenger seat. The cabbie reversed and pulled away. Maksim stared after them.

I came alongside him. "Don't you think you're overreacting a little?"

He pivoted. "Excuse me?"

"Andrei's scams are way worse than what we did tonight. Y'all's boss probably realizes that."

"Is that so?" His eyes went squinty. "I suppose that's your way of justifying what you've done. Because at least breaking and entering isn't as bad as scamming people, right?"

"Is it as bad as what *you* do?" I folded my arms. "What you used to do, supposedly?"

Maksim's jaw flexed. He brushed past me. "Have a safe flight home."

His icy tone left me with a chill that sank into my bones.

I hugged myself, trying to figure out what to do. I had so many regrets from last night—not being able to thank him, not telling him goodbye—and tonight was turning into a repeat.

He passed beneath a band of light, which stemmed from the pub's sign. As he glanced back, I noticed a fresh cut along the top of his eyebrow. Bluish marks speckled his cheek.

Heaviness sank between my rib cage. Those must have been from last night. From Émilien.

Maksim swung his leg over the bike and donned his helmet. Using the heel of his boot, he wrenched up the kickstand and turned the key. The engine growled to life and settled into a rumble.

The heaviness inside me twisted. I walked forward. "Maksim, wait."

He looked at me.

"I'm—" What? Sorry? An idiot? All the above?

He braced the handlebars, waiting. But every time I thought

of something to say, my brain countered with a reason I shouldn't say it.

He blipped the throttle, and the motor thundered. Without a word, without even a glance my way, he dumped the clutch and shot across the parking lot, a smear of black with silver streaks.

He did a head-check, crouching low, and careened onto the street.

I ran to the sidewalk. Taillights smoldered red all the way to the next intersection. Maksim lane-split the two lines of traffic, riding between them.

Regret poured into me. "Awesome. Perfect way to end the night." I threw up my hands and let them fall at my sides.

"Focus, Kat." I back-burnered my emotions and slipped a finger into the key pocket of my pants. "Go to the hostel. Get the refund. Rebook your flights. You can do this. It's not—" I groped for my cash.

My finger detected fabric and nothing else.

"What the—?" I tugged on my waistband. I'd brought fifty lei, which I'd folded and tucked into the key pocket, but the money was gone. So was my room key.

They must have fallen out. It was the only explanation, but where? When? Should I go looking for them?

"You know what? It doesn't matter." I made fists and stormed into the parking lot. "Did you hear me?" I shouted. "I said it doesn't matter! None of this matters!"

Whoever I was talking to—God, luck, this city—I really believed what I was saying. None of this mattered anymore because I was going home. End of story.

My feet stalled. No, this wasn't the end of the story. Because not only had I lost my money and room key, I also had no idea how to get to the hostel.

"The pub probably has Wi-Fi," I said as if to reassure myself. But that moment of comfort fled when I realized... I didn't have my phone. There'd been nowhere to keep it, and Andrei had insisted I leave it behind.

That meant I couldn't download walking directions. I literally had no way to get to the hostel.

I was stuck. In Bucharest. In the middle of the night.

My stare shot to the traffic jam that filled the one-way street. I swore and launched into a sprint. "Maksim!"

16. VULNERABLE

The traffic was gridlocked. I slowed to a jog and scanned for Maksim's bike. A long row of parked cars blocked my view.

I ditched the sidewalk and raced through traffic. A driver honked. Another driver shouted. I ignored them, still scanning.

There. Maksim was idling at the front of the line. The light burned red while traffic from an adjacent street flowed through the intersection. I needed to get his attention, but how? He wouldn't be able to hear me over his engine.

An idea sparked.

I raced alongside a hatchback, jumped up, and slid across the hood—same way I did a sliding tackle in soccer. The driver lambasted me with his horn.

A sedan idled in the next lane over. I leaped up and braced a hand on the sturdiest part of the hood, along the outer edge, while kicking my legs to the side.

I glided over, and an orchestra of honks went up.

Dave had shown me that move—called a "speed vault"—and I hoped it would be enough to get Maksim's attention.

It was. Maksim straightened, looking around.

"Here!" I waved. "Right here!"

He locked onto me.

The stoplight splashed down to green. Maksim shot forward and cut to the right, pulling alongside a parked car. I reached him, out of breath and covered in sweat.

"Changed my mind." I gulped air. "Can I get that ride?"

"Tell me about your father." The helmet muffled his voice.

My chest rose and fell. Exhaust fumes burned my nose and lungs. I wasn't unwilling to answer his question—not this time—but I wasn't sure where to begin. The result was a lengthy silence.

He rolled his eyes and let off the clutch.

"Wait!" I caught his jacket, and he braked. "Look, I'm sorry. Really. I'm a high-speed train wreck." I inhaled a shaky breath. "What exactly do you want to know?"

"Everything."

I frowned. So much for finding a starting point.

"Okay, well... my dad lost everyone he knew in the revolution, and I think it must have traumatized him because he never wanted to talk about Romania. He wouldn't teach me the language. He wouldn't even let a friend of his speak Romanian around me. All that changed this past fall."

"In what way?"

"When I was a kid, my dad sometimes mentioned Transylvania, but always in a way that seemed unintentional. Like he'd let a thought slip out. I assumed he had a connection to that place, but I never knew how. Come to find out, he was from Transylvania and had lived in Braşov for a while."

"Braşov?" Intrigue glimmered in Maksim's eyes. "Did he say when?"

"After he finished college. He wanted to stay there, but his father secured a job for him at the polytechnic university. That was how he ended up here in Bucharest. He moved to America during the revolution and decided he was never coming back. That also changed.

"See, my dad had this rule about not taking European-based projects. He wouldn't even accept clients with a European branch. There were times when we needed the money—like when we lost our house—but he refused to make an exception no matter how desperate we were. Last Thanksgiving—"

"Remind me when that holiday is? November?"

"End of November. While we were making dinner, he started opening up about his old life for the first time ever. He shared stories all weekend, and the following week he announced a work trip to Romania. I couldn't believe what was happening, so... I found ways to test him."

Maksim unfastened his chin strap. "How?"

"I asked him questions he wouldn't have normally answered and suggested things he wouldn't have normally allowed. Like doing a Romania-themed Christmas tree." A lump formed in my throat. "I had begged him to do that when I was a kid. Back then, he got upset."

"But not this time." Maksim removed his helmet. Damp hair matted his face, and sweat rolled off his hairline.

I averted my gaze. "Right. Not this time."

A bus sped through the intersection. Hot air blasted us, rustling our clothes and kicking up debris. Maksim killed his engine, dismounted, and pushed his bike up onto the sidewalk.

I joined him. "My dad and I played a scavenger hunt game when I was a kid. He would make the clues, and I would solve them. Two weeks after he died—"

"One moment. You've not explained that part yet." Maksim rested the bike on its kickstand. "How he died."

"Plane crash." The lump in my throat solidified. "His flight crashed in the mountains of western Romania, near Timişoara, when he was on his way home."

"That was why you became upset when I mentioned Timişoara." He exhaled, pushing a hand through his wet hair. "I didn't realize—"

"I know. It's okay." Pressure coiled in my chest, but I did my best to keep going. "Two weeks later, one of his scavenger hunts arrived in the mail. There was no note, nothing to indicate why he'd sent it, but everything was in his handwriting. There was also —" I was about to mention the gold locket when Andrei's warning twanged in my memory.

"Don't tell Maksim about the Gypsy thing. Don't tell anyone, but especially not him."

"There was a postmark," I said, changing course. "My dad sent the package from Braşov, which is strange because he was supposed to be in Bucharest for his work meetings."

"That's interesting, to be sure, but how is any of this related to the employment records?"

"Some of the clues were anagrams that alluded to finding an address. Another clue referenced the polytechnic university. I knew he was talking about his old address in Braşov because—"

"Because the package had been mailed from Braşov"— Maksim's expression turned thoughtful—"and because he had spoken of Braşov before the trip."

"He was also living in Braşov when he received the job at the university, and employment files are supposed to have the person's address from the time of hiring. That's what I was told by a professor."

"Find the file, find the address. It makes sense."

"You think so?" I perked up. "You don't think it sounds silly?"

"It would be rather ambiguous without the extra details, but there's cleverness in such subtlety. I can appreciate that for a scavenger hunt."

A ray of excitement glimmered within me.

But then reality dragged me back into the muck and mire. Without the address, my problem-solving skills were useless.

Maksim held me with a steady gaze. The lines of his face had softened, his expression warm.

He passed me the helmet. "Put that on. I'm taking you to your hostel."

Maksim's leather jacket smothered me, and sweat drizzled down my back and arms. My breaths came fast, fogging the visor of his helmet.

I death-gripped him as he followed a line of traffic into Union Square.

Stone buildings towered over us. Neon signs and LED billboards glittered, creating a bubble of light over the city. I vacillated between admiring our surroundings and squeezing my eyes shut in terror.

Motorcyclists are twenty-eight times more likely to die in a traffic-related accident than someone driving a car. I'd come across that statistic months ago, and my brain refused to let me forget it now.

Maksim did a head-check, hair wild, and accelerated into a roundabout. The bike boomed, pure power shuddering through me.

I tightened my grip. My fingers detected rock-hard abs beneath his shirt, and a fresh fog clouded my vision. I had sighed on the visor.

He circled through a roundabout, merging with the river of headlights flowing around us. The movement left me feeling disembodied, weightless.

I gritted my teeth.

We reached a standstill behind a line of traffic. Maksim rested his boots on the pavement and peered over his shoulder. "How are you feeling?"

I wrestled with the visor and forced it up. "Do you want, like, an overall average or...?"

One side of his mouth lifted. "You remembered to keep your feet up when we stopped. That's good." He faced forward. "Don't forget to lean with me when I corner. Try to relax. I won't be going fast."

Guilt slinked through me. I hadn't told him I was an experienced rider. Honestly, I didn't feel like one anymore. My fearlessness had abandoned me, right along with every fragment of my old self—whoever she was. I couldn't remember anymore.

We cruised through the narrow streets of Old Town until we reached Strada Olimpului. A soft glow burned into the darkness around the hostel's back gate. Maksim parked in the warm light.

I peeled myself off him and grappled with the helmet. He reached over and popped the chin strap.

"Thanks," I whispered as the helmet lifted off. My hair bulged.

"Were you serious about going home?"

I nodded, stripping off his jacket. "My best friend is helping me with the upfront costs. Once the trip insurance goes through, I'll reimburse her."

"Is there any chance you'd change your mind?" He punched his way into the jacket, one arm at a time, then zipped himself in.

"The clues have to be solved in order. Without my dad's old address, I'll get stuck."

"Are you certain? Because I have friends in Braşov. I lived with them last summer, and I came to know the city well."

I responded with a heavy dose of side-eye. "Are you offering to help me with the scavenger hunt?"

"I am." He donned the helmet and turned the bike around. "We could stay with my friends. I'm sure they would love to help."

Hope and fear played tug-of-war. Would firsthand knowledge of the city be enough to solve the clues out of order?

Possibly, but... no. I was going home. Brandy would be crushed if I didn't make it there by Sunday. That was the right thing to do. The sane thing.

"There's a rapid train leaving for Braşov at 8:10 tomorrow morning." He adjusted the helmet's chinstrap. "I'll be there, at Gara de Nord, in case you change your mind."

"I won't."

"But in case you do." He revved his engine.

Suddenly, I remembered... There was one last thing I'd been

meaning to look into. If I wanted an answer, he could probably give me one.

"Hey, Maksim?"

He eased off the throttle. "Yes?"

"Do you happen to know—?" I didn't have to do this, I could let this go. "H-how long was the revolution?"

"Our revolution?" His eyes turned thoughtful. "Ten days, although pockets of fighting did carry on after that."

My center pinched. That was basically what the cab driver had said. "And how many people died? Ballpark figure."

"One thousand, a bit more." Maksim scanned our surroundings. Darkness cloaked the neighborhood beyond our halo of warmth. "These are oddly specific questions to be asking in the middle of the night while we stand outside your hostel." He focused on me. "Context?"

I didn't respond. Couldn't. Dad had lied to me. Why?

"I'll leave you to your thoughts." Maksim gripped the handlebars. "Eight ten tomorrow morning. Platform seven. I'll have the tickets."

He dumped the clutch. His tires gripped the pavement and catapulted him down the street. His engine roared, echoing long after his taillight disappeared.

16½. SHAKEN

Maksim and I hiked a set of switchbacks. The rocky trail pressed against the soles of my shoes. The smell of pine and churned-up soil infused my senses.

Maksim broke from the trail and entered a patch of forest. I followed him.

"Can't believe you talked me into this." I stepped over a dead tree. "We should be working on the scavenger hunt."

"This will be worth it." Maksim climbed onto a rock ledge and reached down for me. "Careful. Mind your step."

I gripped his hand, braced a foot on the ledge, and let him pull me up. Our bodies collided, and I found myself tangled in his arms.

The side of his mouth hitched up. *"Bună ziua."*

"Bună ziua." Every inch of my body glowed. "Why'd you bring me here?"

"It's the most beautiful view in Transylvania, and I wanted you to see it." He carefully, with that oh so gentle touch of his, turned me around until I faced away from him.

I pulled a soft breath.

Evergreens stretched on either side of us, covering the mountain. Down below, orange rooftops set the valley on fire. He was right. The view was amazing.

Confusion crowded my thoughts as the rooftops turned fuzzy. I rubbed my eyes. Nothing else seemed to be out of focus. Only the rooftops, as if the scene had been uploaded into a photo-editing program and then blurred.

Maksim rotated me in a slow turn, bringing us face-to-face again. Blue sky cocooned us. The sun burned at midday, and Maksim's eyes shimmered like the earthy layers of a desert landscape.

Sweat leaked down his face and skidded along his jawline. One of the droplets teetered before continuing its journey down along his throat. I pictured myself lifting up and placing my lips to the same spot the dampness had kissed.

A jarful of butterflies cracked open in my tummy.

His gaze wandered the planes of my face and settled on my mouth. I eased closer, heart drumming out a solo.

Movement blipped in my vision. I peered past Maksim, and a stab of fear slashed the fluttery feeling to bits.

A lion sat on a ledge higher up the mountain. The animal swatted its tail, its golden mane catching the sunlight.

"M-Maksim? There's a lion." I pointed over his shoulder. "Right there. Look."

His attention was on something skyward. I traced his gaze to a commercial airliner coasting into the valley.

My eyes fogged up. No. Not again.

Maksim hopped off the ledge. I stayed anchored, my entire being filled with dread. The wind kicked up. The clouds rolled in, and four black wedges dipped out of the storm.

The funnel clouds lengthened into ropes, twisting around Dad's plane. A fifth appeared and joined the others.

Maksim hiked down the mountain, following the switchbacks.

"Stop!" I cupped my mouth. "Maksim, don't go down there!"

Tremors rolled under my feet. A slow rattle shimmied up my legs and deposited into the rest of me. Clumps of dirt and rocks bounced around my feet.

The mountain shuddered, and everything shifted—a rug pulled out from under my feet. I toppled off the ledge and face-planted on the trail.

Rocks stabbed my hands and knees. Tears plucked at my eyes.

Maksim's frame quaked in the distance. The tremors grew, and the trail in front of him sank and swelled at once, like the ground was taking a gigantic breath.

My eyes widened. "Oh, God."

An explosion erupted, blasting up dirt and rocks while a pillar of dense smoke swallowed everything it touched... including Maksim.

"No! *No! Maksim!*"

<hr>

"KAT, WAKE UP." A hand gripped my shoulder. "Kat."

My eyes wrenched open. Maksim sat beside me, a book lying face down in his lap. The 8:10 to Braşov swayed beneath me, scraping along rough tracks.

I looked around. Passengers murmured to each other. Everyone's eyes were on me, and heat crawled into my face. Had I screamed out loud?

"You've been stirring for a bit." Maksim glanced at the onlookers. "Are you all right?"

I hugged myself and shook my head.

"Do you remember what you were you dreaming?"

The heat spread, stinging my eyes.

I turned my attention to the world rushing past my window. We'd left the gray cityscape behind us. Now emerald forests filled the scope of my vision.

The tree line broke, and jagged mountains jutted up from the earth and climbed into the crystal-blue sky. Wooden cottages with thatched roofs sprinkled the foothills.

"Kat?"

"I don't want to talk about it," I said. Then I took the dream, wadded it up, and shoved it so far into the depths of my mind I hoped the memory would never resurface.

PART TWO

BRAȘOV

UKRAINE
HUNGARY
MOLDOVA
ROMÂNIA
Brașov
SERBIA
București
BULGARIA

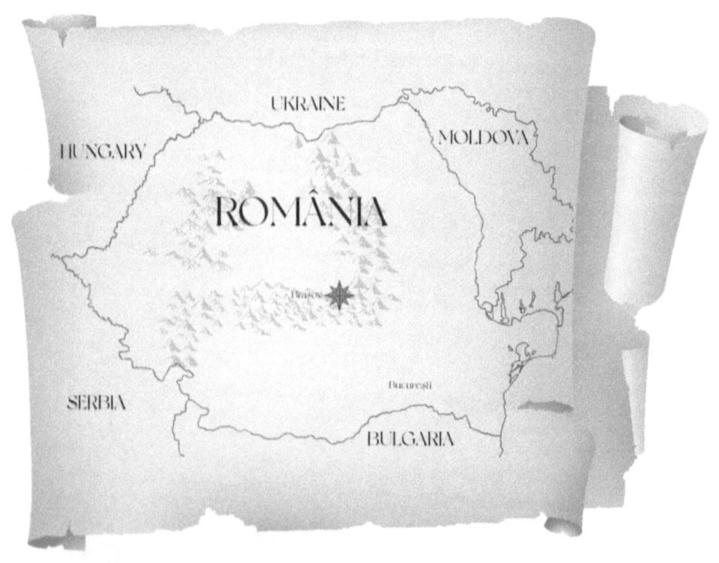

17. Headway

Gray daylight filtered through the windows of the Braşov train station. Passengers hurried in all directions.

I squeezed through a line of people waiting to buy tickets and followed Maksim outside.

Elderly men in fedoras loitered around a newspaper kiosk, sipping on something steamy while smoke curled up from their cigarettes.

We veered right, past the kiosks, and headed for a line of taxis. In Bucharest, the cabs had been New York yellow. These were white.

One of the cabbies walked forward. Maksim handed off a leather duffel and climbed into the back seat. I climbed in after him.

"You didn't bring your suitcase," he said.

I set my backpack and travel purse between us. "How did you know I have a suitcase?"

"You were wheeling it through the airport." He arched an eyebrow. "The day we met."

"Right. I knew that." I forced a smile and pretended like my brain *didn't* have a glitch. "I packed light and left everything else at the hostel. Couldn't get a refund, anyway, so…" I shrugged.

Maksim's attention shifted to my purse. "May I see the scavenger hunt?"

I retrieved the list of clues. He took the paper and unfolded it.

Our driver pulled out of the parking lot and merged with traffic on a four-lane road. I held my breath, taking note of every billboard, every shopping center, every apartment building.

The cabbie popped a cigarette between his lips and cracked his window. Chilly air circulated through the car.

"What's up with the weather?" Goose bumps rippled over my arms and legs. "You said Romania was having a drought and heat wave."

"Braşov is in the Carpathian Mountains, and their weather can be somewhat different from the rest of the country."

"Somewhat?" I rubbed my arms. "Maksim, it's freezing."

"Twenty isn't freezing." My expression must have blanked because he added, "That's nearly seventy degrees in Fahrenheit. Most days it's been warmer than this and with little rainfall." His gaze drifted to his window, then to the city breezing past us. He angled a glance up. "The clouds come, but the rain is elusive. That's what my friends tell me."

I studied him. He seemed relaxed, genuine. If he was lying, I would've never guessed it.

But why would he lie about the weather? Why would anyone?

"Any chance the forecast might change?" I peeked down at myself. The gray sky had my legs looking extra pale. "All I brought were shorts and T-shirts."

"Braşov has plenty of shops. We'll leave our belongings at the guesthouse and then go shopping."

Our taxi veered into a residential area and circled through a roundabout. Tower-block-style apartments sprouted up around us. These buildings were smaller than the ones in Bucharest and sprinkled the neighborhood in bright colors. One building had a fresh coat of lime green. Others had been doused in coral or canary yellow.

The apartments gave way to two- and three-story stucco villas. Decorative gates and stone walls bordered the properties. Terracotta roofs crowned the homes.

Our driver parked beside a wrought-iron gate accented in fleurs-de-lis. Maksim had his wallet out. "This is us."

"Do you want some money? I can split the fare with you."

"*Nu, mulțumesc.*" No, thank you.

"Okay. If you're sure." I gathered my things. "Thank you. For paying, and also for coming. And for talking *me* into coming."

He was counting out the cash, and his gaze wandered to me. "*Cu plăcere, dragă.*" *Cu plăcere* meant "with pleasure." I wasn't sure what *dragă* meant, but he followed it up with a wink that made my body flicker.

I fought a smile and pushed open my door as a herd of females ambled through the wrought-iron gate. They were layered up in cardigans and jean jackets, and one of them wore a blush-colored beanie with a gaudy flower.

I would have killed for a beanie. Even a froufrou one.

The girls gathered on the sidewalk, whispering to each other. I thought they were talking about me but then realized they were staring at Maksim.

The cabbie collected the duffel.

Maksim took it and then started toward me. He pulled up short when he found himself blockaded by flirty smiles.

"Hi there." Beanie Girl flipped her hair, eyes glittering. She looked like she wanted to put on a little music and invite him in for a drink.

"*Bună dimineața.*" Maksim squeezed past her, nodding to the other girls. "*Bună.*"

They giggled. One of them exclaimed, "You think he's staying here?"

My eyes rolled so far into my head I thought they might stay there permanently.

The girls left us—him—with a round of cutesy waves before wandering up the sidewalk.

"Is this a hostel?" My attention wandered to a sign. Pensiunea La Madălină. "I thought we were staying with your friends."

"We are." Maksim angled for the gate and jimmied the latch. "They run a guesthouse out of their home."

"Oh." In other words, we'd be seeing those girls again. Terrific.

The gate creaked open, and Maksim ushered me through. Stone pavers marked out a walkway to the house. We were halfway there when a man old enough to be Maksim's dad barreled through the front door.

He charged forward with a laugh and a shout. Maksim hugged him.

They bantered, and my ears detected a distinct difference in how they spoke. Maksim had the same sharpness I'd noticed before, his accent popping across the words. This man spoke more slowly and had a familiar musicality to his voice, his words strung together like a song.

Memories of Mr. Kotfas flooded in. Dad's friend had rarely spoken Romanian around me, but when he had, it'd been similar to Maksim's friend.

The man beamed a smile, switching to English. "You must be Kat. I'm Daniel."

"Nice to meet you." I hoped I didn't look as awkward as I felt.

"I was wondering, Kat"—he led us to the entrance—"is your name short for Katherine?"

"Uh, yeah. Sure is."

"Did you know Katherine comes from the Greek word *katharos*, which means 'pure one'? In Hebrew, the name is Zakiah."

"That's... interesting." I stifled a shiver and tried to catch Maksim's eye. He was putting away his phone. "Apparently my dad's mom had an odd name like that. Zora, I think."

"Oh?" Daniel's mood brightened even more. "And what kind of name is that?"

"Romanian. My dad and his family were from here." Hadn't Maksim told him that part?

"I don't believe Zora is a Romanian name." Daniel scratched along his jawline. "I suppose it could be—"

"Why don't we go inside?" Maksim stepped between us. "Kat comes from a very warm climate. This weather feels cool to her."

"Oh dear." Daniel's attention fell to my bare legs. "I wasn't paying attention at all. I'll show you to your rooms." He gestured for us to follow him.

We passed through a den that had been outfitted, floor to ceiling, in leather and wood. A pine-colored chandelier, complete with golden, flickering LEDs, hung above us. Metal-studded leather chairs encircled a solid-wood table, and everything else—couch, coffee table, bookshelves—carried on the medieval look.

Well, everything except a menorah, which sat atop a bookshelf. The spines of several books showcased a script that might have been Hebrew.

"The kitchen is there." Daniel gestured at an open doorway. "It's small, but we make up for it with our selection of gourmet coffees and teas. Maksim can show you that. Your rooms are upstairs."

We ascended a wide staircase that curved around to the upper levels. Daniel bypassed the second floor and continued to the third.

"My wife is eager to meet you, Kat." Daniel's voice echoed through the stairwell. "She was needed at our other business, but she'll be returning this evening." He pulled out a key ring and stationed himself in front of a door.

I lingered on the top step, admiring a painting on the wall. There were others, most of them colorful with dreamy landscapes, but this one was darker, more ominous.

Gnarled branches extended from gray tree trunks. Deep

shadows had been layered into the scene, but a cluster of flowers in electric purple sprang up along the forest floor.

"My wife painted that." Daniel had been reaching for the door handle, but his attention was now on me. "These are all her original works." He nodded toward the other paintings. "She is a gifted artist."

"There's something special about this one." I reexamined the painting. "I love how the forest is shadowy but the flowers are glowing. Like they've found their own magical life amid the death and decay."

"She will be pleased to know her inspiration conveyed with such clarity." He turned to Maksim. "She painted that when you were with us. Do you remember?"

Maksim held a soft smile. *"Da."*

Daniel placed a hand on Maksim's shoulder and gave it a squeeze. They seemed to be having an unspoken exchange. Daniel's eyes misted.

He swallowed his emotion and returned to the door. "This will be your room, Kat. I hope you'll find it comfortable. And warm."

The door opened to a cozy room with a twin bed, bedside table, and lamp. An upholstered chair sat in the corner.

"There's one extra blanket." Daniel gestured at a wool blanket folded in the chair. "We have others in case that's not enough. Maksim, you'll be in your old room." Daniel handed him a key. "The bathroom is there"—he pointed at the end of the hall—"shared between the two of you."

I wasn't sure how I felt about sharing a bathroom with Maksim. Even at Brandy's house, as crowded as it was, we girls had our own bathroom, which we shared with Brandy's sister. Their little brother had to use the bathroom downstairs.

Maksim's gaze met mine from across the hall. I ducked inside my room.

"I'm late for an appointment," Daniel said, "but Madă and I

hope to hear more about this scavenger hunt Maksim has mentioned."

I dropped my stuff in the chair and returned to the doorway. "Madă is your wife?"

"Madălină, actually, like our guesthouse. But you may call her Madă, as we do." Daniel switched to Romanian, giving Maksim's shoulder a fatherly pat. They hugged, and then Daniel broke away and plodded down the stairs.

Maksim ambled closer and propped his shoulder against the wall. He folded his arms and crossed one foot in front of the other, relaxed—except that he was fighting a smile the entire time. "You don't mind sharing a bathroom, do you?"

I gave him side-eye. "Was I that obvious?"

"A bit. You do realize—"

"No, I don't." I held up a finger. "And I don't want to realize or talk about realizing if it involves mutual use of the bathroom."

"What if it involves a clue I've solved?" He bounced both eyebrows.

"You solved a clue?" I perked up. "Already?"

"Possibly." He plucked the scavenger hunt from his back pocket, unfolded the paper, and placed his finger next to the clue.

X marks the spot

X marks the spot. That was the main part of the clue, but there were two drawings as well.

Maksim's finger moved to the drawing on the left—a picture of a sailboat with a number sixteen scrawled into the sails. There was something odd about the way Dad had drawn it, something I'd noticed the very first time I studied the clue.

"Does the answer involve the number four?" I asked. "Because I've always thought this sailboat looks like a square root symbol over the number sixteen. Square root of sixteen is four."

"I noticed that, too," Maksim replied, "except I believe it's a play on words."

"A pun? How?"

He gestured at several hand-drawn tickets, each labeled with the Romanian word *bilet*. Ticket. Most of these tickets had been drawn directly above the sailboat.

"They look like our train tickets," I said, tilting my head. "They're similar, anyway. Do we need to purchase tickets for a sailing trip or...?"

"I've been wondering the same thing. But Brașov is nowhere near the sea, so I don't believe that's the answer. There is, however, a local establishment where transportation tickets are commonly pinned to the walls."

One of the hand-drawn tickets was featured front and center in the clue. Dad had also drawn an arrow that pointed left and was aimed at a clearly defined X. "***X marks the spot***," I said, reading the clue aloud.

Maksim nodded. "Perhaps he visited that establishment. He could have hidden a message in the tickets."

"That's where the arrow must be pointing." I focused on Maksim. "But what about the first part of the clue? Why would he draw the sailboat this way? And why the square root of sixteen? There has to be a connection to the number four somewhere."

"That's the pun I was referring to. The place with the transportation tickets is called For Sale Pub. As in, it's for sale." He hesitated. "It's not *actually* for sale, mind you. That's just the name."

I thought about it. *For sale.* The number *four* and a *sail*... as in, a sailboat. The pun was silly—borderline ridiculous—but it was so Dad. "Maksim, you did it. You figured it out." My attention wandered to the X. "I think you're right. My dad hid something for me at that pub."

A TAXI DELIVERED us to a row of yellow buildings near the city's Old Town. Steep terra-cotta roofs slanted their way across the tops. Grand archways and skinny rectangular windows hinted at an age and architecture I wasn't familiar with.

"Braşov is a medieval city," Maksim explained. "These buildings are Saxon and were referred to as merchant houses."

A piece of burnt driftwood, which had been repurposed as a sign, hung at the entrance to one building. For Sale Pub. Black torches trimmed the door, and a strong sooty odor irritated my nostrils.

Maksim gripped an iron ring and dragged the door open. A draft swept through the pub, rustling countless pieces of paper.

Transport tickets. They covered the walls and windows and spilled up onto the ceiling.

"*Bună dimineaţa.*" The greeting came from a skinny guy sweeping around the bar. Maksim replied, and the two of them had an exchange.

I waited beside a table, taking note of a melted-down candle.

"The pub is lit entirely by candlelight," Maksim said, breaking away from their conversation. The skinny guy had tossed a book of matches on the bar, and Maksim snatched them up. "Which is why we need these."

He led me down a pine staircase. Stale cigarette smoke saturated the stairwell before giving way to a dank odor. Shadows closed over us.

A familiar white light streaked the darkness. "Why don't you get started?" Maksim said. "I'll light a few candles and then join you."

"Start where?"

He aimed his phone at a raised platform. "That's the stage where live bands perform. The X in your father's drawing is very clearly on the left side of the room, so anywhere left of the stage would be good."

I pulled out my phone. After figuring out my flashlight app, I began thumbing through tickets pinned to the wall. What if we were wrong? What if this wasn't the right place? Worse, what if the thing Dad had hidden was gone? It'd been five months since he'd been here. The clue could have been torn down. Someone could have taken it.

I made myself take a breath. The transportation tickets were pinned in layers, and I needed to pay attention or else I was bound to miss whatever I was looking for.

Maksim piled candles onto the nearest table and struck a match. The flame sizzled, releasing hints of sulfur. One by one, he lit the wicks until a halo of light formed.

Neither of us spoke much as we searched—a comment here, a question there. The ceiling was low, and Maksim was able to check the highest tickets without a chair. I checked the tickets midway and lower.

"Look at this." Maksim plucked several tickets off the wall and moved to the table. I joined him, pushing the candles back.

I joined him, pushing the candles back.

He nudged two yellow tickets toward me. "These are bus tickets. Look what's written on them."

I angled my flashlight. *NB* had been scribbled in red ink. Nicholas Barrett.

"These have the same." Maksim gestured at a handwritten receipt and a business card featuring a white taxi. Dad's initials had been jotted on everything.

Maksim lined up the tickets one way and then reshuffled them. "Was your father a hiker?"

"Not that I know of."

He picked up the business card and flipped it over. "You're certain?"

"I'm not certain of anything at this point. Why?"

He handed me the business card. The words **Porumbacu de Sus** scribbled the back, along with Dad's "go to" arrow—except there was something odd about this one. There was something odd about the whole thing.

→ Porumbacu de Sus

"This means 'go to Porumbacu de Sus,'" I explained. "It's another clue, but this isn't my dad's handwriting."

Maksim's eyes widened. "It's not?"

I shook my head. "And I have no idea what Porumbacu de Sus means."

"That part I do know." He reclaimed the business card and placed everything on the table. "This is a bus ticket from Sibiu to Avrig. And this." He pointed at the address listed on the business card. "This taxi company is based in Avrig. They likely drove your father to Porumbacu de Sus."

"What makes you say that?"

"Driving is the only way to get there. The area is very rural, and public transport is nonexistent." Maksim moved on to the handwritten cab receipt. The edges were frayed and dirty, and there was a notation of *times two* on the front. "I think this is an abbreviation for two rides—there and back. And we have a second bus ticket as well, dated for the following day, which shows the destination as Braşov."

"Let me get this straight." I squeezed my forehead, willing my brain to work. "My dad—or whoever this was—traveled to that Porumbacu place one day and then to Braşov the next day? And he—they, whoever—kept all these things to use as clues afterward?"

"That appears to be the case."

"But why?" I stared at everything. "Why would anyone do that?"

"I can't answer that about your father, but I do know hikers travel to Porumbacu de Sus because it's the launch point for Negoiu Peak."

"Negoiu Peak? What's that?"

"The second-highest summit in Romania."

18. HEADWIND

I felt like a frosty mug by the time we left For Sale Pub.

Fortunately, there was a mall nearby, and their camping store had residual winter clothes. *Un*fortunately, the only thing close to my budget was a thin fleece pullover that came in one hideous color—banana yellow—and was overpriced despite being marked down.

The clerk found beanies in the back. They were fire engine red and also not cheap. "One hundred fifty lei? For *this*?" I inspected the beanie, which was thin enough to be a Fruit Roll-Up.

"SmartWool," the clerk said simply.

I wrinkled my nose. Not only was I going to be cold, I was going to look like a banana split with a cherry on top.

Maksim didn't comment on my selections, but he did do a double take, blinking hard and shaking his head. "There's a coffee-supply shop I'd like to visit." He dragged his stare from the yellow-and-red disaster the clerk was bagging. "It's on the first floor."

"Aren't we on the first floor?" I glanced around. "Seems like we walked straight in here."

"This is the ground floor. In Europe, the first floor begins at the next level."

"So the second floor is called the first floor." I tucked away my debit card and grabbed the plastic bag. "I guess the third floor is called...?"

"The second floor." His mouth angled up. "As you may have surmised."

"Yeah, well, my brain is about to explode with all this surmising I have to do." I reached into the bag and yanked out the pullover. "Either way, I'm glad you suggested coffee. I could go for a hot drink."

"It's a supply shop. They don't serve drinks." I must have done the blank-expression thing because he added, "For the scavenger hunt." He unfolded the paper and pointed at a set of clues.

ORIENTATION – EAT – SEE   COFFEE PRESS   NUMBERS

"I thought your father may have been referring to a french press or something similar. This shop specializes in those sorts of things."

Every time I'd looked at this clue, I had assumed Dad was talking about a café. I'd never thought of coffee supplies.

"What do you think?" Maksim asked. "Should we give it a go?"

"Absolutely. We leave no stone unturned." I ripped off the price tags, donned the beanie and pullover, and followed Maksim out of the camping store. I probably looked ridiculous wearing winter wear with shorts, but I was a little warmer. For what it was worth.

The main department store looked like any other—racks of clothes, mannequins, shoes on display. We passed through a sugary-sweet cloud that hovered over the perfume counters and stepped onto an escalator backlit by indigo lights.

The blue-lit stairs ascended, carrying us to the second—A.K.A. "first"—floor. Another department store fanned out, but this one had small shops sprinkled in between the various sections.

We stopped in front of a wine and liquor store. Lines formed across Maksim's forehead. "This was it."

I looked at him. "This was what?"

"The coffee-supply shop." He continued to a souvenir shop and then backtracked to where I stood in front of the liquor store. "It's should be right here."

"You're sure it was on this floor?"

"I have a type of photographic memory called didactic. It's more difficult for me to forget details than it is for me to remember them."

"Oh. Gotcha." Teachers used to say I had photographic memory. I didn't according to a test I'd taken, but my score had classified me as Exceptional.

That was before Dad died. Now I had the memory of an amnesiac snail.

Maksim and I entered the liquor shop. I thought the clerk might greet us, but he was putting the final touches on a whiskey display.

"Daniel needed help choosing an electric kettle for the guesthouse." Maksim circled through the store. "We paid for it here." He stopped in front of a glass case full of cigars. "I returned once more on an errand for Madă."

A pebble lodged in my throat. Had the supply shop closed down? Was the clue gone?

Maksim approached the clerk and asked him something. The man answered.

"He doesn't know anything," Maksim translated. "We should check the rest of the mall in case the shop relocated."

And so we did. We checked every store on every level, all the way to the top. Seven stories? Eight? I'd lost track.

We didn't come across any coffee-supply shops, but we did find a coffee machine inside a chocolatier. There wasn't anything special about it, nothing related to the scavenger hunt. Maksim said these types of coffee machines were everywhere in Romania.

He gave me two lei and showed me how to select a *cafea cu lapte.* Coffee with milk. Brown liquid dispensed from the machine, filling a disappointingly small paper cup.

My lower lip quivered. "They don't have a bigger size?"

"You can get two if you'd like." He reopened his wallet.

"It's... fine. Thanks, anyway." I picked up the microsized latte. Warmth seeped into my fingers.

Maksim put away his wallet. "I wouldn't worry just yet."

I blew on the coffee. "Who said I'm worried?"

He looked down at my foot, which was tapping the parquet floor.

I stilled myself. "Okay, I might be a little worried."

"Don't be. We have a full day ahead of us, and I have a few ideas yet." He motioned for me to follow him.

We left the chocolatier and worked our way through the department store on that level. The mall was busier now, and we had to push through a swarm of shoppers.

"There's a café I'd like to visit." Maksim ushered me onto the down-escalator. "It's located at Piaţa Sfatului. Council Square. I've seen french presses there."

"And after that?"

He held up his phone. "Working on a plan now."

I finished my coffee by the time we reached the ground level. Maksim led me through the main department store, his attention divided between his phone and our surroundings. We found the exit, and I tossed the paper cup in a trash can.

Lunchtime traffic motored through the streets. Pedestrians hustled around us. We passed an entire block of merchant houses, but these were earth-toned and more weathered than the yellow ones we'd seen earlier.

I paid extra-close attention to everything. But nothing made me think of the clues.

Five minutes later, we reached a sprawling patch of green broken up by walking paths. A small park. Manicured shrubs and wooden benches dotted the compact space.

Maksim stopped beside pedestrians gathered at a crosswalk. "There are four coffee-supply shops in Brașov." He upped his volume, making himself heard over the rumble of traffic. "There were five, but the shop we've been searching for went out of business." He held his phone toward me.

The screen displayed a list of businesses. One of them had a red strike-through that read permanently closed.

My insides turned to gravel. "What if the clue was in that shop? I-I'm not sure what to do."

"I believe we should visit the other four." He pocketed his phone. "Your father surely understood that businesses come and go. If I had been in his position, I would have duplicated the clues and left them in multiple locations."

My heart came alive. "You mean as a fail-safe. In case one of the places closed down."

"Or simply to stack the odds in your favor. Leaving the same clues at multiple businesses would increase your probability of success. And if one of those businesses happened to close down—"

"I wouldn't get stuck." It sounded like the type of thing Dad would think of. "We should check out those other supply shops. Forget the café."

"I believe it would be wise to visit the café," he countered, "if only for the sake of eliminating it."

Traffic ground to a halt. The crosswalk panel activated, and a white stick figure blinked in time with an electronic chirp. Pedestrians filtered into the street.

"Of course, it's your scavenger hunt." Maksim watched the

foot traffic flowing through the crosswalk. "But if we do visit the café, we'll be using Strada Republicii— Republic Street—to get there."

"Is there some significance to that street?"

"It's a very popular thoroughfare, with shopping and dining, and I believe it's worth checking out—if not for this clue, then potentially for the others."

"How far are we talking?"

"It's just there." He tipped his chin toward a billboard. Fashion ads glittered on a massive screen, blinking from one set of models to the next. The sign stood outside a wide cobblestone corridor similar to the corridors of Old Town Bucharest, but this passageway appeared to be lined with merchant houses.

Didn't seem like the kind of place Dad would have chosen. He wasn't into shopping, and he disliked crowds. But Maksim had a point. We should visit the café if only to eliminate it.

"Leave no stone unturned, right?" I joined him at the curb.

His mouth slipped into a gentle smile. "Right."

The crosswalk figure sped up, blinking in time with the quickening chirps. We darted across the street, veered toward the billboard, and then entered the cobblestoned corridor.

LATER THAT EVENING

A chime rang through the dark, startling me. Another chime followed. I rolled over in bed and checked the incoming messages. They were from Brandy. I'd texted her from the train, explaining that I'd changed my mind about Brașov. She hadn't replied until now.

I pushed onto my elbows and launched the messages.

> I gotta be honest, babe. None of this makes sense to me. I get that you wanna finish this thing (and honor your dad's memory) but... idk, I guess...

> I guess if it was my parents I'd do the same? Yeah. I don't know. But do what you need to do, and we'll be cheering you on from here (best we can).

Another message chimed.

> P.S. Try to have a happy birthday, okay?

I deleted her last message and flopped onto my back. My gaze flicked to the date and time stamped across the top of my screen.

SUNDAY, JUNE 2 - 12:06AM

Muted laughter filtered up through the floor. Those girls were staying in the room below, and they'd been rowdy all night.

I navigated to my music. If I couldn't ignore them, maybe I could drown them out. Had I brought my earbuds?

My eyes shifted toward my purse. The lump of black sat in the upholstered chair, strap dangling off the side.

I swung my legs out of bed, hit the light, and rummaged through my things. My fingers brushed smooth, hard plastic.

I pulled out my wireless earbud case and flipped the lid. I could *really* drown out the noise with these—but then I had another thought.

What if I went for a jog? Working out always helped me sleep, and the girls might be passed out by the time I got back.

On the other hand, it was after midnight, and I didn't know the area. But, well...

"Screw it. I'm going." I sifted through my backpack. Sleek, stretchy material swathed my fingers.

I yanked out my leggings. They were capris—not ideal for

chilly weather—but they'd work. And I wouldn't have to worry about being hit by a car, either. Between the red beanie and my yellow pullover, I was going to look like a moving stoplight.

After layering up as much as I could, I laced up my running shoes and slipped out of my room.

Maksim exited the bathroom at the end of the hall. He was supercasual in soccer pants, and a paper-thin undershirt clung to wet patches on his chest.

He was tossing a towel over one shoulder when our gazes locked. Something made him think twice, and he moved the towel to his other shoulder instead.

"*Bună seara.*" Good evening.

"Hi," I said. "You're back."

"I am. For about twenty minutes now."

"And Daniel?"

"Likely taking a shower. The casinos were smoky."

Maksim and Daniel had been investigating the **three of clubs** clue. I'd hung back, doing internet research—which I had continued to do until my eyes started to cross. Then I'd called it a night.

Maksim raked his wet hair back. His tattoo flexed, and my heart trilled. "Are you going somewhere?" His gaze trailed over me. "Workout?"

"Can't sleep. Thought a jog might help." I focused on my running app, trying not to ogle him too much. "It's safe, right? I mean, this is a really nice neighborhood, and I've felt safe since we've been here."

"It's perfectly safe, even at night."

"Cool. I won't go far, anyway." *Couldn't* go far, because I had stopped working out more than a month ago. I didn't say that part out loud. "So what'd you guys find at the casinos?"

"Nothing, unfortunately."

Tightness squeezed my midsection. "Nothing at all?"

He shook his head. "We went inside each one to be sure.

Neither Daniel nor I could discern anything connected to the scavenger hunt."

"What about card games? Since the clue looks like a *three of clubs*—"

"None of them had card games." His upbeatness waned. "Only slots and sports betting."

Disappointment slinked through me. I swallowed past a lump in my throat and forced a weak smile. "Thanks for checking. Sorry it turned out to be a waste of time."

"It wasn't. Anything we can eliminate is worth the effort." His smile returned. "And I... I didn't mind to go." His tone slipped into a different emotion I couldn't pinpoint. Or maybe it was just earnestness I was hearing. Whatever the case, he followed it up by clearing his throat. "Daniel didn't mind, either. It gave us a chance to catch up, which we both appreciated."

"Good. I'm glad." I tried really hard but couldn't hide the disappointment in my own voice. "It's late. I better get going." I broke away and activated my GPS.

Silence followed me halfway down the staircase. Suddenly, Maksim called out. "It would be best to stay within two kilometers of the guesthouse. If you can."

I managed a halfhearted wave.

Lamp light greeted me on the first floor, but I didn't see or hear anyone. Daniel and his wife lived on the other side of the house, and I couldn't even detect a shower running.

I crossed the living room, entered the hallway, and let myself out. After wrestling with the wrought-iron gate, I stepped onto the sidewalk and fixed my beanie and earbuds. My music player promised inspiration, but dull gray disappointment overshadowed my mood.

Finding those clues at For Sale Pub had reignited my hope. Now we were stuck again.

I selected a workout playlist and started my jog. Streetlamps dumped harsh light onto the road, leaving thin stretches of shadow in between.

The next intersection funneled into a roundabout. I cut through, calves burning, lungs struggling. I grimaced as a cramp formed in my side. When exactly was the last time I'd worked out? It must have been closer to two months ago.

It was, I realized. End of March—my infamous last soccer practice.

The first tear escaped. The heaviness of that day—the humiliation, the pain—returned and stripped away my strength.

"Barrett, get back here now. Barrett!" Coach Jules's fury had left an imprint on my psyche and a wound in my heart. I still felt both two months later.

My knees buckled. I stumbled forward.

A club anthem pulsed through my earbuds, interrupting the memory with big beats and epic female vocals. The music seemed to catch me. I straightened. My legs were wobbly, but as the singer soared into the next octave, her voice carried me with her.

I pushed harder, driving my knees and commanding myself into focus. I passed through the glow of one streetlamp and then another. The neon lights of a hotel burned into the darkness. Headlights zoomed through an intersection.

At the next corner, I snapped forward and braced my knees. Tears leaked, but a laugh rose up and spilled over. Not bad for my first run in two months. Not perfect, obviously, but not horrible.

I sniffled, wiping my face, and checked my music app. The title of the song glowed on my screen. Wake. The vocalist had been singing about fire in her eyes, the streets burning bright, and waking up on the inside.

Strangely, that was how I felt. Like I was waking up, too. Just a little.

The track switched, transitioning to something deeper and bass-heavy. I turned to head back, but a blue sign held me in place.

Centru. Downtown.

I smashed my Down Volume button, giving myself space to think. Maksim had taken me downtown earlier. That street he'd mentioned, Strada Republicii, had been total chaos, full of shoppers, tourists, and too many distractions.

But what if I went now? The crowds should be gone, and I'd be able to focus.

I followed the sign. The street curved to the right, and a patch of green appeared—the park I'd seen earlier in the day. I hung a left, searching for the crosswalk Maksim and I had used. Landscape lights brightened a section of sidewalk, and a building made of natural stone shone in the darkness.

Block-style letters bracketed the entrance. Caffe News.

Caffe? As in, café?

I pressed my face to the glass. The interior lights were off, but I could see tables, chairs, and something boxy and silver. An espresso machine?

I opened my camera app and backed up, snapping pics of the entrance. I'd have to look up their hours. Hopefully, they were open on Sundays.

The crosswalk waited around the corner, and traffic was sparse—one car driving past, two taxis idling at the curb. My feet carried me at a fast clip.

I reached the other side and followed the cobblestones into the corridor.

A long row of merchant houses spanned either side of me, the buildings converted into storefronts, bars, and restaurants. The stores were closed, but the exterior lights were on, casting an icy glow over the cobblestones.

I plucked out my earbuds. Ultrachill EDM—electronic dance music—pulsed from a bar. Chatter hummed in the outdoor patio of each restaurant while the waiters handed out little red blankets.

"Time to focus, Kat. You can do this." I pushed out a breath and mentally reviewed the remaining clues.

Shops lined the next section of the corridor. I snapped photos and took video, documenting anything that might be significant.

KALO. A boutique.

DIGIALL. Electronics store.

MADAME SHOES. Women's shoe store.

MEGA LEU. Miniature supermarket, something akin to a corner grocer.

INET. Internet café.

The corridor branched off in both directions. Maksim and I had checked these side streets earlier, but we hadn't gleaned anything at the time. I decided to check them again.

ZAPPHIRE FALAFELS.

CASA BRUTARULUI.

GELATO GHEORGE.

FUSION BAR.

AMORE CHOCOLATES.

MONEYXCHANGE.

BRASSERIE DE L'ARTE.

THE CREATIVE EGG.

MAGAZIN POP.

Twenty minutes later, I wandered into Council Square. Lampposts created a plume of golden light over the plaza. Restaurants filled the air with a stream of chatter and the clinking of silverware and glasses.

I found a bench and parked myself there. Really needed to head back before my muscles cooled off, but thoughts of Dad nudged me to stay. He'd mailed the scavenger hunt from Braşov. Had he visited Council Square during his trip? Could he have sat on this same bench?

Footsteps scuffed the cobblestones.

A man hurried past, and my heart clenched. His profile looked like Dad's. So did his gait, his stride, the way he swung his arms.

Wait, was it Dad? It couldn't be, right?

I hopped up and took a step, about to call out. The man looked over without breaking stride. Salt-and-pepper dusted his head. Wrinkles aged his face.

He was older than Dad. Much older.

A dark-stone church stood beyond the plaza, forming a bulk in the shadows. The man strode in that direction.

I turned away, warming with a flush of embarrassment. Couldn't believe I'd thought he was Dad. Just like I'd thought the man in the peach shirt had been Dad.

I sent a final glance over my shoulder. Wasn't sure what I expected to see—maybe that the man had a different gait after all, or that he was a different height and build. If I was imagining things, I wanted to know.

But the man was gone.

I scanned the plaza. A handful of people loitered on benches, and none were in a hurry like the man had been. They also weren't anywhere near that dark-stone church.

Heaviness sank between my ribs and anchored in the pit of my stomach. Could I have imagined him completely? Not just that he'd *looked* like Dad but that he'd been nonexistent—not really walking past me, not really in this plaza.

I wasn't sure if that was possible, but as I stood there, wondering where he'd gone, I had the strangest, most distinct feeling I was being watched.

19. ADMISSION

My calves burned. I panted, sweat gathering under my beanie, as I checked my GPS for the millionth time. Where was I?

Yellow light pooled beneath a streetlamp at the next intersection. I slowed to a walk. The street had stucco homes, but they were small. Too small to be in the guesthouse's swanky neighborhood.

Voices intruded on the stillness. I headed that direction and stopped at a waist-high fence. Several guys were gathered on a playground, which sat adjacent to a towering apartment building.

One of the guys hunched over, panting.

Another guy fixed his beanie, tugging it down over his ears, and launched into a sprint. He cut left and dove over a red bench. His body folded, tucking midair, as he entered a roll—but not just any roll. A parkour safety roll.

Safety rolls can break a fall, even a long fall, by transferring the person's built-up kinetic energy and allowing the roll itself to absorb most of the impact—as long as the person does the roll correctly, of course, which this guy did.

He angled himself, landing on his right shoulder and rolling to the opposite hip, his hands braced for support. He came full circle and popped up, still running.

I opened my camera app. My phone showed low battery, but I had to get a recording for Brandy and Dave.

Beanie Guy powered up the slide. He reached the top and flung himself off. His body stayed in layout position while he flipped backward, rotating through a twist.

He landed on his feet and let his momentum carry him forward into another safety roll. His friends shouted, grabbing their heads and high-fiving each other.

"It's official. Parkour is in Romania." I held my phone steady on the guys. "What do y'all think? Should we recruit him for Dave's team?"

Beanie Guy popped up and brushed himself off, stare drifting. He noticed me and waved.

"Uh-oh. I've been spotted." I pressed Stop and lowered the phone. "Sorry, uh—*nu vorbesc românește.*" That was supposed to be "I don't speak Romanian." I butchered the pronunciation.

Beanie Guy grabbed one of his friends, a guy with pale skin and a ginger beard, and pointed at him. Then he pointed at the playground.

"You want me to record?" I held up my phone.

Beanie Guy nodded. *"Da. Video."* Sounded like he said *vee-DEY-oh.* The ginger guy stretched his arms and shook out his legs.

I gave a thumbs up and pressed Record.

A blip of movement pulled my attention from the guys. Black soccer pants and a navy hoodie emerged from the adjacent parking lot. Someone's tall form walked into the light, and a familiar rugged face became clear.

I grinned and circled around the playground, meeting Maksim on the other side. "You found me," I said. "Didn't mean to stay out so late. Think I took a wrong turn on my way from—"

"Centrul Vechi?"

"I guess so? The signs said Centru."

"Centrul Vechi is a reference to the old city. Centru is simply the city center."

"Gotcha." I rocked back, glancing around awkwardly. "How'd you know I went there? And how'd you find me just now?"

"I came looking for you and heard voices. When I entered the parking lot, I saw you walking from that direction." He nodded toward the narrow street I'd been on. "You're not difficult to spot in that outfit." His gaze shifted to my fire-engine-red beanie, then to my banana-yellow pullover. A tiny grin sparked.

I chuckled. "Mission accomplished."

"I gather you've been working on the scavenger hunt?"

"Yep." I held up my phone. "Got photos and videos. Wanna see?"

He leaned forward and rested his arms on the fence. The links gave under his weight. "Weren't you recording these guys?"

I looked at my phone. The video timer counted up, and I swore. "Well, I was supposed to be." I pressed Stop. "This is why I'm never put in charge of this stuff."

Maksim threw up a questioning eyebrow.

"My friend has a parkour and free-running team, and they always need someone to record. They stopped asking me because my videos come out tilted and shaky"—I jiggled the phone—"or nonexistent."

"You're familiar with parkour?"

"I... guess you could say that." I wasn't sure where to begin with an explanation. I'd only ever done parkour to improve my agility for soccer, but I definitely didn't want to get into *that* conversation.

Maksim's expression turned thoughtful. He gripped the back of his hoodie and dragged it over his head, leaving him in a long-sleeved shirt. "Would you mind holding this?"

I took the lump of navy. "What are you doing?"

"Nothing too very foolish. I hope." He backed up and ran

straight at the fence. He caught the rail with one hand and kicked his legs to the side, soaring over.

Speed vault. A good one.

He landed with ease and crossed to where the guys had gathered. They greeted him, and after a brief back-and-forth, Beanie Guy gestured at the playground. They were letting him have a turn.

Maksim stationed himself at the foot of the slide. He bent forward, gripping the curved lip, and kicked himself into a handstand.

I slung his hoodie over my shoulder, woke up my camera, and pressed Record. A new video started.

Maksim held the handstand, shoelaces dangling, and added a vertical pushup. And another. His shoulders strained against his shirt, his biceps flexing through the thin fabric. My mouth popped open. I peeked out from behind the phone.

One of the guys called out what sounded like encouragement. I straightened out the phone, which had tipped sideways, and focused on the screen.

Maksim gritted his teeth, the tendons in his neck straining, and launched himself out of the handstand. His shoes touched down on the lip of the slide, and he flung himself into a backflip, adding a flash kick midair.

He landed on the playground, turned, and speed-vaulted over the red bench. From there he circled around, angling for the jungle gym, and launched into side flips and cork twists before leaping up to the monkey bars.

Using his momentum, he thrust his legs and flung himself up to a much higher pull-up bar. As his fingers grabbed hold, he cried out and released the bar with his right hand. I couldn't see his face, but from the back, it looked like the move had been painful. I wasn't sure why. Maybe he'd injured his hand? One of his fingers? I'd had my fair share of jammed fingers while doing this stuff.

I kept recording as he shook out his right hand and arm,

hanging by only his left. I assumed he would turn himself around and face this way, maybe do a dismount onto the playground. But when he regripped the bar with his right hand, he began to swing and build momentum still facing the other direction. *Away* from the playground.

I raced along the fence line.

He pumped his legs a final time and let go. Just as I reached him, I saw his face contort, his back arching. His feet came together, and he landed on top of the fence.

The chain links rattled. I jumped back.

He flailed, swaying, but managed to thrust himself into a forward flip. He landed beside me with an *oof*. Cheers went up from all the way across the playground.

Maksim's face was red and sweaty as he straightened. He was grinning—but then his eyes flashed toward my phone, and his smile disintegrated. "Are you recording me?"

"Was." I pressed Stop. "Points off for the playground equipment you failed to utilize"—I pulled the hoodie off my shoulder—"but your form and execution were off the charts. Ten out of ten for that." I held the hoodie out to him.

"You wear it. I'm a bit sweaty."

"Are you sure?" My gaze flicked to the hoodie.

"I'll be fine, and I know this weather is cool for you."

"Thanks." I snuggled into the oversized hoodie. It smelled like him, his natural smell mixed with sweat and whatever soap he'd used. I tried not to breathe him in too much. "In Georgia—"

He slipped an arm over my shoulders and guided me away from the playground. A soft glow lit up my body. Whatever I'd been planning to say vanished into thin air.

"How was your run?" he asked. "Did you manage to solve any of the clues?"

"Not yet," I peeped. "But, um, I did come across a café. Might be a good starting point for tomorrow. Today. Later this morning." I navigated to my photo gallery and showed him the pics of Caffe News. "I'm not sure how we missed it. It's by that park."

We turned onto a sidewalk. This road was wide and well-lit, and large homes with fancy gates and stone walls lined both sides of the street.

The guesthouse's neighborhood.

"Oh, and check this out." I pulled up my videos. "We might want to—"

Maksim touched my hand. "Go back to that café."

I returned to the pics of Caffe News. He took my phone and swiped through the photos. "***Coffee press***."

"Huh?"

"*Caffe* is Italian for coffee. 'Press' could be another term for news. As in the free press."

"Wait, what? You think this café's *name* is the answer to that clue?"

"It may be." He handed me the phone. "We'll need to confirm the secondary clues to be sure."

"Wow. Can't believe I didn't catch that." I gazed up at him. "You're amazing, and your parkour skills are seriously impressive. You killed it back there."

Pride shone through in his eyes.

We continued up the road, our shoes scuffing the sidewalk, our clothes rustling. Apart from that, the neighborhood was quiet.

I wrapped an arm around his waist and leaned against him. He must have been wearing some kind of undershirt because my fingers detected bumpy fabric under the long-sleeved top.

His voice broke the stillness. "There's something I need to ask of you. A favor."

"Sure. Anything."

"Don't send that video to anyone."

I snorted a laugh. "How come? Not ready to go viral?"

He didn't answer.

I peeked up at him. His expression had fallen grim.

"I was only going to share it with two friends. The ones who do parkour and free-running."

"I need you to promise you won't send it to them or post it anywhere. Not on social media. Not even on a storage drive connected to the internet."

"What about a direct message?"

He brought us to a stop. His expression held an edge of gravity I hadn't seen before. "You can show them in person, from your phone, but you cannot transmit that video over the web."

"Why?" My vocal cords constricted. "Is this because of Ştefan? Because of the scamming operation?"

Maksim's stare drifted until the full weight came to a rest on me.

Another puzzle piece snapped into place. I swallowed. Loudly. "Y'all are more than a scamming operation, aren't y'all?"

"And I'm more involved than you may realize. Than I've allowed you to realize." He removed his arm. His gaze struggled to meet mine, and I suspected I knew why.

Dampness formed behind my eyes. "Your cousin, the one you've been talking about... it's Ştefan, isn't it?"

The cords in Maksim's neck tightened, and my heart skidded down into my rib cage. The club. The taxis. Those were business fronts to hide something illegal.

A criminal enterprise, I realized. The epiphany made my stomach bottom out. My own words came back to me. *So it's a family-run scamming operation?* That was what I had asked Maksim when we were at Kebap. His answer? *Something like that.*

"Are y'all a mafia crime family?"

My question landed like a stone tossed into still waters. The ripple spread through Maksim's features. "My parents had no criminal dealings, but they died when I was very young, and I was raised by Ştefan and his father—my uncle, Vladimir. I was three when these things transpired, and I had no say in the matter." He reached out, finger curled to cup my chin. I recoiled. It was unintentional, a knee-jerk reaction, but it was enough to make him withdraw his touch.

My heart clenched. "I'm sorry."

"I'm the one who's sorry. I should have found a way to tell you sooner. I wasn't sure how."

Guilt pinched my center. I wanted to say I understood, that I didn't know how to talk about certain things, either. Before I could try, hinges creaked somewhere behind me. *"Bună seara"* came a melodic voice.

I peered between the bars of a wrought-iron gate. The guesthouse's gate, I realized. We'd been standing outside La Madălină.

A brunette waved to us from the doorway. Her stick-straight hair stopped at her chin. A fleece robe wrapped her petite frame.

"That's Madă." Maksim levered the latch on the gate. He hesitated. "There are things I need to explain, and I will, but she has been wanting to meet you." He pushed open the gate, eyes pleading.

I nodded, mouth dry, and walked through.

"Is this the *americanca*?" Madă had a smile that could have warmed the coldest winter day. "It is so nice to meet you, dear. I am hearing many positive things about you." Steam swirled up from a mug she carried.

She took a sip, backing into the hallway, and motioned for us to join her.

"We are grateful for you, Kat." She entered the living room, crossed to the couch, and perched on the edge. "Your adventure has returned our Maksim to us."

The front door snapped shut, and Maksim emerged from the hallway. "I'm happy to be here," he said, squeezing past me.

"I understand this is for a few days only." Madă peered up at him. "I hope it's enough time for a visit."

"We'll try to make time." Maksim stopped beside her. "Perhaps tomorrow evening?"

"That would be wonderful. I wish to show Kat my artwork." Madă set her mug on the coffee table and faced me. "I was very excited to learn how much you love *Maksim*."

I tensed. "You were excited for— Wait, what?"

"How much you love *Maksim*." Her smile wilted. We both looked at Maksim.

"She means the painting." He rubbed his neck. "The one of the forest."

"With the purple flowers," Madă said. "The scene depicts the heart of our Maksim as I saw it during that time." She smiled up at him. "There are many more flowers today, *da?*"

"Perhaps not as many as we had hoped." His voice dulled. His smile had gone bland with shades of gray and black. Did Madă know about Maksim's cousin and their criminal enterprise?

She rose from the couch and stood in front of him, searching his face. "The hour is late. Rest. While you can." She switched to Romanian. He nodded in response.

I waited for them to finish and then followed Maksim to the curved staircase. My foot was on the first step when Madă called out. "Kat, dear? May I speak with you?"

I sent a questioning look to Maksim.

He reached out, slowly, and brushed his thumb along my jawline. Shivers flowed through me.

I covered his hand with mine. "We still need to talk," I whispered.

"I know. But what you need to hear from her is more important." He leaned in and placed his mouth by my ear. "We'll talk," he murmured. "I promise."

He turned his head and placed a tender kiss on my cheek. His lips lingered, and my heart thumped out a soft, fast rhythm. My next breath caught.

He pulled away and whispered, *"Noapte bună."* Good night.

His brown eyes glistened as he broke away and continued up the stairs. I returned to the living room. Madă held a genuine smile, her face shiny in the lamplight.

"Sorry about that," I said. "We were talking about—"

My explanation choked off as she took my hands. Warmth poured out of her palms, and a strange sensation, like an electrical current, streamed.

I recoiled, but she hung on.

"The hour is late," she repeated—except now the words sifted through me like a warning. "You carry much sorrow and grief. Disappointment. I see the missing pieces to this strange puzzle of yours. They are hidden, not lost as you have believed, and they will reveal themselves when you ask the right questions, seeking your answers with the right perspective."

"I-I don't know what that means."

"You will." She closed her eyes and began speaking in another language. It didn't sound like Romanian yet rang familiar.

The secret poem.

My heart came alive. Whatever Mada̧ was saying sounded like what I'd heard the other day, the language Maksim had been speaking when I was crying outside that restaurant.

She transitioned to English. "You were the best daughter you knew how to be. Take heart in that, for the trials that lie ahead will require everything you possess—all your strength and all your weakness. Remember"—she opened her eyes—"fear is never the answer to a problem, but it can be the beginning of one."

Her words penetrated my being, a bucket dipped into a deep well. My racing thoughts settled into calm.

She searched my face the way she'd searched Maksim's. "All matters will be settled in time. What lies in the darkness will be exposed by the light." Her expression softened. "You and Maksim are so alike—secrets long kept, brokenness of the heart. I see it clearly." Her cheeriness ebbed. "But you must tell him, dear."

I sniffled, dabbing at my eyes. "Tell him what?"

"Everything." She took my hands again. The electrical current returned, and one of my arms twitched. The muscles arrested all the way to my shoulder.

I gasped and pulled away. This time she let go.

20. BREAKTHROUGH

Maksim held the door to Caffe News. I walked inside, and an earthy aroma awakened my senses.

The barista hustled behind the coffee bar, wiping down the counter and setting out mugs. Chairs stood stacked in the corner. A broom and dustpan leaned against the wall.

The woman stationed herself at a touch screen computer, greeting us in Romanian.

"*Două cafele cu lapte.*" Two coffees with milk.

Maksim handed her a fifty-lei bill. She took the money, splitting a tentative look between us. "Are you in need of information *turistica*?" she said in accented English.

Could she tell I was a tourist?

The woman pointed at a wooden display case across the café. "The Ministry of Tourism provides complimentary touristic resources. You are welcome to—"

"We're okay," I said. "Thank you, though."

She replied with *cu plăcere* and started working on our drinks.

I unzipped my purse and claimed the stool beside Maksim. He had his phone out, responding to messages. I'd been groggy this morning and had decided to wait until after coffee to mention his... what? Criminal history? Illicit dealings? Andrei had said he didn't do that stuff anymore, but that wasn't what Maksim had indicated last night. I needed clarification. And I needed a way to get that clarification without insulting him again.

He finished punching out a text and slept his phone. "Any thoughts on the supporting clues?"

I pulled out the scavenger hunt and set the paper between us. Even if **Coffee Press** really was codespeak for *Caffe News*, we had to confirm the supporting clues. I reread them for about the one-millionth time.

ORIENTATION – EAT – SEE   COFFEE PRESS   NUMBERS

I gave the café a once-over. Nothing about the place stood out. "My brain isn't fully functional until after coffee," I said to Maksim. "What about you? Do you have any thoughts?"

"I suppose **See** could be the view." Maksim swept a hand toward the windows. They spanned floor to ceiling and offered a picturesque view of the park. "**Eat** could be the food they serve."

I inhaled through my nose. "I don't smell anything cooking."

Maksim addressed the woman, who replied in Romanian. "Our coffees come with a cookie," Maksim translated. "They do have croissants, which they get from a bakery, but everything else is drinks. As for **numbers**"—he grabbed a single-page menu off the bar—"perhaps a reference to their prices?"

"Or their—"

The espresso machine rumbled to life, muting my answer.

"Or their address and phone number," I tried again, pushing my volume higher.

"I've been wondering about **Orientation**." Maksim set the

menu down. "I simply don't correlate that word to coffee in any way."

"Same. Like, oriented to what?"

The espresso machine switched off, settling into silence. Something happened then, like a tectonic shift that pushed my thoughts into place. It must have happened to Maksim, too, because we looked at each other and then rotated on our stools until we faced the tourism display.

I hopped up and crossed the café. Maksim dogged my heels. The display case held pamphlets, maps, coupon books, guidebooks, all in a variety of languages. The sign above the display read Centru de Informare Turistica.

Maksim grabbed one of the pamphlets. "***Orientation.***"

"Bingo." Because who needed to orient themselves in a city? Not locals. Tourists.

I grabbed a coupon book and flipped through it. Maksim exchanged his pamphlet for a pocket-sized book on the bottom shelf.

"That is a very informative guidebook," the woman called from the bar. "It comes with a self-guided tour of Braşov, which is accessible online with audio options. It is supposed to cost forty lei, but the tourism agency who created this resource insisted we sell it for less. You can purchase one for twenty or two for thirty. I can only accept cash due to restrictions by the agency."

Maksim pulled out his wallet.

"One sec." I touched his hand. "Why would a tourism agency require cash-only payments? And why would they insist on selling the book for less?"

Maksim sent a fleeting glance to the woman. "She may be scamming us."

I snapped to attention. "Really?"

"She said the government provided these resources. It may be that she was issued the books to give away but is attempting to profit from them."

"Then why are you pulling out your wallet?"

He pointed at the title of page one.

ORIENTATION

My heart stuttered.

He flipped through the next pages. "This section offers dining suggestions, and it's titled 'Places to Eat.'" He skimmed the next pages and stopped again. "This one is 'Things to See.'"

Orientation, Eat, See. They were all there.

He approached the woman and handed her the cash. We flipped through the rest of the book until our coffees arrived.

"Well?" I picked up my mug and blew. "Anything else jump out at you?"

He returned to his stool. "Let's go over the clues again. In order." He set the scavenger hunt on the bar and placed his thumb beside the first clue in the Braşov section.

"Talk to me about these," he said. "Does anything come to mind now that we've discovered the guidebook?"

"My dad and I weren't exactly close. We were when I was a kid, but my mom—" I fidgeted with a string on my shorts. "She caused a lot of friction and... honestly? I don't think my dad would have known most of my favorites."

"*Your* favorites? I assumed these were favorites of his."

"I... hadn't really thought of it that way before, I guess since I'm the one doing the scavenger hunt." I peered down at the clue. "It's definitely possible he'd been talking about himself."

"Framed within that context—of his favorites and not yours—does anything come to mind?"

I pushed out a breath until the air rolled across my lips. "I do know soccer was his favorite sport. And burgers were his favorite food... I think. Oh!" I thought of something and snapped my fingers. "He used to eat at this place called Gypsy Django. It was his favorite restaurant. He went there every Monday."

A crease formed along Maksim's forehead. "What was the restaurant called?"

My brain took a full three seconds to catch up. Andrei had warned me not to bring up Gypsies around Maksim. I hadn't been thinking of that when I mentioned Mr. Kotfas's restaurant.

What do I do? I considered lying, pretending he'd misheard me, making up a fake name—Hippy Mango, Tipsy Tango—but I couldn't bring myself to go that far. Not after Maksim had been so kind to me.

"The restaurant was called, um, Gypsy Django." I lifted the glass mug to my lips. "But I stopped going there when I was old enough to stay home by myself, so I don't think he would have used it for one of the clues."

Maksim's eyebrows formed a deep V.

"He ate there because the food was cheap. That was why he liked it." I took my first sip of coffee. The hot earthy drink burned going down. "Mm, and the owner sold the place before my dad died, so it became a completely different restaurant. Too fancy for my dad. Way too expensive."

I waited for Maksim to say something or ask a follow-up question. His shoulders were stiff. Actually, his entire six-one frame had gone rigid.

The tension suddenly lifted. He withdrew his intense stare and pointed it at his mug. "Forgive me," he said, massaging his eyes—and he did it surprisingly hard for someone who wore contacts. At least, I assumed he wore contacts. I hadn't seen the grandpa glasses since that first day.

He brought his fingers together at the bridge of his nose, and the overhead lights revealed blue marks on his knuckles. Bruises. From that night at the club.

His stare followed mine, and he clenched and unclenched his fist. "Doesn't hurt too badly. This, however, is rather painful." He touched the edge of his eyebrow. The cut swelled pink with a fresh layer of scab. Blue marks speckled the exterior, trailing around his eye and down along his cheekbone.

"Is that why you haven't been wearing your glasses?" I asked.

Surprise crisscrossed his face. He reached for his coffee. "About those," he said, picking up the mug.

I brought my own mug to my lips, waiting. By the time I took a sip, he still hadn't continued. "What about them?"

He finished taking a drink and lowered the mug. "They're not actually necessary. I can see without them."

"Huh." I set my mug down. "Then why do you wear them?"

"Habit, I suppose." He smoothed the scavenger hunt. "Can you think of anything your father enjoyed, any hobbies or 'favorites' that could be considered vintage? Cars? Comics?"

I tilted my head. Maybe I was crazy, but I had the distinct feeling he had sidestepped my question.

I put away the thought. "My dad was a history buff. History itself could be considered vintage, couldn't it?"

"That's a bit of a stretch. What else?"

"He was a TV junkie, mostly news and political stuff. Guess there's nothing vintage about that, is there?"

Maksim considered it. "I'd have to think about it more. Anything else?"

"Art. When I was packing his room, I found books about famous painters like Van Gogh, Monet, Matisse."

"That's a possibility. Brașov does have art museums and galleries."

"Any history museums?" I scooted forward on my stool. "He loved anything to do with history but especially museums."

"We can visit both the art and the history museums. We'll stop by the galleries in between." He folded the scavenger hunt. "I have a plan, but we'll need to hurry." He downed a swig of coffee and plunked the half-finished drink on the bar. His mug clinked.

I tried to down mine. The coffee scorched my mouth and throat.

Maksim was across the café by the time I drank past the froth. He pushed open the door and slid an expectant look my way. "Art galleries keep irregular hours, and the museums may close early on Sundays. When I say we need to hurry, it's not hyperbole."

21. DEEPER

aksim led the way to a merchant house nestled between two cement buildings. A Romanian flag hung above the entrance, fabric rustling in the breeze.

Muzeul de Artă. The Museum of Art.

Maksim had warned me this museum was small. I hadn't realized how small until we were doing a walkthrough of the final exhibit twenty minutes later.

"We went through too fast." My gaze wandered over decorative glassware and porcelain vessels. "Should we do a walkthrough of the paintings again? I don't think my dad would have been interested in these vases."

"I think it's safe to move on to the next museum." Maksim waited by the stairs. "I've been taking photos of everything, and I've memorized the placards."

"You have?" I joined him. "All of them?"

His mouth tipped up. "Didactic memory. Remember?"

"Oh. Right."

"We can go over everything later. For now I believe we should move on to Muzeul de Etnografie. It's a textile museum with exhibits that explore the history of our textiles—clothing, tapestries, those sorts of things. There's a vintage element, and I believe the focus is on *Transilvănean* history."

Now that sounded right up Dad's alley. The textile museum was in the same building, so we had nothing to lose by going.

Maksim and I weaved our way through traditionally dressed mannequins and historic textile machines—everything from personal spindles to factory looms. A handful of black-and-white photos hung the walls, but nothing seemed tied to the scavenger hunt.

A male mannequin had been stationed in the final exhibit. Bright blue thread embroidered his shirt and vest while a matching cobalt scarf tied his waist.

He stood beside his female counterpart, who was dressed in a long wool skirt and white blouse. Red roses embroidered her neckline while a long scarf wrapped her head and flowed down her back. Her lifeless stare held steady on a glowing green sign. Ieșire. Exit.

We weren't in the right place. She knew it. I knew it.

"There are other museums in Centrul Vechi." Maksim checked his phone. "I'm seeing four around Council Square and others nearby."

"Can you read the names? Maybe if I hear them, something will click."

"Council House History Museum. Museum of Urban Civilization. Rope Street Museum." He scrolled. "Ștefan Baciu House."

"Who's Ștefan Baciu?"

"A poet. He was born in Brașov."

"My dad wasn't into poetry." That I knew of. "What about the rope place?"

"Strada Sforii, the Rope Street. It's one of the narrowest streets in Europe; though, the museum is more of a café and souvenir shop."

"Anything vintage about it?" I pressed.

"The street itself is very old."

"Could be worth a visit." I tapped my foot. "What about war museums? Anything with World War I or World War II exhibits?"

"The National Military Museum has exhibits from those wars. Unfortunately, it's located in Bucureşti. As far as I know, there is nothing like that here in Braşov."

"Can you double-check? My dad was obsessed with the world wars, especially World War II."

Maksim navigated to his messages. "I'll SMS Daniel."

MORNING DISSOLVED INTO AFTERNOON. Afternoon into late afternoon. Around three p.m., Maksim's warning came to fruition.

The curator of an art museum exited the building the moment we arrived. She was locking up and wouldn't let us go in. Maksim offered to make a "donation" toward the museum if she would make an exception. She refused.

We tried an art gallery after that. It was closed by the time we got there.

Daniel helped remotely, checking online and calling around. Braşov didn't have any war museums, but he hoped there might be a special exhibit somewhere.

There wasn't.

"He has suggested a monument commemorating soldiers from the First World War." Maksim slept his phone. "It's on the far side of Old Town near Biserica Sfântul Nicolae." He offered up a smile. "That's Romanian for Saint Nicholas's Church."

I perked up. "Nicholas. Like my dad."

"Yes, and let's hope it's the confirmation we need."

We took a taxi to the monument—which, as it turned out, was a single statue depicting a soldier. The placard was in Romanian, and the monument had been built on a type of stone dais, the statue elevated with steps around it.

I stood beneath the soldier, scrutinizing his rifle, his uniform, the way he charged forward.

Maksim came alongside me. "Anything?"

"Not yet." I circled around the monument, trying for a different angle.

People ambled through the plaza. Behind us, the slender columns of Saint Nicholas's Church rose up from behind a wall. Tourists toted kids, cameras, and backpacks through an impressive archway, following a path to the churchyard.

Chatter hummed. A bus chugged up the street.

I ignored the distractions and kept studying the statue. "Can you read the placard again?"

"'Gratitude to the heroes of the nation.'" Maksim recited the placard from memory. "'Erected by the Assembly of the Women of Brașov, neighborhood Șchei, with the support of Brașov City Hall.'"

I lowered myself to the monument steps. Mountains stood watch over the city, filling the horizon with a forest landscape. Sunlight broke through the gray haze, but any warmth vanished as clouds scrolled across the sky.

I tugged on the insides of my sleeves, hugging myself.

"So." Maksim joined me. "What's next?"

"I'm thinking we should move on to the three-of-clubs clue. We might need to split up to cover more ground."

"I was referring to you." He inserted a smile that was as dull as his voice. "When do you go home?"

My stomach tumbled into a free fall at the mention of going home. "I fly out from Bucharest on Wednesday." My throat constricted, pinching the words. "I'm supposed to stay the night at the airport in London, then my flight to Atlanta is on Thursday." I played with a frizzy tendril, twisting it around my finger. "Probably could've stayed in Romania an extra day, but the government liaison mixed up his part of the booking."

Maksim's expression went from somber to... I would have said thoughtful, but he seemed alarmed. "The American government is involved in your trip?"

"It's the Romanian government."

His alarm heightened. Took me a second to understand why.

"No, no. It's nothing you would need to worry about. The government is only involved because they botched the cleanup efforts after the plane crash. When the liaison found out I couldn't afford this trip, he got permission from his boss to book one of my flights."

"By that, do you mean—?" He gave his head a subtle shake. "What precisely do you mean?"

"Flights from Atlanta to Bucharest were fifteen hundred dollars. Flights to London cost half that. The liaison told me to purchase that leg—between Atlanta and London—while he covered the leg between London and Bucharest."

"You're saying someone from our government paid for your flight?"

"Just the one leg."

He blinked. "Why?"

"Probably to avoid a lawsuit. It's been six months, and the cleanup crew still hasn't recovered all the remains. They can't even account for all the passengers. Whatever incompetency is going on—"

Maksim's pocket chimed. He held up a finger and pulled out his phone. "It's Daniel," he said, reading the message. He punched out a reply and stood.

A taxicab cruised in our direction. Maksim put his hand up and gave a sharp whistle. The cabbie paused at the curb.

I stood and brushed off my shorts. "Where are we going?"

"The guesthouse." Maksim held the back door for me. "Daniel thinks we need to reassess our strategy. He wants to talk it over with us."

I climbed in.

Maksim circled around the car and climbed in on the other side. The driver started up the road. He and Maksim went back and forth over something. I assumed they were negotiating the fare, but a different thought occurred to me.

"Does he work for Ştefan, too?" I tugged on my seat belt. "Like the cabbies in Bucharest?"

Maksim's eyes flashed toward me. I didn't want him to know where I'd gotten that tidbit—or anything else about my conversation with Andrei—so I added, "We never paid for those rides in Bucharest. I put two and two together."

"Ştefan doesn't own any taxis in Braşov." Maksim dragged his seat belt across his chest. "It's a single company, a small one, and includes a small portion of the taxis in Bucureşti." He slanted a curious look across the back seat. "Since we're answering each other's questions now, I'd like to know something."

I waited. "Okay?"

"Why did you become angry with me at the club?"

I'd been angry with him? When?

Whatever information had been lost in the blur suddenly came back to me. "Oh, um... you were staring at a girl." The admission sounded weird and jealous, so I added, "Not that I care who you stare at. It's more about— She reminded me of someone my ex hooked up with." I looked down at my hands. "He cheated on me with her. After my dad died."

A moment of tense silence passed. Finally, Maksim said, "I assume you don't mean the waitress."

"It was the dancer, the one who'd been wearing the red costume."

"I know who you're referring to. Understand, my response to seeing her wasn't what you're thinking."

"I-I don't think anything." Nothing I was going to share with *him*, anyway. "It's none of my business."

"She transitioned to a new role, or so I was told. That's why I took notice of her. I was surprised to see her dancing that night."

"It's fine, Maksim. It doesn't matter."

"It doesn't?" He reached over and brought his hand to a rest beside mine. Our pinkies touched, and my heart trilled. I wondered if he felt something, too, because he tangled our fingers together. Sparks of electricity ignited everywhere my skin came into contact with his.

I withdrew my hand. "My dad's death wrecked me, and Ty's betrayal was the final crushing blow." I closed my eyes, and a stream spilled over. "I don't mean to be such a mess. But no matter how hard I try, I am."

Our driver circled through a roundabout and entered a two-lane street where traffic flowed in both directions. Parked cars lined the curb.

"I understand the kind of betrayal you speak of," Maksim said. "I've experienced it."

I looked at him.

"My ex is a model with aspirations beyond the runways of Paris. She began sleeping with a French filmmaker while we were together."

"You dated a model?" My mouth twisted. "Like, a supermodel?"

He rolled his eyes. "This isn't easy for me. Can we keep on topic?"

I toned down my shock. "Sorry."

"A mutual friend informed me of what happened. Thankfully, he felt more of an allegiance to me than to her; otherwise, I would not have learned the truth as quickly as I did."

"Well that's ironic." I huffed a laugh. "The way you found out about your ex, through a mutual friend, is the same way I found out about Ty. Except I've never known who the mutual friend was."

Maksim's head tilted. "Oh?"

"It was after the scavenger hunt arrived. My best friend, Brandy, received an anonymous text." My insides tightened. "There was a pic."

"Of?"

"My boyfriend, Ty. *Then*-boyfriend. He hooked up with some

European snow bunny during a ski trip. The pic was a selfie of them, making out before they..." I wrinkled my nose.

"Ouch." Maksim drew a sharp breath. "Was she the one who sent the photo?"

"I don't think so. She wasn't anyone he knew, and there's no way she could have gotten Brandy's number. Ty didn't even have it. Brandy disliked him from the beginning, and she refused to share her contact details with him."

Our cab reached a line of traffic and rolled to a stop.

"Best we can figure," I continued, "Ty must have sent the pic to someone we both knew, someone he thought he could trust, and that person must have felt compelled to let me know—but they probably didn't want any drama, so they used an anonymous number. The thing is, I have that blocker app on my phone, so I can only receive calls or messages from people in my contacts."

"Hence the need to involve your friend."

"Exactly. It had to be someone Brandy and I both knew, someone who realized the messages wouldn't get through to me. The snow bunny wouldn't have known that." I leaned against my door, letting my gaze wander beyond the cab. Earth-colored merchant houses lined this side of the road. People hustled past inns and cafés.

A man carrying a yellow flag led a group of tourists toward a bulky dark-stone building. A steeple rose up from the slanted roof. Might've been the church I'd seen the night before. If so, that meant we were near Council Square.

We were still sitting in traffic when our driver broke the silence.

"He thinks there may be construction ahead." Maksim craned his neck. "But I don't see any heavy machinery."

I lowered my window and listened. "I don't hear any, either."

Our taxi inched forward, and the source of the traffic jam became clear. Trailers had been parked beside a plaza—Council Square, as I'd suspected—and because there wasn't a shoulder, cars had to circumnavigate the trailers one at a time.

Men in work uniforms were unloading huge, freestanding billboards made of solid wood. One of the billboards displayed a map of the plaza. Another advertised a hotel.

The workers shuffled forward, hauling the billboard to the end of the trailer. The signage tipped, and the worker lost his grip at the same time our driver accelerated.

The billboard toppled.

I braced the seat in front of me. "Watch out!"

Crack. The billboard landed on the pavement. The wood broke apart, and our cabbie braked.

I launched forward. My seat belt caught me across the hips and chest.

"Are you all right?" Maksim had a hand braced against the driver's seat.

"Fine." I peered out my half-open window, watching as the workers scrambled to gather the busted pieces.

Our driver honked again and veered left, circling around the mess. That was when I noticed another billboard waiting to be unloaded. An ad for a brasserie splashed the backside. I recognized the name, but I didn't know why.

The colorful plaza stretched to our right, the cobblestones shining silver in the afternoon sun. Our driver cleared the trailers and continued up the street. I faced forward.

I gasped, swiveling in my seat. The name. The clue.

That's it.

"Tell the driver to stop."

My request met silence. I twisted around and found Maksim on his phone, expression blank. "Maksim, please."

He addressed the cabbie. The man picked up speed, pointing at the road. "There's nowhere to pull over," Maksim translated. "He's concerned about the traffic behind us."

"It'll take two seconds for us to get out." I leaned forward. "Please, sir. This is important."

Maksim translated for me. The driver raised his voice and

waved his hand, thumbing behind us. We reached the next block, and the plaza disappeared behind a wall of dull merchant houses.

"Look. You can go there. Right there." I pointed at the curb. "Please."

Maksim kept translating. The man barked at us, face pink, and all the while his cab carried us farther away from Council Square.

"That's it." I unbuckled my seat belt and jimmied the lock on my door.

Maksim straightened. "What are you doing?"

I cross-bodied my purse, yanked on the door handle, and shoved my foot against the door. The driver gasped, swerving.

I hung on, bracing myself, and then launched out of the cab.

"Kat!"

22. PROPAGANDA

I landed on the pavement and rolled. Sort of. Actually, it was more of a flop. Pain flared in my arm and shoulder. Cars swerved around me. One of the drivers blasted his horn.

I swore and scrambled onto the sidewalk.

Bells tolled somewhere nearby. The sound grew louder, pealing in rich, deep tones. I sprinted in that direction. Weathered merchant houses spanned my left, their facades cracked and peeling.

I passed the last building and hung a left. Council Square fanned out in front of me. People swarmed the plaza.

Maksim pulled me to a stop. "What the hell was that?"

I fixed my purse and motioned for him to follow me. We zigzagged through bodies until we reached a short tunnel.

"I assume you know where you're going?" Maksim's voice echoed around us.

"Think so. Pretty sure." I held up a finger, still trying to catch my breath. "Give me a second, and I'll explain."

We exited the tunnel, and sunlight poured over us. I squinted, shielding my eyes. A handful of restaurants had Italian-sounding names. I was looking for French.

"When my dad left Romania," I began, "he ended up in Paris.

He didn't have much money, but one brasserie let him have all the onion soup he could eat when they found out he was a refugee."

Our path split as we reached a brown stucco building. Another row of restaurants stretched to our right. I turned that way—to the right—and Maksim stayed at my side.

"He shared the story over Thanksgiving," I continued, "when he started opening up about Romania. Fast-forward to last night. I came across a brasserie during my jog, and one of those billboards back there"—I jammed a thumb over my shoulder—"had an ad for the very same brasserie. Plus, you'd been talking about your ex in Paris, so..." I shrugged. "Something must've clicked."

"I saw the billboard. It was for Brasserie de l'Arte."

"That's the one. Doesn't that mean 'Eatery of Art'?"

"More like Art Brewery." He paused. "We're still working on the *Vintage* supporting clue?"

"Well, yeah. Art is one of the things we agreed could be vintage. Isn't that why we've been visiting art museums and galleries?"

"Yes, but this is a restaurant. I don't imagine they'll have real artwork, just an artsy theme."

"But we should check," I countered. "You've been saying that. Process of elimination."

"Yes. We should check." He sighed, glancing behind us, and raked at his hair. "Just don't be so reckless. You could have been hit by one of those cars."

I touched his arm—a silent "I'm sorry"—as we came upon a yellow stucco building. Pink flowers sprang up in flower boxes while vines ran along the exterior. Elongated, retro-looking letters curled across the entrance.

Brasserie de l'Arte.

Smooth jazz floated through the restaurant. Accented voices tinkled.

"Over there." Maksim gestured toward abstract art hanging on the wall.

I shook my head. "My dad hated abstract art. Definitely not

one of his 'two favorites' of anything." I craned my neck, searching for other forms of artwork.

A cocktail bar stretched along the back wall. To our right, a woman's intense gaze locked onto me. Her red bandanna wrapped her head and tied on top. She pursed her lips, eyebrows sharp and serious. Her blue sleeve was rolled up, biceps flexed.

We can do it! Rosie the Riveter.

I beelined toward her. The World War II poster hung in a black frame. A *Joan of Arc Saved France* poster—World War I propaganda—hung beside her. I was familiar with Joan. At one time, Dad had a smaller version taped to his closet door.

People dined at tables along the wall. I stood to the side, studying Joan. *"The quintessential American housewife,"* Dad used to say, *"but with armor and a sword."* Joan's gaze beheld something in the heavens, like she had been sent on a mission by God. In reality, for this Americanized Joan, she had been sent by the US government.

Their slogan for this wartime poster:

WOMEN OF AMERICA
SAVE YOUR COUNTRY
BUY WAR SAVINGS STAMPS

Maksim edged beside me. "Vintage art."

"Exactly. And my dad had both of these prints at our old apartment."

Maksim examined a third poster, which hung to the left of Rosie. The artwork depicted three faces over an open book, a sun rising up from the pages. Cyrillic text lined the bottom.

Soviet propaganda.

"Knowledge to all," Maksim said. Correction: *read*. He was reading the poster.

My brow furrowed. "You know Russian?"

"My parents were Romanian, but we have family in Russia. The name Maksim has Slavic origins."

"My dad always had not-so-nice things to say about Russia, I guess because of communism, so he never collected any Soviet—" My explanation stalled as the overhead lights cast a shimmery glaze over the poster, drawing my attention to one section. The sunrise had been drawn like a burst of sunbeams, and those beams had been depicted by...

"Lines." I shot a look at Maksim. "The clue. **Read behind the lines.**"

"I see it, and I would be willing to bet there's something behind this poster."

I squeezed past the table standing between me and the answer to the clue. A woman sitting there hopped up. The man shouted.

"What is this you are doing?" A woman in black trousers and a white blouse hurried over.

I had a solid grip on each side of the frame. "We need to look behind this poster."

The woman shoved a hand to her hip, eyes narrowing. "There is nothing to look at. I assure you."

"Can we check, anyway?"

She slid a pencil behind her ear. Curtain bangs framed her round face, giving her a friendly look in spite of her scowl. "This print belongs to someone. It was purchased—"

"Last December?" I asked.

Her jaw slid out of place. "How did you know this?"

"Was the buyer named Nicholas Barrett?" Maksim asked. "Or perhaps Boris Funa?"

I tilted my head. "The clue?"

"Boris is a Slavic name, and this is Soviet propaganda." Maksim shrugged. "Perhaps it's an alias of your father's."

My dad didn't have an alias. That's what I'd been about to say, but I couldn't actually say it. Because what if he had? He might've had a bunch of aliases, and I would have never known.

The woman offered that couple a strained smile. They didn't respond in kind.

"I'm unsure what this is about"—the woman halved a glare between Maksim and me—"but I must ask you to leave."

"Couldn't you let us look behind the poster first?" I clasped my hands. "Please?"

Maksim switched to Romanian. The woman replied, and Maksim was quick to say, *"Da, da, da."* Yes, yes, yes.

She huffed and dragged a chair out, setting it to the side. The patron who'd been sitting there was still on her feet, now with her arms crossed and mouth pursed.

Using both hands, the manager—or whoever she was— gripped the frame and jostled it loose from the wall. She backed out of the space, letting me have a glimpse of what was behind the poster.

My heart sank. The wall was blank.

"Are you satisfied?" The woman went to rehang the poster when a yellow piece of paper flapped. Someone had taped a sticky note to the back of the frame.

"Wait!"

The woman froze.

I peeled off the note. The number fifty-seven had been scribbled on the yellow paper, along with the initials *NB*.

"What did you find?" The woman set the frame on the floor and propped it against the wall. She stepped closer, and I showed her the sticky note. "An accounting record?" she asked.

"We're not certain," Maksim said, "but we believe it was left by her father. What more can you tell us about his purchase?"

"I was approached by this man—he called himself Nicolae— in December. He took great interest in these prints. We had them for a special event, and he requested to purchase them. I explained they were not for sale, but what could I do? He was with Invest Romania."

"Invest Romania?" Maksim repeated.

"The nonprofit organization he works for." When Maksim and I shared a quizzical look, the woman added, "They are helping local businesses here in Braşov."

"Do you mind?" Maksim pulled out his phone. "I need to document everything."

The woman motioned for him to go ahead, and he began to snap pictures of the posters. To the people we'd disrupted, the woman apologized profusely and encouraged them to return to their table. Then she led she me away from the dining area.

We stopped beside the bar. "Our representative from Invest Romania said it would be best to keep our financial problems a secret," she said, lowering her voice another notch. "He said this kind of publicity could be bad for our business."

"We'll be discreet." I matched her volume. "You were having financial problems, and Invest Romania helped?"

"Yes, of course. This is the mission of Invest Romania. Have you never heard this from your father?"

"I... didn't know much about his work." Clearly, that was true. "Can you tell me more? It might help me figure out what the sticky note means."

"Invest Romania finds local businesses that are having big financial problems. They are then pairing us with angel investors who want to help. Recipients are never required to repay this assistance. In return, we fulfill a short list of obligations."

Maksim joined us. "What kind of obligations?"

"We were required to provide five years of accounting records and detailed information about our bills. Invest Romania also required us to take a course in finance and a business-management course specific to the restaurant industry."

I raised an eyebrow. "And these were courses *they* provided?"

"Oh no, dear. Invest Romania are doing investing." She said it like she was talking to a fifth grader. "We chose these classes for ourselves. They were free at the university." She folded her hands. "Popescu said we had six months to complete this requirement, so my husband and I took these classes during the autumn semester."

Maksim's brow pinched. "Who is Popescu?"

"Our representative. We gave our records and all the information about our debts to him. He said our bills would be paid for six months. Upon the conclusion of this time, we were supposed to receive an evaluation."

"Did you?" I asked.

"No, which was very strange. Popescu said the angel investors wish to reward positive behavior changes, and so if our finances were in order, Invest Romania would continue payments for six more months. This would have given us one year without the worry of bills."

My eyebrows shot up. "Wow."

"Yes, but he never returned for this evaluation."

"So what happened? The payments stopped?"

"They continued for a time. Our past-due bills, our taxes, all were paid for ten months. This month would have been eleven, but the payments have stopped."

"Any idea why?"

"I hoped you would know. We fulfilled our agreement and completed the classes. Our spending is much better, and we have a savings account now. We're doing everything Invest Romania has asked."

"What contact information do you have for that man Popescu?" Maksim asked. "Did you communicate with him by email? Telephone?"

"I have no contact information for him."

Maksim's mouth drilled down into a frown. "He gave you no way to contact him? And you did not find that strange?"

"They have no office, no secretary to receive the calls, and the angel investors do not wish to be contacted." Pink dusted her cheeks. "I understand I should have asked more questions, but I was too happy for our bills to be paid. And they were."

"What about your initial application?" I asked. "Was that done online, or did you have to go somewhere?"

"Invest Romania does not receive applications. They stay informed of local businesses and choose who they wish to help.

When they learned of us, they sent Popescu. He came into the restaurant to inquire further."

Maksim muttered and rubbed his eyes. He looked like he wanted to scream. I felt about the same.

"Do you have any other information that might help us?" I asked. "Popescu's last name, maybe?"

"That *is* his last name," Maksim mumbled. "It's probably the most common surname in Romania."

Crap.

"Okay, then a first name?"

"He may have mentioned it during our first meeting," the woman said. "I don't remember, and we only ever called him Popescu."

I exhaled. "I suppose you don't have the name of your angel investor, either, huh?"

"Popescu said the investors wish to remain anonymous, but I believe we met ours. I think he was your father." She took my hands. "Please will you tell him everything I have told you? I want him to know we are good people like him and that we have done everything we were told."

I searched for words.

"What makes you think he was your investor?" Maksim interjected. "Did he say something about it?"

"No, but his request was unusual. Those are replica prints, nothing special." She waved a hand toward the posters. "But he insisted on purchasing them and made a very generous offer. More generous than a working person could have afforded."

Maksim tilted his head. "How much?"

"Two thousand euros, in cash."

"*Two thousand euros?*" I repeated at a shout. The bartender froze. The dining room fell silent.

"Did her father appear to be under duress when he made this offer?" Maksim asked. "Did you have the impression anyone was with him?"

"I saw no one else, and... yes, he did seem agitated. I assumed he must be in a hurry." She placed a hand to her chest. "I can see this situation involves something of great importance. Allow me to look behind the other prints in case we may find something helpful." She left us and returned to the dining area.

Maksim waited until she was out of earshot. "I find it strange this Invest Romania company would do these things without expecting something in return."

"You think *that's* strange? I couldn't even afford the full flight over here while my dad dropped two grand on posters he already owned."

"How could there be no application?" Maksim pinched at his throat. "And how were these investors privy to the financial status of a small private business?"

"The government would have that kind of information, wouldn't they? Like if a business was past due on their taxes?"

"Certain individuals in the government would." Maksim parked himself on a stool. "Perhaps this man, Popescu, knows someone who can keep him abreast of struggling businesses."

"But why?" I watched the woman remove Rosie from her spot on the wall. There didn't appear to be another sticky note. "Who would think to look into that kind of thing?"

"Who would think to do any of this"—Maksim gestured around us—"and without providing a single piece of contact information?"

His phone chimed. He checked the message, and his head slowly tilted. His eyes went squinty.

"Oh, no. What now?"

The woman suddenly called out. The bartender rounded the bar and made his way over to her. After their exchange, the guy gathered all three posters—Rosie, Joan, and the Soviet propaganda—and carried them into the kitchen.

The woman returned. "Those prints are taking up wall space that could be used for original art. Since your father was the buyer, I would like to ask you to take them please."

"Um, sure. I don't have a way to carry them, though."

"We have transport canisters. My employee is unmounting each poster, and he has instructions to search carefully for more accounting notes." She excused herself and disappeared through the kitchen door.

"I'm talking to Daniel," Maksim said as he punched out a text message. "Do you mind if I take a picture of that?" He gestured toward my hand.

The sticky note clung to my finger. I held it toward him.

He snapped a pic. "I thought, perhaps, we could make a stop before returning to La Madălină. Would that be all right?"

"I guess so. As long as it's quick."

"It should be, and Daniel is busy with something anyway. Apparently one of the guests failed to use a voltage converter while drying her hair, and the bathroom nearly caught fire."

"Are you serious? Just now?"

"A moment ago, yes. Everything is fine, but the electricity is out, and he needs time to deal with that. Since we still have other matters to discuss, I thought we could go someplace quiet."

"Where did you have in mind?"

His eyes twinkled. "How do you feel about surprises?"

23. CROSSING

Maksim pushed through a turnstile. *"Scuzaţi, vă rog!"* Excuse me, please!

The man operating the *telecabină*—aerial cable car—waved us over. Maksim jogged forward, tickets raised.

I trailed behind him. "You're sure we have time for this?"

"I'm sure." Maksim handed over our tickets.

The man motioned for us to board. Passengers crowded the windows, everyone talking and readying phone cameras. Maksim ushered me to the center of the cabin.

The lady at the brasserie had agreed to hold the posters, and Daniel needed time to get the electrical issue fixed. Still, every minute that ticked by increased the pressure bearing down on me. We were running out of time.

I peeled off my pullover and tied it around my waist. "Not a fan of heights, by the way."

"Ah, but the view is incredible, and the fresh air will be good for us."

The *telecabină's* ticket office lay nestled at the foot of a forested mountain. "Mount Tâmpa," Maksim had said. At the top of the mountain, massive white letters spelled out Braşov, à la the Hollywood sign.

I hadn't seen the letters before today—there'd been too much fog—but the sun had managed to break through the haze and burn off the dreary weather.

The operator slid the doors shut and latched a bar. Our cable car lifted, carrying us over the emerald forests. Emerald with splotches of brown, rather. Some of the trees were looking kinda crunchy. Maybe Maksim was right about the drought.

I stood at the back window. The ticket office drifted farther and farther away while fiery-orange rooftops spread across the scope of my vision. Oohs and aahs circled through the cabin.

The higher we climbed, the more disoriented I became. I grabbed Maksim's sleeve—another long-sleeved knit shirt, which he'd pushed up to his elbows.

He slipped out of my grasp and placed his arm around me. "It may help to look where we're going"—he turned me around—"rather than where we've been."

Outside the cable car, beyond the passengers crowded around the front window, a radio tower sprouted up from the mountain and reached into the sky. Movement tugged at my peripheral. My gaze shifted to a line of people passing through a clearing. The leader carried a long hiking stick. The next person had trekking poles.

"Are there trails on the mountain?"

"There are." Maksim let me go. "I used them as part of my recovery process last summer, first hiking and later running."

I looked up at him. "What recovery process?"

"I thought you knew." He raked a hand through his hair. "I assumed Madă spoke with you about it last night."

"I'm not sure what she was talking about, honestly, but she didn't say anything about recovery. Were you... a drug addict?" I held my breath, waiting for his answer.

"This wasn't addiction recovery."

I exhaled a relieved sigh. "Oh. Good."

He looked like he had more to say, but he hesitated as our cable car neared the top. Everyone shifted toward the exit.

Maksim went the other way, stationing himself by the back window. His gaze swept over the other passengers. "I suppose you've already seen this." He gripped his sleeve and tugged it up and over his elbow—not on the arm with the tattoo. His other arm. Puckered skin, paler than his natural olive, appeared. It was the scar I'd noticed the other day, and it was bigger than I'd thought, stretching all the way around his biceps and triceps.

"I was in an accident." He rotated his arm and dragged the sleeve higher. Scar tissue mangled his skin.

I drew in a surprised breath. "What happened?"

"I'd been in Braşov, on business for Ştefan, when I learned of my ex's infidelity. I decided to fly to Paris to confront her and in my haste to leave lost control of the bike. It was a low-side crash— meaning the bike came out from under me when I cornered."

I knew what a low-side crash was. But I didn't say anything.

"I was wearing light armor that day—protective jacket, double-lined pants, my helmet. Nevertheless, the pavement tore through my skin, all over the right side of my body."

I clapped a hand over my mouth.

"Daniel and Madă witnessed the accident. They were driving behind me when I lost control."

Our cable car lurched to a stop.

I lowered my hand and looked around. We were hanging in front of a cement building the size of the ticket office. A man met us on the platform and disengaged the lock. The doors slid open, and everyone piled out.

Maksim pushed off the window, and we followed the other passengers into the building. Sunglasses and bucket hats filled a bar area, the people sucking on water bottles and fanning them- selves. A bartender served drinks from an industrial-size fridge.

Maksim slid his hand into mine and pulled me through the crowd. We waded through sweaty bodies, past an outdoor bar, past a covered patio and then a souvenir table.

He did a U-turn, asking the souvenir lady something. She ducked down and rustled through a box. When she stood, she held a flat piece of foam with a cluster of lapel pins formed into Romanian flags.

Maksim handed her a five-lei bill. "This is my gift to you," he said, selecting one of the pins. "So that you'll always remember your trip."

I took the pin between my thumb and index finger. Silver filament outlined the design. Sunlight reflected off the enamel.

A hint of sadness swelled. "My dad and I decorated our Christmas tree with blue, gold, and red lights. We made flag ornaments."

"I don't want you to be sad, *dragă*." Maksim took my hand and drew me away from the souvenir stand. "Let me show you the viewing platform. In my opinion, it's the most beautiful view in all of Transilvania."

The last thing he said rolled through my mind—once, twice. Why did I feel like I'd heard him say that before?

Maksim turned onto a rocky trail. A wooden sign stood to the side, displaying trail maps and information about plants and animals. Big, bold letters stamped the top. Wildlife Warning.

For some reason, a lion came to mind.

I brushed off the strange thoughts, slipped the pin into my pocket, and did my best to match stride with Maksim. My shirt bunched beneath the pullover, which was still tied around my waist. My travel purse bounced against my hip, the strap looped across my body.

Our path carried us down and then up a rocky hill. The terrain leveled off and led us around a bend. To our right, steel beams bracketed the mountain, displaying six gigantic outward-facing letters.

We were behind the Braşov sign.

Maksim didn't stop until we reached a wide viewing platform. People stood around, snapping photos. One guy appeared to be meditating on a boulder.

I walked onto the platform and peered over the railing. Dense forest spread below us, a green wave rolling down the mountain and washing up against the city. Way in the distance, along the horizon, the faint outline of mountains reached up and kissed a crystal-blue sky.

I unzipped my purse and dug out my phone. "This is amazing."

"It is. I've missed this view." Maksim leaned forward and rested his forearms on the rail. His expression softened into tranquility.

I tried various angles with the phone camera. When I zoomed out, the merchant houses became tiny. When I zoomed in, the shots turned grainy.

Maksim watched me. "We should take one together."

I snorted. "What, like a selfie?"

"Why not?"

"Um..." I gave a little chuckle. "Because you're worried I might post stuff on the web?"

"It's habit for me to worry about such things." His peaceful gaze floated over the landscape. "I'm not worried now."

"Really?" I checked my reflection in the selfie camera. "Ugh, I look terrible."

"You look beautiful. Your cheeks are rosy in the sunlight, and your eyes sparkle like sapphires."

Heat bloomed in my face. I checked the screen again. Sure enough, the patches of pink on my cheeks had darkened.

"I'm not very good at selfies," Maksim said. "You'll have to direct me."

"We should probably stand like this." I turned us around and held the phone up and out. Maksim stepped closer, bringing himself into view.

Fiery orange rooftops created a distant backdrop.

"I'll count to three and take the picture. Ready? One, two—"

"On three or after three?"

"Three." *Click.*

A preview appeared. Maksim's mouth was open, his eyes closed. My mouth was twisted.

We tried again. Maksim strained a smile, teeth showing. I went for a cutesy pose, one shoulder hitched. The whole thing looked phony as hell.

Maksim played photographer for a while. That didn't work out, either.

We resigned ourselves to goofy faces. I stuck out my tongue. He crossed his eyes. I puffed my cheeks. He squinted dramatically.

We paused our session and swiped through the photos. I wrinkled my nose. "Am I imagining things, or did these turn out blurry?"

"There's a slight blur." He stopped on a photo. "Actually, this one came out nicely."

I used my hand to block the glare. Maksim had managed to capture us midlaugh. We were looking at each other, not the camera, and the angle was decent. No blur.

He returned the phone. "Send me that one."

"You're sure?" I angled the phone so he could see the screen. "Last chance to stop me."

"I'm sure."

I created a new message and pressed the paperclip icon. I wasn't sure what to write for the text, so I opted for a red heart.

No, red was way too romantic. Yellow was more casual, but so was blue. Or... what about all three?

My lips tugged into a grin. I inserted the hearts, putting them in the same order as the Romanian flag—blue, yellow, red. I pressed Send, and Maksim's pocket chimed. He checked the message, and his mouth lifted into the biggest, shiniest smile I'd seen yet. The glimmer in his eyes made my heart throb.

He leaned back against the railing and pointed above us. I traced his finger to a Romanian flag mounted higher up on the mountain. The fabric caught a breeze, showing off the colors I'd just texted to Maksim.

"We can hike up there if you'd like." He arched an eyebrow. "Care to?"

"How far is it?"

"Five minutes. Ten if we're hiking slowly."

That wasn't far at all, and when would I ever be in Romania again? When would I be here, in this spot, with Maksim again? Probably never.

Sadness swelled, a toxic friend who comes around when there's not enough drama going on in her life.

I firmed up my jaw. No. I would not let regret win this round. Not today. Not with this. "Let's do it. Let's hike up."

We backtracked to a narrow path carved into the mountain. People passed us, a hum of excitement moving toward the viewing platform.

We left them behind and began our ascent.

Sweat saturated my scalp. My thighs and hamstrings strained. It wasn't long before Maksim pulled ahead.

"You never finished your story," I called. "About the bike accident."

He paused beside a tree. "I was unconscious for most of the ordeal. I do remember waking up en route to the hospital. Each time my eyes opened, I discovered an angel praying strange prayers over me. The angel was Madă. She had convinced the medical personnel to let her ride in the ambulance. Daniel followed in their car."

"Did you know them yet?"

"It was our first meeting, but they refused to leave my side until they knew I was okay." Maksim gripped the tree and pulled himself up a steep section. I noticed he used his left arm—the one that wasn't scarred.

I echoed the technique, grabbing a branch and hauling myself up to the next level. "What injuries did you have?"

"Concussion, fractured wrist, sprains and bruises. The right side of my body received the worst of it. The road rash was second degree, and I sustained muscle and nerve damage. The pain— I cannot begin to describe to you this pain. Even medicated, I could feel everything when they scrubbed the dirt and the gravel out of my skin."

I grimaced. "Did you need skin grafts?"

"A few. I required intensive physiotherapy in order to walk and move normally again. Though, I've never fully recovered my strength and mobility."

The last bit of trail brought us to a narrow staircase. Maksim climbed up, his movements smooth and easy.

"You seem okay to me."

"Most people would never notice my present limitations. I've trained myself to continue moving and working through the pain."

I followed him up the staircase. "You're still in pain?"

"Sometimes. The nerve damage is extensive."

The trail forked. Each path led to a viewing platform constructed of two-by-fours. We angled for the one on the right.

"How'd your cousin react?"

"He was understanding and offered to extend as much time as I needed. Supposedly, anyway. In theory."

"And... what? He wasn't so understanding after all?"

"He didn't anticipate the amount of time I would be absent, nor had I. Among other complications." Maksim stepped onto the wooden platform. A thick banister served as the railing.

He leaned against the banister, arms resting on top. The bruising on his knuckles became clear in the sunlight.

I stood beside him and looked out. The landscape rolled into the distance, the hills jutting and growing into mountains. Orange rooftops filled the valley, adding a splash of fire to the sea of green.

Maksim was right. This view was unbelievable.

I peeked over at him. "What other complications? You mean, with your recovery?"

"The best hospitals are in București, but Daniel had heard of a new treatment being introduced to the hospital in Brașov. He offered to let me stay with him and Madă so that I could try it. Over the coming weeks, something began to shift from within the depths of me. It's—difficult to explain." He focused on me. "You've met Daniel and Madă. What do you think of them?"

"They've been really nice. And not fake-nice, either. They seem genuine."

"I've only known people to be cruel, deceptive, and always with ulterior motives. Daniel and Madă are different. In the weeks that followed, I found myself sickened by the thought of doing the things my work required of me. My updates to Ştefan lessened in frequency and fervor, and he noticed. One day he was waiting for me at the hospital."

"Was he mad?"

"He was concerned. I'm second only to him, and I have a wealth of knowledge that can destroy everything his father built should I ever turn against him."

My torso tightened. "He thought you had turned against him?"

"He wondered." Maksim used his boot to sweep a pebble off the platform. The tiny rock swished through tree branches and plummeted down the embankment. "I had to explain myself and do so without implicating these innocent people I was staying with."

The tightening turned into a sharp twist. "Daniel and Madă were in danger?"

"They could have been had Ştefan decided they were a threat, but I shouldered the blame and said I had become preoccupied with recovery and this new treatment method."

"Did he believe you?" My throat rasped. "What about Daniel and Madă? Did they ever find out?"

Realization dawned across his features. He reached out and brushed his thumb along my jawline. "They know. I was honest with them, just as I'm being honest with you." He lowered his hand. "You have nothing to fear, *draga mea*."

A burst of laughter rang out from the tree line. We turned.

Someone stood at the top of the skinny staircase, his arm curled, biceps flexed. He switched arms, and more laughter rattled from somewhere unseen. Somebody must have been taking his picture.

"There's one more spot I'd like to show you," Maksim said. "I discovered it during one of my hikes. We can stop there on the way down."

"We're not taking the cable car down?"

"The line will be long, but if you prefer the *telecabină*—"

"I'd rather hike, but I want to make sure we don't keep Daniel and Madă waiting."

"Daniel said he would SMS as soon as he's finished." Maksim checked his phone. "Nothing yet. I think we'll be fine."

We made our way past the guy and his entourage, down the skinny staircase, through the forest, and down to the main trail behind the giant Braşov letters.

Picture-happy people chattered excitedly on the viewing platform. Maksim led me in the other direction.

Gravel crunched under our shoes. Thick forest encased the landscape on our left. Maksim followed a trail straight into the forest.

I paused at the tree line and sent a backward glance over my shoulder. People trickled this way, but they were all headed for the viewing platform.

I pushed out a breath, situated my purse, and marched into the forest.

24. CONFESSION

Maksim hiked a ways and then made a sharp turn. I thought he was doubling back until I noticed he was one level down.

Switchbacks. We were going down the mountain.

He pushed his sleeves higher, face red and slick. My attention moved to his right arm. "Is that why you wear long sleeves all the time?" I pointed. "The scars?"

He shrugged. "It's been cool in the mornings."

"Maksim, you wear long sleeves even when it's one hundred degrees outside."

He didn't offer an immediate response. The ground dipped down into a bushel of tree roots. Maksim hopped over and landed on a fresh patch of trail, one level down.

He held out his hand.

I took it and leaped over the roots. "Well?" I straightened and slanted a look.

"People knew about the accident, but the extent of my injuries has remained a secret. Only Ştefan knows." He raised an arm and rubbed the sleeve across his face. Sweat transferred onto the gray fabric. "The scars make me vulnerable."

"To who?"

"A host of people who would enjoy seeing my family's demise —enemies, tenuous allies." He continued down to the next switchback. I fell in step behind him. "The scars communicate a weakness, which can then be used against me and, ultimately, against Ștefan."

"Then why are you hiding them from me? I've already seen them, and I'm not someone who's looking to bring down your cousin's empire."

He risked a glance but then refocused on the trail. Sunlight broke through the canopy of leaves, dusting him in golden light. His stride remained steady, relaxed, but his posture had gone rigid.

We hiked in silence for a lengthy span before he said, "I want out."

"Of this conversation?"

"Of my cousin's operation."

"Oh." I edged along a narrow section of trail. "Can you... do that?"

"Under normal circumstances, the answer would be no. However, I've become something of a liability to my cousin, and so he— We've come to an agreement of sorts."

"Maksim, that's great."

"It's a bit premature, actually. Some aspects of our agreement are yet to be settled, and I'll be required to meet his conditions."

"Oh yeah? One final impossible job like John Wick?" I pumped playfulness into my tone, making it clear that was a joke.

He didn't laugh. He didn't say anything at all.

I cleared my throat. "So, um, what do you plan to do after you're out?"

"Normal things. Find a job. Travel." Maksim stopped at the next switchback, and I came alongside him. "I've never been to the United States. I've always wanted to go."

"Would you want to visit Atlanta? I could take you to Civil War museums and introduce you to Brandy and Dave." I smiled up at him. "Dave will definitely try to recruit you for his parkour team."

"That all sounds wonderfully normal." A sunbeam penetrated the forest and fell across him. His eyes shone like the earthy layers of a desert landscape. "What about you? Are you certain you'd want a criminal hanging around?"

"*Ex*-criminal. And yeah, I'd love that." That last part came out whispery and full of hope. He looked hopeful, too.

His smile widened as he gripped the back of his shirt and dragged it over his head. The sleeves peeled off his arms, leaving him in a thin white undershirt.

He raked at his damp hair. His sleeve lifted, revealing the pale, crinkly skin.

My gaze brushed over his scars. "There. Was that so hard?"

"I'm disinclined to answer that." He wadded up the knit shirt and motioned for me to follow him—except he didn't continue onto the next switchback. Instead, we entered a patch of forest.

"Since I'm being vulnerable," he said over his shoulder, "I have a confession. I told you Brașov is safe, and it is, but—"

I waited. "But what?"

"The city came under a terror threat some months ago."

My feet lagged. "While you were living here?"

"I was living in București by then, but our media reported on the incident, and of course Daniel—being a local—was aware of it. None of this occurred to me until after you had left the house last night."

I exhaled a laugh. "It's fine. Really. I appreciate your honesty, but terrorism can happen anywhere."

"That part wasn't the confession." He braced his foot on a thick log lying on the forest floor and hiked over it. He motioned for me to do the same. "I may have overreacted when I realized my error, and I... I followed you."

I stalled out on the other side of the log. "You did?"

"That was how I knew you'd gone to Centrul Vechi." He eased closer. "When you turned onto the wrong street, I continued to the guesthouse. You never arrived, so I went looking for you."

"You were behind me that entire time? Until I took that wrong turn?"

He offered up an apologetic smile. "I'm proficient in tailing people, whether on foot or by car, and when the person is listening to music, it makes my job that much easier."

I cringed. Coach Jules used to warn us about listening to music while running. She'd said it was safer to keep one earbud out.

Sometimes I did. But I hadn't last night.

"I hope you can forgive me. The terrorists took the lives of a civilian and a police officer before they were neutralized." He rubbed his neck. "It's all I could think about after you left."

"Well... I appreciate the sentiment." I mustered up a smile. "It's probably good you were watching out for me. That terror attack sounds kinda crazy."

"I'm surprised you hadn't heard about it. The terrorists included a notorious ex-politician and his assistant. The politician was extraordinarily corrupt. In my opinion, for whatever it may be worth, I believe he reaped a harvest of the evil he sowed— during communism and since. He is the reason—" Maksim pushed out a breath, hands on hips, and let his gaze fall to the forest floor.

He shook his head and restarted our hike.

I quickened my steps, coming alongside him. His jaw was tight, hardening his other features. "Maksim?"

"That man, the ex-politician— He was behind the death of my parents."

The explanation rattled me to the core. My feet stuttered. "I've actually been wondering about... that. I haven't known how to ask. About your parents, I mean. I've wanted to, but I haven't wanted to pry."

"You're welcome to ask me anything. If I don't wish to answer —or can't—I'll tell you."

"Okay." That was easy enough. "So what happened?"

"Sometime in the nineties, that wealthy politician began bankrolling the efforts of a radical activist known as the Traveler. Together they organized protests and stirred up mobs in an effort to revive various factions of the workers party. My parents were pro-democracy and decided to counterprotest one day. They were killed."

My eyes widened. "How?"

"The Traveler ordered his men to drive a large van into the crowd. The vehicle had pro-democracy signage, making it appear as if pro-democracy advocates had committed the act. Most of the people who died were the Traveler's own supporters, but my parents were struck down, as well."

My blood froze. "Why would he attack his own supporters?"

"To gain sympathy for their new worker's party. Apparently, it's an effective method. The court cases of several communists—associates of Ceaușescu—were postponed. Some who were in prison had their sentences commuted."

I thought back to what Andrei had said about Maksim's parents. He'd never mentioned any of this. Maybe he didn't know the whole story.

The forest thinned, and a clearing opened up. Maksim headed that way. "This is the spot I mentioned." He draped his knit shirt over a low-hanging branch. Then he angled for a ledge, climbed up, and reached back for me. "Careful. Mind your step."

I took his hand, bracing one foot against the rock. The gesture felt familiar, like I'd done this before.

He pulled me onto the ledge, which was barely big enough for both of us. My purse bounced against my hip. I wobbled and rocked back. My heel found air.

I clutched Maksim's arms. He winced—the tiniest of winces. I might not have noticed except that his attention flicked to my hand.

I let him go. "The nerve damage?"

"It's nothing to worry about." He let his gaze drift over the emerald-green landscape and down to the orange rooftops. He was still holding on to me, and his tribal band flexed.

I'd been into tattoos ever since I'd seen David Beckham shirtless on a soccer field. Maksim was just as much of a heartthrob, and his tattoo took him from hot to nuclear—but it was his scars I couldn't stop thinking about.

I slipped my hand under the thin sleeve of his undershirt. My fingertips connected with tough, creased skin.

His stare shot to my hand.

My fingers bumped along thick sections and chaotic patterns. I moved to his biceps, then his triceps. The muscles were solid, bulky—though not as bulky as his other arm. His long sleeves had been concealing the difference.

I found a patch of soft flesh along his inner arm. My fingertips grazed the border, slipping between rough and smooth, damaged and undamaged. Scarred and not scarred.

He tensed, bowing his head.

I paused. "It hurts?"

"No... and yes." He met my gaze. "The damage is extensive, and the nerves are firing faulty signals."

I withdrew my hand. "I'm sorry."

"Don't be." He laced our fingers. His gaze wandered over my face, starting with my eyes and drifting to my nose and cheeks, to my mouth. His expression turned thoughtful. I could see an idea forming behind his eyes, a question. He was wondering if he should kiss me.

I pushed up onto my toes and brushed my lips over his with a feathery touch. A spark ignited, and heat electrified every part of my body.

He drew back, surprised. I was kind of surprised, too. Had I really just kissed him?

I lowered my heels. Maybe I shouldn't have done that. It was too much too soon, and—

His lips swept down, angling for mine. My heart vibrated into a drumroll. I gathered his face in my hands, and day-old stubble scraped my palms. Our lips brushed a second time, then a third. The warmth radiating from his mouth sent a shiver through me.

He tightened his hold. I tilted my head, making room for him.

Polyphonic techno punctured the silence. I jumped, startled, and buried my face in his shoulder. His mouth landed against the side of my head. We stayed that way, breathing heavily, his front pocket vibrating against my thigh. Three beats passed. Four.

He fumbled for the phone. "I'll turn it off."

"You should answer it." I lifted my head. "What if it's Daniel?"

He checked the name. "You're right. It's him." He placed the phone to his ear. "*Da*. Uh-huh. Yeah." The rest of the conversation unfolded in Romanian.

I slipped out of his hold and hopped down. My legs shook so badly they nearly gave out.

Maksim lowered himself to the ledge and dangled his legs off the side. He reached over and reeled me in. I thought he might try to kiss me again, but he seemed content to hold my hand while he listened to Daniel.

Suddenly, his demeanor shifted. He looked at me, and his eyes widened.

"What?" I mouthed.

He pushed off the ledge, snatched his shirt, and strode into the forest. I chased after him. *"Da da da. Pa. Pa-pa."* I knew *da* meant yes and *pa* meant bye. I wasn't sure why he said it all rapid-fire, but his tone, even his posture, held a serious edge of gravity.

I touched his arm. "What's going on?"

"We're going to La Madălină." He pocketed the phone. "Right now."

"What about the posters? I told that woman we'd go back for them."

"We'll have to go later."

"Why?" I pulled him to a stop. "Maksim, you're scaring me."

He exhaled deeply. "Daniel was able to fix the electricity, and

he's been studying everything I sent to him. He believes—"
Maksim's stare fell to the wadded-up shirt in his fist.

"What?"

"Your father may have been in danger during his business trip. More specifically, he may have come to Brașov because he was fleeing from someone."

My surprise ballooned. "Who?"

"Daniel doesn't know. But whoever it was, he believes they were trying to kill him."

25. ACCUSATION

"Daniel thinks someone was trying to kill my dad?" My mind blanked. "How? Why?"

Maksim pointed me forward and led me through the trees. "Daniel's family is Jewish, and he's very familiar with the language and writings, their history. The phrase *awaken the dawn* seemed familiar to him, and he realized it's from a collection of ancient songs and poems called the Tehillim. He—" The pink in Maksim's face darkened. "Never mind about that part."

"Maksim, what?" I drew him to a stop. "I want to know."

"Daniel showed me these writings and taught me how to read the script, enough so that I could learn a handful of lines. I still remember them, and... that day you were upset, when you chased that man into the restaurant, I may have recited one of them."

"You... What?" My mouth hung open. "You recited ancient Jewish writings? Why? Are you Jewish, too?"

"No, but I find the words strangely comforting, and I wondered if they may have the same effect for you."

His explanation sparked a memory. The secret poem.

"The writings are divided into five sections," he continued, "and then several subsections or chapters. Would you like to guess which chapter contains the phrase *awaken the dawn*?"

I squeezed my forehead, thinking—but I didn't have to think long. I reached into my pocket and pulled out the sticky note that had been attached to the Soviet propaganda. "It's this, isn't it?" I held up the note. "Fifty-seven."

"Precisely. Chapter fifty-seven of the Tehillim was written by a man trying to flee from someone in authority."

"Like the cops?"

"Like the king. His protégé was set to take the throne, and the king became paranoid and murderous. The protégé escaped into the wilderness and to other cities."

"Wait, so..." I shook my head. "Maksim, it's an ancient writing. A lot of people were probably in danger back then. And anyway, we're not Jewish."

"But your father *was* a history buff. What if he, while studying ancient history, learned about the Tehillim?"

"Except my dad wasn't into ancient history. He was into the world wars, especially World War—"

Maksim waited. "Two?"

My head gave a slight up and down. World War II had centered on Hitler's annihilation of the Jews. Could *that* have led Dad to a study of Jewish history? Had he come across these ancient writings?

"Tell me about the people who hired your father," Maksim said. "Did he know them prior?"

My insides tightened. "They were a new client."

"Were they referred by another client of his?"

"I-I don't know. I don't think so."

Hikers ascended the mountain. Maksim moved to the side, letting them pass. I edged in beside him.

"This is purely hypothetical"—Maksim drew me along—"but let's pretend this new client desired your father's programming abilities for nefarious purposes. Would he have complied even if it meant doing something unethical or illegal?"

"Anything's possible, I guess."

"I don't want to know 'possible.' I want to know *likely*. Tell me the first answer that comes into your mind—would he do something unethical or illegal?"

"No. He wouldn't."

"Is there anything you can share about the client? Their name? A point of contact?"

"My dad never told me. I'd be willing to bet the information is on his computer, but that thing was locked down after he died. I tried every password I knew and nothing worked."

"I may be able to help with that if you're still in possession of the computer. I'm trained in network security. Rather, anti-security."

"Are you a hacker?"

"Not specifically, but I was trained by one. My cousin. He's the truly skilled one when it comes to hacking, but the knowledge I possess is enough to be of use." He checked his phone. "We can discuss that later. For now, Daniel wants to explore this hunch he has about the Tehillim."

Walking paths and park benches greeted us at the base of the mountain. We passed the ticket office and a fancy-looking restaurant. As we exited the park, Maksim turned onto a side street. Parked cars dotted the road. A familiar multilevel building towered over the area.

We were behind the mall.

Polyphonic techno pulsed from Maksim's pocket. He pulled out his phone and placed it to his ear. *"Da."* He listened, and the spark in his eyes dimmed. "Ah, Ştefan."

Ştefan? Why was he calling?

Maksim listened, expression lifeless. He lowered the phone. "I neded to take this." He gestured at a *farmacie.* "It's a private matter. Forgive me."

A pharmacy didn't strike me as the most private place to take a call, but I didn't want to seem clingy or pushy.

"Sure. No problem."

"Thank you." He started for the pharmacy.

As he neared the door, he did a one-eighty and returned to

me. I was more than a little surprised when he pulled me in for a hug and then wouldn't let go. I slid my hands around his waist, hugging him back, trying to reassure him. But reassure him of what?

"Maksim?"

He drew back, placed a finger to his lips, and shook his head. My gaze flicked to his phone. Whatever was going on, it must have been pretty serious.

He steered the phone away from us and leaned in. "I need to speak with you about something," he whispered. "But I must speak with my cousin first."

Tension twisted my insides the way someone might twist a towel to wring it out. I didn't have a good feeling about this. Even so, I nodded that I understood.

He planted a quiet kiss on my cheek. I hugged myself, thoughts racing, as he disappeared into the pharmacy.

I forced myself to focus—as best I could—and retrieved the scavenger hunt from my purse. Assuming Daniel was right, where did the guidebook fit in? And what about the **numbers** clue?

I reviewed the list. It would've been nice if Dad had used more anagrams. Those were easy compared to other types of clues. When I was a kid, I could glance at a scavenger hunt and tell, almost immediately, if he'd turned a word or name into a—

"Wait." I homed in on ***Boris Funa***. Maksim and I had thought this was someone's name, but what if it was another anagram?

The letters shuffled themselves in my mind's eye. I dug through my purse, found a pen, and jotted a list of new words in the margin.

Abrus Info
Bain Fours
Bonus Fair
For Unbias

Fibrus Na

"Na" was the abbreviation for sodium on the periodic table. I made a note and kept going.

The letters swirled, creating new words. ***Fur Bosnia***. I paced the sidewalk. Had I seen any Bosnian shops?

A muffled shout went up. I tuned it out initially, but then a shriek pierced the otherwise still street. I wheeled around. A motorcycle had toppled over, pinning the rider to the ground. A woman with white hair and round hips squatted, trying to lift the bike.

"Wait wait wait!" I darted across the street. "You can't lift it like that."

"You're American! Oh, thank heavens." The woman stood. "I was going to call the police, but I can't get our phone to work." She pulled out an archaic-looking flip phone. "Can you call them for us?"

"We don't. Need. The police." The man huffed from beneath the bike. He and the woman looked old enough to be somebody's grandparents, and they sported matching Hawaiian shirts. "Get. This. Thing. *Off*," the man growled.

Ty's dad had taught me proper lifting technique, in case any of his bikes fell over, but I hadn't done it with a person trapped underneath. Plus, this bike was huge, something like a touring bike for cross-country travel.

I tucked away the pen and paper and unhooked myself from the travel purse. "Hold this," I said, handing my purse to the lady. Then I mentally reviewed the checklist Ty's dad had made me memorize.

The old man squirmed, face red, and pushed on the bike. It lifted an inch before resettling on him. He moaned.

"Sir? I'm going to need you to hold still." I engaged the kickstand and checked the ignition. The engine was already off.

I squatted beside the bike and then, using my right hand, I gripped the fender. With my left, I gripped one of the handlebars.

Then I backed my butt up against the seat, took a breath, and used my legs to push.

A grunt tumbled out.

I tried again, rocking it back and forth, trying to build momentum. The man screamed. I gritted my teeth and pushed, locking my knees. The bike lifted into a forty-five-degree angle.

The man crawled out. The woman rushed to help him.

When they were clear, I walked the bike back using baby steps. Finally, I had the thing upright and let it drop onto the kickstand.

"Holy crap." I fanned my shirt. "What kind of bike is this?"

"I don't know." The woman dusted off the man's pants. He shooed her away. "Whatever they gave us at the rental place."

"This thing has to weigh seven hundred pounds. If you can't handle a bike this size, you shouldn't be riding it."

"We *weren't* riding it," the man barked. "I couldn't figure the damn thing out, so I was walking it back to the rental agency."

That explained why the engine was off. I was about to offer to drive it back for them when I remembered Maksim.

I pivoted toward the pharmacy and froze. Maksim stood directly behind me, staring at the bike. "Four hundred kilograms."

"Huh?"

"That's how much this bike weighs." He was wearing the long-sleeved knit shirt again. The gray fabric was wrinkled. His hair was disheveled, pointing in all kinds of directions. "Four hundred kilograms. About nine hundred pounds." He pointed a sharp look at me. "Amazing you could lift it."

His sarcasm hit me like a battering ram. I was busted.

"Thank you for helping us." The woman shuffled over and returned my purse. "We're going to leave the motorcycle here and let the rental company come get it. Do you think that will be okay?"

"It has to be okay," the old man snapped. "'Cause that's what we're doin'!"

"Do you need an ambulance?" I asked.

The man harrumphed and waved me off. "Come on, Barb. We're gonna find us one of them rooftop bars. I need a drink." He hobbled up the sidewalk.

The woman followed, fussing over him. He kept shooing her.

Maksim's frosty gaze rested on me. I owed him an explanation.

"My ex was... into bikes. We went to a local bike track occasionally." A lot. "I rode with him a couple of times." More than a couple of times, and plenty by myself. "His dad was paranoid about his bikes falling over, so he taught me proper lifting technique."

"You've said nothing of this." Maksim's expression stabbed cold. "You allowed me to believe you had never ridden before."

"I didn't mean to. This was my ex who cheated on me, and it hurts to talk about or even to think about. All I've wanted to do is forget."

Maksim went silent, but his stare remained chilly. Finally, he said, "We need to work on the clues. I have limited time now."

A black hole opened up in my chest. Emptiness swirled, threatening to suck me in and rip me apart. Was this about the phone call? Was Ştefan making him leave? I wanted to ask, but Maksim's callousness deterred me.

I fumbled with the zipper on my purse. "I-I've been working on the ***Boris Funa*** clue." I pulled out the scavenger hunt. "It might be an anagram rather than someone's name. I've been—" Before I could finish, the old guy's last words came back to me. *"We're gonna find us one of them rooftop bars."*

Bar.

I dug out my phone and navigated to the photos. The ones from Mount Tâmpa appeared first, and my heart wrenched. Maksim had been laughing and smiling just a few minutes ago. Now he was acting... different.

I swallowed the feelings and swiped to the photos from last night. The path I'd taken—up and down Strada Republicii, down each side street—scrolled across my screen. I stopped on the one

I'd thought about. Shadows concealed the building, but a glowing purple sign marked the entrance.

I double-checked the *Boris Funa* clue, and the words reshuffled themselves yet again.

B-A-R...

...and then...

F-U-S-I-O-N.

"This is it!" I lifted my gaze. "***Boris Funa*** is an anagram for Fusion Bar. Maksim, I came across that place last night. See?" I showed him the photo.

His icy stare held steady, his brow furrowed. Dread filled my stomach like dirty, stinky dishwater in a clogged sink.

I lowered my phone. "Maksim?"

He blinked, eyebrows parting. "Fusion Bar. I've heard of it." He turned away. "Daniel can wait if you'd like to go there first."

26. KEY

We found Fusion Bar tucked away in a narrow alley, which branched off from Strada Republicii. Neon-lit beer signs decorated the walls. Stale cigarette smoke saturated the air.

A dark-haired woman watched us from behind the bar. "Drink?" she asked, rolling her *R*.

Maksim held up a finger. *"Apă."* Water.

"Can I get one, too?" I asked, fanning myself.

His jaw tightened, and a wave of emotion crashed into me. I reached for him. He dodged, and the sharp tip of a dagger slid into my heart. I was about to tell him "never mind" when he turned to the woman and changed his order.

She set two bottles of water on the bar. Her bored stare held steady while Maksim fished out his wallet. She glanced at me, and then her expression widened.

I smiled politely, despite feeling like I might cry.

Maksim handed her the cash and grabbed the bottles. "Here," he said, passing me one.

I broke the cap and lifted the bottle to my lips. The woman was still staring at me, so I did an about-face and crossed the room, gulping my water along the way. A purple couch sat against the far wall. Pool tables filled the rear of the bar.

Maksim gravitated to a TV mounted in the corner. A soccer match was on, and he paused to watch before continuing to the pool tables.

I angled for some black-and-white photos displayed on a wall. The pictures weren't framed, and I didn't recognize the people or places, but I figured I should examine them.

Footsteps approached. A hand gripped my arm and pulled me around. My bottle tipped, and water spilled out. "Hey!"

The woman had followed me. She was jabbering in Romanian.

Maksim returned and held up a calming hand. She directed a question to him, and he replied with my name. The woman crossed herself, muttering, and hurried behind the bar.

"What's going on?" I asked.

"She seems to know you."

"How? My dad?"

"I'm trying to figure that out." Maksim's expression was a blank slate.

Papers rustled. Glasses clinked. The woman returned from the bar, and Maksim translated what she said next. "A man came in here and provided her with your name. He showed her a photo of you." Maksim waited, listening. "You were young in the photo, a child, and you were with a friend. He would not allow her to have the photo, but he insisted she take notes about your description"—another pause as he listened—"so that she would know who to give the key to."

"What key?" I asked.

The woman opened her hand, revealing a key. The blade was skinny, the tip flat, while tiny ridges ran along one side.

I plucked the key from her hand, and she started jabbering again. Maksim's eyes lit with surprise. "The man who gave her this was with Invest Romania. He was here last December and asked this favor of her. She complied for the same reasons as the owner of Brasserie de l'Arte."

"Because Invest Romania had been helping her business?"

"Precisely."

My emotions swelled. "She has to be talking about my dad. He used to carry old photos of me in his wallet."

The woman said something else. Maksim perked up.

"The man used her mobile phone to call and SMS someone." Maksim let her continue. "She thinks he was contacting... you." He focused on me, eyes squinty. "Is there something else you're not telling me?"

"What? No."

"Are you certain?" His jaw flexed. "Because if there is, now is the time to share it."

"Why would I—?" My argument skidded to a stop. "The blocker app," I said as the epiphany crash-landed. "If my dad tried to reach me from someone else's phone, he wouldn't have gotten through. Any calls or messages would have been blocked."

His squint deepened. "Wouldn't he have known that?"

I bit on my lip. Heat seeped into my eyes.

"No. Do not become emotional." He grabbed me, harshness cutting into his features. A shadowy tone cloaked his voice. "You need to concentrate. This is important."

"Maksim, stop." I tried to twist out of his grasp. "Why are you acting like this?"

The light returned to his eyes. He released me and stared at his hands.

"I never told my dad about the app." I sniffled, massaging my wrist. "He would have been really upset if he'd known why I was using it. It had to do with my mom and her creepy friends."

The woman said something and extended her phone. Message bubbles from a text-messaging thread filled her screen. I clapped a hand over my mouth.

Kat, darling, it's me again. I have been trying to call. I cannot get through.

Have you received my other messages?

I'm running out of time. Text or call this number as soon as you receive this.

"Oh my God." A tidal wave of emotions swelled, threatening to snap my composure in half. "I can't believe it."

"We need to know what's in those other messages," Maksim said. "How are they blocked? Does the app autodelete them, or are they stored somewhere?"

"Stored, but I rarely check that folder. I didn't check it all after my dad died. I knew Ty would be texting, and I didn't want to see his messages."

"Are the blocked messages purged after a time?" Maksim's attention fell to my purse. "Do you think the app may have saved them since December?"

"The app saves them, but this isn't my phone." I touched the outer pocket, pressing on the pint-sized smartphone. "It's an old one Brandy kept as a spare."

He leveled a look at me.

"It's true. I couldn't afford to lose or break mine."

"You told me you have the app on *that* phone." He said it like I might have been making the whole thing up.

"I do, but it's not a cloud-based service. If those messages still exist, they'd be on *that* device. Not this one."

His intense stare relented. He sighed, wiping a hand down his face. "So then we would need to physically have your other phone."

"Brandy has it." I gasped. "She knows about the app. I could have her check the blocked messages!"

"Do it." Maksim grilled the woman while I yanked out my phone—Brandy's spare phone—and swiped a text.

> Need you to power up my phone and check the blocker app.

> There's a folder where the blocked messages are saved. Can you tell me how far back they go? Looking for something my dad might've sent.

"Brandy's good about—" I hesitated.

Maksim was listening to the woman, and a new level of confusion twisted through his features.

"What's wrong?" I asked.

"Your father told this woman to be expecting you. But he also told her to be expecting me."

"You? That's impossible."

My phone vibrated.

BEE

> OMW to work. What's up?

> Anyone else home?

"Let me see the scavenger hunt." Maksim held out his hand.

I slipped the paper out of my purse and passed it to him. My phone vibrated again.

BEE

> My dad went to Mass. My mom's helping with a baby shower. No idea where Bianca and Brady are.

I groaned. Brandy had two siblings—a younger brother named Brady who wasn't even driving age and an older sister named Bianca who was a bookworm with no social life. They were almost always home. Except for today, apparently.

Maksim was going over the clues with the woman. She pointed at one, and he asked her something. When she replied with "*da*," Maksim produced his wallet and pulled out a stack of lei.

"Why are you giving her money?" I asked.

"Your father promised her additional payment upon delivery of the key." He counted out several two-hundred-lei banknotes.

My jaw went slack. "He wouldn't have promised her *that* much."

"Perhaps not, but I believe she just solved one of the clues." He showed me which one.

"*Three of clubs?*" I said. "You mean, the casinos?"

"Not casino," the woman said, her accent dripping. "Club. Eez called Trinity *Club*."

Maksim woke up his phone and did a search for *Trinity Club Braşov*. The club's online listing had photos, and he'd stopped on a pic of their entrance.

I gasped.

TRINITY CLUB WAS six hundred meters from Fusion Bar. We navigated the crowds of Strada Republicii and turned onto a side street.

A long line of traffic stacked a road called Poartă Şchei. We followed pedestrians through the crosswalk, and Maksim angled for a two-story merchant house.

We entered the building and found ourselves in a foyer. A set of double doors stood to our right, each marked with a logo. Same logo Maksim had shown me online.

A white number three scrawled into a black suit of clubs.

Maksim yanked open one of the doors. Normally, he would have held it for me. This time, he walked straight through and let the door fall shut in my face. Uneasiness filled every crack and crevice of my being.

I pushed through the door and stepped inside. The club dropped down into a lounge with leather couches and chairs. Lo-Fi electronica streamed through overhead speakers.

A bartender greeted us, saying something about drinks. Maksim declined, and the man went back to cleaning glasses.

"We're here." Maksim treaded down the staircase. "So what's the strategy?"

"Same strategy we've had this entire time—look around, see if anything reminds us of the clues."

"Except you never found your father's old address." He paused at the bottom of the staircase. "That may be vital in light of that key you now possess."

"Yeah." I tightened my grip on the key, which I'd been carrying since Fusion Bar. "I know."

He waited, as if I might say something else. When I didn't, he muttered under his breath.

A knot tangled in the pit of my stomach. "Maksim, please. You know I'm bad at talking about stuff, and I don't think you're holding the bike thing against me. What's really going on?"

A pained expression drew lines across his forehead. He averted his gaze.

"Is this about the call you got? From your cousin?"

He nodded.

"What happened?"

His mouth formed around an answer. He hesitated, refusing to look at me.

"Things aren't working out as I had hoped," he finally said.

Was he talking about leaving their operation? Something to do with me? Both?

I touched his arm.

He removed himself from my reach. "You look around here," he said, backing up. "I'll check the other side of the club." He pivoted and angled for a row of slot machines.

Movement tugged at my vision. I turned in time to find a guy descending the staircase. The bartender offered him the same greeting he'd offered us.

The guy held up a hand, bypassing the bar and entering the lounge area. "I don't speak Romanian, mate." He sounded British. His accent was working-class—clipped, informal.

"Would you like a drink?" the bartender said, switching to English.

"Not right yet, mate. I'm meetin' someone." He craned his neck, scanning the room. I was the only one in there, and we naturally made eye contact. I managed a smile. He gave a polite nod and parked himself on a leather couch.

A mural on the wall depicted a roulette wheel, stacks of chips, and playing cards. A row of slot machines glittered in the corner, flashing cherries, sevens, stars, and pots of gold.

The sound of a door shutting echoed in the background. *"Sunt aici!"* I'm here.

A guy plodded down the staircase.

"Dead chuffed to see ya, mate." The Brit stood and greeted the newcomer with a handshake that turned into a guy-hug, the kind that's quick and followed by a pat on the shoulder or back. "Shall we go check out the flat, then?"

"Let's go. I am ready." The other guy sounded local, his accent dense and rich.

They headed for the stairs.

Maksim loitered on the other side of the club. He had the travel guidebook out while he studied the slot machines. After making his way down that row, he aimed for a spiral staircase and twisted his way to the top.

He reappeared a minute later and descended. "Toilets are upstairs," he said, striding across the club. "I haven't found anything of significance."

"There's a mural on the wall if you want to—"

"Oi! You."

I pivoted toward the shout. The Brit was coming down the main staircase while his Romanian friend waited at the entrance. I thought they'd left.

"Do ya see me wallet o'er there, love?" the Brit asked.

I pointed at myself. "Me?"

"Yeah, you. Do ya see me wallet?"

I scanned the floor. Sure enough, a lump of leather sat on the floor. I scooped it up.

"Now don' go nickin' me quid." Both sides of his mouth cranked up. He closed the gap and plucked the wallet out of my hand. "Thanks, love." He winked. "Try an' stay out of trouble, right?"

My attention darted to Maksim. I watched his expression go from slightly perplexed to W.T.F.

"That was cozy," he said as the Brit jogged up the stairs. "Friend of yours?"

"He was in here a second ago. I have no idea why he talked to me like that. I literally never said one word to him."

Maksim rolled his eyes.

"What? It's true. I was looking around while he was waiting for—" My stomach did a somersault. "He was waiting for his friend. I overheard them say they were checking out a flat. Doesn't that mean apartment?"

Maksim's attention swung to the entrance. "Did he say if the flat was in this building?"

"He didn't, but this building is pretty big. Too big for just a club."

Maksim was across the room before I could finish the sentence. I chased him up the stairs and through the double doors.

"There's no elevator," I said, my voice reverberating through the foyer.

"I'm aware." He angled for a door I hadn't noticed until then. It opened to a stairwell. The Brit's voice echoed from above us, fading until a door snapped shut.

We followed the same path and pushed through a door that dumped us into a hallway. Maksim split his attention between the doors lining each side of the hall. He had the guidebook out, and he seemed to be checking the apartment numbers.

"What are we looking for?" I asked.

"Page numbers."

My eyebrows converged. "Why?"

"The page number for *Orientation* is one. *Eating Out* is three. *Things to See* is seven."

The answer socked me in the gut. We were looking for apartment 137.

Apartment 117 appeared on our left; 118 on our right. We continued until the hallway ended in a T. We turned right, then doubled back.

We stopped. There, at the very end of this side hall, stood a single door all by itself. Apartment 137.

I walked forward, fingers wrapped in a fist, the key biting into my palm. Hope hung in the air. I inhaled a shaky breath, desperate for the key to fit in the lock.

And it did. The slender brass rectangle slid into the handle. I twisted... and twisted and twisted. I wasn't sure how many rotations I'd done before...

Click.

I looked at Maksim, and he looked at me. Neither of us spoke for a long moment. Eventually, he said, "We should probably go in."

I pushed open the door, and we stepped inside. The living room was bare—no furniture, no TV.

Maksim closed and locked the door while I continued to the bedroom. "There's no bed," I called, "but there is an office desk."

I tugged on the drawers—there were only two—and peered inside. "Empty."

"Kat."

I returned to the kitchen and found Maksim holding up a lockbox. A combination lock fastened the lid shut. "Any idea what the combination may be?" he asked.

"I guess... try one-three-seven."

He examined the lock. "It's a four-digit combination."

"Put a zero in front."

He tried and then shook his head.

"The zero in back?"

That didn't work, either.

"Try my birthday—June second, 2001."

"You mean today." Maksim slanted a look. "Precisely when were you planning to share that bit of information?"

My emotions had been swirling, but this struck a nerve. "You want to know when I was planning to share that?" I snapped. "Never, okay? Because I don't celebrate my birthday." I stepped up and stared at him, dead-on, until he met my gaze. "I don't like to talk about my birthday or even *think* about it because it brings back horrible memories of ambulance rides and ER visits. Would you like to know why?" I folded my arms and cocked my head. "Well?"

His Adam's apple dipped. He didn't otherwise move.

"Because of my mom, Maksim. My selfish, drug-addicted mother managed to do something traumatizing every year, and now I can't even enjoy my own birthday. *That's* why I didn't mention anything—not because I was hiding some big secret from you."

Remorse flickered in his eyes. He blinked it away and shoved the numbers into place. The lock didn't budge, and he knocked the metal box aside. *"Este vrăjeală."* It's a scam.

We tried my dad's birthday.

Our old address.

Old phone numbers.

The last four of my social—I couldn't remember the last four of Dad's.

"Are there any locksmiths we could—?" A memory whispered to me, interrupting the question I was about to ask. *The archives room. My conversation with Andrei.* "How did you order the numbers for my birthday?"

"Two, six, zero, one," Maksim said.

That was the European way—two and then six. Second of June.

"Try switching the first two numbers. That's how we write it in America—six and then two. June second."

He pushed the digits into place and tugged. This time the lock released. His mouth popped open, and he took a surprised step back.

I rushed forward and opened the box.

A stack of folded-up papers popped out, expanding like an accordion. Dad's chicken scratch filled each page, front and back.

Maksim stationed himself by a window in the living room. He parted the blinds and peeked outside, as if checking for something. Or someone?

I was about to ask him what he was doing when he reeled in his attention and pointed it at me. "I need you to read all of that. Out loud."

27. REVELATION

"'To my darling Kat,'" I read. "'If you're reading this, it means I have not made it—'" I faltered, skimming the next lines and down into the next paragraph. Apologies and I-love-yous sprinkled the page.

My eyes misted. "He's apologizing for stuff that happened when I was a kid, stuff to do with my mom. Maksim—"

"It's private?" His expression dulled another degree. "Begin with what's relevant to the scavenger hunt and his business trip. Do not leave anything out."

I moved to the second page. "'As you know, I left Romania during the revolution, but not for the reasons you believe. My father, your grandfather, is Vasile Braţiu. He was a high-ranking member of the Nomenklatura—the elite within the Party.'" I peered over at Maksim. "What's he talking about? What party?"

"*Partidul Comunist Român,*" he said flatly. "The Romanian Communist Party."

I gripped the papers. My grandfather was a communist?

"'My father and I have been estranged since 1989. Many years went by where he did not search for me and many more where he did. This was why I never accepted any European projects. I had hoped he would never find me, but one day he walked into Gypsy Django—'"

I hesitated, attention flashing to Maksim. His eyes darkened. There was no covering up the restaurant thing now, and I decided to come clean before the letter revealed much more. "Um, Maksim?"

"Keep reading."

"But I have to—"

"Keep. Reading." He turned away and propped his shoulder against the wall.

"'My father sought my forgiveness,'" I continued weakly, "'as well as the forgiveness of Kotfas, whose family he had wronged in 1950 when he sent Kotfas's relative to'"—I struggled to read Dad's chicken scratch—"'Pitesti, uh...?"

"Piteşti," Maksim corrected. "It was a prison the Stalinists turned into a gulag. Communist reeducation. Horrific things happened at Piteşti. Unspeakable things."

My insides shriveled.

According to Dad, Vasile had tried to make restitution to Mr. Kotfas's family by paying their business debts and helping with the restaurant. Same thing he'd done for Fusion Bar and Brasserie de l'Arte.

"'My father returned home to Sibiu, and we carried out our communication secretly. This was difficult for me, but I felt obligated due to a terminal cancer diagnosis he has received. To further complicate matter, my older brother died just this past year, and his son—my nephew, who has a terrible reputation here—isn't to be trusted. He would commit great evil with so much wealth, and my father cannot conscionably permit such a bequeathal upon his passing. Therefore, he—my father, your grandfather—has made me the sole inheritor of his estate.'"

My mouth dropped open. He... *what?*

"'We planned for him to meet you upon his next visit,'" I read in a rush, "'but his health deteriorated, and returning to the United States wasn't possible. There was more legal paperwork that needed to be filed as well as other business to attend to, but instead of conducting our business long distance, I decided to visit him in person. That was when I announced my trip to you.'"

I squinted at the next lines. Dad's squiggles were near-impossible to read, as if he'd suddenly realized he needed to hurry. *Or he abruptly realized he was out of time.*

"What does it say?" Maksim demanded.

"Two of his father's men picked him up from the airport and drove him to Sibiu—I guess that's where Vasile's estate was. The men took my dad's phone and wouldn't give it back." I squinted harder and gasped. "They locked him in a room with Vasile, who was already being held captive. Someone helped them escape. Vasile's... assistant?" I shook my head. "Personal assistant."

Maksim crossed the room and snatched the papers.

"What are you doing?"

He read them silently until he finished every single page, including everything I had skipped over. "Your grandfather has been liquidating his assets and moving the funds to a foreign bank," Maksim said. "He's been doing this gradually over several months because he's afraid of his grandson. His fear heightened after the cancer diagnoses when suspicious things began to happen."

"What suspicious things? Why won't you let me read it?"

He ignored me. "Do you not realize who your grandfather was? Do you not understand any of this?"

"No! I don't!"

"I suppose you don't know about a locket either." His attention fell to the papers. "The one your father sent with the scavenger hunt."

My throat closed.

He pushed the papers into my hands. "Where is it?"

"At my hostel in Bucharest." I ambled into the kitchen. "I didn't want to lose it, so I left it there."

"Why did you never mention it?" Maksim followed me.

"Andrei said your parents were killed by Gypsies, and I think maybe the locket's inscription might be written in the language of the Gypsies." Bile rose in my throat. I set the papers aside. "That's why I didn't want to talk about Gypsy Django. Andrei warned me not to broach the topic."

"How does your father know Levi Pavel?"

"Why? Was that in the letter, too?" I glanced at the pages.

Maksim stood behind me, his back and shoulders stiff, hands on hips. "Answer the question."

"I'm not sure how they met if that's what you mean." I faced him. "All I know is that Levi was an old friend of his who died during the revolution."

"No. He did not." Maksim's matter-of-factness plowed into me.

I blinked. "He did."

Maksim snatched the papers and sifted through them. He held one of the pages toward me. "Go ahead. Read it for yourself."

I read through Dad's explanation and lost the ability to breathe. The woman at Fusion Bar had been expecting someone to arrive with me. She'd assumed it was Maksim. It was actually Levi Pavel.

"His name was on the customs form," I whispered, more to myself. "It was a clue. Dad had made everything else on the form illegible so I would focus on the name." I should have realized. Everything was right there the whole time.

Silence filled the kitchen. I looked up from the letter and found myself alone. "Maksim?" I raced out of the kitchen and rounded the corner. The front door was open, and Maksim was going through it.

I chased him down. "Where are you going?"

He stopped but wouldn't look at me. "I put my hand in the fire for you."

"Maksim, I'm so sorry. I swear I didn't mean to—"

"Ştefan has learned of your father's connection to the Traveler. He tried to tell me." Maksim clenched a fist. "I didn't want to believe him."

"The Traveler? What are you talking about?"

"Your father's friend, Levi Pavel"—Maksim's eyes pinched shut—"*is* the Traveler, the same man who killed my parents."

His words hung there, suspended between us in the stagnant air. I wanted to grab them, to tear them down until they weren't words anymore, until they weren't real. But all I could manage to say was "Wh-what? How is that—? *What?*"

"Andrei told you Gypsies killed them. It's true, but Pavel gave the order. He is not ethnically Gypsy but is something of a cult leader to them. So they did as he said..."

"No."

"...and drove the van into the crowd. I don't blame them. I blame the Traveler and the man who funded his radical agenda. Your grandfather, Vasile Bra\u0163iu."

Maksim's explanation slammed into me. I swayed. "That can't be right." *Can it?* I touched his arm. "Maksim, please. There has to be another explanation. Maybe—"

He caught my wrist. His other hand squared against my chest, and he drove me against the wall. I let out a cry. "Your father left you a warning in the letter—do not involve the police. I'm giving you the same warning." Maksim's voice fell into a dark whisper. "They are corrupt to the highest echelons, and my cousin is deeply connected to the most dishonest among them. If you go to them, they will inform him. You do not want that to happen."

Blood pulsed in my ears.

"Do not contact me. Do not attempt to follow me. If you do, you will find yourself in deep waters with no way out. Do you understand?" He slapped the wall, and I flinched. "Answer me."

"Yes." The word spilled out, more of a wisp than a reply. I swallowed and tried again. "Y-yes."

His knifelike expression smoothed. He released me. "You need to go home. Do not stay in Romania, and do *not* go looking for the Traveler." He turned the corner and disappeared into the main hall.

His footsteps faded, taking my tattered heart—and any sliver of hope I'd been hanging on to—with them.

———

DAD'S LETTER stared up at me. I stared back, bleary-eyed and heartbroken.

> I'm so sorry for lying to you, my darling. I couldn't risk my family finding me. Finding us. I had to protect you and your mother, and the only solution I could devise was to live this lie, saying (and believing at times) that my loved ones had perished in the revolution.

I leaned against the window on my right. The landscape moved at the pace of the train—not fast or slow but somewhere painfully in between. Jagged mountains reached into the sky, the sun dipping below the peaks and leaving a burst of deep gold in their wake.

I blinked away my grief and skimmed another part of the letter.

> My father has done many evil things for which he carries tremendous guilt. Eight years ago, he set out to make things right with the families he wronged.
> These families would not receive him. One woman cursed him, saying he had killed her parents and

*that he should never be permitted to ease his
conscience.*

*My father realized, if he was ever going to
make recompense, he would need to do so in secret
(how I've wished he had done this with Kotfas).
And so, with the help of his assistant, he created
something called Invest Romania...*

Vasile had been the angel investor behind Invest Romania. Popescu had been his personal assistant. They hadn't been keeping tabs on local businesses. They'd been looking for ways to help the families of the people my grandfather had wronged during the Ceauşescu regime.

Two sliding doors swished open.

A man in a blue uniform and navy cap entered the train car. He carried a handheld machine and paused at each row while passengers showed their tickets.

I focused on the last part of the letter.

*I hope you've brought the locket. If not, have
someone ship it to you as quickly as possible
(important information is contained within it). Show
it to Levi if you haven't already. Years ago, when
we took a day trip to Sighişoara, an old peddler
attempted to sell us a locket just like it. This one
opens in the same manner.*

*When you get to where you're going, think about
the fables I told you as a child. One in particular
is supposed to assist in locating a lockbox similar
to the one containing this letter.*

This other lockbox was hidden on or perhaps very near to a hill. We don't know where, precisely. Even Popescu doesn't know. He and my father planned it this way in case any of us are captured.

Kat, you must find the lockbox. It has the passcode needed to access the bank account my father set up. That is the only way to gain control of his assets, and you must do so before his grandson (my nephew) devises a scheme for seizing the funds. I don't see how he could, but my father is convinced he will manage a way in due time.

Know this... I believe the gold locket to be a clue. If I'm correct, Levi's assistance will prove especially useful.

My phone vibrated from inside my purse.

BEE

Checked the blocker app. There was one message, and it was from Ty. Dave thinks you did a factory reset. Could that've deleted what you're looking for?

Disappointment sank to the bottom of my being. Now I'd never know what Dad had said.

The conductor reached my row, and the people across the aisle held up their tickets. I held up mine. Daniel had bought it for me, which was really nice of him considering what happened. He and Madă had a confrontation with Maksim, and they'd still been shaken up when I reached the guesthouse. By that time, Maksim had been long gone.

The conductor returned my ticket, tipped his hat, and continued to the next row. I clutched the letter and stared out the window. Coolness seeped from the glass, spreading across my face. Emptiness spread through my heart.

The scenery breezed past as the train skated along the tracks. Day dissolved into night, and the sky melted into layers of rich orange and tea rose pink.

"Do not go looking for the Traveler." Maksim's warning shook loose from the fallout. I didn't believe Dad could have been friends with someone who was so dangerous. That was the whole reason he'd estranged himself from Vasile. Still, what if Maksim was right? What if there were things Dad hadn't known about Levi? His friend might have been living a double life.

But that didn't make sense, either.

I sifted through the pages, looking for the scavenger hunt. I had one more clue to solve, and now I knew how to solve it. But should I? Because doing so meant finding the one person I wasn't supposed go looking for.

The Traveler, Levi Pavel.

BUCHAREST

UKRAINE
HUNGARY
MOLDOVA
ROMÂNIA
Brasov
SERBIA
București
BULGARIA

28. REPEAT

I powered up the walkway and headed for the rectorate. My eyes stung. My heart felt like it had been smashed into a million pieces.

Morning sunlight glistened over the dewy grass. A slight chill hung in the air, and for a split second, I thought I was in Braşov.

But I was in Bucharest, not Transylvania. And I was alone, not with Maksim. My insides tangled.

People in business attire carried satchels and messenger bags up the front steps. Each person paused at the entrance, as if checking something. I couldn't tell what.

I drew in a breath, fixed my travel purse, and forced my shaky legs to climb. If I could find someone to help me—someone other than the Wicked Witch of Bucharest—I'd know if I had really solved this last remaining clue.

I had already figured out the anagrams—*drs sade* being "address" and *dreads finds* being "find address"—and I thought I had figured out the main part of the clue, too.

„*Am fost profesor la Universitatea Politehnica din Bucureşti.*"

Translation: **"*I was a professor at the Polytechnic University of Bucharest.*"**

I'd been *sure* Dad was referring to himself. But when he started talking about Levi in the letter, I realized this clue had been pointing to *him*. To Levi. That was why Dad had listed Levi's name on the custom's form. These were all subtle clues I had missed.

If I was right, that meant Levi had also been a professor at this university. That could have been how they'd met, why they'd become friends. I honestly wasn't sure about that part, but if that was the case, then it was Levi's address I should have been looking for. Not Dad's.

And that was the reason I'd come back, despite everything that happened last time. Instead of trying to get Dad's records, I was going to see if I could get Levi's. Somehow.

I pushed out a breath, reached for the door... and froze. An announcement had been taped to the entrance, and a picture of me—eyes round, mouth open—filled the center.

"What the—?" I picked at the tape and peeled the paper away from the glass. Bold red letters blotted the page, forming sentences I couldn't read. But there was one word I recognized.

Poliţia. Police.

I dug out my phone and plugged the other words into a translator app. The notice instructed anyone who saw me to call the police and notify the administrators.

My shoulders slumped. I'd been hoping the secretary was bluffing, or at the very least that she hadn't had time to follow through. Clearly, I'd been wrong.

Someone exited the building. I threw my hand up and turned my head, pretending to block out the sun. The woman bypassed me and shuffled down the stairs. Her dress shoes clacked across the pavement.

I moved away from the door but not before someone else came through it. I swore under my breath, turning again.

The girl hoisted her backpack and sashayed down the steps. My gaze drifted over her petite frame, her raven hair, her faded corduroys. Shock rattled through me. "Paty?"

She wheeled around. Our gazes locked, and her jaw collapsed. "You should not be here," she said, waving me away from the entrance.

I double-timed it down the stairs and followed her onto the sidewalk. We passed students and a professor. Paty offered a friendly greeting to each person. I feigned extreme interest in something in the distance.

Paty veered off the sidewalk and ducked behind a tree. I joined her, my running shoes squishing in the wet grass. Weird. The ground hadn't been this dewy since I'd been in Romania.

"Well." I held up the announcement. "Looks like things haven't calmed down."

Her expression fell. "Is big problem."

"I'm really sorry. I didn't mean to cause any trouble."

"Problem is not with you. Problem is with the hearts of peoples." She patted my arm. "You come back because you need the file of your father, yes?"

"His friend's file, actually. I think he must have worked here, too." I navigated through my phone, searching for an old photo I'd taken of the customs form.

I found the photo and showed Paty. She gasped.

"I know this man." She pointed at Levi's name. *"Gadjo dilo."*

"I don't speak Romanian."

"Is not Romanian. Is Romani Cib. The language of *my* people. Roma people."

"Roma?"

"We are called *Țigani*, Gypsies, but you can say Roma. Is better maybe." She dipped inside her neckline and pulled out her cross, fidgeting, glancing around. *"Gadjo dilo* is meaning 'stranger crazy.' No... 'Crazy stranger.' This *gadjo* is living with my people, but he is not one of us. He did crazy things during communism days, dangerous things. I hear stories."

Her English broke across her accent in hard-to-understand pieces, but when she said that last part my last glimmer of hope disintegrated. Levi really was a dangerous man. Maksim had been right.

"What will you need from his file?" She glanced at the building. "My friend is working. She can help."

"I-I needed his address, but—"

"Oh! I can give to you this information. We don't need file. I show you." She pulled her backpack around and tugged on the zipper.

A moment later, she had her phone out and a web browser loaded. *"Gadjo* is living here, in Crețulești. Is going near Pitești." She held the phone toward me.

Tiny red dashes marked out a supersmall section of the map.

"We are here. See?" Paty zoomed out and pointed at Bucharest. "Pitești is here. Do you know this city? There is a museum and tours." She used two fingers, dragging the map until Pitești appeared.

Maksim had mentioned that place. He'd said it was a prison.

"And here, *gadjo dilo* is living in Crețulești." Paty centered the map between the two cities and pointed at the red marker. "I take you."

"Sorry, Paty. I'm not—" I felt myself go pale. "I can't, um—"

Paty peered at me. "You no feel good?"

"Yeah." I looked away. "I'm not feeling good."

"I give you my telephone number, okay? And when you are feeling better, I go with you to see *gadjo dilo*." She nodded, spurring me on. "Maybe tomorrow. After classes."

"I don't think that's—"

"Take number. Please." She nudged me.

I sighed and pulled out my phone. She entered her name and number in my contacts and pressed Save.

"I have to go now." I tucked away my phone. "I'll... message you later."

Paty's mouth lifted on both sides, her expression all flowers and sunshine. "I am happy to see you. I hope for good days for you. No more rain in your heart."

A tide swelled against my sternum. I tried to smile and then powered down the walkway—except now there was less powering and more *try not to have an emotional breakdown.*

I wadded up the announcement as I crossed campus. A plastic bin bracketed a telephone pole on the adjacent sidewalk. I chucked the piece of paper. Okay, so now what?

Hostel. I should go back to the hostel and think, process. This was the end of my trip, so going home early would be a waste of money—but Paty's offer was still on the table. Then again, that was more of a temptation. No matter how crazy this whole thing was, the end result wasn't worth risking my life over.

Right?

I trekked up the sidewalk. Parked cars crammed both sides of the street. One car had been driven up onto the curb—fully, with both front tires—in order to squeeze into a space. The rear of the car jutted into the street.

The Uber driver must have dropped me off on another side of campus, because I didn't recognize this street. I reached for my phone and then hesitated. I didn't have internet, so I wouldn't be able to log into the ride-sharing app.

A line of traffic waited at the next intersection, and a blaze of bright yellow plucked at my vision. "Hey!" I hurried across the street, waving.

The cabbie's back seat was empty. He rolled down his window, and I could have sworn I detected an eye roll.

"*Nu*," he snapped. "Taxi is not—" His stare trailed over me, and he drew back in his seat. "You... need ride?"

"To Strada Olimpului. Near Old Town."

He nodded, pressing a button. His door locks disengaged.

I dropped into his back seat as the traffic light slipped into green. The cars ahead of us moved forward. My guy picked up speed, navigating the dense traffic.

His gaze met mine in the rearview mirror. "Uh, you are...?" He didn't seem to know the word he needed.

"Tourist," I said. "Not a student."

"Ah." He reached for his phone, which was mounted on the dash. "Address?"

I gave him the address of my hostel. I might have been off by a digit, but the sequence was close enough to get us into the neighborhood.

A buzz rumbled from my purse. I pulled out my phone, thinking it was probably Brandy while pathetically hoping it was Maksim. I woke up the screen, and disappointment slinked through me. There was no message. I must have heard the cabbie's phone.

The thought of Maksim tore at my insides. I dipped into the pocket of my shorts—same shorts I'd been wearing yesterday— and fished out the Romanian-flag lapel pin. Sunlight glistened over the tricolored bands. *"It's my gift to you. To remember your trip."*

A stab of pain, hot and fresh, entered my chest. My bottom lip quivered.

I unzipped my purse, planning to tuck the pin away. The cabbie took a hard right, banging me against the door. The pin popped out of my fingers. My purse tumbled across the back seat, contents spilling.

The driver straightened us out, and I finally sat up and took notice of our surroundings. Cement tower blocks rose up on either side of us, an array of antennas and satellite dishes sprouting from the rooftops. Graffiti covered the ground floor of each building.

"Excuse me, but... where are we?"

The cabbie's attention returned to the rearview mirror. "Who?"

"Where?" I said, correcting him. *"Unde?"*

The man smiled and nodded. Did he not understand?

I leaned forward. "Sir? This isn't Old Town."

"Yes, yes. We take shortcut. Less traffic."

What was he talking about? There was no traffic. We were the only vehicle on the road. Correction: the only *functioning* vehicle. There were plenty of stripped-down, abandoned cars sitting off to the side. Trash blanketed the streets and sidewalks, and a sour odor crawled up my nose. My stomach lurched.

The cabbie turned down a side street and crushed the brakes.

I grabbed my phone. I'd saved a memo with important info, including my hostel's address and phone number. "I'm getting you the exact address, okay? Just give me a second."

He didn't reply.

I was about to repeat myself when a lanky form emerged from an alley up ahead. Was that... Drago?

A stocky frame appeared in the rearview mirror. I twisted around, and my eyes bulged. Émilien.

I banged on the driver's seat, screaming for him to go. He killed the engine.

Swearing, I fumbled for my phone and whatever else I could grab. My purse ended up strapped across me and then I launched out of the cab.

Footsteps pounded the pavement. Drago and Émilien were chasing me. Why? Something to do with Maksim? I didn't know the answer, but I had definitely been delivered here, and now these guys were after me.

I knew myself well enough to realize I couldn't outrun them. But I might be able to outmaneuver them.

An alley appeared on my left. I turned in... and slammed straight into a ten-foot cyclone fence. The links rattled, and tears climbed into my eyes. "Dammit!"

Drago and Émilien rounded the corner. Black and blue marks rimmed Émilien's eye. The cheek below was puffy and pink. From that night at the club.

"Wh-what are you doing here?" I backed against the fence. "What do you want?"

A sly grin played across the Frenchman's lips. He and Drago shared a look that made my gut churn.

A shadow suddenly fell across them. Heavy footsteps treaded up the sidewalk. Someone was coming.

"Help! Please help me!"

Émilien peered that direction and chuckled.

The source of the footsteps reached the alley. Broad shoulders appeared, and a tall, sculpted silhouette took shape in the morning sunlight. The guy placed a hand on the Frenchman's shoulder—a friendly greeting that said *I'm here*.

My heart cracked all the way down the middle. It was Maksim.

29. RUN

"No!" I slumped against the fence.

"Aww." Émilien made a pouty face. "Did the American believe someone was here to rescue her? Mm?"

Maksim's eyes remained dull, lifeless—the same way they'd looked in Vasile's secret flat.

Drago grinned and stalked forward.

"Stop." I put a hand up. "Don't come any closer. I'm warning you."

Drago hesitated.

Maksim said something sarcastic in Romanian. Drago barked in response, pointing at me. Émilien stood by with a smirk.

I was about to start pleading for my life when Maksim's attention shifted. He tilted his head, eyes focused on something behind me.

I traced his line of sight to a gate. It was secured with a padlock and chain, but the chain was loose.

I threw myself at the gate and rammed it open. Hands swiped at me. I slipped through but then jerked to a stop, held in place by my purse. I lifted the strap over my head and crashed to the ground. One of my arms landed in a puddle.

I twisted around. Maksim had my purse while Émilien and Drago stood on either side of him, scowling.

My attention moved to everything scattered on the ground—phone, wallet, locket, passport. Dad's words rushed back. *I hope you've brought the locket. Important information is contained within it.*

Maksim's gaze followed mine.

I swore and lunged. He lunged, too, reaching through the gate—but he went for my phone while I went for the locket. I clutched the necklace, scrambled to my feet, and sprinted deeper into the alley.

The chain-links clattered, and footsteps stampeded after me. I risked a glance. Émilien and Drago had jumped the fence. Where was Maksim?

Trash cans blurred past me. My feet splashed through another puddle. I counted... one, two, three, four, five.

Splash, splash. Splash, splash. Drago and Émilien went through the same puddle. They were only five seconds behind me.

Smaller alleys branched off to the sides. I hung a right, still clutching the locket, and found myself sprinting through a narrow corridor *full* of hypodermic needles. Queasiness swept through my stomach.

I kept running.

The alley dumped me into a courtyard surrounded by crumbly cement apartments. A dilapidated fire escape hung from the backside of one building. Vines crawled up the wall.

I stopped beside a cracked cement fountain. Was this the same fountain from the other night? I didn't have time to figure it out before Maksim materialized on the other side of the courtyard.

My attention shifted to a grimy door. I dashed for it and tried the handle. Locked.

Émilien and Drago barreled into the courtyard as my attention returned to the fire escape. The ladder was too high, but a wall climb might give me enough upward momentum to reach the first rung. Maybe.

I stuffed the locket in my pocket and backed up. Then I launched into a sprint with Émilien and Drago bearing down on me. Maksim closed the gap on my left.

I aimed straight for the wall without slowing down, without easing up at all, just like Dave had taught me. That was the only way to get the vertical lift I needed.

I leaped toward the wall. *"Bend your knee, not too much. Keep your back straight. Don't lean forward."* Dave's lessons reverberated in my psyche. My running shoe gripped the wall, and my forward momentum launched me straight up. I grunted, reaching. Stretching.

My fingers caught the first rung.

I jerked my legs up, dodging a swipe by Émilien, and braced my feet against the building. Drago attempted his own wall climb. He hesitated, losing the momentum he needed. His shoe slipped, and he slid to the ground.

I'd never had the arm strength to pull up my own body weight, but Dave had shown me a workaround. I closed my eyes and pushed off the wall, swinging in an arc. The momentum carried me up, just a little, and at the top of the arc I stretched for the next rung.

Caught it.

I did the same for the third rung, then the fourth. Finally, I was high enough to step onto the lowest rung and do a head-check.

Émilien glared up at me. Drago and Maksim were nowhere to be seen.

I climbed onto the first landing and ducked inside the building through an open window. Glass crunched under my shoes. The smell of death and rot, of bodily fluids, suffocated me. I snapped forward, dry-heaving, then stumbled into a hallway and down a winding stairwell.

Glass ruptured as I reached the ground floor. Sunlight poured inside the building, and a stocky silhouette stepped into the light. Émilien had found a way inside.

I sprinted into the nearest hallway. Darkness closed over me, and my attention shifted to a nebulous mass. It looked like a mound of garbage, and it filled the entire hall.

Émilien growled as he caught up. "I have her," he called.

I focused on my breathing—in through my nose, out through my mouth—and stared down the mass. What would Dave do? Hurdle it?

No. He'd do a dive-roll. It wasn't my strongest move, and the mound was pretty big, but...

"It's all about your form." Dave's voice rushed back. *"Good form helps your body bend and contort the right way, and if you land wrong, you can always safety-roll out of it."* I neared the mound, totally focused on my form.

Step. Plant. *Push.*

I dove headfirst, flinging myself up and over the pile. Darkness blinded me, and I had no way to know if I had cleared the obstacle or not. I closed my eyes, tucked myself into a roll, and braced myself for the impact.

My right shoulder landed first.

My hands met cool floor.

I circled around, popped up, and kept running.

Shoes skidded behind me. A cry went up, followed by a clatter, and I knew Émilien had slammed into that disgusting pile of refuse.

"Merrrrde! I am going to kill you!"

The hall emptied into a foyer. A door stood to my left; stairs rose on my right. I angled for the door until Maksim and Drago barreled through it.

I doubled back to the stairs. The wide staircase circled around an open shaft. I sprinted up, keeping as close to the center as possible. Drago and Maksim charged after me.

I stretched for two steps at a time while clutching the railing and pulling myself up and up and up.

Second floor.

Third floor.

Fourth.

I wheezed, legs shaking. This wasn't sustainable. I needed a new plan, otherwise they were going to corner me on the top floor. *If* I could make it to the top floor.

My attention moved to the railing. Skinny vertical bars supported the banister. Some bars were rusty and broken, others missing completely.

I reached a section with several missing bars, which created a gap wide enough for my legs and feet. Or so I hoped, because this was the only way I could think to stall.

I gripped the railing and hopped over, twisting around while keeping hold of the banister. My feet landed on the spot where the broken bars had been. I was still on the staircase, but on the outer edge.

I directed my gaze to Drago—or who I assumed was Drago. Turned out to be Maksim. Our eyes locked, and my composure collapsed. I choked on a sob.

His face ballooned. He was in shock.

Drago was, too, apparently. He stood one stair down, hunched over, panting, and all the while he kept his wide eyes on me.

I gulped air and glanced around, searching for a way out. A height-drop down the center shaft was out of the question—I was way too high for that—but I might be able to do a cat leap down to the next level.

Drago knocked Maksim aside and lunged. I dodged him and pushed off the banister, leaping through the center shaft. I landed hard against the railing on the next level. My fingers curled around the banister in desperation. My foot found a gap between the vertical bars. Unfortunately, that gap wasn't big enough for both legs, and my knee crashed into a bar that was sturdier than it looked. Fire scorched my kneecap.

I screamed, sucking in a sharp breath, and cat-leaped to the next landing. I managed to repeat the move all the way to the ground floor. The fire flared every time I landed, but I kept going.

Maksim and Drago stampeded after me.

I limped through the foyer and entered a shadowy hallway. A voice huffed and puffed, muttering in French.

No.

I doubled back. The next hallway dumped me into a foyer. Sunlight poured through a window with burglar bars. A chain and padlock secured the exit doors, locking me in, but there was an interior door with a push bar that led to another stairwell. I barreled through that door and began my ascent. *Dammit!* This would put me in the same position I'd been in moments ago—with nowhere to go but up—but I had no other option.

The shadows thickened as I climbed. My right knee throbbed. My leg muscles trembled, burning with each step and luring me to give up. But I couldn't. I wouldn't.

Someone entered the foyer. It was Émilien, and as I peered down the shaft, I found him peering right back up at me. He growled—a low, menacing rumble—and powered up the stairs.

I picked up the pace. Each floor contained a split hallway—probably leading to the old apartments—but fear drove me upward. I couldn't risk hiding and getting caught. Then I'd be trapped.

The upper floors grew darker as the last remnants of sunlight trickled up the center shaft. Suddenly, two more sets of footsteps scurried into the stairwell.

Maksim and Drago.

I reached the next landing and groped for the banister. Nothing. All I found was air. I was on the top floor, which meant there was nowhere else to run.

Émilien panted, muttering. He was still a few floors down.

My attention moved to the split hallway. I abandoned the stairwell and stepped deeper into the shadows. This was a new level of darkness, the kind nightmares are made of, and I had to force my feet to carry me into it.

The hallway stretched left and right. I went left, pushed

through a door, and found myself in another hallway. I eased the door shut, and pitch blackness closed over me.

Flick. Swish. A golden glow sparked.

The light went out.

Flick-flick. Swish. The amber light reignited. Someone was in here.

I crept forward, feet bumping into cans and bottles, cardboard. I stepped on something small and thin that rolled under my shoe.

Fear gripped me. A syringe. It had to be a syringe.

The hallway took a sharp left. I peered around the corner and found a woman sitting against the wall. My hope reignited until I noticed the straw held between her lips. She was smoking something off a sheet of tinfoil.

A familiar smell—like vinegar, but sweet—made my blood freeze. The girl was smoking heroin, and memories of Mom tumbled down on me. I couldn't think. I couldn't move.

The girl placed the flame to the underside of the foil. The aluminum crackled as she sucked on the straw. I shook myself out of the daze, rushed past her, and hurried down the hall. Doors lined both sides of the hallway—probably apartments. I tried a handle and poked my head inside.

A tidal wave of death and disgust sent me hurtling backward. I retched as the druggie's lighter went out, dousing the hall in blackness again.

A glass bottle clanked and rolled from that direction. I clapped a hand over my mouth and clenched my muscles, going completely still. A can crunched under a heavy shoe. My lungs constricted.

Émilien was in the first hall. Any second, he'd turn the corner and be in *this* hall. With me.

I reached out until the tips of my fingers detected wall. I could keep going, keep feeling my way... somewhere. Into an apartment?

The mere thought stoked my gag reflex.

I bit down on the urge to vomit and forced myself to walk forward. This hallway might lead to another wing, and then I could work my way around and sneak past Drago and Maksim.

I kept my hand on the wall, feeling my way through the darkness. My heart hammered with each step. I moved slowly, silently, extending my foot and feeling around for bottles or cans. I detected pieces of cardboard. Nothing more.

The woman moaned.

I looked back in time to see a beam of white light streak the darkness. The light bounced around and landed on the druggie.

A struggle ensued. Her moans heightened. Had Émilien mistaken her for me?

I quickened my steps. He was close—twenty-five feet? Thirty? If he pointed his flashlight this way, he'd see me. I needed to find the next—

My shoe kicked a bottle. Glass clinked, rolling, and I froze as the scuffle behind me stilled. I grimaced, glancing back. The white light landed on me.

Shoes scraped the floor. The light bounced, growing bigger, brighter. The footsteps rolled toward me at a jog, then at a run.

I took off in a sprint. The hallway didn't wrap around like I'd hoped, but Émilien's light careened off a door straight ahead. It didn't appear to be an apartment. Was it a janitor's closet?

Hope sparked. It might be, and if I could find a mop or broom, I might be able to use it as a weapon.

I abandoned the wall and aimed for the door. My feet slipped on slabs of cardboard and crashed against bottles and cans.

I reached out. My palm slammed against the door handle. *Please be unlocked.* It was, but this wasn't a janitor's closet. The door opened into a tiny stairwell that went one direction. Up.

The roof access.

I clambered up the steps, plowed through another door, and stumbled onto the roof. Sunlight burned my eyes. Fresh air choked me.

I rammed the door shut, darted to the backside of the building, and peered over the edge. The courtyard stretched below—way below—and the fire escape I'd used was unreachable from here.

I searched for another landing. All I saw were ripped-out chunks of cement where screws and mounts had been.

I ran the perimeter of the roof. There weren't any pipes attached to the building, no stepping balconies.

What else? *Think, Kat.*

I surveyed the roof gap between this building and the next. That building was two stories shorter than this one. Even if I could clear the gap, there was about zero chance I'd make the landing without breaking bones.

I returned to the side with the fire escape. The nearest landing put me at a five-story drop straight down to a rickety, rusted-out piece of uncertainty.

Or I could try the two-story roof jump. Even if I broke a bone, I'd have a chance at getting away.

A third option wormed its way into my thoughts. I could surrender and beg these guys for mercy.

Émilien burst through the roof access. He locked onto me, eyes wild, and screamed. There was no third option. These guys were *not* going to show me mercy.

My legs exploded in a dead sprint, and I ran in the only direction I could go. Toward the roof gap. The Frenchman powered after me. I glanced back as Maksim and Drago flocked behind him.

I focused forward. The roof had a raised ledge. I'd have to leap up, plant my foot on the ledge, and jump—and I'd have to do it with my left foot because my right knee was jacked.

Everything within me said this was impossible and that I was going to die. Something else told me that what Émilien had in mind was worse.

The Frenchman grunted, fingers catching on my ponytail. The tendrils pulled taut, and my head drew back.

I gritted my teeth and leaned forward, pumping my arms, lengthening my stride. My knee pinged, threatening to give out. *God, if you're real—*

That's all I could think. I was out of roof.

30. TREACHERY

*S*tep. *Plant. Push.*

I launched off the ledge with every bit of strength I had. With every last bit of hope.

The alley stretched below as I arced toward the other building. *I'm not going to make it.* Gravity took hold and drew me down. The alley rushed up. My stomach lurched, and the fall dragged a blood-chilling scream from my lungs.

My eyes slammed shut. I forced them open, focusing on where I needed to land. The roof drew closer as every technique Dave had shown me, every tidbit of knowledge he'd ever shared, bubbled up.

I lifted my legs, clearing the other roof's ledge. Barely. My feet touched down. I angled myself, hands braced, and tucked my body.

"Don't roll on your spine." Dave's warning echoed. *"Roll at an angle, or sideways if you have to. But never on your spine."*

I entered the safety roll. My right shoulder landed first. I found the correct angle, and my left hip grazed the rooftop as I circled around. I popped up and out of the roll... but instead of coming to a stop, my momentum carried me forward... and kept carrying me. I was about to face-plant.

I tucked my arms, straightened my legs, and flattened myself until I was rolling longways. *Oof!* The paved rooftop scraped my arms and legs.

Everything stilled.

My eyes peeled open. I found myself lying face down, breathing in dust. My knee throbbed. My hands were scraped up, and I felt like I'd been body-slammed.

Anything else?

I pushed up, trembling, and felt around—arms, legs, ankles. Nothing was broken, and a laugh spilled out of me. I couldn't believe it. I'd made a two-story roof jump.

My concern shifted to the front pocket of my shorts. I reached inside. The locket felt like it was intact. I could check later.

Émilien, Drago, and Maksim glared from the other roof. Any relief I might've been experiencing went *poof!* the moment Maksim motioned for his companions to move aside. Then he backed up.

Memories from Brasov trickled in. Maksim knew all the parkour moves I knew and beyond. He was going to make that roof jump, and he wasn't injured like I was.

"No, no, no." I sprinted for a roof-access identical to the first one. I had a grip on the handle by the time Maksim launched himself over the roof gap. He landed and tucked himself into the most flawless safety roll I'd ever witnessed.

He jumped up, wincing, and signaled to his companions. They were still on the other roof, watching. Émilien nodded, and they both disappeared.

I redoubled my grip on the handle and yanked. The rust broke loose, and the door flew open. Shadows absorbed me inside the stairwell. My right knee gave out on the first landing. I collapsed.

Two hands grabbed me. I slipped out of Maksim's grasp and backed against the wall. He lunged. I brought my leg up and jammed my foot into his gut. He snapped forward, and I darted past him. He reached over and hauled me around. I screamed.

"Kat, stop!" He forced me to face him. "We don't have time for this!"

I hesitated, waiting. "You're n-not going to hurt me?"

He raised an arm, wiping his sleeve across his brow, and shook his head.

I threw myself against him. "I'm sorry," I said into his chest. "Maksim, I'm so sorry."

He pushed me away. "I'm not here for that."

Rejection socked me in the gut. I swayed under the blow.

"Do you have the photo of that girl?" He winced, grabbing his shoulder. "The one your ex slept with?"

Confusion splintered my thoughts. "You're asking me about that now? Why?"

"Because I need to know. Do you have it or not?"

"It's on my phone. Brandy's phone." I sniffled, wiping my face. "I kept it in case Ty ever tried to get back together with me."

Maksim reached into his pocket and fished out my phone. "Show me."

The screen had a fresh spiderweb. Apart from that, the phone was working. I navigated to the special folder I'd created—a duplicate of the one on my real phone—and showed him the pic.

His expression went from curious to confused and then to deeply concerned. He rubbed his chin. "It's her."

"Who?"

"The dancer from the club."

My insides sank. "How's that possible?"

"I don't know." He dragged a hand through his hair. "Ştefan promoted her to a new rank in our operation. I never knew why."

"The girl at the club has a tattoo. This girl doesn't."

"The tattoo is new, a sign of her new position. We all have them according to our roles." He glanced at his left arm. The tribal band remained hidden under his sleeve. "When did your ex go on that ski trip?"

"Over Christmas break. He was there for New Year's."

Maksim swore under his breath. "She was gone during that time. She received the tattoo soon thereafter."

"Um, Maksim?" I hugged myself. "How do you know all this?"

His gaze met mine, and for a split second his eyes hinted at guilt. He looked away. "Don't ask questions you don't want the answers to."

My heart tumbled down into my rib cage. They'd been in a relationship—and then a very broken part of me added *Or just sleeping together.*

The revelation injected a fresh dose of nausea into my stomach.

Maksim moved to the doorway and peered out, checking the other roof. "Where is the Traveler? Have you figured it out?"

"Why do you want to know?" My voice broke. "And why are y'all chasing me?"

"Ştefan has placed the entire city on alert for you—police, taxis, every associate and employee he has. They were told to convene on the area around Politehnica and report to him when you were seen. The taxi driver who picked you up works for us."

"It's the Braţiu fortune. Now that he knows about it, he wants it for himself."

"I have not told Ştefan about the Braţiu fortune." Maksim met my stare dead-on. "I have said nothing of your father's letter, to him or anyone."

A distant *clank* echoed up the stairwell.

Maksim leaned forward, listening. "They're in the building. Scream, right now, like I'm hurting you."

"I-I—"

"Do it." Maksim gripped my arms. "Now."

I closed my eyes, took a breath, and reached deep down inside myself. A scream pealed out before devolving into a pathetic cry. It wasn't hard to do because it was how I really felt.

Maksim held up a finger. I quieted.

Distant scuffs drifted up the stairwell. Someone called up.

Maksim called back before dragging me onto the roof. "Here. Take this." He had his wallet out and handed me a stack of lei and euros. "You'll need to hitchhike to Bulgaria. I know someone there who can help you."

"Are you crazy? I'm not hitchhiking to Bulgaria."

"Listen to me." He grabbed me again. "If my cousin thinks, if he even suspects, you know the location of the fortune—if he has learned of these things and has decided it's something he wants— he will torture the information out of you."

"I don't have the information. My dad didn't even have it. He said so in the letter."

"Ştefan won't care."

"But how did he find out in the first place? And how did his operative, whatever she is, end up at the same ski lodge as Ty?"

"I don't know! Okay? I don't know anything." He released me. "But if you don't give my cousin what he wants, whether by sheer willpower or because you truly do not know, he *will* kill you."

"Why would that matter to you? Why put yourself at risk?" I wanted him to say he still cared, that I meant something to him.

He didn't.

"Something is amiss, and I must know what it is." He focused on me. "Kat, please. Do you know where to find the Traveler or not?"

"I do." My chest swelled until I could barely speak. "Someone at the university told me."

"And?"

"I'll show you." I held the banknotes toward him. "I need answers, too, and—I'm not interested in your money."

He snatched the bills. "Fine. But you'll do exactly as I say, or I will let *you* deal with the consequences of your bad decisions." He shoved the bills into his wallet. "Understood?"

I nodded.

He jogged the roof's perimeter. "We have to ditch our phones."

"Why?"

"Ştefan has people in telecommunications. He'll have them ping the SIM cards, and they'll think they've found us. That will buy us time to get out of the city." He pointed at something on the building's exterior. "That pipe is our way down."

I joined him. "Is it secure?"

"I'm about to find out." He hoisted himself onto the ledge, swung his legs around, and lowered himself down.

He gripped the pipe and braced his boots against the building. "It's secure enough," he said, peering down. "We'll only need it until we reach the fire escape."

I followed his gaze. The fire escape started halfway down the building—not as far down as the other one I'd seen, but far enough that the distance made me swoon.

"I-I don't think I can do this. My knee is messed up—"

"We don't have any more options." He began his descent. "I'll help you," he said with a glance up, "but we must hurry. Otherwise neither of us is going to make it."

PART THREE

CREȚULEȘTI

UKRAINE
HUNGARY
MOLDOVA
ROMÂNIA
Sibiu
Brașov
Cozfev
Argeși
Pitești
Crețulești
București
SERBIA
BULGARIA

31. STRANGER

Dark clouds hovered, draping a cool shadow over the countryside. An earthy smell hung in the air. Maksim and I had managed to hitchhike out of Bucharest. I hadn't been able to recall the name of the village, but I knew it was on the way to Pitești.

"Pretty sure I'd remember it if I could see it on a map."

Maksim turned to the driver and asked him something. A moment later, we had the man's phone and were studying an online map. Our phones were back in Ferentari—Maksim's in an abandoned building, mine in a trash can. That would keep Ștefan busy for a while.

"It's somewhere here." I zoomed in on the area Paty had shown me and crawled along the highway. "There." I pointed at the name. Crețulești.

Maksim paid the man to take us there. Five hundred lei later, we were being dropped off. We'd thought the hard part was over, but we encountered a brand new problem when we started asking about any Gypsies in the area. The villagers, who'd been friendly and helpful up to that point, would then hurry away without answering.

"These people don't want any trouble," Maksim explained

after speaking to an elderly lady he referred to as a *bunică*. Grandmother. The woman didn't seem angry or upset. She simply clutched her woven basket and waddled away.

"Why would they think we're causing trouble?" I asked.

"Most people don't come looking for Gypsies. The times they have, there've been incidents."

"Like what?"

He merely shook his head. "She mentioned a settlement on the outskirts of the village. I believe that's where we need to go, but she would not say where it is."

"Try telling them we're meeting my dad's friend. Act like he's expecting us."

Maksim tried that with the next villager, a fortysomething in loose khakis and a faded shirt. The man balanced a garden hoe on his shoulder and led us to a tree line. "The settlement is on the other side of these woods," Maksim explained. "That's all he'll say."

We left the village behind and entered the forest. Maksim was on high alert, glancing around, checking over his shoulder. "Do not wander off. And don't go into any of the homes."

"Okay."

"I mean it." He let a stern look fall on me. "Something about this feels off. You're certain your father's letter wasn't in your purse? No pictures of it on your phone?"

Maksim had been worried—borderline paranoid—that Ştefan was going to figure out what we were doing. Right now he didn't know anything, so we were safe. But Maksim said that could change at any moment.

"It was just the scavenger hunt in my purse," I assured him. "The letter had too many pages. I didn't want to lose one, so I left it at the hostel." My insides tightened. "You don't think Ştefan would go there, do you? Could he or his goons sneak into my room?"

"They wouldn't sneak. They would have the police escort them in and give the staff a fabricated story." Maksim picked up his pace. "I don't think they would glean much from the letter, but they could figure out we've come *here* to find the Traveler. We need to hurry."

I hobbled after him. "Not sure I can go any faster."

His attention fell to my knee. "It's amazing you have only that injury. You could have been killed doing that roof jump."

"This isn't from the roof jump. It's from when I did that cat leap through the stairwell, and it's not the worst injury I've ever had. Probably just a bruised kneecap." I slowed a bit more and pressed on my knee. It was tender, and I pulled a sharp breath.

"Perfect." Maksim threw his hands up and let them fall. "We haven't a second to waste, and now this."

"This wouldn't have happened if *you* hadn't been chasing me." I straightened. "When exactly were you planning to help me, anyway?"

"I was trying to figure that out." His stare circled the forest. "Drago and Émilien were armed. They were told not to use lethal force against you, but I guarantee they would have used it against me. I had to play the part."

"You had the element of surprise. You don't think you could have taken them?"

"I'm not armed. My Glock is at the apartment, and I had no time to go back for it."

The tightness in my torso crept toward my lungs. "What were they going to do to me?"

"Deliver you to the lion's den." His stare met mine. "From there I don't know, but at that point I would not have been able to intervene."

My next breath choked off. I was almost kidnapped.

Ten minutes later, we entered a clearing and followed a dirt road to a cluster of shacks. A man approached. He had a mop of black hair and a bushy mustache that reminded me of Mr. Kotfas.

Sadness pricked me. My grandfather had bailed Kotfas's family out of debt and paid for Gypsy Django to be renovated. Then, without telling anyone, Kotfas had sold the restaurant.

That part of Dad's letter filtered into my thoughts.

> *Kotfas was angry after I reconciled with my father. I continued to visit him on Mondays, but I would go to his house instead of to the restaurant. His wife always received me. Sometimes Kotfas would, too. Other times not.*
>
> *I'm sorry I didn't tell you any of this before. I thought it best to wait until my return before doing anything that may alter our lives or perhaps even give a false hope. I would not accept so much as a penny from my father until these legal matters were settled and I could officially share this news with you…*

Maksim's voice drew me back to the present. The black-haired man perked up at the mention of Levi Pavel. He motioned for us to go with him. The road dipped and rose under our feet, a mixture of clay and mud. My running shoes sank into the softness.

The villager stopped in front of a shack and gestured at a silver-haired man sitting on the front porch. A woman relaxed beside him. Thick braids spilled onto her shoulders from beneath a cobalt headscarf. A matching skirt cascaded over her legs and brushed the weathered porch.

The gray-haired man noticed us and waved. The woman stared.

"Are you Levi Pavel?" I called.

"I haven't gone by that name in many years." The man sat straighter. "I'm curious how you know it."

"It's the name my dad gave me."

The woman rose and stepped down off the porch.

Levi hardly noticed as she lumbered away. "Who are you, young lady? Who is your father, and how is it that you've come to find me?"

"My name's Katherine Barrett. This is my friend, Maksim." I gestured. "A student at the polytechnic university told me you live here."

"And your father?"

"His name was Nicholas Barrett. He asked me to find you."

"Barrett. Barrett." Levi rubbed his chin, mouth twisted. "I'm sorry, my dear. I cannot recall anyone by that name."

"Braţiu," I amended. "You would have known him as Nicolae Braţiu. He changed his name when he moved to the US."

"My God." Levi rose from his chair. "Come closer, child."

I started toward him.

Maksim caught my arm. "She'll speak to you from here."

Levi blinked in confusion. But, to his credit, he simply craned his neck and leaned across the banister. His eyes trailed over my face before drifting toward my frizzy curls. A few pieces had worked loose from my ponytail. I smoothed them back.

A smile split the man's face, deepening the lines around his eyes. "You have your father's hair."

I nodded.

He threw his head back and laughed, clapping his hands together. "Goodness me. Where is your father? How is my old friend?"

"It's a long story." My gaze flicked to Maksim. "We have more questions than answers."

"Then please come and make yourself comfortable. Are you thirsty? I do have an advanced filtration system if you'd like a glass of water."

Maksim didn't budge. So I didn't either.

Levi's attention shifted. "You are of course welcome to join us, young man," he said to Maksim. "Are you—?" Levi squinted. "Have we met before, son?"

Maksim's jaw flexed. "I am *not* your son."

"Forgive me. I meant nothing by it." Levi's cheeriness ebbed. "Will you be joining us, young man?" He gestured at the two chairs on the porch. "I don't mind to stand."

Maksim scanned the immediate area. He must have decided everything was okay because he walked me onto the porch and directed me to one of the chairs—the chair nearest to the steps, I realized. Probably so we could make a getaway if things went south.

Levi tried to offer Maksim the other chair.

"I'll stand," Maksim said flatly.

"The better for me, I suppose." Levi parked himself in the other chair. "Now, young Katherine. What is the news of your father?"

"Something happened to him last December. He said he was coming here on a business trip, but—" My voice cracked. Would this ever get any easier?

"We're not certain what has become of him," Maksim finished. "It's possible he's been captured. More likely, he's dead." He said it like he thought Levi had something to do with it.

Did he actually think that?

If there'd been an accusation, Levi didn't seem to notice. "I assumed Nicolae was dead all these years. To think him alive, even for a moment, resurrects many emotions within me." He sniffled, dabbing a knuckle to his eye. "Please, can you tell me what has happened to my old friend?"

"Maybe I should start from the beginning?" I peeked up at Maksim, and he gave a curt nod.

I told Levi everything I knew, starting with the way Dad had been acting weird before his trip. I told him about the scavenger hunt, the things we'd found in Brașov. Finally, I reached the part about the letter in the apartment. "It was a secret flat of Vasile's, which nobody knew about except Popescu, Vasile's personal assistant. Vasile had started doing things in secret because of his grandson. My dad's nephew."

"Ah, yes." Levi gave a firm nod. "The son of Nicolae's elder brother, Vladimir. I'm well aware of him."

The name Vladimir rang familiar, although I couldn't figure out why. Dad hadn't named names in the letter. Why, I wasn't sure. Maybe he was too short on time. Or maybe he was afraid I'd go snooping around too much.

"My dad said Vasile was diagnosed with cancer," I continued. "It was around that time that the assistant, Popescu, uncovered a plot to take over the estate, so Vasile started liquidating his assets and putting everything in a foreign bank. My dad came here to conclude the legal paperwork, but Vasile was already being held captive by then."

Levi's eyes widened. "Was your father taken captive, as well?"

I nodded, and his whole face ballooned.

"They did escape," I said, "at least initially. Popescu snuck into the compound and knocked out the guards, and then they all worked together to devise an escape plan while doing what they could to protect Vasile's assets."

"They decided to create a scavenger hunt," Maksim chimed in, "something only Kat could solve, by using local businesses Vasile had been helping in Braşov—"

"One moment." Levi held up a finger. "Vasile Braţiu—*the* Vasile Braţiu—was helping local businesses?"

"He was trying to find ways to compensate people," I said, "any families he had wronged during communism. A lot of them rejected his efforts, though, so he started to be more secretive about it."

"Fascinating." Levi scooted forward in his seat. "And how did he manage this?"

"He and Popescu worked together, visiting people and finding ways to help them—like by purchasing property for more than its current value or pretending angel investors wanted to invest in the family's business."

"Bear in mind, he wasn't doing it for the sake of kindness." Maksim folded his arms. "He was assuaging his own guilt."

"He tried to make things right," I countered. "That has to count for something."

"Does it? Can forty years of crimes be erased by throwing money at people?"

My eyes narrowed. "You mean the way you threw money at me today?"

"I was trying to *help* you."

"And Vasile was trying to help those people. I get that you hate him, but you're judging him by his actions and yourself by your intentions, and that's not fair."

Maksim was about to fire back when Levi gave a cough. "You were saying something about a scavenger hunt, weren't you?" He divided a concerned look between us. "Before we wandered off track?"

"Right. Sorry," I said, lowering my volume. "So while my dad and Vasile were setting up the scavenger hunt, Popescu was hiding a lockbox that contains the account details."

"It's supposed to contain a special passcode," Maksim corrected, "which is the only way to claim and access the funds. Popescu didn't have the account number itself."

He was right. Dad had said exactly that in the letter. I'd forgotten.

I turned to Levi. "Vasile delegated tasks so that no one person had all the details. My dad never saw the passcode, and Popescu never saw the account number. And none of them—not my dad, Vasile, *or* Popescu—knew the exact location of where the second lockbox had been hidden."

"None of them knew?" Levi's eyebrows converged. "And how is *that* possible?"

"We don't know, and neither did my dad. I've been batting around ideas—like maybe Popescu sent it down a river or placed it inside something being transported. Whatever the case, Vasile trusted him enough to let him make that call."

"According to Kat's father," Maksim said, "Vasile was paranoid about being captured. He felt the less each of them knew, the better off they'd be. Nicolae thought all this a bit extreme, but as their situation deteriorated, he realized his father was right to be so cautious."

"Indeed." That was all Levi said—but the intensity of his expression said so much more.

"You don't think they were going too far?" I asked.

"There are reasons why Vasile experienced such paranoia, why he would go to such lengths to protect himself and others." Levi's gaze turned distant, like he might have been remembering something. He breathed a sigh and then shook his head. "That's a story I'm happy to share later. For now, please do continue."

"We have one final piece of the puzzle to solve. At least, I think it's the final piece." I reached into my front pocket and pulled out the locket. "There's an inscription inside."

Levi pressed the latch. The locket's front face sprang open.

"I've never been able to translate it," I said. "Do you know what it says?"

"It's a Roma proverb, one I don't care for due to its divisiveness. 'In the village without dogs, the farmers walked without sticks. Rom with Rom. Gadje with gadje.'" Levi peered over at me. "*Gadje* is a reference to non-Roma people or 'strangers.' *Rom* is a man who is ethnically Roma."

"Gypsy," Maksim said as if to correct him.

"I know that word is commonly used in Europe"—Levi's smile slipped away—"but it is derogatory."

"And *gadje* isn't?" Maksim guffawed. "Are we not considered unclean to them simply because we're not of their ethnicity? That is the nature of the proverb, is it not? That *gadje* are the dogs they're alluding to?"

Levi sighed. "Not all Roma carry on the old traditions."

"Oh they don't? What about child brides? And what about—?"

"Hey." I hopped up. "Can we bring this down a notch?"

Maksim shrugged me off. "What about the men who drove that van into the crowd? Will you make excuses for them, as well?" He stood over Levi. "Or perhaps they should be making excuses for you."

Levi drew back in his seat. "I'm unsure what you mean, young man. Is this an allegation?"

"Do not feign ignorance. You know precisely what I'm referring to."

"I don't."

"Liar." Maksim bit down on the word. "You ordered those 'Roma' men to drive into the crowd of protesters, *your* supporters, the people who were there for *your* cause. They were killed because of you, and my parents were struck down with them!"

"You mistake me for somebody else. That or someone has lied about me." Levi pushed up from the chair. He was nearly the same height as Maksim. "How did you come to hear these things?"

"I am of the family Răzvan, and we know all about your treachery."

"Răzvan? I thought—" Confusion twisted through Levi's features. His gaze flicked to me. "Are you two married? Did you take her family name?"

Maksim's eyes went squinty. "Excuse me?"

"Her family—Vasile and his family—are the family Răzvan. That's more of a recent development, after the fall of communism, but they have been Răzvan since."

My confusion heightened. "Wait, what?"

"I didn't believe you two were blood relatives." Levi lowered himself into the chair. "You certainly don't look like a Răzvan, young man. Your facial structure is like mine, more Slavic."

Maksim tensed. "Our family lineage extends to Russia."

"That's preposterous if we are, in fact, speaking of the same family. Vasile Răzvan had business dealings in Russia, but none of his family were from there."

"H-hang on," I said. "Vasile's last name was Brațiu... not Răzvan."

"It was both. Not simultaneously, but at different times."

Levi's expression and tone were plain, matter-of-fact. "I've always known your father's family as Braţiu. After the revolution, Vasile thought it best to change the family name so that he and Vladimir could have more—leverage, you might say—for doing business in this new pseudocapitalist society."

Maksim's confusion dissolved into horror. "Vladimir," he whispered, seemingly to himself. Then again... "Vladimir." The second time escaped as a puff, hardly audible.

"Vladimir was Vasile's eldest child," Levi said. "He was Nicolae's older brother. Kat's uncle. He is dead now to my understanding, having passed away—"

"Last summer," Maksim finished. "*My* uncle was Vladimir of the family Răzvan. He died last summer."

"It may be a coincidence. Vladimir is a common name after all." Realization sparked in Levi's eyes. "Ah, but Vladimir does have a son, Ştefan, if that may be helpful."

"*What?*" I pointed at myself. "Are you saying Ştefan is my—? That he's—?"

"Your cousin," Levi finished for me. "Indeed. He is the son of Vladimir and thus the nephew of your father." Levi shook his head. "It seems you two are under the cloud of some misunderstanding."

Maksim backed himself against the nearest post. I reached for him. His hand connected with my arm, and he shoved. I stumbled backward as he staggered down the steps.

Levi stared after him. "I hope he's—?" Levi's eyes brightened, lit by some epiphany I didn't understand. He hopped up and chased after Maksim. "Young man, don't go." He pulled Maksim to a stop. "May I ask... who are your parents?"

Maksim's lips moved. His answer came out as a mumble.

Levi turned an ear. "Can you repeat it?"

"Petru *şi* Iulia Răzvan," Maksim finally said.

"My God!" Levi placed a hand to his chest. "I know *precisely* who you are. I cannot believe it. I cannot believe it! You are

Maksim Ćosić, son of Croatian journalist Petar Ćosić. I knew I recognized you. You look exactly like your father."

I jumped off the porch. "Maksim is Romanian, not Croatian, and Ştefan is definitely his cousin. He helped raise him. The reason Maksim has a Russian name is because—"

"Maksim is a *Slavic* name," Levi said, "and Croats are South Slavs. Maksim is a very common name in Croatia. He is Romanian—by way of his mother—but his father was Croatian. I met them both." Levi gripped Maksim's shoulders. "They were slain because of your father's work. You went missing."

The color drained from Maksim's face. He looked like he was about to throw up.

"The police determined you had been killed," Levi continued, his eyes misting. "I have always believed otherwise due to the exposé."

"What exposé?" I asked.

"About the kidnapped children. It was the story his father was working on when he was killed." Levi's expression fell. "No, Maksim is *not* of the family Răzvan. His surname is Ćosić, and he has been missing for twenty years."

32. DISCLOSURE

There's a saying in Romania: *A-ți pica fisa*. It means to "drop your coin," but it isn't a reference to money. It's when someone has an epiphany. Instead of saying they figured it out, they might say, "I dropped my coin."

If there was anyone in the history of Romania who had ever dropped their coin, it was surely Maksim when he realized the truth about who he was. He bent forward and vomited before slumping to the ground.

"Maksim?" I placed a hand on this back. "Can I get you anything or...? Do you just need a second?"

He was on all fours, face in the dirt while he muttered in Romanian.

"Let's give him a moment." Levi made his way to the porch and plunked himself on the steps.

I joined him. "Not to change the subject, but... What should I call you since you're not the Traveler and you don't go by Levi Pavel?"

"I've been using Pavelić since the revolution. This is the name my family had when they immigrated here from Croatia many years ago, and I thought it best to carry on with a name different from that in my file."

"What file? At the university?"

"This was a different type of file. A secret police file. All Romanians had one during communism." A smile drew up the corners of his mouth, but his eyes held a glimmer of sadness. "You're welcome to call me Pavelić or simply Levi."

"Think I like Levi better."

"Your father called me Levi. We were very close." He fished the locket out of his pocket and tried to hand it to me.

I stopped him. "My dad said there's another clue inside."

"The inscription?"

"That might be part of it, but he was referring to something else, something that's only accessible by opening the locket a certain way. In his letter he said you'd know how to do it, that the locket is similar to one a peddler tried to sell y'all in Sighi-something."

"Sighişoara?"

"That's it. He said y'all took a day trip there."

"Mm." He turned the locket over in his hand.

"Also..." I swallowed. "There was a lady at the university who saw the locket and freaked out. I think she might have realized there was something distinctly Gypsy—sorry, Roma—about it. Pretty sure she recognized the language."

"Or this perhaps." He held up the locket, showing me the wagon-wheel design on the back.

"What is it?"

"A dharmachakra, or wheel of dharma. It's a symbol used in India, where the Roma originate, and it was modified into something akin to a cartwheel for the Romani flag."

"Flag? For what country?"

"The Roma are unique in that they have no country, so they have devised an ethnic flag containing this symbol. Perhaps the woman you met recognized it." Levi's attention returned to the inscribed inner plate. "Now, for the special way this must open."

He pressed on the top, the bottom. He tapped the inner plate and all along the sides. He squeezed the outer edges.

Clouds settled over the area. Lightning flickered, followed by a soft rumble. Humidity plucked at my pores, coating my skin in stickiness.

Levi tried pressing on the inner plate again, twisting it counterclockwise and then clockwise.

The plate shifted.

"Oh my." He tried again, and the plate twisted away from the main part of the locket.

A tiny scrap of paper dropped out. Levi retrieved it and handed it to me.

"Kopernikus," I read. "This doesn't look like Dad's handwriting, and I don't know what Kopernikus is." I pinched the paper and turned it around, showing Levi. "It's spelled with a K."

"That's the German spelling. Kopernikus is a highly exclusive bank for the ultraelite in Europe. They have a reputation for secrecy, safe deposit boxes, those sorts of things." He tipped his head sideways. "I didn't realize they offer passcode-accessible accounts."

"There's a long number scribbled underneath. Do you think that's the passcode?"

"I would assume it's the account number, but I don't have personal experience with such things."

I looked over at Maksim, wanting his opinion. He sat on the ground, shoulders slumped, head down.

"Ah, a moment. What do we have here?" Levi squinted at the paper. "There's something written on the other side."

I flipped over the scrap. "Mihailo Ksorba," I read aloud.

"Goodness." Levi rubbed his forehead, brow crinkling. "My goodness."

"What's wrong? Who is that?"

"Mihailo Ksorba was a Roma child slain in Serbia when a group of men set fire to the family's home. It was a brutal murder of the most tragic kind—a defenseless family with young children." Levi's gaze turned distant. "As the fire drove the family out of the house, the men fired upon them with AK47s."

I gasped.

"The lone survivor was the twin brother of Mihailo, who only lived because his father collapsed on him, shielding him from the gunfire and hiding him in the moments thereafter. The men left feeling sure they had killed everyone, but this other child remained."

Movement tugged at my peripheral. Maksim was on his feet, looking dazed as he brushed himself off.

"The twin brother—forgive me, I don't recall his name," Levi continued, "was brought to Romania to live with extended family. But the killers were never charged, you see, and these family members feared for their own safety and for the child's. They then moved to an obscure Roma settlement deep in the Carpathian Mountains."

"That's all horrible, but"—I held up the scrap of paper—"I don't understand why the dead twin's name would be written here?"

"I would proffer that, perhaps, it's directing us to the same settlement."

"The one that family moved to? Why?"

"And where?" Maksim stopped in front of us. His color had returned, but he still looked kinda sick. "Where exactly is this settlement located?"

"Between Braşov and Sibiu," Levi said, "in the area of Negoiu."

Maksim and I shared a look. The clues at For Sale Pub had pointed to Mount Negoiu.

"And the name of the settlement?" Maksim asked.

"It has none officially, nor is it listed on any map. In a way, it's permitted to be self-governing—though it's such a small settlement even people in the Roma community know nothing of it. Those who do refer to it simply as Village Ksorba in memory of the dead family. The brother of Mihailo grew up there and became a prominent elder. He was known as their protector and defender."

"What makes you think that's where we're supposed to go?" I asked. "Why not Serbia where the Ksorba family were from?"

"Because Village Ksorba was called something else in time's past, a nickname used to deter strangers from going there. Satul Câinilor. Village of the Dogs."

Understanding lit Maksim's face. "The locket."

My brain was slow to catch up. When it finally did, the light bulb activated. The locket's inscription said something about dogs.

Levi pushed himself to standing. "There is yet another reason Nicolae may have sent young Katherine to find me—if, in fact, he kept up with European news over these many years." Levi let a questioning look fall to me.

"He watched all kinds of news," I said, "all the time. I caught him watching French news sometimes, but he played it off like he didn't understand much."

"Your father was fluent in French. He spoke more languages than I do, and I speak four—Romanian, Croatian, English, and Romani Čib." He turned and climbed the steps of the porch. "After the Yugoslav wars, I joined a special team of volunteers who sought to help with the demining efforts. I had a keen interest in Croatia because it's the homeland of my grandparents."

"Demining?" I followed him up the steps. "Like coal mines?"

"Antipersonnel mines," Maksim said, "otherwise known as land mines. The Yugoslav Republics deployed them to cover rural areas." He came behind me on the porch. "What could this possibly have to do with the Roma settlement we're discussing?"

"In order to complete my work," Levi said, "I received specialized training that would be remarkably useful for a trip to Village Ksorba. I'm happy to explain more, but... you may want to sit down for this part." Levi gestured at his door. "Shall we?"

All of Maksim's warnings fell away, and we followed him inside the house.

Levi made his way into a kitchenette area. He didn't have a fridge, and his stove was woodburning.

He lifted a bucket and poured the contents into a shiny canister. Then he grabbed a glass, placed it under the nozzle, and twisted the handle. A stream poured out.

He did the same with two more glasses and set them all on a rustic-looking table. "Please. Have a seat," he said, gesturing at the chairs. "The water is filtered, purer than the water in Bucureşti."

Maksim nodded in thanks and parked himself in a chair. I took the chair across from him.

"Near the end of communism," Levi began, "Ceauşescu initiated something he called systemization. It was an attempt to fulfill the communist vision by making everyone and everything uniform. Things that lent uniqueness of identity had to be destroyed for the 'greater good' of society.

"To accomplish this, Ceauşescu decided to raze villages and move the residents into new 'cities' with apartments much like the ones seen in Bucureşti and also in Russia and North Korea. In fact, it was during a trip to Pyongyang that he became inspired with this vision for systemization." Levi's brow crinkled. "When the people in Village Ksorba learned of these plans, they took certain... measures."

A look of understanding glinted in Maksim's eyes. He wiped a hand down his face and swore.

I gulped my water and lowered the glass. "Did I miss something?"

"The mines." Maksim's answer fell in a near-whisper. "He's talking about the mines."

I sent a wide-eyed look to Levi, who nodded.

"The man who became an elder of the village," Maksim said, "the twin brother of Mihailo Ksorba. You said he was known as their defender and protector. Why?"

"Some mines were deployed in 1989, but there was no need to continue the project because the revolution happened and Ceauşescu was executed. When the twin brother became an elder of the village many years later, he worked tirelessly to obtain mines from his homeland of Serbia and then finished the project. With the wave of hate crimes targeting the Roma people, he was heralded as their savior."

"How do you know all this?" I asked.

"One of the villagers sought me out—oh, I'd say eight or nine years ago. I have a reputation for being a risk-taker thanks to my exploits during communism. This man had heard the stories and knew about my work in Croatia with the NGO."

I thought back to what Paty had said, how she'd called Levi the crazy stranger. Did that have anything to do with the exploits he mentioned? I wanted to ask, but he was already moving on to the next part of the story.

"This villager," Levi was saying, "sought my help with strategic demining after several villagers died in a series of accidental detonations. Sadly, he was unable to obtain the cooperation of the elders, and I never heard anything more."

"Did you ever go there?" I asked. "Like, to survey the area?"

Maksim was pushing back from the table, about to stand. My question brought him to a standstill. "No." He pinned me with a severe look. "You cannot go."

"You heard Levi. He can demine the area."

"I'm trained in demining," Levi said, "but unless you have tremendous manpower, funding, and time, demining is not an effort any of us can undertake."

"Oh."

"I can, however, navigate the terrain. My team and I were trained on single-sensor metal detectors for the Croatia project. I still have mine. I continue to do a little metal detecting in my spare time."

"No." Maksim shook his head. "She cannot go."

"It's not your decision." I turned to Levi. "I'm willing to go if you are. My dad obviously trusted you, so... I do, too."

Maksim slammed his hands on the table. Our glasses rattled. Levi and I flinched. "What is the matter with you?" Maksim screamed.

"Me?" I pointed at myself. "I'm doing what I came here to do —solve the scavenger hunt."

"At what cost? It's money. It's not worth your life."

"It's not about the money!"

He guffawed. "Of course it's not."

"It isn't. It's about keeping Vasile's wealth out of the wrong hands. What if Ştefan finds the lockbox one day? He has the scavenger hunt, and he could get my dad's letter. He could figure the whole thing out."

Maksim averted his gaze. "I don't think so."

"What's that supposed to mean?"

He went quiet.

"The villager," Levi said, "the one who came to me, drew a detailed map with notations of where the mines were deployed. I may yet have the map with my papers." His bushy gray eyebrows arched. "Would you like for me to check, young Katherine?"

"That'd be great," I said. "Thanks."

Levi rose and disappeared into his bedroom. From what I could tell, it was the only other room in the house.

Maksim held me with a pained expression. "You don't have to do this," he said flatly.

"Neither do you."

He threw his head back with a sharp laugh.

"What? Maksim, you shouldn't go if you think it's a bad idea. But I have to. This isn't something I can walk away from." I lowered my voice. "I couldn't handle that kind of regret."

He stood there, hands on hips, looking annoyed. "I need some air," he finally said, and I watched him wander outside and hop down from the porch.

Levi appeared, arms full of papers. Some were loose, others rolled up. "This is all the documentation I have of the region where Village Ksorba lies. I believe the hand-drawn map is here." He shoveled everything onto the table. "Now then, let's examine this situation a little more closely."

33. HISTORY

aksim, Levi, and I bounced along in the back of a freight truck. The driver had said he could take us to Sibiu. From there, we'd have to find a ride to Avrig.

Levi balanced his metal detector against a stack of crates, fanning himself with a fedora. "How are you doing, Katherine?"

I sat across from him, leaning against a large crate. My knee ached, and I was sweating like it was midsummer in the first circle of hell. Apart from that...

I mustered up a smile for Levi while fanning myself. Sweat soaked my shirt. Well, Maksim's shirt, which I was currently borrowing. I'd rolled up the sleeves the way he always did and had the bottom placket tied at my waist. That helped, but I was still hot.

"You two won't be needing those disguises again for a while." Levi motioned between us. "There was a concern while we were hitchhiking, but I believe we're safe now."

I unbuttoned the shirt and then removed an old fishing hat I'd borrowed from Levi. My frizzy curls spilled out. I plucked at the damp, sticky mess. Maksim stripped off a rugged-looking fisherman's shirt and tossed a fedora to the side. His scars shone through his undershirt.

The truck dipped, jarring everything in the cargo hold. A stack of crates swayed, and Levi's metal detector toppled over. He picked up the device and checked the knobs. Maksim and I exchanged a worried look.

The metal detector seemed fine, but Levi strategically laid the device beside him instead of trying to prop it up. "Well then, shall I continue the story I began earlier? Where did we leave off?"

"It'd be really helpful if you could start at the beginning," I said. "How did you meet my dad?"

"Your father was living in Braşov at the time. My wife was Roma, and your father met us while visiting a nearby village. There was a woman who lived there—beautiful, a kind soul, and she had become good friends with my wife." Levi angled an eyebrow. "Things were looking serious between this woman and your father, the reason he often visited that village."

My mouth tumbled open. "My dad was *dating* someone?"

"More like courting, but yes. Then one day Nicolae received a letter from his father 'explaining' that he—your father, that is— would be moving to Bucureşti. Vasile had secured a job for him at the university, and whatever Vasile said always went. There was no questioning it. Nicolae, aware that I had a knack for teaching, used the opportunity to secure a job for me. A month later, my wife and I were moving to the big city.

"Now, this was around the time when the reign of Ceauşescu turned tyrannical. Vasile Braţiu was deep into his dealings with the Nomenklatura, the elitist segment of the Communist Party, and with Nicolae's older brother, Vladimir, rising within the ranks of the Securitate, the Braţius were becoming the most powerful family in Romania, second only to Ceauşescu himself."

Maksim scooted forward. "Vladimir was Securitate?"

"He was the foremost among them. It's said he was trained by the KGB." Levi directed his attention to me. "Do you know of what we speak, young Katherine?"

I shook my head.

"The Securitate were Romania's version of the Stasi or SS—

state secret police. They were a callous bunch, and Vladimir Brațiu was especially ruthless. As a very young man, he worked with the KGB during the Pitești Experiment. No one was able to prove it, as was often the case for Vladimir Brațiu, because he had an unnatural ability to know when trouble was imminent. Nearly all the records from Pitești disappeared prior to the program being shut down."

"I thought Vasile was to blame for the atrocities at Pitești," Maksim said. "That's what Ștefan has always said."

"Vasile provided the authorization Vladimir needed in order to arrest people and imprison them."

"On what grounds?" I asked. "What laws did they break?"

"Many were deemed enemies of the state, enemies of communism, but Vladimir was known to exact revenge on his personal enemies, even those from his childhood. He used the Pitești experiment as retribution. His father—your grandfather—signed off on all those arrests." Levi arched his eyebrows. "But it wasn't until the eighties, when construction ramped up on the People's Palace—otherwise known as the Palace of the Parliament—that the terror truly began."

"I saw the Palace of Parliament," I said. "A cabbie told me his father and grandfather died building it."

"As did many Romanians. Ceaușescu was obsessed with this project, and when Vasile was put in charge of it, he drained the prisons and forced those prisoners to work at the construction site. When that was not enough, he asked Vladimir and the Securitate to find a way to source more workers. They did so by conducting raids on individuals, couples, and then entire families. When this, too, failed to meet Ceaușescu's demands—the goal being round-the-clock labor with twenty thousand workers at any given time—Vladimir took the plan a step further. He had a particular distaste for Roma people, and because they formed their own communities—a result of forced settlement and failed assimilation policies—they became an easy target." Levi's mouth had fallen into a straight, serious line. As he paused, he managed a weak smile, which he settled on me. "This was when I learned about Nicolae's heart for the Roma. You see, his mother—your grandmother—was Roma."

"No way." The words escaped as a whisper. "Are you serious?"

"I am. And because she was half-Roma—her mother being Roma, her father being Romanian—she managed to keep her lineage hidden. Her name was—"

"Zora," I said in a whisper.

"Why yes." Levi perked up. "Your father told you?"

"He mentioned her once, but he never said anything about her being half-Roma. In fact, he always said Gypsies weren't real."

"Perhaps it was too painful to speak of, dear. Or perhaps he was being overly cautious considering what happened—the details of which I'll be getting to shortly." Levi leaned forward and patted my leg. "Zora's parents," he said, settling back, "ensured that a traditional Romanian name—Andreea—was listed on their daughter's birth certificate; and although Zora's complexion was not especially dark, they kept it light by dressing her in sunhats and long sleeves. When she was old enough, they began dying her hair blond, further securing her identity as Romanian rather than Roma. Her father's side of the family was well-educated, accomplished in the arts, so Zora—as Andreea—was permitted to attend college. She was a brilliant woman, admired by all, and this brought tremendous admiration to Vasile Brațiu upon their engagement... but he did not know Zora's ethnicity, nor did her in-laws or even her own children. For many years, only her parents knew...

"Until one day Zora realized her younger son—Nicolae, your father—had grown a natural fondness for the Roma around Sibiu. He was a teenager and, by no prompting of Zora's, somehow felt compelled to be charitable to those people, giving them food, clothes, and sometimes money. Zora decided to share her secret, and they did this charity work together, outside the purview of Vasile and Vladimir. Years later, when Vladimir began to raid the Roma communities, Nicolae and Zora took it upon themselves to do something about it. My wife and I helped."

"What'd y'all do?"

"Zora oversaw the maidservants in Vladimir's villa, and she noticed where he stored important papers. The first time she dared to look was the time she discovered notes about a coming raid. She took the information to Nicolae, who brought it to me, and I was able to get a warning to the right people. It was all very reckless. We went about it ignorantly, and any one of us could have been caught and arrested. Thankfully, it was the holidays, and Vladimir believed the members of that community had dispersed for Christmas gatherings. But from that point onward, our small group—Zora, Nicolae, my wife, and myself—were far more careful, inventing make-believe events—typically out of town—to explain why entire communities would be gone when the Securitate agents arrived."

Maksim scooted forward, clearly enthralled. "What kinds of events?"

"Birthdays, funerals, weddings. We created invitations, flyers, notecards, even handwritten letters—*anything* we could leave behind to explain why the community had suddenly left. This was the only way to protect Zora. We couldn't allow Vladimir to know his plans were being leaked." Levi's smile faded. "But he eventually realized these could not *all* be coincidences. He suspected he'd been betrayed, presumably by one of his maids. He was convinced he knew which one. But she was sick on the day he decided to falsify notes about a coming raid."

I gasped.

"His men were watching two locations, both of which had been mentioned in the notes. Vladimir was clever, you see, and he understood there was a better chance of a misstep if the betrayer felt rushed. This was precisely what happened. Believing the raids to be that night, across two different Roma communities, Nicolae and Zora split up and made contact with those communities outside our normal channels."

"And Vladimir's men were waiting for them," Maksim said.

"Yes, and imagine their surprise when the culprit turned out to be Vladimir's own mother. Across the city, Nicolae was also seen but not recognized because he had disguised himself as a produce vendor. It didn't take Vladimir long to figure it out, but the extra precaution bought him a little more time."

"Is that when he fled to America?" I asked. "When he was trying to get away from Vladimir?"

"It was when he disappeared. I never knew what had happened to him or where he had gone. Not until you and Maksim arrived."

"What about my grandma? Did she get away?"

Levi's posture, his entire mood, fell. "I was told she endured many days of psychological and then physical torture before they broke her."

"No." My heart cracked. "They tortured her?"

"Using techniques developed by the NKVD and GPU—Russian secret police, pre-KGB. Vladimir employed the most heinous of their methods, and when she broke, she disclosed everything about our operation and even her own secrets. When Vladimir learned she was half-Roma, he placed a gun to her head and—" Levi's voice pinched. He swallowed and shook his head. "She died instantly."

My stomach roiled.

"Unless you were involved in the interrogation," Maksim said, "how would you know these details?"

"Some months after Bloody Christmas—after the Ceauşescus were executed—a Securitate agent managed to locate me. He claimed to have experienced the terror of God in the days and weeks that followed Zora's death. After the revolution, he felt compelled to seek me out."

"But why?" Maksim pressed. "And how did he have your name or whereabouts?"

"Everything, every facet of my life, was noted in my secret

police file because—" Levi paused, his expression pained. "Zora informed on me. During her interrogation."

Maksim straightened. I clapped a hand over my mouth.

"I would be lying if I said it didn't hurt," Levi continued. "But anyone can succumb to those kinds of torture techniques. They're designed to cause people to give up information. She did what she did under extreme duress, and I cannot fault her for it."

Maksim's gaze drifted to me. Our eyes met, but he quickly looked away.

"And this brings us to your story, young Maksim. Rather, the story of your parents." Levi pushed up a smile. "They were lovely people. I do believe you have your mother's eyes, but you look like your father in every other way."

Maksim's jaw tightened. He ran a hand over mouth and then his cheeks. Seemed like he was having a hard time keeping his emotions in check.

"They moved to Bucureşti toward the end of the Yugoslav Wars. Petar was already an investigative journalist and continued his work in Romania. One day, when I was in court to reclaim a property I had lost during communism, Petar slipped me his business card with an address written on the back and a note that said to come alone. I hadn't any idea what this could be about, but I had hoped it may be news of Nicolae, so I went. Iulia let me in, and I found your father"—Levi nodded at Maksim—"chain-smoking and pacing the living room." A hesitation. "I met you that day, as well. You were a smart little thing. We had an exchange in English, your parents and I, and you walked in and proclaimed that you speak English, too, and that you wanted to talk about important things like your *tată* did."

Maksim lowered his hand. His jaw remained tight, and his eyes had gone moist.

"That was the last time I saw you," Levi said. "The story your father had stumbled upon was bigger than any he'd ever broken. He claimed he was being followed, and he suspected his phone was tapped."

"What was the story?" I asked. "Was this the exposé you mentioned?"

"It was indeed. Petar had discovered a human trafficking ring, a large one, involving children from Romania, Moldova, Bulgaria, and other east-European countries. Mothers were told they had received hardship grants and that their children would be attending top-rated schools. Others were promised hefty amounts of money in exchange for work in the entertainment industry– TV, films, modeling. The families were always presented with documents and official-looking credentials, and they needed the money, so they were inclined to acquiesce." Levi whipped out a handkerchief and dabbed at his sweaty forehead. "Eventually, it became clear that the children were missing, but the authorities would never investigate the cases. Or they would conclude the investigations prematurely."

"How did my father discover this?" Maksim asked.

"By falling down a rabbit hole." Levi huffed a laugh, but it was mirthless. "I'll tell you what I said to him that day, and I still believe it. He was chasing down one rabbit, and he found himself with another that was *much* bigger."

Maksim brow furrowed.

"Petar had been troubled over the treatment of Roma people," Levi explained. "He'd been writing stories, detailing the ways Roma people had been turned into scapegoats and how the government had set them up for social failure. While investigating more of those stories, he kept coming across distraught families with missing children. He branched out, following leads to Bulgaria and Moldova and discovered the same phenomenon. He inquired with the police each time, but most of the cases were closed or had never been opened.

"*That* was when the phone calls began—heavy breathing at first, then a sinister voice speaking veiled threats. Then the threats became not-so-veiled. When his editor killed the story. Petar decided to submit to an American paper. Their editor was willing to run it, but he required more research and eyewitnesses, more documentation that the police were covering these cases up. That was why Petar sought me out. He had heard about our group—myself, Zora, Nicolae—to help the Roma community during communism, and he thought I could assist."

"Were you able to?" I asked.

"I tried, but then news broke about the murder of Petar and Iulia. They had been shot, as had their two closest neighbors, all of them at point-blank range." Moisture filled Levi's eyes. "By the time their bodies were discovered, Maksim was missing."

"It was Vladimir. It had to be." My attention landed on Maksim. "You said he died recently, right?"

"*Da*. This past summer. It's why Ştefan is now in charge of our operation." Maksim focused on Levi. "Do you have any theories as to why Vladimir chose to kidnap me? Why not kill me along with my parents?"

"Vladimir had a wife and child, but he was also said to have a mistress. When his wife learned of this other woman—and of the son she had borne to him—she threatened divorce." Levi wagged a finger. "Ohh, but that would not have been good for his new business ventures."

"Business ventures?" I said.

"If Vladimir was Securitate," Maksim chimed in, "he would have come under intense scrutiny after the revolution."

"That's right," Levi said. "And yet many hoped to take advantage of this pseudopolitical shift, and so they registered businesses under the names of wives and girlfriends. Vladimir's companies were key in the rebuilding of national infrastructure—taxis, waste service, telecommunications—and they were all registered under his wife's name. This made her threats rather inconvenient, and one day she was the tragic victim of a bombing. The circumstances indicated *he* had been the intended target, but he was 'coincidentally' called away on business.

"Sadly, his wife was not the only one to perish that day. Their young son was with her instead of the nanny, and he, too, died."

Levi's attention trailed over Maksim. "He was three years old. Yet another strange coincidence."

An epiphany sparked behind Maksim's eyes. "I was three when my parents died."

Levi nodded. "Indeed."

"You believe Vladimir kidnapped me out of guilt? Because I don't believe he was capable of guilt."

"Even the cruelest of men have aspirations for their sons. Perhaps you reminded him of his son in some way. Perhaps he thought you could be the fulfillment of what he lost."

"What about his other son," I asked, "the one he had with his mistress?"

"That was some years prior. The boy was a preteen by the time these events transpired." Levi tipped his head. "Can you guess who *he* was?"

My mouth slipped open. "Ştefan."

Levi gave a decisive nod. Maksim echoed the movement, confirming that Levi's story jived.

The truck shuddered, and everything around us lurched. A handful of crates toppled. I ducked, covering my head.

Footsteps approached. The locks disengaged, and the doors swung open with a loud creak. Sunlight poured inside the cargo hold. The driver said something in Romanian.

Levi replied with a wave. "This is our chance to use the toilet," he said, putting his handkerchief away. "We'll need to be ready by the time he is finished refilling the petrol."

Maksim was on his feet and reached down.

"Thank you, young man." Levi let Maksim pull him up.

I shifted myself onto all fours, about to push up. My knee made contact with the floor, and pain spread like fire. I pulled a sharp breath.

Maksim walked over and reached down. "Your knee?"

"Yeah." I took his hand, grimacing, and he pulled me up.

"Here. Take this." He reached for his wallet and fished out

two one-leu banknotes. "For the toilet," he said, placing them in my hand.

I stared at the money. We had to pay to use the toilet around here?

"The petrol station may sell pain medicine," he said. "I'll get you some, plus bottled waters and whatever we may need for—" Uneasiness sank into his features. Under normal circumstances, he might have called our trip a hike or excursion. But he'd made it clear he thought of this as a suicide mission.

He turned away and hopped down from the cargo bay. I watched him stride toward the bright yellow gas station and follow Levi inside the building.

KSORBA

UKRAINE
HUNGARY
MOLDOVA
ROMÂNIA
Sibiu
Brașov
Ksorba
Neamt
Pitești
Crețulești
București
SERBIA
BULGARIA

34. ABANDONED

It was late afternoon by the time we arrived at a lodge nestled in the foothills of the Făgăraş Mountains. This was one of the launch points for Negoiu Peak, and the place was full of hikers who looked like they belonged in an REI commercial.

We stayed the night and began our journey early the next morning. Levi led us down a path called the Dragon's Trail, which took us into pine forests, over a rusted bridge, and along a razor path carved along the brow of a cliff.

Midafternoon we hit a barren, rocky stretch called Cleopatra's Saddle. We'd been encountering other hikers the entire time. They went one way, heading for Negoiu Peak, while we went the other.

The sun sizzled, casting heat waves over the stony terrain. My knee cooked inside a stretchy black knee brace—something Maksim had picked up inside the gas station—and every step I took drove stabbing pain into my kneecap.

As if that wasn't bad enough, my thighs and calves were shredded from the flights of stairs I'd climbed yesterday, and they were getting sorer.

Levi paused our trek and distributed water and protein bars. I tipped my face up and dumped water, trying to cool the burn setting into my skin. Maksim poured water on his head and gulped the rest.

"I believe we're getting close." Levi twisted a knob on his metal detector. The device chirped. "Many blast mines contain fifty grams of TNT. That is enough to take off your foot. The Soviet mines used here contain five times that amount—enough to destroy your entire leg. Step on one and you will probably die out here." Levi removed his backpack and held it out to me. "Would you mind to carry this, dear? So I can concentrate."

I gaped.

"I'll carry it." Maksim intercepted the backpack. Our eyes met, and he flicked his gaze in the direction we'd come. His stare intensified, burning into mine. A silent plea. *Let's get out of here.*

That was what the look said. It was also what he'd said when he cornered me in the kitchen this morning.

I swallowed and shook my head.

Disappointment flickered through his features. He brushed past me, stationing himself at the back of our line.

Levi took the lead, sweeping his metal detector back and forth. The device emitted soft, electronic clicks. "Follow right behind me. In a straight line now. That's it."

Our pace grew slower as the afternoon faded against a crystal-blue canvas. We were hours from sunset, but the mountains were huge. We were going to lose daylight as soon as the sun dipped below the peaks.

Brown objects appeared in the distance, forming man-made shapes against the natural landscape. The village.

Levi's metal detector went from clicking to whirring. The thing screeched, and Levi zigzagged our trajectory. "Do not step there." He pointed. "Careful now."

My lungs squeezed.

We stopped outside a dilapidated fence. Levi called out in Romanian, then in the Roma language. The echo of his voice was the only response.

"I suppose we'll let ourselves in." He stepped over saggy barbed wire and motioned for us to do the same.

A rusty chime hung from a porch, swaying in the breeze and playing a dull out-of-tune song. The shacks went from decrepit to blackened, and the smell of soot and charred wood wafted over us. We didn't hear any voices or signs of life. The place was abandoned.

Our path dead-ended at a tree line, and for a long moment, none of us said anything.

Maksim broke the silence. "We have water, don't we? Extra protein bars?" He unhooked the backpack and tugged on the zipper. "We'll have to ration everything for the hike back."

"We won't make it by nightfall." Levi scanned our surroundings. "We'll have to take shelter in one of these homes. Those near the entrance are the most intact."

"So that's it?" I divided a look between them. "We came all this way just to turn around and go back?"

"What would you suggest?" Maksim wiped a hand down his face, wicking away sweat. His olive skin was singed pink. "The villagers are gone, apparently due to a fire."

"Yes, and who knows where they could be," Levi added. "Perhaps they've scattered to other parts of the region or other parts of the country. They could be anywhere."

My thoughts spun. Vasile had taken so many precautions with the scavenger hunt. Popescu, too. Dad had said—

"Wait. Guys. What if *this* is what Popescu was talking about?"

Levi tilted his head. "How do you mean?"

"What if he came here, found the village like this, and... I don't know, had the lockbox hidden someplace nobody would think to look since the village was destroyed? Maybe his explanation is some kind of riddle. It could be another clue."

Levi turned to Maksim. "She has a point."

"Does she?" Maksim trained an annoyed look on me.

Levi's gaze drifted over the tree line. "Perhaps we can think about it as we—" His eyebrows cinched. "A moment," he said, extending his metal detector. Then he disappeared into the forest.

"How is your knee?" Maksim asked.

"Not great." A shrug. "But I've played through worse."

He was about to take another drink. "Played?"

"Soccer. Football," I amended. "I used to play."

He stared at me, the plastic bottle raised to his lips. He guffawed and chugged the last of the water.

"What?" I asked.

"You ride bikes, you do parkour—"

"*Used to do* parkour, and only the basics. It was great agility training for soccer."

He looked like he had more to say, or ask, when Levi's voice rang out. "There's a trail!"

The clicking returned, and Levi materialized from the forest. "I've found a trail, and I can hear running water. Perhaps the villagers moved closer to their water source. We should investigate."

I started forward.

Maksim gripped my arm. "Is it safe?"

"I did come across two detonated mines, and there could be more." Levi gave the metal detector a lift. "I'll go first of course."

"It's better than staying the night here"—I jammed a thumb behind us—"in a burned-up shack."

Levi gave a firm nod. "Locating the new settlement would be ideal."

Maksim didn't argue. He must have realized it was the better option.

The forest was dense and offered a cool reprieve from the heat. Slivers of sunlight broke through the thick canopy.

The trail widened and then narrowed again, the forest spreading on either side of us. A hole appeared in the middle of the trail. Levi stepped over it. "This is one of the detonated mines." He glanced back. "It's okay. There aren't any mines around it."

I followed him over. The earth lay freshly bared, and the smell of gunpowder hung in the air. "Did it detonate recently?"

"It would seem so."

"When?" Maksim called from the back.

"It's hard to say." Levi faced him. "Out in the open, the cordite would disperse quickly. However, this forest is dense, without much wind flow, and so the cordite could be lingering in the air from much earlier in the day."

"Meaning someone has come through here recently," Maksim said.

"I've been seeing footsteps." Levi gestured. "They likewise appear to be fresh."

Maksim's jaw tensed. He looked at me, then peered past Levi as if checking the trail for something. Or someone.

Levi traced Maksim's gaze, peering that way before returning his focus to us. "Since I haven't seen the scavenger hunt, I must ask—did the clues imply anything that could lead Ştefan Răzvan here?"

"Not specifically," Maksim said.

"Not at all," I interjected. "The locket was the only thing that hinted at this place. But the reference was vague, and Ştefan doesn't have the locket. We do."

Levi scanned the trail. "The villagers may have trekked through here today. It's possible they detonated mines by accident or that an animal did it."

Maksim didn't seem convinced. Even so, he stepped over the hole and joined us on this side. His eyes clung to worry. I slipped my hand into his, and he looked at me. "You don't understand what would happen if we were to be wrong, if Ştefan—" He couldn't seem to finish.

"Then we'll be careful. And if we come across the settlement, we'll check it out first before making ourselves known."

"That's a good idea," Levi said. "We'll remain quiet, now and hereafter."

I gave Maksim's hand a squeeze. He inhaled, nodding, and fell in line behind me.

Levi circumnavigated a skinny tree in the middle of the trail. He tipped his chin toward the ground. "Mind the roots," he said, stepping over the bumps and ridges.

We copied him.

The metal detector whirred and then settled into clicking. Another hole, similar to the one we'd stepped over, appeared on our right. This one was off the trail, and a scattering of weeds sprang up from within it. Hopefully, that meant the detonation wasn't recent.

The metal detector's clicking stretched into an earsplitting screech. Levi put up a fist. "Hold," he said, pulling up short.

I froze.

He swept the disk, inching forward. The screeching pitched, and fear drained the strength from my knees.

"I think I've found it." Levi angled his metal detector toward another tree, one that grew beside the trail. The screech settled into a *beeeeeep*. "There it is." Levi craned his neck. "It's on the edge of the trail, on the other side of this tree." He motioned for us to back up.

Maksim stopped next to the skinny tree. I stopped in front of it.

Levi headed our way, metal detector whirring and clicking. "It seems the villagers have used these trees as markers. Allow me to go ahead for a—"

The metal detector gave way to a screech.

Levi went still, his device angled in my direction. The screeching edged into the beep we'd heard a second ago.

He scanned the area around our feet. His eyes widened. "Katherine? I need you to walk this way. Very carefully now."

Maksim swore. I pivoted to face him, and his eyes bulged. "Don't move!" he said.

"Katherine, do not move!" Levi shouted at the same time. I finally realized why.

An uneven clump of earth lay in front of the skinny tree, mere inches from where I stood. My heart leaped.

"Come this way, Katherine. Toward me." Levi's voice faded into the background. Fear flooded every crevice of my being, from bottom to top, while something like static filled my ears.

I staggered. My shoe caught an irregularity, and I stumbled. My other foot came down on uneven ground. My ankle rolled, releasing a sharp pain into my bad knee.

My leg muscles, which had been straining to hold me upright, gave out. I fell backward, arms flailing.

I slammed my eyes shut, trembling as Levi's warning took hold. *"Many blast mines contain fifty grams of TNT. That is enough to take off your foot. The Soviet mines used here contain five times that amount—enough to destroy your entire leg."*

This was it. I steeled myself.

Oof. Something hard and scratchy broke my fall.

I opened my eyes and found myself propped against the second tree, the one growing on the edge of the trail. The bark bit into my back and shoulders, my butt. My shoes had gotten tangled in the tree roots.

Maksim stood to my left, wide-eyed, hand extended. To my right, Levi posed in a similar way, like he'd been about to grab me.

I exhaled. "I'm okay," I said, pushing off the tree—and then the trunk moved. Had I imagined it?

Rapid fluttering punctured the stillness. My gaze traveled into the canopy of branches, to the birds taking flight, and I noticed the tree didn't have any leaves. The bark was white.

Levi tipped his head back, and his mouth tumbled open. "Dead tree!" His panicked stare fell to me. "Run! Run!"

Snap. Swoosh.

A gnarled branch plummeted from the treetop. The branch was falling on the other side of the tree, the same side where Levi had been standing. The side where he'd spotted a mine.

I pushed off the tree. My shoes tangled in the roots, and I face-planted on the trail.

Levi darted past me, a smear of khaki and tan. I jumped up, scrambling, trying to follow him. A hand caught my forearm.

My gaze connected with Maksim's. He was in front of me, gripping my forearm with ferocity, and yanked hard.

My shoes broke free from the roots. I flew forward, sailing past him, when a force slammed me to the ground.

35. UNEXPECTED

A blast ripped through the air and rumbled the earth. Dirt rained down. Branches snapped. The entire forest sounded like it was coming down around me.

The rumbling settled into a steady hum. Blood pulsed in my ears.

My eyes opened to pinpricks of light throbbing against a black sheet. I was on my stomach and tried to flip over. I couldn't. A tree had fallen on me.

Levi shouted. His voice grew louder, clearer.

The stars dissolved, and Levi's hiking boots and khaki pants appeared. "Don't move. He may have a spinal injury."

My eyes widened. *He?*

I reached a hand back and discovered... not a tree, but a body. My fingers detected denim, and a sick feeling flooded me. "No! Maksim!"

"Do not panic, Katherine." Levi stooped.

I couldn't tell what he was doing, but I heard something soft hit the ground. The backpack?

Levi squatted in front of me, bringing himself into view. His eyebrows were knit together, deepening the creases in his forehead. "Katherine, I need you to place your hands beneath you. Pretend you're doing a pushup."

I worked my hands under me. Dirt ground into my palms.

"I'm going to hold Maksim's head and neck stable," Levi continued, "in case he has a spinal injury. I need you to push up, slowly, so that he rolls off you. Come now. Up."

"I'm... trying." I gritted my teeth and pushed, grunting. My arms trembled, and I collapsed. "He's too heavy."

"Oh goodness." A hesitation. "Try pushing up onto your forearms."

I did what he said. It was enough to roll Maksim off me.

He landed on his back.

"Now bring me the backpack. It's just there." Levi held Maksim's head straight and directed his eyes toward the backpack. The heap of brown blurred behind a veil of dust and tears.

I swiped at the dampness and snatched up the backpack. The smell of gunpowder wafted up, and a fresh wave of nausea rolled through me. The tan fabric was singed black in one section.

"Levi, look." I held the backpack toward him.

He inspected it. "Indeed, the pack may have protected him to some degree. And I don't see any blood, so I don't believe the mine contained shrapnel. All very good signs."

Levi tucked the backpack under Maksim's head and shifted the contents until they conformed to the right shape. When he finished, the water bottles and spare clothing cupped Maksim's head, holding it stable.

"What are we going to do?" I asked. "We can't just stay out here."

"We need a better sense for Maksim's injuries. We'll have that when he wakes." Levi stepped away and plunked himself on the trail. "Ideally, Maksim will be able to walk and we can continue to the village. Perhaps someone there has a mobile phone."

"You don't have one?"

"I've managed to stay hidden all these years only by avoiding technology."

"This is horrible." My gaze settled on Maksim, and a sharp twist pierced my intestines. "I really thought we'd be okay once we got to the village. I didn't realize— I didn't—"

"None of us realized. When I found the map, I assumed I had the knowledge we needed for a safe journey." He pushed a hand through his sweaty hair. "Assumptions are nothing but trouble. I should know this."

"You don't understand. Maksim didn't—" Heat permeated my eyes. "He thought this was a bad idea from the start, but this morning, while I was making coffee in the kitchen, he came in there to talk to me about—"

Levi peered up at me.

I felt myself blush. Levi had seen us in the kitchen—right along with the rest of the lodge—and Maksim and I hadn't been talking. We'd been kissing.

Levi must have noticed my embarrassment because he said, "You were having a conversation? While you were brewing coffee?"

Regret spilled over and soaked my cheeks. "We were." At one point. "Maksim had a bad feeling, and he begged me to reconsider. I said I couldn't and that he was free to leave if he didn't want to join us. But..."

"But Maksim, caring for you as he does, insisted on accompanying us." Levi's brow crinkled. "Is that right?"

I nodded, sniffling. "I should have listened to him."

Voices reached us from somewhere farther down the trail. I gasped, looking at Levi. He pointed his ear that direction, and hope returned to his eyes. "I do believe that's people speaking in Romani Čib."

"The villagers?"

"Perhaps so. They must have heard the explosion." He called out in the Roma language and then stopped to listen. His brow furrowed.

"What is it?" I asked.

"One of them is speaking in French."

Dread poured into me. "Are you sure?"

A man appeared in the distance, and he was followed by a line of people. They drew closer, weaving their way along the trail. Levi called out.

They kept coming. Tattered jeans and a faded polo shirt came into view. His skin was dark, his hair black as night. He looked like he might be a villager.

He paused at a wide section of the trail and pointed around him. Another villager walked forward, then another.

Levi craned his neck, trying to see who was next. Terror eclipsed his face. "My God. Is that... Vladimir?"

"Vladimir's dead. Maksim said he died last summ—" My explanation dropped off when a stocky form came into view. A lanky form and black hair followed.

"Oh God." I dropped beside Maksim and scooped up his hand. "Please wake up. They're here." I squeezed. "Maksim, they're here. You were right."

He groaned.

Émilien and Drago stationed themselves between the villagers. Émilien's eyes locked on mine and narrowed.

The dread in my stomach hardened.

A lean form with sooty-blond hair swaggered forward. Black slacks fell around dusty chukka boots similar to the ones Maksim had worn one night. His eyes were red-rimmed like he hadn't slept, and his beard looked like he was two days past due on a trim; but his button-down dress shirt was tucked neatly into his belted pants, giving him a put-together finish.

He drew a massive—and I mean *huge*—handgun from some type of leather holster strapped across his shoulders. A strip of sunlight glinted off the pistol's gold plating and cast a soft sheen across the man's haggard face.

"You must be Kat. I have heard so much about you." His smooth timbre slipped through the tension in the air. His eyes blinked to me, and his icy-blue irises chilled my blood.

My attention moved to a swirl of black curling across his hands and fingers. The skin was covered in tattoos, and I gasped.

His gaze flicked past me. "The infamous Levi Pavel, I presume. You're a difficult man to find."

Levi swallowed his horror and pushed himself up.

Ştefan's icy gaze fell on Maksim. "Tell me, what has happened to my cousin?"

"He's not your cousin," I snapped. "And you know it."

Ştefan's lifeless gaze returned to me. Fear tingled in my throat. Émilien said something in French.

Ştefan listened while inspecting the fingernails on his free hand. Then he glanced at me and flitted his pistol in my direction.

Émilien's lips curled up in a sly smile. He marched toward me.

I whimpered, backpedaling.

Levi stepped between us. The Frenchman gripped his shoulders and flung him into Drago, who trailed three steps behind. They both staggered, and Ştefan went rigid.

"*Aveţi grijă!* Idiots! There are mines in this forest."

A gentle hand with a familiar touch came to a rest on mine. I looked to my right and found Maksim, sitting upright and reaching for me.

I knelt beside him and cupped his face. "You're okay?"

"Apart from seeing two of everything." He blinked hard and shook his head. His mouth parted as if he had more to say, but then his eyes locked onto something. Some*one*.

Ştefan stood over us.

He placed a boot on Maksim's chest and shoved him to the ground. Maksim landed on his back.

"Leave him alone!" I clambered, trying to get between them.

Someone dragged me away. I screamed as Ştefan stomped on Maksim's shoulder and arm, grounding his boot down into his scars.

Maksim's grimace gave way to a scream.

Ştefan ground a final time and rocked back, hair flopping into his face. He raked the greasy locks back and used his pistol to beckon the villagers. Two of them walked forward, carrying rope.

Levi called out to them in the Roma language. The men looked at each other, confusion passing between them.

"They are surprised to hear a *gadjo* speak their language." Ştefan's mouth hitched up. "They also speak Romanian, and I was able to forewarn them of what would befall their families should they fail to do as I say."

"You are just like your father," Levi said. "Nicolae always said Vladimir was quite the manipulator."

"What say you, Pavelić? Would you like to know what happened to my uncle, Nicolae?"

"He didn't die in that plane accident, did he?" Levi's voice swirled with shock and revulsion. "When I heard the story, I wondered if he was perhaps alive."

"He is not alive anymore." Ştefan's eyebrow angled up. "But he was."

A tremor took hold of me. "He... wasn't on that plane?"

"Your interactions with a certain liaison were not as you believed." Ştefan ambled over to the backpack. "You were speaking with one of my people."

I drew back. The liaison worked for Ştefan.

"Your father needed to disappear as far as the Americans were concerned." Ştefan snatched up Levi's singed backpack. "I was in possession of his passport, and so I hired a man who resembled him to take his place on the flight. This man thought he was traveling to the United States. Of course, he didn't quite make it there."

I had no idea what he meant by that. Levi didn't seem to either, but then his face blanched. "You. You were the one who sabotaged the flight."

"He... What?" I gaped between Levi and Ştefan. "He did what?"

"It was a simpler solution than manufacturing a fake story," Ştefan said. "All it required was a call to the right person to approve a change of aircraft. There was one in the fleet that was known to have a certain software issue." He waved the gun at no one in particular. "My people were able to gain access to it before the flight and were thus able to ensure a successful… mission."

I focused on Levi. "What's he talking about?"

"The EU was set to ground a particular aircraft"—Levi eased closer—"a model that contained a fatal flaw in the flight-control software. It's the same issue that brought down commercial jets Ethiopia and Jakarta."

"A sensor malfunction triggers the nose-down command and keeps the aircraft locked in that state," Ştefan said casually. "In case you were interested in the specifics."

Levi narrowed his eyes. "You took advantage, didn't you? You understood the nature of the defect, and you exploited it. You killed those innocent people!"

"Where's my dad?" I demanded.

"My men captured him en route to the Braşov *postă*. He was in possession of a package, which we intercepted before he could mail it." Ştefan swaggered toward me. "I needed to understand this scavenger hunt he and my grandfather created, and I tried a variety of methods to extract the information—sleep deprivation, stress positions, fear induction, fingernail excisions, light effects, sound effects.

"On the third day, as his will was beginning to fracture, we experienced an unfortunate… accident." Ştefan pursed his lips. "One of my employees used blunt force that was too great for Nicolae to bear, and the final blow killed him."

I held a fist at my side. "You're lying."

He slid a hand into his pocket, pulled something out, and tossed it at my feet. It was a wooden crucifix, the same kind Paty had been wearing. The same kind Dad used to have.

But it didn't just look like Dad's. It *was* Dad's.

A wave of nausea barreled into me. I hunched over and heaved hot, watery vomit into the dirt.

"Vasile was already dead"—Ştefan's voice drifted into the background—"having thrown himself in front of a bus. His assistant died during an altercation with the police. With Nicolae dead, I was left with one option—to send the package to our dearest Kat and then wait, and watch, and let *her* do the work for me."

I wiped my mouth and straightened. "That was you—somebody working for you—who was texting me, pretending to be my dad."

Ştefan's smug look told me everything I needed to know.

"I thought I was being paranoid, but someone really was following me, weren't they? And—" I gasped. "You hacked my phone! You were the one opening my emails, my text messages, everything."

Maksim pushed himself to standing, and another epiphany plowed into me. Maksim's behavior, certain things he'd said or asked, the way he'd insisted on knowing about the scavenger hunt.

But... no. He couldn't be part of this. Not him.

He limped over to us, saying something to Ştefan. I heard Ty's name.

Ştefan replied, still hanging on to that smug smile.

"He set your ex up," Maksim translated, "with the dancer. To ensure Ty wouldn't come with you on this trip. He wanted you to come alone."

"He told you that now?" I swallowed. "Or did you already know?"

Maksim stopped beside me. Anguish tore through his features.

"I can't believe this." My voice broke. "You knew, didn't you?"

"Kat, please—"

"No! You knew, and you never said anything!"

Ştefan laughed maniacally. "Ohh, now isn't this intriguing? Perhaps Maksim was also the employee who sabotaged the flight." He gestured with his pistol. "Perhaps *he* was the one who tortured your father to death."

My eyes heated. I glared at Maksim.

"It's a lie. I knew nothing of your father nor of Ştefan's involvement with the plane crash." He leaned in and lowered his voice. "I was distancing myself from the operation during that time. I've been trying to get out."

"Did you tell her *how* you planned to do that?" Ştefan leaned in and lowered his voice, clearly mocking Maksim. "Does she know about our little arrangement?"

Maksim looked away, and the truth came crashing down.

"I thought you wanted to help me," I said as the first tear spilled over. "I thought... I thought you cared about me!"

His Adam's apple moved with a loud swallow. "I do."

"No, you don't. You've been spying on me!" My stomach bottomed out. "And that was the arrangement, wasn't it? To feed information about me, about the scavenger hunt, to Ştefan, and then he would let you out."

"Yes." Maksim's answer rang hollow, pinging through my mind and leaving me disoriented. He reached for me. "Kat, please. There's more I need to tell you."

"Don't touch me." I jerked away as shadows fell across us. Émilien and Drago were moving in on Maksim. Drago held a pair of handcuffs.

Maksim took one look at Ştefan and then held out his hands. Drago slapped the cuffs on him.

"Coward," I muttered.

Maksim shot a look at me. "What else am I supposed to do? He's got a piece. They all do."

Émilien reached back and pulled a plain black pistol from his waistband. He gave the gun a playful jiggle.

One of the villagers grabbed my hands and bound them together with rope. Levi was next. They retrieved Levi's metal detector while Ştefan ordered us into formation.

I scanned the ground. Dad's necklace was on the trail, the tiny crucified figure lying face down in the dirt.

I squeezed past the villagers, past Ștefan and his goons, and scooped up the necklace. Emotion pressed on my throat.

I pocketed the necklace.

When I turned again, I rammed straight into someone. My gaze trailed up the buttons of a burgundy shirt, over a blond beard, and stopped on ice-blue eyes. My courage dissolved.

Ștefan reared back, gun raised. The metal gleamed, sailing toward me, until the butt connected with the side of my head.

Crack! Pain flared in my skull.

Scuffles and shouts faded into the background.

36. TOGETHER

A golden glow warmed my eyelids.

I cracked open my eyes and blinked against sunlight. A dirt floor stretched around me. A drumbeat pulsed somewhere far away.

But it wasn't far away. The horrible throbbing was in my head and cheek.

I moaned and peered down at the rope digging into my torso. My arms were numb, tingly, as they hung at my sides.

"Katherine?" It was Levi's voice. "Are you awake?"

I nodded and then realized he couldn't see me. We were seated back-to-back. "Yeah," I mumbled. "I am." We'd been like this all night, each of us tied tightly to a chair. Drago had then tied those chairs together using more rope, ensuring we couldn't help each other.

"How are you feeling?" Levi asked.

"My head hurts really bad. So does my cheek."

"I'm sorry to hear that." Levi shifted behind me. "My legs are asleep, as are my hands."

"Mine are asleep, too." I tried to lift my leg. The rope pulled taut against the chair and bit my bare ankle.

"Do you see any signs of Maksim?" Levi asked. "Did they ever bring him back?"

I craned my neck and peered out the window. I could see into the next shack over. "He's not there, and I haven't heard anything since—" Memories from last night choked me. I pinched my eyes shut, wanting to forget what I'd witnessed.

"I suppose you wouldn't know what time you fell asleep," Levi said, "would you? Approximately?"

"It was sometime after Maksim— After they—" I couldn't get the words out.

Drago and Émilien had strung up Maksim and used him as a punching bag. When they'd done all the boxing they could, Émilien had retrieved a plank and used it as a baseball bat, focusing on the scarred side of Maksim's body.

Maksim's screams echoed in my ears.

Noise reached us from somewhere outside the shack. The door flew open and slammed against the wall. I started and threw a look over my shoulder.

Drago strode toward us. He was carrying a knife, and I screamed.

"Shut up!" He yanked on the ropes and sawed through them. The restraints broke and fell away.

He lifted me up and pushed me toward the door. I collapsed, legs on fire with pinpricks, my hands and arms tingling.

I grimaced, rubbing and moving everything while Drago cut Levi's ropes.

"Hurry up," Drago barked when he was finished.

I pushed up and helped Levi. He could barely walk.

Heat cloaked us outside, the sky clear and blazing blue. A group of silhouettes gathered in front of us. I squeezed my forehead, desperate to soothe the headache, and squinted against the morning light.

"Maksim." Surprise ricocheted through Levi's voice as he gaped at a tall silhouette.

Maksim slouched, head drooping while a middle-aged couple

—villagers, I assumed—held him up. The villagers scampered away and disappeared into one of the shacks.

Maksim swayed, his arm cradled in a sling. He was still wearing his jeans and boots from yesterday, but someone had dressed him in a red plaid shirt that made him look like a lumberjack.

Ştefan shoved him.

Maksim stumbled forward and dropped to his knees.

"Oh dear." Levi took a step, then snapped forward. "Katherine, my legs." He rubbed them. "Go and help him."

"But—"

"Please. He needs help."

I swallowed my argument and approached Maksim. Dark circles ringed his eyes. A five-o'clock shadow tinged his sun-kissed face.

I squatted beside him and hitched his good arm across my shoulders. "Try to stand up," I said. "I don't think I can hold your body weight."

He placed one foot in front, and we both pushed up to standing.

"You good?" I asked, and he nodded.

I turned, planning to return to Levi. Maksim caught my arm and reeled me back. "I had nothing to do with sabotaging that flight."

I tried to pull away.

He held on. "I've done terrible things in my life, and I was fully capable of such a thing in the past, but not anymore. I could not have lived with myself." He loosened his grip. "The same is true about your father. I knew nothing of him."

"Guess you were just spying on me then."

"Ştefan always investigates Americans traveling here. He did the same with you, or so he told me, and then pretended you may be a spy, saying the scavenger hunt was suspicious. He wouldn't let it go, and I became concerned for you."

I rolled my eyes.

"It's true. He did promise to release me from my obligations if I helped you solve the clues, but he was already considering it beforehand"—Maksim glanced at his arm in the sling—"for this very reason. I'm a liability. I took the easier way out, I admit, but I was also doing what I thought best for you. So that he wouldn't see you as a threat."

My chest swelled. "How do I know you're not making this up?"

"You don't. But I had to tell you this before—" Moisture pooled in his eyes.

He brought his fingers to my cheek, and his calluses skimmed the spot Émilien had hit. Why hadn't my knee—or anything else for that matter—healed like my cheek had healed? What was the difference?

I'd always recovered from sports injuries quickly. Not overnight, but faster than my teammates. Last night I'd been willing my body to heal itself again, to re-create whatever super-fast healing I'd experienced after the club.

Nothing had improved. In fact, the headache was worse.

Maksim lowered his hand. "I'm sorry for all of this and even more so for the way I've treated you. Will you forgive me?"

I nodded, emotions spilling over. He drew me in for a hug.

"We're going to die out here, aren't we?" I buried my face in his shirt as the tears flowed. "That's why you're saying this stuff. Because you know we're going to die."

"Shh." Maksim's lips came to a rest on my head. He was saying something, whispering. His words danced into my psyche and soothed my frazzled thoughts.

The secret poem.

My cries dispelled into nothingness. I rested against him, letting him hold me.

Someone did a slow clap. We pulled away from each other.

Ștefan was swaggering up to us. "Bravo. A beautiful perfor-mance." He lowered his hands, his attention on me. "And since you two have reconciled, *you* shall have the lovely task of helping this traitor."

"Helping him with what?"

He ignored my question, beckoning two more villagers. They rushed forward, each carrying a backpack. One of them held a metal detector. "Ion and Vano have knowledge of the mines around this village. They shall be accompanying us on this hike."

"Maksim can't hike," I insisted. "He can barely stand up."

"Hence the need for your assistance," Ştefan said dryly.

Drago placed a knuckle to his cheek, pouting dramatically, and mimed like he was crying. Émilien had his arms crossed, his steely gaze fixed on Maksim.

Ştefan thrust Levi's metal detector into his hands.

Levi took it. "And if we refuse to comply with your demands?"

"Think not only of yourself, Pavelić, but also of your friends. Your death may be a painful one, and I can make theirs exponentially worse." Ştefan lit a sly smile on Levi. "Is that clear enough for you?"

Levi sent a fleeting glance to Maksim and me. "Perfectly clear."

Ştefan formed our line and put Levi in front.

The crime boss's goons were stationed in back. Maksim and I ended up in front of them, and Émilien kept his pistol trained on Maksim the entire time.

Drago had a pistol—I'd seen it in his waistband—but he held some kind of retractable riot stick. He stuck his hand through a strap and clenched the handle. With a flick of his wrist, the riot stick snapped to full length.

"Insurance," Maksim whispered.

"The riot stick?" I looked up at him. "Why?"

"I've disarmed him in training—on several occasions—and he doesn't appear to be taking chances today in spite of my condition." Maksim grimaced, holding his shoulder. "Notice the wrist strap. That will help him maintain possession, but if I did manage to take it, he still has his pistol."

"So do the other two," I whispered back.

"*Da.*"

Drago made eye contact. Maksim faced forward and draped his unslung arm over me. I wrapped an arm around his waist.

Jagged mountains chiseled the landscape around the village. Levi's metal detector clicked for a hundred yards. We rounded a bend, and the device slipped into whirring and clicking.

"Stay in a straight line," Levi called to us. "Do not stray from the trail we're forging."

I tightened my hold on Maksim. His sober expression intensified.

We trudged along until the landscape opened up into a valley. The smaller villager—pretty sure he was Vano—pointed at a cluster of hills.

Levi faced us. "Nicolae said the lockbox should be buried on or near a hill. There aren't any hills around the old village, and so" —Levi gestured—"this is where Vano has suggested we come."

Ştefan raised his hand and beckoned someone.

Steel jabbed me from behind. "You are being summoned, *ma chérie.*" Émilien pushed, and the pistol dug into my back.

Maksim withdrew his arm and nodded for me to go ahead.

I walked forward until I reached Ştefan. He cut me with side-eye, and a swirl of darkness seemed to hover around him. My heart trembled.

He reached into his pocket and produced several sheets of paper. Dad's letter, I realized. He must have found a way to access my room at the hostel like Maksim had said.

Ştefan unfolded the pages and began to read one of them. "'When you get to where you're going, think about the fables I told you as a child. One in particular is supposed to assist in locating a lockbox similar to the one containing this letter.'" He read like he was doing an audition for high-brow theater.

"'This other lockbox was hidden on or perhaps very near to a hill,'" he continued. "'We don't know where precisely. Even Popescu doesn't know. He and my father planned it this way in case any of us are captured.'" Ştefan stabbed the pages at me. "It seems that you, dearest Kat, are the only person who knows how to discover this lockbox."

"I-I don't. I don't even know which fable he could have been referring to."

Ştefan's eyes narrowed to venomous slits.

A hand touched my shoulder. "I am certain we can figure it out," Levi said, guiding me to the front. "We will try," he called back before focusing on me. "Katherine, do not argue with the man. These are not people to be trifled with."

"I'm sorry, but I really don't know and—" I pressed on my left temple. "Levi, I have the worst headache."

"I understand. I have pains in places I haven't used in decades, but we must concentrate." He dropped his voice another notch. "Perhaps if you can find it, there will be a way to negotiate with him, or perhaps we'll have an opportunity to—"

"What is this?" Ştefan shoved past Ion and Vano. "Conspiring, are we?"

"No, no." Levi shook his head. "I'm merely advising her to cooperate. That is the best and easiest way to go about this." Levi's brow crinkled. "Isn't it, Katherine?"

I swallowed and nodded.

Ştefan didn't act like he believed us, but he didn't question us further.

"All right now. Have a look." Levi turned me toward the valley. "Think about the fables your father told you and analyze those in comparison to what you see here."

"Okay." I kept two fingers pressed to my temple and studied the landscape. "Are y'all sure it's this area?"

Levi said something in Romanian. The taller villager, Ion, answered.

"There is another hill heading east," Levi translated, "but it's farther from the village."

"Okay, then let's pretend the hill is down there in the valley. How do I figure out which one it is?"

"That is the very question we need you to answer."

Sweat seeped along my neck and dripped down my shirt. The previous day's hike had left my arms and legs pink.

I inhaled a ragged breath. Hot, dry air swam around in my lungs. A second breath, deeper. I couldn't organize my thoughts.

Levi sent a concerned look to Ştefan. "Katherine?"

"I'm trying. It's just— I can't think with this headache. The heat is making it worse."

Levi cleared his throat and turned toward Ştefan. "May she have some water? She is having difficulty concentrating, but water may help."

Ştefan's blue gaze sharpened.

He cut a sideways look at his goons. Drago and Émilien grinned, turning their attention to Maksim.

My eyes bulged. "Wait!"

Drago raised the riot stick and slammed it against Maksim's slung arm. Maksim staggered, crying out.

"The mines!" Levi scrambled.

Ştefan grabbed him.

Drago landed the riot stick behind Maksim's knees, taking out his legs, then Émilien pistol-whipped him across the face. The steel butt connected with Maksim's mouth. His head snapped to the side. Blood sprayed.

Émilien delivered a final blow, and Maksim collapsed in the dirt.

"Move!" I shoved my way past Ion and Vano.

"Do not stray from the trail," Levi called.

Maksim lay face down in the dirt, muttering.

"Maksim?" I squatted beside him. "Can you hear me?"

He turned his head. Dirt crusted his nose and forehead. His mouth and cheek were smeared with blood. I wasn't sure what to do. He was a mess, but I didn't have anything to clean him up with.

But... I did. I had my bare hands.

I cupped his face and used my thumbs to wipe away the bloody, crusty mess. That night at the club came back to me, and tears filled my eyes. He had done this same thing for me—cleaning me up, taking care of me. I had never in a million years thought I would be doing it for him.

Ştefan stood over us. "Has your ability to concentrate improved?"

The dam ruptured, and tears leaked down my face. I made a failed attempt to answer, unable to talk past the knot in my windpipe.

"Shall I have them continue?" Ştefan asked coyly.

I glared up at him. "Leave Maksim alone, or I'll... I'll throw myself into a mine and you'll never get that lockbox."

Ştefan's eyes ignited.

"Give her a moment please, for pity's sake," Levi said. "Just one moment!"

Ştefan stepped past me and called Drago and Émilien away from our group.

"Kat." Maksim breathed my name so quietly I almost missed it. I helped him into a sitting position. As I did, he placed his mouth to my ear. "Run," he whispered.

I drew back. "What?"

"Run. While they're distracted." He glanced at our captors as they whispered among each other. "I'll charge them, take them by surprise. That should give you enough time if you run hard."

"The mines. Maksim, I would need Levi's metal detector."

"You won't. I've been dragging my shoe." He glanced in the direction we'd come from, and I could make out a long line carved into the dirt. "Go to the village. Ask for a woman named Vadoma. Her brother in Avrig owns a taxi company. They can drive you to Hungary. You *must* hide in their trunk at the border crossing. Do you understand?"

My gaze lingered. I envisioned myself following the trail, running to the village, getting out of the country...

Then I envisioned Maksim and Levi, still here. Still captured.

"I-I can't."

"You can." Maksim turned his head and spit. Blood spattered the dirt. "Run. Follow the trail. Don't look back." He tensed, about to jump up.

I gripped his shoulders and held him down. "No. I can't leave y'all behind. I won't." My voice quavered. "We're in this together."

"You don't underst—"

"*Together.*" I raked my fingers through his damp, dirty hair. "No matter what."

37. TREK

Stefan slanted a look at us.

I pushed myself up and did my best to ignore the throbbing in my head. My knee cooked inside the stretchy black knee brace.

I'd played through stuff like this before. Back then I could push the pain into the background and will myself to concentrate on whatever strategy Coach Jules had given us.

My only strategy now was to buy us as much time as possible, which meant working on the scavenger hunt. Maybe it wouldn't do any good. But maybe it would.

"I'm ready," I said.

Drago hauled Maksim to his feet.

Maksim's desperation lingered. His eyes were pleading, his lips shaping around something he wanted to say.

Émilien trained his pistol and said something that made the color drain from Maksim's face. Maksim's eyes flashed to me.

"Katherine." Levi waved me to the front of the line.

I made my way to him as he gulped from one of the canteens. When he finished, he held the canteen toward me. "Have some."

I took it and tipped my head back. Warm water sloshed into my mouth.

"Look what we've found." Levi stole a glance at Ştefan and his goons before slipping a square packet into my hand. My fingers detected two round, flat objects inside. I read the label.

Aspirină. Aspirin.

I tore open the packet. "Where'd you find this?"

"Vano's backpack. The pills are old, so I cannot guarantee their effectiveness."

I popped both pills and washed them down with another gulp. A backward glance revealed Ştefan striding toward us. I crumpled the empty packet.

"Try to concentrate, Katherine." Levi pointed, letting his aim drift over the mountains and then down toward the valley. "Think about the fables your father mentioned. Better yet, let's talk about them."

"When I was a kid, he used to tell me Aesop's fables. I didn't know they were Aesop's fables until later, when I read them for an assignment in my freshman English class. All that time, I thought Dad had made them up."

"Did any of the fables involve a hill?"

"I don't think so, but some of them involved animals, and I'm trying to think if any of those characters might have climbed a hill."

"Or a mountain, perhaps?"

"I think— I'm not sure, but there might have been a fable about a volcano." I glanced at Ştefan, who was glaring. "Are there, um, any volcanoes in Romania?"

"Not in this region," Levi said.

I studied the jagged mountains in the distance, the rocky ground around us, the dwindling creek winding through the valley.

A bird soared overhead, and two fables blinked into my thoughts.

The Fox and the Crow.

The Eagle and the Arrow.

But Dad had said something about a hill, not a bird.

"Wait." I faced Ștefan. Our eyes locked, and a chill flowed into my veins. "Can I, um—?" I managed a stiff swallow. "Can I see my dad's letter?"

Ștefan fished out the pages and held them toward me. As soon as I reached, he withdrew them. "I have thus far withheld the full force of my wrath against Maksim. But you *will* see it should I suspect you are being less than cooperative." He grabbed my hand and wrestled my fingers open.

The crumpled-up packet fell. Ștefan nudged it with the toe of his chukka boot.

"Just aspirin." I barely managed to get the words out. "M-my head hurts."

He rolled his eyes and thrust the papers at me.

I read through them, hands shaking. Then I had to read them a second time. Then a third. Sweat dribbled down my face and neck. I flapped my shirt, fanning myself.

"Katherine?" Levi's voice strained.

"Sorry. I need a second."

That second turned into thirty and then sixty. Finally my brain switched on, and I was able to do more than read the words. I was able to picture Dad writing them, putting myself there with him. I imagined what he might have said, what he might have been thinking.

This was how he'd taught me to solve the scavenger hunts. *"Put yourself in the other person's shoes. Think as they think. Imagine you are them."*

The epiphany I'd been searching for pinged.

Well, I hoped it was an epiphany. There was only one way to know for sure. "I don't think the fable involves a hill," I said. "Pretty sure we're assuming that."

"What would lead you to such a conclusion?" Levi asked. Ștefan didn't say anything, but I had his full attention.

"When Dad used to create these scavenger hunts, he had a way of making one thing seem like another—like when he was referring to you in that one clue. He made it seem like it was pointing to him, but that was part of the puzzle, a complexity to ensure no one else could figure it out."

"Do you find such a complexity now," Levi asked, "with regard to the hill?"

"The exact opposite. He's talking about the hill like— It's almost like the hill was just a parameter for hiding the lockbox. He doesn't even sound very sure about it."

Ştefan snatched the pages, reading them again. He cast a disbelieving eyebrow at me.

"You don't see what I'm talking about? If the fable had involved a hill, I think he would have come up with something more clever than that."

Levi glanced around. "Specifying the terrain—a hilly area, for instance—would give you an idea of where to search, otherwise the lockbox could be anywhere. It's possible, however, this was merely a general instruction for the hiding place. Perhaps the assistant—Popescu was it?—had free rein to decide the specifics from there."

Ştefan pointed the pages at me. "Get on with it."

I inhaled a shaky breath. If a hill had been a parameter for hiding the lockbox, what other requirements could there have been? And which fable?

A large bird, something like a hawk, coasted into the valley and swooped down, landing in the branches of a tree. I shielded my eyes. The tree grew on one side of a hill, while a smattering of gray sprinkled the other.

"Do you see that?" I pointed at the gray.

Levi traced my gaze.

Ştefan did the same, passing between us and stopping beside Ion. The two of them had an exchange, and Ion's eyes widened. The villager shook his head. Ştefan grabbed him by the collar. Vano raced over, pleading.

"Ştefan inquired about those gray objects on the hill," Levi whispered.

"And?"

"They're headstones." Levi replaced the canteen lid. "Those are the graves of the villagers who perished in the accidental detonations. A woman and three children."

"Is that why Ion and Vano are so upset?" I stared at the distant splotches of gray. "Are they afraid we're going to disturb their dead?"

"They are more concerned that we may join them." Levi's eyebrows lifted into fuzzy gray arcs. "There are mines around that hill."

"Are you serious?" I gawked. "Why?"

"Of that I'm unsure."

Ştefan marched up to me. "What conclusion have you come to?"

I blinked. "Am I supposed to focus on that one hill or...?"

Ştefan grabbed me. His manicured nails dug into the fleshy underside of my forearm.

"Ouch!"

"Now." He gritted his teeth. "It's up to you to decide. Is *that* the hill we seek or not?"

Maksim's voice reached us. He sounded like he was speaking in Russian.

Drago whipped the riot baton around and slugged him in the gut. Maksim snapped forward and dropped to his knees.

My heart clenched.

Ştefan redoubled his grip—but then he let go. Levi managed a single question, or what sounded like a question. Ştefan's answer was lengthy.

The crime boss snatched the canteen from Levi and marched over to his goons. Maksim was still on his knees.

"Do you remember the story I told you?" Levi asked. "About the surviving Ksorba brother who became an elder of this village?"

"Who finished the mining project. I remember."

"They were discussing him just now. Apparently, his efforts to secure the village came back to haunt him, for those are the graves of his wife and children. They died in a series of detonations."

My hand flew to my mouth.

"I'm unsure what became of him—Miroslav was his name—but the man must have lost his sanity." Levi wiped a soiled handkerchief across his brow. Dirt smeared. "After burying his family there, he mined the entire hill in a final means to 'protect' them."

I lowered my hand. "Then there's no way the lockbox could've been hidden on that hill. Right?"

"I've seen my share of impossible things, young Katherine. That said, I cannot fathom a scenario where such a thing would happen." He didn't sound sure, but I clung to the hope that he was right.

That hope turned to dust as a certain fable came to mind. Tears plucked at my eyes.

Levi's attention settled on me. He straightened. "What is it, Katherine? Have you thought of something?"

Ştefan stormed toward us, sans the canteen. "Well?" he demanded.

My attention returned to the hill. "I don't think you're going to like this." The statement was directed at Levi, but it was Ştefan who responded.

He wrapped his long fingers around my arm, teeth gritted, and yanked me in. "Which. Fable?"

"It's called 'The Miser and His Gold.' A man sells everything he owns for a lump of gold and then buries it. Some versions say it's buried by a wall, others in a garden." Fear gnawed me from the inside out. "In my English class, we read a version where it was buried at the foot of a tree."

"There are other trees in the area." Hope infused Levi's voice. "We could begin with those and—"

"Quiet." Ştefan scanned the valley. "Into formation. All of you. The same order as before." He called for his goons.

"If that's the right fable," I said to Levi, "then I'm pretty sure that's the right hill. None of the other hills have a tree."

"And I suppose the mines would ensure the security of the lockbox." He lifted his arm and rubbed his forehead against the sleeve. Sweat doused the fabric. "God help us."

Ştefan had us tighten up our formation. Maksim and I were the only ones still side by side, and only because he could barely walk. His full weight bore down on me. His feet dragged, one and then the other.

Levi's metal detector reverted to clicking at the entrance to the valley. As we neared the hill, the device skipped between whirring and screeching.

Tension crept into my shoulders. I clutched Maksim's waist. "That's it," I said, trying not to grunt. "We're almost there. You're doing great."

Levi held up a hand and brought our trek to a halt. "This hill is heavily mined," he said, "and the mines were deployed too close together. Detonating one would set off a chain reaction that would kill us all. We must watch for irregularities, trip wires, anything that looks unnatural." His attention drifted to Maksim. "Do try to lift your feet as you walk. Try not to kick up dirt or rocks. Does everyone understand?"

We responded in hard-edged silence. Yeah. We understood.

Levi took us up a steep section layered in chunks of rock-fused earth. We used these juts as stairs, pausing while Levi swept his metal detector in slow, meticulous arcs.

As we neared the top, someone at the front of the line grunted out an *oof*. I peered past Ştefan.

Ion's shoe had caught on something. He slipped, falling forward, and the sole of his shoe flung dirt and pebbles behind him.

The spray flew past Ştefan, past Maksim and me. I turned in time to see the pebbles sail past Drago and Émilien and plunk down the slope.

I snapped my eyes shut, waiting for the explosion. Electronic screeching filled the air. Anxiety filled my chest.

I peeked through one eye. Drago and Émilien stood frozen,

their faces wide in alarm. When I turned, I discovered Levi standing on a large jut behind us. His tan face had gone as gray as his hair.

"Careful please." His Adam's apple dipped. "Everyone."

We crested the hill, and the screeching settled into clicks. I didn't dare relax until we were gathered under the tree.

Maksim collapsed against the trunk. Levi hunched over, hands braced on his knees.

Ştefan marched up to Levi and barked something. Levi straightened and continued across the hill, sweeping his metal detector. Vano joined him. They must have been checking the perimeter.

Ştefan produced two hand shovels from Ion's backpack and tossed them at my feet. "Get to work."

I grabbed one of the shovels.

"The top of the hill is clear," Levi called as he made his way to us. "Vano says the mines are only deployed along the slope—" He pulled up short, his attention divided between the shovel in my hand and the one on the ground.

Ştefan kicked the shovel. "Start digging, Pavelić."

38. CHAOS

Émilien passed one of the canteens to Drago.

Maksim lay beside the tree, knees bent, good arm slumped across his forehead. His other arm was still in the sling and rested on his torso. He hadn't moved in a while.

I used the inside of my shirt to wipe my face and forehead. It didn't help much. My shirt was soaked through, and using my dirty hands would have turned the sweat into sludge.

Levi and I had been digging around that stupid tree for hours. We'd made five holes so far, and my arms felt like they were about to break off.

"Can I have some water?" I asked.

Drago let a smug look fall on me. "No," he said flatly, then took another drink.

Asshole.

Chip. I struck the ground. *Chip chip. Crack!* The shovel jarred my hands, and the spade snapped off. All that was left was the handle.

I swore.

Ștefan stood over us. "Can you not dig any faster?"

Levi and I glowered at him.

He rolled his eyes, grabbed one of the backpacks, and pulled out another canteen. He tossed it.

I flinched, catching the canteen.

"Three-minute break." He pushed a hand through his greasy blond hair and checked his watch. "Beginning now."

I twisted off the lid and chugged. Warm water flowed down my face and neck and doused the inside of my shirt. I swallowed and brought the canteen down, panting. "Levi?" I held it toward him.

He took the canteen and sucked on it, but not with the same fervor I had. When he finished, he handed it back and kept digging.

I climbed out of the hole and stepped over the pile of dirt we'd excavated. Pebbles and potato-sized rocks littered the mounds. This had not been easy ground to dig in.

"Hey." I squatted beside Maksim and touched his leg.

He twitched, eyes peeling open.

"Have some." I held the canteen toward him.

Ştefan swept between us and grabbed it. "The traitor does not get water."

"Yes, he does." I jumped up and snatched the canteen. "Or you can dig these holes yourself."

He narrowed his eyes.

Maksim pushed up. "Kat, no."

"Why not?" I demanded. "You need water."

Ştefan grabbed the canteen. I held on, and he slapped me in the face. Without thinking, I slapped him back. His head whipped to the side.

He straightened, dirt smeared across his cheek. Fury kindled behind his eyes, and my stomach clenched.

"I found it!" Levi tossed his shovel and clawed with his hands.

Ştefan staggered, tripping over the dirt pile. Levi handed him a metal lockbox, similar to the lockbox Maksim and I had found in Braşov but smaller. This one had a built-in lock.

"This is it," I whispered. "As soon as he gets that thing open, he won't need us anymore."

Maksim was sitting up, staring at the entrance to the valley. I couldn't tell if he'd heard me.

He focused forward. "Help me up."

I knelt down.

He grabbed my shoulders, and we rose together. "Stay close to me."

"Why?" I glanced in the direction he'd be staring. "Is someone coming?"

"I thought perhaps—" He grimaced. "I had been hopeful."

Hopeful about what? A villager coming to help us?

Two villagers, I realized. He'd mentioned a woman and her husband. But... what would two villagers do against three criminals with guns?

Ştefan fiddled with the combination lock built into the metal box. Looked like he was trying different combinations.

When none of them worked, he reached into his pocket and pulled out a scrap of paper. He squinted, as if reading something, then entered a new combination.

Click. The soft noise reached my ears, and Ştefan flipped open the lid. A malicious grin split his rugged face as he wrestled a misshapen planner out of the lockbox.

He skimmed the first page and cocked his smile in my direction. "My thanks to you for this, dearest Kat." He held up the scrap of paper.

It was the scrap that had been hidden in the locket.

"My men discovered it in your belongings," he said. "The number was too long to be a bank account, as I had first suspected, but it seems the first four digits were intended as the combination for this lockbox."

"I suppose you've outwitted everyone." Levi hoisted himself out of the hole. "The monster has won."

"Ohh, but this monster is in a generous mood and may

permit you to choose how you will die on this day." Ştefan tucked his hands behind his back and strolled toward us.

Maksim tightened his hold on me.

I wrapped an arm around his waist and stole another glance at the valley's entrance. The ground sloped down and then up, the rocky terrain silvery in the sunlight.

No sign of any villagers yet. We needed a way to buy some more time.

"Before you kill us," I blurted, "I have to know something."

"Oh?" Ştefan brandished his pistol. Sunlight broke through the tree branches, and the gun's golden barrel gleamed. "And what is that you must know?"

"Y'all didn't follow us here, at least not that we could tell. That means you already knew to come to this village. But how?"

"I have my methods."

I frowned. "You're going to kill us. The least you could do is answer my question."

"Since you put it that way." He gave a blasé shrug. "With the help of—you might call him a relative—I was able to decipher this location based on what we knew. It was purely a guess at that time; however, various bits of CCTV footage confirmed you were traveling in this direction."

Maksim swore under his breath.

"Okay," I said, "but... how did you even think of this village? It couldn't have been the scavenger hunt, and it wasn't in my dad's letter."

"Ohh, but it was, when he said Pavel's assistance would be useful." Ştefan angled toward Levi. "My relative is fully aware of your past demining work, and it wasn't difficult to deduce why you may have been needed for this excursion."

"Which means your relative had to know of the *existence* of this village," Levi said sarcastically, "and I find that to be highly —" He hesitated, pulling a sharp breath. "It's Vladimir. He is alive."

Maksim's eyes widened. "Impossible. His death was discussed in the news."

"It was. As planned." Ştefan snorted a laugh. "We needed Vasile to believe my father was dead, to ensure his and Nicolae's next steps resulted in errors. It worked. Had Vasile thought my father to be alive, I assure you, he would not have brought Nicolae to Romania."

My throat pinched. I fought against the tide of sadness, of anger, barreling into me.

"And so," Ştefan continued, "with my father's knowledge of this village, along with my surveillance of our dearest Kat, I was able to piece this portion of the puzzle together."

"What surveillance?" I demanded. "I didn't know about this place, and neither did Maksim."

"But you forget I was in possession of the locket after intercepting your father's parcel." Ştefan's lips slid up. "I did not understand what it meant at the time—which was why I needed *you* to solve the scavenger hunt—but my father and I began to suspect there was something more, something we had missed, when you sent photos of the locket to a certain professor."

"Professor Ionescu," I whispered. I had emailed him, asking for his help with the inscription. Ştefan must have intercepted the email. "Did you kill him, too?"

"Why would I kill someone who would have *helped* you solve the scavenger hunt? Hm?" Ştefan let his surly gaze drift over each of us. His face reddened, and he waved his gun. "That was the point in all of this! To ensure you were able to lead me to these things!"

"Whatever happened I wasn't involved," Maksim said, his attention falling on me. "But I do know someone who may have been. If I'm right, it was Andrei."

My eyes went round. Andrei?

"He was given an assignment to tail someone," Maksim said. "I knew very little about it—only that the man was a professor and that something had gone wrong, some kind of unplanned altercation." Maksim focused on Ștefan. "So? What happened to the man?"

"Presently? He's in a coma." Ștefan straightened his shirt. "My father prefers to avoid more attention with this case, but if the professor does wake, we have men standing by, ready to terminate him. A final loose end to tie up."

"And Andrei?" A hint of worry flickered through Maksim's features.

"Andrei has made enough missteps for our operation"—Ștefan seethed—"and has thus been dealt with."

Maksim swayed. He looked like he was going to be sick.

"What about... me?" I cleared my throat. "What if I had, um, gone home? I almost did." I sent another fleeting glance over my shoulder. Still no sign of villagers entering the valley. "My friend convinced me to go home early," I continued. "What if I would have done that instead of staying and solving the scavenger hunt?"

"Andrei and Maksim were able to convince you otherwise," Ștefan replied. "And if you had *not* been convinced, my people would have been waiting for you at the airport."

Pressure coiled behind my sternum. He really had covered all his bases—and I was out of questions.

"How...?" *Come on, Kat. Stall.* "How will you—get off this hill? Levi's your best bet at doing that, but you're planning to kill him."

Ștefan snapped his fingers.

Émilien walked forward with a black-and-yellow device the size of a smartphone, except bulkier and with a stubby antenna. The Frenchman pressed buttons and handed the device to Ștefan.

"The need to hike was necessary only while we searched for the lockbox—but walking is not, in fact, how we came here." He tipped a smile my way. "How else do you think we arrived ahead of you?"

The hum of a distant motor broke the stillness. My ears detected a rhythmic noise, like something sturdy punching the air. As the sounds grew louder, understanding sank to the bottom of my being.

A helicopter. That was how they'd gotten here, and that was how they planned to make their getaway.

Émilien said something in French. He was talking to Ștefan, but he was looking at me.

"Don't do it." Maksim's throat seemed to close over the words. "Ștefan, please. Not with him."

Ștefan offered a cool reply to Émilien, who didn't even try to hide his smugness.

"What did they say?" I tightened my hold on Maksim's waist. "I-I think they said something about me."

"You must focus on survival, Katherine." Levi stepped up beside us. His attention fell to me, and his eyes went damp. "Do everything you can to survive."

My insides tumbled into a free fall.

Maksim pulled away, approaching Ștefan. The crime boss backed up two steps and took aim with the pistol.

"No!" I ran forward.

Drago whipped out the riot baton and flicked his wrist. *Snap!* The rod released, and he unleashed a blow on the back of Maksim's legs.

Maksim collapsed, grimacing, and Drago delivered the next blow to his slung arm. Maksim toppled over.

I tried to throw myself between them. Ion grabbed me. I fought back, punching, kicking. "Don't touch me!"

Levi launched forward.

Drago faced him, riot baton raised. Levi skidded to a stop and then backed up, hands raised.

Ștefan stood over Maksim and started speaking in... Russian? Again? Why weren't they speaking in their native language?

It occurred to me that no one else had spoken Russian. Whatever they were saying, I got the impression they didn't want anyone else, not even Émilien and Drago, to know.

Maksim grimaced, lying on his side. He glanced in my direction.

Ştefan knotted his fingers in Maksim's shirt and rolled him forward until both of their backs were facing us. Their exchange continued.

Ştefan released him a moment later. Maksim nodded about something, and the crime boss rose to standing. He waved his hand, and—to my amazement—Ion let me go.

"Come here." Maksim beckoned me.

I crept forward, waiting for someone to stop me. Nobody did.

Maksim took my hand and pulled me into a hug. I buried my face in his chest. "We're running out of time," I whispered. "Whatever the plan is—"

"There is no plan." He held me tighter. "I had hoped the villagers would come out to take a stand, but... They may be too afraid." Maksim pulled back a little and cupped my face in his hands. "Don't look."

"Where? At the valley's entrance?"

"At me." His eyes, so red and puffy, swam with regret. "Ştefan is going to take me across the hill, to that grave site, and shoot me."

"No." I shook my head. "Maksim, no."

"Don't look, and for God's sake do not go over there." His gaze roamed my face before settling on my filthy, frizzy hair. He reached over, caressing a tendril that had worked loose from my ponytail, and then tucked the strands behind my ear. "Promise me."

"We can't let them do this. There has to be another way."

"Do as Ştefan commands. Don't argue with him." Worry pressed lines into Maksim's forehead. "In exchange for our cooperation, he is going to kill me quickly, painlessly, and he's going to let you live."

"Stop talking like that." I knocked his hand away. "What did he say to you? What are they going to do to me?"

"I admire your courage, your refusal to abandon us... but you should have fled when you had the chance." He glanced in the direction of Ştefan and his goons and then lowered his voice. "Émilien has asked for you, that you would belong to him."

"What, like marriage?"

"More like a transaction. He will own you. Ştefan has granted his request."

The ground, the entire world, seemed to wobble. I staggered.

Maksim grabbed onto me. "I begged Ştefan not to do it. He cannot show weakness before his men, and he will not go back on his word to Émilien, but he has privately agreed to ensure your safety and well-being. As long as we cooperate."

Fear swelled, mounting into a sob. "I don't want to go. Please don't let them take me. Maksim—"

"Listen to me." He placed a hand on each of my shoulders and looked me square in the eyes. "Do not give up, no matter what happens. Do you understand?" He placed his mouth by my ear. "There may come a day when you'll be able to escape. Never stop looking for that day."

A steely grip with tattooed hands dragged me away. Maksim shouted, lunging. Tears blurred my vision as a lanky frame with lush black hair stepped between us.

Ştefan thrust me toward Ion and Vano. They caught me and held me in place while he followed Drago, Émilien, and Maksim across the hill.

"We have to do something!" I looked at Levi. "They're going to kill him! Somebody—" A sob choked me. I pressed a hand to my chest, despair flowing. "Somebody has to do something."

"What can we do?" Levi asked weakly. "Anything we attempt could make things worse for Maksim. And for us."

"But they're already going to kill him. What's worse than that?"

"What Vladimir did to your grandmother was worse. Ştefan would do the same to us."

Maybe Levi was right. If we intervened, they wouldn't just shoot Maksim. They'd torture him. And Levi. And me.

But... if I had to go with Émilien, if he "owned" me, I couldn't imagine a worse kind of torture. My stomach churned. Bile rose in my throat.

Without thinking, I raised an arm and drove my elbow into Ion's gut. He snapped forward with a grunt, and Vano released me.

I broke into a sprint.

"Katherine," Levi called.

Émilien and Drago wrestled Maksim to his knees. They caught sight of me and pointed. Ștefan wheeled around.

I charged straight for the crime boss.

He drew back, eyes round, and trained the pistol on me. His inked finger hooked the trigger...

He hesitated.

I pumped my arms, ignoring the soreness in my knee, the throbbing in my head, the exhaustion in my body. Maksim jumped up and raced toward me. Drago and Émilien chased after him.

The barrel of the gun stared me down. My heart crashed, and for a second I thought Ștefan had fired. But I was still running, still charging ahead.

He was within arm's reach.

I knocked his hand to the side, pistol and all, and slammed my shoulder into him the way I'd seen football players do it.

The pistol parted from his hand. I had exactly one chance to grab that thing and only a second or two to do it.

I angled that way.

Someone screamed a warning. "Watch out!" The words echoed as brain-splitting pain entered the back of my head. A shrill ringing pierced my ears and vibrated my eardrums.

My feet lagged. My vision shuddered and crossed. Everything around me degenerated into slow motion... and froze.

38½. INTERVAL

I rubbed my eyes. Shook my head. Tried to process what I was seeing.

Ştefan had been falling, but he was frozen midair.

Maksim had been running toward me. Now he was motionless, his eyes wide, mouth open. Émilien and Drago were both locked in place behind him.

I scanned the hill, hoping I wasn't alone in this. Whatever "this" was. Ion was behind me, frozen midrun. He looked like he might've been chasing me. Where were Levi and Vano?

I returned to the tree and found them completely still. "Levi? Can you hear me? I-I don't know what to do."

His gaze remained locked on something across the hill. I stepped to one side and then the other, waving a hand in front of his face. His stare didn't follow me.

Movement plucked at my peripheral.

I whipped around. A man I'd never seen before stood on a ladder, threading a string through a photograph. Then he attached the photo—something like a Polaroid—to a tree branch.

Other photos dangled from other branches, as if the man had been at this for a while. But I hadn't seen him until now.

"Who are you?"

The man met my gaze. "Hi." That was all he said. From what I could tell, he didn't have an accent.

"Do you, um—?" I blinked. "What's going on? How is all this happening?"

"Are you a friend?"

"A friend of who?"

He slipped a string around a branch and tied a knot. The photo twisted, swinging under a breeze. When he finished, he reached for a pile of photos stacked on the ladder's fold-down pail shelf.

He didn't answer my question. He didn't even acknowledge me.

Something shifted on my right. I turned and froze. There, lying under the tree, was a lion.

Slivers of sunlight broke through the leaves, casting a gold shimmer over the lion's mane. My pulse spiked.

The animal swatted its tail. Apart from that, he lay motionless, a bulky beast looking straight at me. I thought of backing up, of hiding behind that man's ladder, but I didn't want to make any sudden movements.

Slowly—ever so slowly—I sent a glance over my shoulder. Both the ladder and the man were gone, and a sea of photos hung from the branches. My gaze drifted north, and I gasped. Polaroids hung all around me.

I lowered my gaze to the lion. He was gone, too.

The Polaroids swung, drawing my attention. I caught a glimpse of a photo that sent a shock of surprise through me.

I reached up and pinched the photo between my fingers. It was a picture of me and Dad. I was a kid, kindergarten age, and we were playing the scavenger hunt game at Gypsy Django.

Another photo had Brandy and me playing soccer. She was crouched in front of the goal. I stood a few paces away, ball under my foot while I pointed downfield.

"Who took these?" My question rang hollow, cloaked in a silence broken only by the photos brushing against each other.

I slipped past Levi and Vano. The images in these photos were much more recent—Maksim and me hiking down Mount Tâmpă; Maksim, Levi, and I talking on Levi's porch.

"Have you seen these?"

My head whipped right. The man on the ladder was back—or had never left? He was hanging photos on the other side of the tree.

"How'd you do that?" I asked. "You weren't there a second ago."

He finished tying a string, and his gaze drifted over a new set of photos. "A seed doesn't grow into a plant unless it dies first." His gaze connected with mine. "Did you know that?"

I was about to ask him what he meant, what any of this meant, when another photo crossed my line of sight.

My stomach twisted. The picture had been taken inside a drug house, the one Mom used to go to in East Point. The one she'd taken me to when I was thirteen.

The memory rushed in. Mom had picked me up from school. *"I only need to stop for a second."* Forty-five minutes later, I was trying to decide if I should keep waiting or go in after her. She had the car keys, her phone, money. Everything.

I had no way to leave. I didn't even have a way to call Dad.

The sprint of my pulse that day, the unsteadiness of my breathing, returned. The photo seemed to suck me in until I was no longer standing by the tree. I was tiptoeing up to the drug house.

THE FRONT PORCH creaked under my weight, the wood threatening to snap. The front door groaned as I pulled it open.

Sunlight spilled inside the dark house, revealing a dirt floor and a room with no furniture. I trembled, not wanting to go in. "Mom?" I whispered. Then a little louder. "Mom."

The smells hit me next—death and decay, rotting wood. I

choked. "Mom?" I repeated, raising my voice. "Mom, I need to make a call."

I stepped inside the house and talked myself into crossing the vacant den. A hallway stretched to my right. I entered it and inched forward to the first room.

The door was off its hinges, propped up against the doorframe from inside the room. I peered through a wide crack and then jerked back. A man and woman were in there, and they were—

"Ew," I whispered, continuing down the hall. The woman wasn't Mom. That was all that mattered.

As I reached the next room, my shoe rolled over something. A sharp stab entered my toe. I yanked my foot back, and a syringe shook loose.

Fear strangled me.

"Mom?" I squeaked, throat closing. "Mom, where are you?"

Grunts and groans trickled from that last room. The urge to turn around, to run to the car, crashed against my will. I needed to look at my toe. More than that, I just needed to be out of this place.

But I really needed to call Dad.

I pushed open the door to the next room. The hinges creaked as I poked my head inside. Mom was leaning against the wall, nodding off with a needle hanging out of her arm.

I stumbled through the doorway and snatched up her purse. Her wallet was missing, but I found her car keys and phone.

"I know you."

I spun around to face the deep, gravelly voice. Mom's dealer was standing in the doorway.

MY BREATHING FELL shallow as I stared at the photo.

The wind kicked up. The photos twirled, colliding with each other. Some of the strings broke, and photos tumbled to the ground. The movement tore me out of my daze.

I looked at the fallen Polaroids—Ștefan and his goons, Levi and Maksim, Ion and Vano. These pictures were from today.

I paused on one of Maksim sitting against a tree. This tree, I realized. His jeans were blood-soaked as he held someone in his arms. Tears streaked his dusty face.

My heart broke in half when I recognized the black curls spilling over his arm. A pale hand hung limp. He was holding... me.

Heat burned my eyes, but then a sense of relief swelled. I was the reason Maksim was here. He hadn't wanted to come, but he'd done it, anyway. To help me. To protect me. I didn't want him to die out here... but maybe he wasn't going to. Maybe that was the meaning of the photo.

"A seed doesn't grow into a plant unless it dies first." The man's words returned to me. I didn't understand them, but they had a strange effect, drawing up deep emotions I hadn't felt in a long time.

I turned around. The man was gone, and I lifted my gaze. Hints of bright blue sky peeked through the branches. A low growl rumbled as frantic voices echoed around me.

The photos vanished. A gust of wind hit the valley so hard the tree swayed. I flinched, holding the trunk. My hands and arms met air.

One blink, and I found myself across the hill, ramming my shoulder into Ștefan, who stared at someone behind me.

Ion. He'd been racing after me and had thrown... the riot baton. It sailed toward me, slowly at first, then faster.

Everything crept into motion, a vinyl record scratching into a higher speed.

Ștefan fell backward, pistol flying from his hand. Even so, his eyes held a smug glint. And then...

Crack. Pain spread through the back of my head.

I collapsed.

39. TRANSITION

Dirt ground into the side of my face. The headache pressed into my skull, from my left temple all the way around to the back of my head. I forced my eyes open. People were shouting, grunting. My ears struggled to parse the voices.

A shout rang out in French. *Thwack!* The sound of skin on skin, of knuckle against bone, rocked me out of my daze. I blinked hard, and Maksim came into view. Ştefan's goons had him pinned not far from where I lay. His eyes met mine and pulled wide. He pointed at Levi, who was tugging on Ştefan's arm, preventing him from aiming the pistol. Vano tussled with Ion, who was trying to retrieve something from the ground.

The riot baton. Ion had thrown it at me.

An idea lit up my thoughts. Drago's back was to me, his pistol poking up from his waistband. Maksim had mentioned disarming him in training. What if *I* could disarm him?

My focus shifted to a multitude of rocks scattered around the hill. That was when the second part of my plan locked into place. *Gun first. Then rocks.* My gaze shifted again. *Then baton.*

Go. Now.

I jumped up, sprinted for Drago, and grabbed his waistband

with one hand while yanking out the pistol with the other. He spun around, patting himself.

I darted left and made eye contact with Maksim. In one swift move, he yanked off the sling and pushed himself to standing. Émilien lunged. Maksim snapped forward at the waist, drawing the Frenchman with him, and then threw an elbow.

Frenchie's head whipped back. He howled and dropped to his knees.

"Gun!" I lobbed the pistol. Maksim caught it left-handed, wheeled around, and crashed the butt into Émilien's head. The Frenchman slumped to the ground.

Maksim grabbed the top of the nine-millimeter and racked it back. The slide snapped into place as he took aim.

A low growl dragged my attention away. Drago was sprinting toward Maksim, but then a shot rang out. I thought Maksim had shot Émilien, but I was wrong. The gunfire had come from Ştefan. Levi was wrestling with him, swiping at the golden pistol. I knew what I needed to do. It was now or never.

I gathered up rocks—as many as I could find in the immediate area—and snatched up the riot baton. Then I raced for the edge of the hill.

The baton had retracted into the handle. I held it up and flicked my wrist. *Snap!* The baton extended, and I flung it over the edge. The metal stick whipped through the air, rotating end over end, and disappeared down the slope. A blast rocked the hill, sending up dirt and rocks and a pillar of black smoke. Another blast followed. Then another.

The entire hill quaked.

Levi had said the mines were too close together. He'd warned us about setting off a chain reaction. But that was exactly what we needed—a chain reaction, something big enough to cause a distraction.

Drago was charging me. Shock waves rolled under his feet. He stumbled, fell, skidded. Maksim angled for him.

I shielded my head and continued along the slope's edge,

tossing rocks as I went. One of them didn't go far, and the subsequent blast shuddered the space on my left. I dropped to the ground and covered my head. Dirt rained down, and something hot and sharp grazed my forearm. My skin heated.

I sucked a breath. The hell was that?

Maksim and Drago were locked together, wrestling. Maksim's bad arm was free of the sling, but he didn't have much mobility. Drago grunted, ducking his head, and plowed forward.

Maksim skidded to the brink. He gritted his teeth, digging his boots into the earth.

Drago pushed again... again... again. Maksim backpedaled down the slope. I screamed before remembering I had two more rocks. I lobbed them. They sailed over Drago and Maksim and tumbled down the hill. A series of mines detonated, one after the other. Drago lost his footing, and Maksim managed to power up the slope. They rolled onto the ground. Drago ended up on top, swinging.

Maksim reeled him in, bringing them body to body. Drago reared back and tried for a rib shot. Maksim tucked his elbows, blocking the blow. Maksim's legs stayed wrapped around Drago's torse the entire time.

A rock the size of a potato lay at my feet. I scooped it up and lobbed it down the hill, directly behind where Drago and Maksim tussled. The explosion wasn't big, but Drago flinched.

Maksim shifted his legs, pulling them in. This effectively freed Drago, who then lunged with sheer determination in his eyes. The look morphed into horror as Maksim planted his boots in Drago's chest and launched him up and back. Drago howled, his lanky body soaring, and disappeared down the hill.

The next explosions made me cringe.

Maksim crawled up the slope. Our gazes met, and fear exploded through his features. "Behind you!"

I pivoted, searching for the threat. Ştefan had broken away from Levi and Vano and was charging me. I turned to run, but it was too late. The crime boss caught me and hauled me toward the slope. His momentum carried us forward, and down the hill we went.

Five feet.

Ten feet.

Fifteen...

40. NIGHTMARE

"Do not come any closer." Ştefan jerked me around until we faced the top of the hill. Steel pressed against my temple.

Maksim slammed to a stop. Pebbles and a clump of dirt glided over the edge. His gaze connected with mine, and I could tell he was going to continue down the slope.

"Don't!" My stare drifted to a metal disk two feet away. I spotted a long wire pulled taut—trip wire—and fear prickled in my throat. "The mines are all around us."

Maksim took a cautious step back.

"Retrieve the lockbox"—Ştefan pinned my arms—"and I will release her."

"Levi!" Maksim called. "Bring me the lockbox!"

Levi appeared. He was holding his stomach, limping, but he had the metal box.

"Throw it here," Ştefan said coolly. "Ensure it lands at Kat's feet."

"Release her first," Maksim countered. "Then we will give it to you."

"No. You will give me the lockbox now or else I *will* throw her into the mines." Ştefan removed the barrel from my head and aimed the gun at Maksim. "And I will end both of *you* where you stand."

Neither Levi nor Maksim moved.

Vano and Ion appeared. Ştefan took aim at the villagers. Ion threw his hands up as Ştefan barked an order. Panic tore through Ion's features. He reached over and snatched the lockbox straight out of Levi's hands.

Levi reacted a second too late. The metal case sailed toward us and landed at my feet. Maksim screamed, trying to fight through Levi, trying to get to Ion. The villager backed away. That lockbox had been our only bargaining chip, and he'd handed it over.

"Ştefan is threatening their families!" Levi did his best to hold Maksim at bay. Vano joined him. "He's afraid for his wife and children. Maksim, he's afraid!"

Ştefan nudged me. "Pick up the lockbox."

"No." I tried to make my voice cool and even. Internally, my heart hammered so hard I wondered if he could hear it.

"Pick it up. *Pick it up.*" Ştefan cracked the butt of his gun against my head—not as hard as he'd done the day before, but hard enough to release a wave of blackness into my vision.

I slumped against him.

Commotion stirred, the voices warbly. Ştefan adjusted his grip, and I felt myself snap forward. But I didn't fall. The crime boss still had me by the waist. There was some jostling, grunting, shifting. As the blackness lifted, I knew without having to look that Ştefan had scooped up the lockbox.

Chopping pulsed the air. I forced my eyes open and spied a black dot entering the valley. The helicopter was getting close.

Maksim focused on Ştefan. "You have the lockbox. Now let her go."

Ştefan clucked his tongue. "Ohh, but I like the idea of Kat joining our operation. I'm certain my father will have the perfect position for her." Ştefan placed his mouth by my ear. "Don't fret, cousin. Our associates will ensure you have the necessary... training." His hot breath crawled across my skin, and my heart rate spiked.

I jabbed my elbow into his gut. He grunted but didn't let go. How? He had a gun in one hand and the lockbox in the other. I should have been able to break his hold.

Then I noticed his left hand was free. Where had the lockbox gone?

Ştefan wrestled me forward. I dug my heels in, squirming, resisting.

"Ştefaaan!"

The frantic shout brought us to a halt.

Maksim stood on the cusp of the slope, raising his hands in surrender. "Your father took everything from me. *Everything*! He killed my parents. He filled my head with lies." A volatile mix of anger and despair swirled through his voice. He paused and inhaled a calming breath. "I believed you to be my cousin," he continued, "but I always considered you my brother. In many ways, you were like a father."

"And you still betrayed me." Disdain oozed from Ştefan. His eyes were wild as I stared up at him. "I entrusted you with all that we have—a lapse in judgment made known to me by my father. Since your unfortunate accident, he has suspected you could not be trusted. I regret that he was right." The crime boss spat what sounded like a curse in Romanian.

"Please!" Maksim brought his hands together, pleading. "This offense you hold is against me. Leave her out of it."

Ştefan pressed the barrel of the gun to my temple. "Should you pay nothing for this betrayal? Should you not pay with all that you have?"

"Then kill me. Enact your vengeance against *me*." Maksim lowered himself to his knees. "I could not give you my loyalty, so I will give you my life. Take that. Do not take her."

Ştefan remained still and quiet. I managed another peek. His jaw was rigid against a deep-set frown. His blue eyes were cold, calculating.

The helicopter descended on the hill. Tree branches swayed, leaves breaking free and swirling. My gaze followed bits of green and brown that settled on the metal disk. Could dirt and leaves set off a mine?

As the helicopter touched down, Ştefan gave me a shove. "Up the hill," he commanded. "Go." I didn't budge, so he pushed harder. My feet stayed planted until he began to wrestle me up the slope.

Maksim's attention shifted to the helicopter. He motioned for Levi and Vano to back away. Ion was nowhere to be seen.

"Don't let him take me!"

Ştefan gave another shove, harder. I stumbled forward and face-planted beside the metal disk. Dust plumed. I breathed it in, eyes fixed on the mine. It lay mere inches from my hand. "Maksim? Levi?" I risked a glance.

They were still backing away.

Ştefan jerked me to my feet and hauled me to the top—but instead of heading straight for the helicopter, which had landed at the center of the hill, he pulled me along the cusp of the slope. "Do not follow me! Do not come near or I will throw her down this hill!"

I peered over the side. Dozens of mines glared up at me.

We inched our way toward the helicopter. I thrashed, trying to break my captor's hold, not caring if he threw me or not. I could *not* go with him.

He yanked me around, doing a one-eighty, and hauled me backward. I squirmed, attempting to break his hold. When that didn't work, I dragged my feet.

"Kat!"

I focused forward. Maksim had been following us, and now he was only thirty feet away. Vano and Levi were angling for the helicopter.

"I need you to pay attention to me," Maksim called. "Can you do that?"

I nodded, and he took up a wide stance, revealing something in his hand.

Ştefan shouted just then. I looked back in time to see him signal to someone. The pilot? Ion or Émilien?

"Kaaat!"

My attention shot to Maksim. He was saying something, but the helicopter's engine drowned him out. The propellers blasted up hot air and swished my ponytail around. Maksim, his voice still muted, held up the object.

A knife.

He wrenched out the blade and lobbed the knife toward me. I had no idea where it had come from, but I realized this was my only chance to escape. *If* I could catch the knife.

Ştefan kept yelling, kept dragging me. I got my feet under me and thrust my butt backward. The move knocked him back a step, and I managed to jerk an arm free.

The knife arced.

Another thrust, and my body came free. I planted my feet, squatted, and then jumped straight up. Sunlight glinted as the knife sailed toward my hand. Sharp steel hit my palm. I clenched, wincing. I had caught the knife dead-center.

Ştefan chained me with both arms. I adjusted my grip and slammed the knife down, burying the blade in his thigh. He screamed, staggering, and began rapid-firing his pistol. Maksim ducked down but continued to charge forward.

"Nooo!" I thrust my hands up, hitting the crime boss's arm. The next shots went airborne. Ştefan growled and twisted me around. As we came face to face, our feet became tangled. He lost his balance and fell sideways...and he pulled me with him.

Down the hill we went, both of us screaming, our bodies scraping over the rough terrain. A rocky piece of earth jutted up. I grabbed hold, and for a split second, I thought I was going to stop. But Ştefan had my wrist, and the dragging continued.

Someone shouted from the top of the hill. I looked up and

found Maksim leaping down to the first drop. Levi and Vano were right behind him.

My foot found another jut, and I dug the toe of my running shoe into the earth, securing my foothold. Ștefan stopped a little farther down. Both of us lay flat on our stomachs.

When the dust settled, I chanced a look and saw red pooling under Ștefan's thigh. His face was pale. I thought he might pass out, but he maintained a steely grip on my wrist.

I tugged, trying to free myself. He tugged back—hard—and tried to yank me down. I gasped and reached for a jut above me. My fingers connected with something sharp. I ignored whatever that might've been—a cactus, maybe?—and clung to the jut. This section of the hill was steep, and every muscle in my body was engaged.

Suddenly, my arm and shoulder strained. Ștefan had slipped off whatever foothold he'd found and was beginning to slide. I felt my body being dragged with him. "Don't!" I pulled with all my might. "Let me go. *Let me go.*"

His frosty gaze met mine. He tightened his grip until my wrist popped.

I grimaced and cried out. "Why are you doing this? *Why?* You can let me go. Just let me go!"

But he wouldn't. This was his final act of revenge against Maksim, Dad, and anyone else who had thwarted his plans. If he was going to die, everyone else had to suffer.

My attention shifted to his thigh. Blood saturated the rocky slope and was pouring along both sides of his leg. The knife, which had been knocked loose, must have hit his femoral artery. But where was the knife now?

I gasped, attention flying to the jut above me. The stab I'd felt wasn't from a cactus. It was from the knife, which must have landed on the jut I was clinging to. I could see the handle poking out from the side.

A vague memory flickered in my mind. *"Just grip something before you swing. Adds weight to your hand and reinforces your knuckles.*" Andrei's voice flooded my senses. He'd used his knife on Émilien—not to stab him, but to deliver a blow strong enough to knock him out. What if I could do that?

No. I would have to let go in order to grab the knife. This part of the hill was too steep—not a straight drop, but a lot steeper than forty-five degrees—and with Ştefan's body weight, there was no way I could let go. The jut was my lifeline.

My right arm ached as Ştefan continued to slide. I pulled hard, attempting to lift him. It wasn't working, and he was *not* relenting.

I shifted my gaze to the knife again and then a little higher to where Maksim had been. Levi and Vano had him restrained, preventing him from going any farther. He fought to free himself, but they were holding on to him as fervently as Ştefan was holding on to me.

"Are you ready to die, dearest Kat?"

My attention fell to the crime boss.

He smirked up at me, looking woozy. "I am not ready," he mumbled, "yet I can feel the life draining from me." He gave a soft chuckle that morphed into rage. "This is because of youuu!"

I screamed as he clawed at me. He was trying to pull me off the foothold, drag me the rest of the way down. We would hit a mine eventually, and then we'd both be dead.

My left hand slipped until I was holding on by only my fingertips. My right foot was still on the jut below, but that wouldn't last long with Ştefan yanking on me. Fear tore at my insides. I had to make a split-second, gut-wrenching decision.

I pushed up on my toes, stretching, and groped for the knife. My fingers made contact. I found the handle and clutched it. With only the lower jut to hold me up—and only on one foot—I brought the blade down on Ştefan's hand. He wailed, releasing me.

With my wrist free, I switched the knife to that hand and did exactly as Andrei had shown me. I gripped the handle as tightly as

I could and sent a quick jab to Ștefan's face. The punch landed at his nose, and his head whipped back.

I pulled my arm around and crashed my knuckles into his cheek. Pain entered my hand and spread into my wrist. I winced, still clutching the knife, and watched his eyes go glassy.

He blinked, giving his head a swift shake...and then he lost his footing. Our stares connected, blue burning into blue, until his gaze wandered past me. His eyes went round and wide as he skidded down the hill, leaving a red trail behind him.

"Up here!"

My attention swung to Maksim, who had broken away from Levi and Vano. He crouched on a ledge. "Back up the way you came! Hurry!"

I dropped the knife and started climbing.

A grunt reached my ears. Then a series of thuds. Ștefan was tumbling. Any second he was bound to set off a—

An explosion ignited somewhere below. The first mine detonated.

41. WICK

The blast slammed me against the hill. The ground shuddered, vibrating against my face. *Ping. Ping-ping. Ping.* Pieces of metal ricocheted off rocks, and searing pain spread across my upper arm.

I grabbed the spot, grimacing, and lifted my gaze. Maksim was on his back, and he wasn't moving.

"Maksim!" Levi charged down the hill. Vano was behind him. They grabbed Maksim's arms and dragged him to the top.

Blasts rumbled along the lower part of the hill.

I looked down. Red flashes burned into the scenery while dense black smoke scaled the hill. I had to climb.

I reached up, grabbed a jut, and pulled myself higher. My arm dripped blood, and pain exploded.

"Ow!" I felt around on the open wound. No shrapnel, at least none that I could detect, but the graze was deep.

Movement blurred above me. Maksim was struggling against Levi and Vano. He broke their hold and skidded down the slope.

Pop!

I twisted around. A puff of white smoke billowed, and an object hurtled up from somewhere just below me. Tiny pieces of metal burst.

"Cover your head!"

I looked up at Maksim. He was back on the ledge. "Your head!" he repeated, motioning.

A force entered my back and hurled me against the slope. Stabbing pain cascaded from the entry point, turning to fire before spreading through my body. The hot metal sank deep, smoldering in my flesh.

I screamed. Tears jumped out of my eyes.

My face landed in the dirt.

I COULDN'T TELL how long I'd been unconscious. Hours? Minutes? All I knew was that the mines had stopped detonating, and something was crushing me. I thought it must have been a boulder until the weight lifted.

Two hands rolled me onto my back.

My eyes peeled open. Maksim was bathed in sunlight, his tears silvery, shimmering, and pouring down his face. A steady buzz filled my ears. Pain filled the right side of my back while thick, slippery liquid pooled beneath my fingers.

He slid a hand beneath me and pressed. A smoldering, stabbing pain ground into my shoulder blade.

I arched, howling. My vision melted to black.

"...MUST GET HER TO THE TOP." Levi's voice echoed from somewhere far away, as if he'd fallen into a canyon.

Hands gripped me. Lifted me. Carried me.

A moment later, I was lying on flat earth.

"The helicopter." Maksim's voice pitched. "Where is it?"

"The pilot left when the mines exploded."

"We need it. She won't make the hike in this condition."

"I know, Maksim..."

STRONG ARMS CRADLED ME. The hold was firm, the voice soft but deep.

My eyes fluttered open.

Maksim came into focus, tree branches stretching high above him. Tears streaked his dusty face. Blood covered his shirt and smeared his cheek.

His mouth lifted in a weak smile. "There you are," he whispered.

I inhaled, needing fresh air. The breath was labored, and a strange chill settled in my body. My eyes dragged shut.

"Don't—" Maksim's voice fractured. He tightened his hold. "Don't go to sleep," he whispered. "I need to tell you something. It's important." He swallowed. "Do you remember when we talked about my scars? About the nerve damage? Things that shouldn't hurt me, that normally wouldn't, do now because the nerve endings are warped."

I blinked up at him.

"When we were in Braşov, when Ştefan had convinced me you were a government agent, I was so angry with you. In that moment, I hated you with an intensity I have rarely experienced— but the real reason I felt so betrayed is because, like my scars, something is wrong with my heart. It's damaged, warped." He choked on a sob, blinking away dusty tears. "I was blinded by pain and pride, and I'm sorry. Kat, I'm so very sorry." He settled a soft kiss on my forehead.

His lips lingered, and warm tears dropped onto my face. I could barely feel them.

Maksim pulled back, and his eyes danced across my face. His next words grew distant, garbled. My vision darkened along the edges, and a soft breath escaped.

I slipped out of my body.

"Kat?" Panic rose in his voice. "Kat, wake up. Kat!"

42. VEIL

I plunged into an ocean and sank. My hair cascaded around me, filling my vision with a tide of black curls.

I pushed the strands back and looked around. Sunlight penetrated the surface. Directly below, an underwater canyon stretched down into blackness.

A current grabbed hold of me and drew me toward the canyon.

I punched at the water, kicking, fighting—panicking—but if this was a riptide, fighting would only make things worse.

I forced myself to relax and hold my breath... except I didn't really need to hold my breath. This didn't even feel like normal water. It had a glossy texture, silky, and seemed to fill every cell of my being.

Purple light appeared below. The current tugged on me, and I found myself drifting down into the light. Bits of purple pulsed, glittering all around me.

The light mounted, gathering, and then dimmed, as if the water itself had taken a breath. Electricity sparked, and the shimmer exploded.

I shielded my face as white-hot light flashed.

Suddenly, I was sitting on something hard. I opened my eyes

and found myself on the brow of an underwater cliff. I scooted closer to the edge and peered over.

Velvet blackness, darker than the darkest of nights, stretched into a deep abyss. Fear grabbed hold and shook me to my core. I shivered and moved away from the edge.

Movement plucked at my periphery.

Soft, flickering light danced in the distance. The effect reminded me of a campfire burning hot on a chilly night, but the flames weren't red and orange. They were silver with flecks of shiny gold embers.

The light drew closer until I realized... it wasn't just light. It was a lion.

I stood up, ready to run. Or swim. But where would I go? Down into the abyss? That was one option—I supposed—but it didn't seem like an appealing one.

The lion wasn't moving particularly fast or slow. It wasn't floating or swimming. It simply stalked forward, silver flames licking at the silky waters.

He stopped in front of me.

I tensed, waiting for the thing to attack. He didn't. In fact, the lion didn't seem aggressive at all. Powerful? Sure, and that power was intense. But I didn't have the impression I was about to be eaten.

The lion ambled closer. I rocked back, gripped by the urge to flee, but a flicker of purple held me in place.

The purple light. I was surrounded by it. Somehow it bolstered my confidence, and I found myself reaching out instead of recoiling.

A tremor moved through my arm as my fingers entered the silver flames. The fire warmed my fingers... but didn't burn.

The lion held me with a watchful gaze, and I considered the possibility that he might not want to be touched. Would he growl? Bite?

Worse?

I shook off the hesitation and closed the gap. My fingers

grazed the lion's mane, and a deep thrum, like a low-frequency sound wave, entered my hand and moved up my arm.

I pulled a breath and drew back as a familiar voice broke the silence. The words were garbled, fading in and out like an FM radio. "...dream... not rational, but... have to try."

Maksim.

"...can't do this... when I say I understand..." This transmission was clearer. The voice belonged to Levi.

People spoke in a foreign language. It didn't sound like Romanian. Was it Romani Čib? A woman's voice filtered into the mix.

"What are they saying?" Maksim demanded. "Are they willing to do it?"

There was no reply.

"Levi, what did they say? Please. I beg you." Maksim's plea devolved into a sob. "What harm would it do to try? That's all I'm... that we..." Static rippled through the last part.

I lowered my gaze to the lion, wondering if I could ask him anything, thinking I should at least try.

What do I do? I had intended to speak the question aloud, but it reverberated through my mind instead. I tried again. *Tell me what to do.* Again, the words rang inside my head.

The purple light enveloped me in thick layers. Pressure surged and pushed me toward the brow of the cliff. *Wait!* The scream echoed in my thoughts.

The surge repeated, pushing me closer to the edge. *Please!*

Another surge, and I tumbled over. *No!*

I sank. My lungs squeezed. My chest, my whole body, ached.

Darkness swallowed me.

Another surge of water struck me from behind—but this time the current changed direction, drawing me upward. I clawed at the water, then at my throat and chest. My lungs burned. *Help me!* I beat the water, which no longer felt silky and thin but cool and thick.

The current gripped me and dragged me deeper into the

blackness. I screamed. It was a real noise—not a thought—that escaped through my mouth in a blast of bubbles.

The purple light twinkled around me... and then the current shifted. Water swelled, and the surge seemed to envelop me from behind and below, and even from the sides, before it gave its next push.

I tumbled upward, bungling my way toward the surface. It was so far away, and I was still surrounded by blackness, but I focused on the sunlight penetrating the waters.

The purple light rippled around me and glided upward. I had to fight now, to swim.

I beat at the water, kicking, struggling, willing myself onward. The first hints of sunlight broke around me. I kept going until I was bathed in warm yellow light. *Almost there.*

The purple light parted—a veil being drawn back—and my fingertips broke the surface. My hand flew out of the water. My arm. My head.

I sucked in a breath, expecting relief— Instead, my chest and lungs caught fire, scorching me from the inside out.

The fire spread, igniting in my back, my arm. I screamed, louder than I think I've ever screamed in my whole life. "It hurts! IT HURTS!"

A flash blinded me.

DAY ONE

DAY TWO

DAY THREE

DAY FOUR

SIBIU

UKRAINE
HUNGARY
MOLDOVA
ROMÂNIA
Sibiu
Brasov
Sighet
Pitesti
Crețulesti
Bucuresti
SERBIA
BULGARIA

43. AWAKE

A high-pitched *beep beep beep*, accompanied by a loud hiss, startled me awake. My eyes cracked open. White. That was all I could see. Pure white all around me.

I blinked. Blinked again. Everything was a thick smear. I went to rub my eyes, but my arms were held down by... something. I couldn't tell what.

My vision focused a little, and I found myself tucked inside a stiff white blanket. My clothes—the last clothes I remembered wearing—had been replaced with a medical gown.

Voices stemmed from somewhere on my right. I managed to turn my head enough to see a lady in pink scrubs walking away from... I would have said my hospital bed except I wasn't in a bed. Not a typical one.

This bed had been set up inside a clear capsule that, strangely, seemed to be pressurized. I felt like I was in an airplane.

The nurse cleared out of the room, revealing a familiar form seated in a chair by the door. He was hunched over, elbows rested on his knees while he held his head. A petite figure joined him. I recognized the dark, stick-straight bob that fell at her chin.

Madă nudged Maksim and held a cup toward him. Tiny

slivers of steam swirled up to greet him. He nodded, saying something, and reached for the cup.

Madă's gaze drifted in my direction. She locked onto me, and Maksim traced her stare. He abandoned the coffee and crossed the room in two strides. He was wearing a fresh set of clothes, and his arm was secured in a proper medical sling.

He lowered himself to kneeling and peered through the glass. The beginnings of a beard shaded his chin and cheeks, around his upper lip. Blue marks colored the area around his eyes. A fresh set of stitches had been sewn along his eyebrow. Same injury from the club, but it looked redder now, more swollen. The wound must have broken open when we were... when we...

Memories rushed in. The hill. The mines. Ştefan and...

Adrenaline flooded me. I sent a panicked look to my surroundings, as if expecting to find myself out in the wilderness, on that hill, under that tree.

"Hey. It's all right." He touched the glass. "We're safe."

I tried to reply. My throat felt like worn out tires driving over desert terrain. I shifted my eyes to the capsule and hoped he understood the question.

"We're in a hospital in Sibiu. This is a hyperbaric oxygen chamber." Moisture filled his eyes. "Do you remember anything?"

Memories flickered—silky water, a strange light, pain like fire spreading through my body. Phantom pain jolted me in response, a spark in my nervous system.

"We thought you were dead." Maksim's voice fell, edging toward a whisper. "You've been in a coma."

I wanted to reach over, to place my fingers on the curved glass separating us. I couldn't free myself from the blanket. "Wh-wh-where...?" That was all I could manage.

"Where is... Levi?" Maksim asked, and I gave a tiny nod. "He's with Daniel."

"*Bună seara.*" Madă eased closer, tentative but with a gentle smile. "I am so happy to see your beautiful face. I have been praying for you."

"Thank you," I mouthed.

"We should call Daniel." Maksim peered up at her. "He and Levi will want to know she's awake."

Mada crossed the room and retrieved her purse.

"One of the villagers had a satellite phone," Maksim explained. "It was an older model, but it worked. She called Sibiu Mountain Rescue, and they dispatched a helicopter with medical personnel who then transported you here."

"H-how...?" I tried to swallow. My throat felt like sandpaper.

Chatter floated into the room. The voices grew louder, more urgent, while softer voices interlaced the chaos. Daniel entered first, followed by Levi and a whole group of people. Americans. My emotions swelled when auburn hair set the doorway on fire.

"Oh my God!" Brandy sprinted for me.

Maksim caught her. "This equipment is delicate, and the chamber is oxygenated. You'll have to be careful."

"Who the hell are you?" Brandy clamped down on a glare. Her finger found its way into his chest. "Are you the asshole who let this happen? I knew there was a guy involved."

"All right, all right. Take it easy." Dave inserted himself. "Sorry about my girlfriend. She's overprotective of Kat." His gaze circled the room. "Can someone tell us what's going on? We've been traveling for twenty hours after getting bare-bones information from an old guy with an accent."

"That would be me." Levi raised a hand.

"We encountered them as we were leaving just now," Daniel explained, glancing between Maksim and me. "I realized they were Americans and asked if they were here to see Katherine. We were off to make phone calls, but those can wait."

Brandy pushed Maksim aside and squatted beside me. "What happened? Why are you in this thing?"

"It's a very long story we would be happy to share," Levi said. "Perhaps we should begin with introductions."

I listened to the muffled voices outside the chamber. Everyone offered their name and how they knew me. Brandy introduced herself as "the best friend who's going to murder the person responsible." That was clearly directed at Maksim.

He pretended not to notice.

Mr. Ballerini—Brandy's dad—was there. So was her younger brother, Brady. At twelve years old, Brady usually looked bored out of his mind and was almost always on his phone. Currently he was gawking at me, and there was no phone in sight. I imagined I knew why.

Brandy's late grandmother had taken the Ballerinis on a Caribbean cruise before she died. It was a big family trip, one they all got passports for, and it was the one and only time they'd ever been overseas. Any of them.

This was no Caribbean cruise. Brady Ballerini was probably freaking out.

Levi did his best to explain—in delicate terms—what had happened to Dad and why he, Vasile, and Popescu created the scavenger hunt. Maksim filled in the gaps, describing our efforts to solve the clues.

They were segueing into Village Ksorba—sans the gory details —when a lean, dark-skinned woman sashayed into the room. Her hair was folded into a neat, professional bun, and her lab coat displayed a name tag I couldn't read.

"I thought I heard English," she said without any hint of an accent. "May I ask what's going on here?" She let a curious look float over each person. "I assume you're all relatives of the patient?"

"We're frie—" Dave began.

Brandy ribbed him with her elbow. "That's right. We're Kat's family."

"Mm." The woman acted like she didn't believe it but also like she didn't care to argue. "I'm Dr. Annette Rhyland. My father is Dr. Alexander Rhyland. He's a visiting fellow at the medical school in Bucharest. We've been traveling to hospitals across Romania, teaching their staff about hyperbaric oxygen therapy."

Her explanation garnered several blank stares.

"We haven't reached that part of the story yet," Levi said. "This nice family has only just arrived."

"This is a hard medical hyperbaric chamber." Dr. Rhyland used her clipboard to gesture in my direction. "When administered in the correct doses, my father and I find this treatment does wonders for wound care and the body's ability to self-heal—as my former patient can attest to." She glanced at Maksim when she said that.

"I received these treatments last year," he said with a glance my way, "after an accident I had in Braşov. Dr. Alexander Rhyland oversaw my recovery there and mentioned expanding his program to Sibiu."

"Sibiu Mountain rescue was going to take Katherine to Bucureşti," Levi elaborated. "Our nation's best hospitals are there, but now I understand why Maksim insisted they bring her here."

"It was the closest," Maksim added, "and I heard a news report that Dr. Rhyland had begun the specialized program."

"That was *partially* correct, a bit sensationalized by Romanian media." Dr. Rhyland smiled. "My father and I have only managed to set up this one chamber, and the staff aren't trained, so I'm personally administering treatments to this patient while my father works on our grant." She straightened her lab coat. "Now please, I've made exceptions up until now, but this is far too many visitors at once." She swept her clipboard in the direction of the door.

Brandy placed her hand on the glass. "We'll be back, okay? Love you so much."

"Love you," I mouthed.

Mr. Ballerini flexed his arm in a silent *Be strong*. Everyone filed out until the hissing of the oxygen was the only sound left.

Maksim paused in the doorway. Dr. Rhyland placed a hand

on his back, saying something I didn't catch. He nodded before peering back at me. I shuffled my arm free of the blanket, nudged my hand against the glass, and inched my fingers up the curve of the chamber. "Bye," I mouthed.

Maksim's lips lifted in a reassuring smile. He winked and disappeared into the hallway.

FOUR (MORE) DAYS LATER

Nurses gabbed to each other, checking my vitals and adjusting various pieces of equipment. I'd been moved to a normal hospital bed inside a normal room. Dr. Rhyland was still administering oxygen treatments, but only for two hours at a time.

"*Ce faci?* How are you?" the older nurse asked.

"Okay. I guess." I tugged at my hospital gown. "I'd be better if I could wear normal clothes."

"Eez better for treatment." She patted my shoulder. A little farther down, along my shoulder blade, a fresh bandage covered the spot where the shrapnel had struck me. "What eez pain level today? Zero to Ten."

"Zero," I lied. Really, my pain level was a three or four, but I didn't want to take any more pain meds. They always made me think of Mom, and I would start crying, wondering if I was a junkie yet.

A knock startled me. "Anybody home?" Brandy poked her head into the room. Dave was behind her.

"Hey," I said.

The nurses cleared out while Brandy pulled up a chair. "Brought you something." She reached inside a heavy-duty paper bag and pulled out a biodegradable to-go box. "Bacon cheese-burger, loaded." She set the box on a rolling table I'd been using for meals.

I smiled. "Thanks."

"Madă has family here and arranged for us to stay with them. We thought lunch would be a nice way to thank her, and I ordered extra for you." Brandy's smile did a U-turn. "My dad ended up paying for Maksim, too. Does the guy not have a job or what?"

Dave frowned. "Come on, Bee."

"What?" she asked. "It's a fair question."

"He has money," I said quietly. "He probably lost his wallet when were out at that village. Ştefan and his goons probably took it."

"They took yours, too, but the villagers supposedly recovered everything. Levi has your purse, wallet, passport—"

"In all fairness," Dave said, "Maksim initially turned down lunch. It was your dad who insisted." He flagged Brandy with both of his blond eyebrows. "*And* he got the cheapest thing on the menu, some kind of soup with cow stomach. *Blech*." Dave made a sour face.

"*Ciorbă de burtă*," I said. "Tripe soup. It's common in a lot of countries."

"Oh, so he's a saint now because he ate cow stomach instead of rib-eye steak?" Brandy harrumphed and folded her arms. "Seriously. Who lets the girl he *supposedly* cares about go off on some wild, crazy—"

Someone cleared his throat from the doorway. I cringed. Dave full-on grimaced.

Maksim entered the room, carrying a bouquet of roses gathered in tan and white paper. Brandy saw the flowers, and her mouth twisted into a scowl.

Dave swatted her and offered a polite nod to Maksim. "Hi. Good to see ya."

Maksim nodded back before extending the bouquet to me. He did it with his right arm, and I gasped. "You're not wearing the sling."

"I'm making use of the physiotherapy department. Dr.

Rhyland wants me to move normally, without the sling, as often as I can. I'm currently up to two hours."

"That's amazing. Maksim, I'm so proud of you." I took in the spray of red, yellow, and orange teacup roses. Their silky buds peeked open, and a sweet fragrance floated up. "These are gorgeous. Thank you."

A loopy smile curled across his freshly shaven face. "I came to tell you"—he risked a glance at Brandy—"I'll be gone for a day or two."

I sat straight. "Why? Where are you going?"

"An errand, one that's time critical. I'll return as soon as I'm finished."

"Actually, that's why we're here," Brandy said. "There's no need for you to keep coming if you have other stuff to do."

"Bee." My jaw fell slack. "What the actual hell?"

"Sorry. I wasn't trying to be rude."

My eyes narrowed. She absolutely *was* trying to be rude, but I didn't want to say that in front of Maksim.

She shifted to the edge of her chair, attention swinging to me. "You're doing better than anyone expected. Dr. Rhyland didn't think you'd be able to fly for weeks, but your injuries are healing so fast she's going to discharge you in a couple more days."

Maksim and I exchanged a look. I felt sure we were thinking the same thing. This was a repeat of what happened after the club.

Then again, it might have been the oxygen therapy. Dr. Rhyland's father had been experimenting with new techniques and time limits. The healing could have been the result of those things. Maybe.

"Babe, are you listening?" Brandy leaned forward, eyes wide with excitement. "Do you know what this means?"

"Um, yeah. I'll be back to normal soon."

"It means we can go *home* soon." Brandy took my hand and gave it a squeeze. "You don't have to be in this hospital for weeks on end like we thought. Isn't that great?"

Heaviness sank between my ribs and filtered into my stomach. My eyes flashed to Maksim. He averted his gaze. "I'll try to return by tomorrow night," he said, angling for the door.

I opened my mouth to say something... but what? He had to go.

He paused in the open doorway. His gaze returned to the bouquet, and sadness flickered through his features. I felt a pinch behind my eyes as he swallowed and walked out. I stared after him.

"Everything's so cheap here." Brandy fiddled with the to-go box and flipped open the lid. "But the food's really good. How do you think they do that?"

"Do what?" Dave asked. "Make really good food?"

"Make the food good *and* cheap. Our lunch was cheaper than fast food in Atlanta, and it was way better."

"Stop," I said. "Please. Just stop."

"What?" Brandy asked. "What's wrong?"

"That. What you did." I gestured in the direction Maksim had gone, and the pinch behind my eyes heated. "You were awful to him."

"I wasn't—"

"Bee, you ran him off, and you did it on purpose."

"My dad can't miss any more work, okay? And *we're* signed up for summer classes at Perimeter College." She flicked a finger between herself and Dave. "I thought we were going to have to withdraw, but now we don't. That's why I was so excited."

"We'd've stayed as long as we needed to," Dave said, "but one of our classes can be hard to get into, so it's better for us to get back if we can."

"I'll be the first to admit I've been hard on your... friend." Brandy scrunched her nose. "So I'll apologize if it makes you feel better. But babe, it wouldn't be right to let him think you're staying for the foreseeable future and then boom, you're gone in a few days. Better to let him know now."

She had a point. But I wished I could have been the one to tell him.

"I'll apologize," she repeated, splitting a sincere look between Dave and me. "Promise."

"And if you're discharged before he gets back," Dave said, "we'll do our best to wait as long as we can. Right, Bee?"

She stiffened.

"Right?" Dave arched an eyebrow.

"Fine." Brandy waved him off. "I'll book our return flight for Saturday."

Dave hip-checked her chair.

"Sunday." She glared up at him. "But it would have to be the earliest flight out if we want to make it to class on Monday."

Today was Tuesday. Wait... Wednesday? Hopefully Maksim really did come back tomorrow night, or at least by the weekend. At the *very* least before Sunday.

"Bună dimineaţa." Good morning.

I opened my eyes. Broad shoulders filled the space by my bed, and a wave of panic crashed into me. Pink rays of dawn spilled in through the window, revealing a strong nose, square jawline, and beautiful, familiar lips.

"Maksim." I struggled to sit up.

He reached over and pressed the recline controls. The hospital bed hummed, raising me into a sitting position.

"I'm so glad you're here," I said. "Honestly I wasn't sure you'd come back."

"I didn't want to risk missing you in case—" He stationed himself on the edge of my bed.

"In case Dr. Rhyland discharged me?"

He pushed a strand of curls behind my ear. "And because I've missed you, and I've wanted time to talk with you."

"I'm really sorry about Bee. She was there for all the stuff with my mom, and she's way too protective."

"That's good to hear. I know you'll be in good hands when you go home."

"About that." I clamped down on my bottom lip. "She's, um — She's booking our flights for Sunday. First flight out."

Silence settled. I waited, wondering what he might be thinking, when I suddenly felt something on my lap. Metal clanked. My fingers detected a warped surface, all dented and scratched.

"No way." I felt along the lockbox's exterior. It was in bad shape, but it was intact. "Where did you find it?"

"Two villagers found it, actually. They were the ones who cared for me the night we spent in the village, after I was—" He didn't finish.

My mind recalled the brutal beating Maksim had taken. The images flashed in short bursts, and I wished I could somehow make myself forget. "I saw everything. Through the window."

I heard him swallow.

He cleared his throat. "Vadoma and her husband attempted to rally the other villagers against Ştefan. Their efforts failed, but when they heard the explosions, they made the trek themselves. Vadoma showed us the lockbox before you and I boarded the rescue chopper. She recognized it because she was the one who buried it. At the request of her brother."

I gasped. "Popescu?"

"Their family is from Village Ksorba. One brother owns a taxi service in Avrig. It's the same service Popescu used to reach Porumbacu de Sus. He made the trek out there because he knew he could trust Vadoma with the lockbox, so he delivered it to her, along with the parameters for hiding it, and *she* chose that hill because she knew it would be safe there."

"And then Popescu went to Braşov to... what? Meet up with Vasile?"

"It seems their trio split up after escaping Vasile's compound. Your father and grandfather traveled to Braşov while Popescu went to Village Ksorba. They all reconvened the next day after Popescu finally joined them."

"But why? Popescu could have hidden the lockbox and then gone into hiding. Or gone on the run. If he hadn't met up with Vasile and my dad, he'd probably still be alive."

"Perhaps, but Vadoma and her husband say he was very loyal to your grandfather. He is the reason Vasile had that extraordinary change of heart, wanting to set right the wrongs he had committed in the past. Vadoma's family are religious, and Vasile came to some kind of faith after Popescu started working for him."

"Just curious...why are *you* still here?" I set the lockbox on the rolling table. "You could have taken this and stolen the money. I would have never known."

"I have plenty of money. I simply won't have access until I'm out of the country. That's what I've been hoping to discuss with you." He scooted closer. "If you desire to claim what's rightfully yours, I would be happy to escort you and your friends to Germany before you depart for the States. That would give me a chance to access my own funds, and it would be better—safer— than booking flights that leave from here."

"Wait, we're not safe?" A fresh wave of panic struck. "Brandy might have already booked our flights. I-I didn't realize—"

"Shhh, it's all right." He cupped my cheek—my left cheek, the one Émilien had hit. Maksim's thumb grazed the cheekbone. "I think everything will be fine even if she did book the flights."

"Are you sure?"

"Not one hundred percent. But Émilien is in police custody, and both Levi and Daniel have been contacting Interpol and following up with EU authorities. That should prevent the Romanian police from quietly or 'accidentally' releasing him."

"What about Vladimir?"

"With so much heat coming down, he will likely stay in the shadows. That's my hope, at least until we can get you home."

Maksim bent forward and planted a soft kiss on my cheek. His hands found mine, and he passed something else to me.

My fingers detected wood shaped into a cross. A leather cord was attached, and my throat constricted. "Is this—?"

"Your father's crucifix, yes, but Levi says it originally belonged to your grandmother, Zora. She gave it to your father. When Levi learned you'll be going home soon, he insisted I bring it to you."

I gripped the necklace. The crucified figurine pressed into my palm, and a flood of emotions swirled within me. "I don't want to go home," I whispered.

"Home is safer for you." He covered my hand and gave a tender squeeze. "Vladimir's network is vast. He has too many connections in Europe."

"What if you escort me to Germany like you said, and then we could... I don't know, disappear." What was I saying? "Not forever, but maybe until—" When? "I'm not sure, actually. All I know is that Bee and Dave—they love me, I know they do, but they don't understand what I've been through. You do. You were with me through this whole thing."

He withdrew his hand, his gaze wandering to the window. The branches of a tree reached up, high enough to be seen from this angle, and I wondered if he was thinking about the tree on the hill.

The space between my ribs ached.

"Where would we go?" Maksim kept his gaze on the outside world, his question suspended between us. He was asking *me?*

"I... don't know. England? It's not part of the EU anymore, right?"

"Vladimir has too many contacts in the UK. Some of his operations are based in London."

"Oh."

The shimmer of dawn filled the hospital room, brightening the space. A long moment passed before he reeled in his gaze and settled it on me. "Where else?"

My heart sped up. "Germany? We could stay there after I claim the account, maybe go to a different part of the country?"

"That's not far enough. We would have to go to Western Europe and stay off the grid."

"How far off? Like, stockpiling guns and food? Or taking precautions?"

"Precautions. Many of them." His expression turned pensive. He was really and truly thinking about this. "We couldn't use credit cards. Your friends couldn't know where we were. Nobody could know, not even—" He cut himself off.

"Levi?"

"I was thinking of Daniel and Madă. I would have to limit communication with them. God, they may be in danger. How would I do this?" He raked a hand through his hair.

"This is why we should stick together. At least until we figure things out."

He massaged his eyes.

"Maksim?"

"I wish I could agree with you, *dragă*, but there's too much uncertainty." He pinched the bridge of his nose. "There are things I need to accomplish, connections I must sever before I can fully be free of this life. I don't know how I could do those things *and* be with you."

The morning lightened into shades of orange that stained everything it touched. I could see creases in Maksim's forehead and worry in his eyes.

"We're in this together." I eased my hand into his, letting my fingers glide over the calluses. "Remember?"

His gaze fell to our hands and then lifted to my eyes. The lines in his face softened.

"I want to go somewhere with you. Anywhere. And when the time comes for you to sever those connections, whenever that may be, I'll go home. You can come visit me when you're done."

He sat motionless, his gaze soft but alert. Then he leaned in and brushed his lips over mine. Tingles ignited around my mouth.

I raised up and closed the connection. Our mouths crushed together, becoming one, and warmth filled me from the bottoms of my feet to the squint of my eyes.

He pulled away, breathless. "I don't wear glasses," he blurted.

My eyes had been heavy-lidded, my lips searching for his. I blinked. "What, you mean the grandpa glasses?"

"Those and others. I've used them whenever I've tailed someone. Then if they see me again, looking as I normally do, they can't place where they remember me from."

"Oh." That very thing had happened to me.

"Kat, I have many secrets like this. I'm willing to bring them into the open—the ones I can—but there are certain things you can never know."

I touched his face, letting his stubble scrape my fingers. "Okay."

"I mean that very seriously." He covered my hand with his. "The less you know about certain things—" He sent a glance to the door, which stood open. "Can you move over a bit? I need to speak more softly, and I want to make sure you can hear me."

I scooted to the other side of the bed while he lowered the incline partway. Then he settled in beside me, boots and all, and tucked my pillows under his head.

"Hey. I was using those."

"Use this." He offered his arm and motioned at the space between his shoulder and chest.

I settled against him and breathed a sigh. It felt like the first real breath I'd taken since waking up, and I wasn't sure why.

He drew me in, wrapping me in a hug, as I nuzzled his chest. My hand slid along his abs, then his ribs, before finding the chiseled muscles of his back.

"The less you know about my world," he whispered into my hair, "the better it will be for you. I don't want you to be entangled with the people I associate with, and I'm not sure if you would understand the things I'll be required to do."

"That might be true," I whispered back. "I might not understand everything. But I would try. Maksim, you're worth trying for."

His hold tightened. My shoulder blade ached, but I didn't want him to let go—ever, possibly, and definitely not right then—so I held in my whimper.

We lay that way, tangled in each other, when he suddenly chuckled. "This is so much better than the bed in the PT department."

"Where?" I looked up at him. "Are you talking about your physical therapy sessions?"

"It's where I've been sleeping, as well. Dr. Rhyland made arrangements for me."

"I thought everyone was staying with Madă's family?"

"The house is far too crowded. Brandy's father didn't have a bed, so"—Maksim settled onto his back, one arm tucked behind his head—"I let him have mine. He's now sharing the room with Levi."

"I didn't know that. Brandy hasn't said anything." My body conformed to his, my head and arm finding their natural resting places. I played with a button on his shirt. "Is this new?"

"Old." He watched my fidgeting. "That was the errand I had to run. I returned to București and went to my apartment."

I stiffened. "What about Vladimir? What if he was watching?"

"I took a lesson from your father and disguised myself as a delivery person. It was a busy time, when other deliveries were happening, so it was easy enough to manage."

"And?"

"The place was ransacked. I grabbed a few needed items, then cautiously made my way here."

"Why would you do that? What if—?" I shuddered. "What if something had happened to you? I never would have known."

"This is what I'm talking about." He placed a finger under my chin and lifted until we made eye contact. "You won't always understand why I do things, and I can't always explain. Sometimes you may have to rely purely on trust. Do you think you can do that?"

Before I could answer, he bent forward and pressed his lips to mine again. My body sparked, a firework with a long fuse that had been lit for way too long. We worked our mouths together, and the kiss deepened. His tongue grazed mine, and I let myself get lost in the kiss—in him—while he whispered against my lips.

"I don't speak Romanian," I said with a chuckle.

He eased away, breaking the connection. "I said... we would have to do this my way."

"'Kay," I mumbled, reeling him in.

He resisted. "There can be no compromising, no breaking rules or making exceptions." He searched my eyes. "Kat, I need to know... Do you trust me?" He held up a finger. "Don't answer unless you've truly considered the question. Because this would require deep, meaningful trust. A mutual trust between both of us."

Memories swept over me. The first ones weren't pleasant—his ulterior motives for helping me, the way he'd used me to broker a deal with Ştefan.

But what about the way he'd helped me escape from Drago and Émilien? The fact that he hadn't wanted to go to Village Ksorba but had anyway? He'd helped me, protected me, been kind and thoughtful toward me.

"I... guess we both have reasons for distrusting each other," I began slowly, "but I appreciate how you've made yourself vulnerable. You could have denied Ştefan's accusation, made it his word against yours, but you took the high road and admitted you were wrong. Not everyone would have done that." I tangled my fingers in his shirt. "So even though I probably don't understand what I'm getting myself into, I do know that I trust you. With my life and also with something else that scares me more than all the other stuff. My heart."

He managed a small smile. "Friendship is the hand that wipes your tears when life hurts." He gathered my hand and guided it to his chest. "Thank you for being my friend in an hour when I needed it. You have my trust and my loyalty. And this, as well." He placed my hand directly over his heart, and the soft thrum pulsed against my palm. "Kat, you have these things even if you go home tomorrow."

"But then I wouldn't have *you*. That's what I want more than anything—a little more time with you."

"Then it's yours." He pulled me in. "And I know the perfect place to go. It's quaint and beautiful, remote. Ştefan knew nothing of it, and I'm certain the same is true for Vladimir. We would be safe there."

"Where is it? Somewhere in Europe?"

"We shouldn't speak of it now." He pressed a kiss to the top of my head and held me close. "I'll tell you everything when we're on the way."

WANT TO KNOW WHAT HAPPENED TO ANDREI?

Did he die? Or did some other tragic fate befall him? The answer lies in the **FREE FOR EVERYONE** section of my Patreon. You'll find other bonuses as well...

Access your FREE GIFTS

www.patreon.com/EllisKPopa
*Look for **FREE FOR EVERYONE**. It's pinned at the top.*

CAN YOU HELP US OUT?

Reviews are incredibly helpful. Ellis and the artists who worked on this book would be grateful for your rating or review.

www.Linktr.ee/ReviewATD

THE ATD TEAM

My deepest, most sincere thanks to everyone who worked on this project...

ATD's *EARLIEST* EARLY READERS

Julie N.
"L"
Bethany O.
Suzy K.
Heather H.
Leigh H.
Andrea B.
Nicola A.
Jacob M.
Nico B.
Nicolae D.
Jonna B.
Ana C.
Daniel D.
Sammy C.
Tessa H.
Sarah G.
Alex O.

Editing & Proofreading

Victory Editing: Anne, Annie, Crystalle, Tami

Creatives

Jonna Blankenship - clue & scene art (standard and limited editions)
Krystal1204 - scene & character art (limited edition)
Brianna O'Keefe - character art (bonus material)
RedXDesigner - Trailer #1
Ray Morgan - Trailer #2
Adrijus at Rocking Book Covers - cover design

ABOUT THE AUTHOR

When Ellis isn't writing, you might find her exploring Belgrade's Design District, taking cover in Tirana's Bunk'Art museums, or planning her next research trip to the Balkans. Her latest obsession is post-Soviet Romania during the Communist era, and she's working on a suspense series set in that time period.

If you enjoy books and travel, she'd love to connect with you on her Substack, The Wandering Author.

Substack.com/@EllisKPopa

For a more immersive experience, you'll want to check out her Patreon channel, Disappear Here. Joining gets you special agent status + top secret clearance to bonus scenes, story art, readalongs, audiobook listenalongs, and so much more.

Patreon.com/EllisKPopa